**Praise for *Reservations*:**

"Packed with surprises, *Reservations* sends reporter Lola Wicks on a trip that sets a new standard for vacations from hell. Gwen Florio uses the stark isolation and rugged landforms of the Navajo reservation to help build tension to an explosive climax. Another winner from a first-rate writer."—Anne Hillerman, *New York Times* bestselling author

"Reservations, the double entendre of its title echoing throughout, speeds to its shattering conclusion."—*Montana Standard*

**Praise for *Disgraced*:**

"A gut-wrenching mystery/thriller that explores prejudice and the incredible stress on soldiers in a seemingly unending war with no clear goals."—*Kirkus Reviews*

"A hallmark of the Lola Wicks series is Florio's seamless weaving of Native American communities into the narrative. The culture of the Blackfeet in Montana and North Dakota, the Shoshone in Wyoming, both on and off the reservation, come poignantly alive in characters."
—*Montana Standard*

"It is the issues and ideas that [Florio] explores that got me invested in this novel ... an entertaining read."—*Missoulian*

"A story that is gratifyingly real."—*Missoula Independent*

"Even as *Disgraced* pinpoints our political reality it never sacrifices its suspense."—*Bozeman Daily Chronicle*

"Lola Wicks is back and better than ever."—*Montana Quarterly*

"With the chops of a world-class journalist and an unsurpassed knowledge of the Rocky Mountain West, Gwen Florio weaves a compelling tapestry that combines family saga, social consciousness, and human frailty, making *Disgraced* difficult to put down."—Craig Johnson, author of the Walt Longmire Mysteries, the basis for the hit Netflix drama *Longmire*

"Gwen Florio achieves what few others can in the field of crime fiction. She creates characters with real depth and places them in a story that is so hard-hitting and believable, it's easy to imagine it being in tomorrow's headlines."—J.J. Hensley, award-winning author of *Resolve* and *Measure Twice*

**Also by Gwen Florio**
*Montana*
*Dakota*
*Disgraced*
*Reservations*

# UNDER
## THE
# SHADOWS

## GWEN
## FLORIO

MIDNIGHT INK
WOODBURY, MINNESOTA

FIRST EDITION
First Printing, 2018

Book format by Bob Gaul
Cover design by Ellen Lawson

Midnight Ink, an imprint of Llewellyn Worldwide Ltd.

This is a work of fiction. Names, characters, places, and incidents are either the product of the author's imagination or are used fictitiously, and any resemblance to actual persons living or dead, business establishments, events, or locales is entirely coincidental.

**Library of Congress Cataloging-in-Publication Data**
Names: Florio, Gwen, author.
Title: Under the shadows / Gwen Florio.
Description: First edition. | Woodbury, Minnesota: Midnight Ink, 2018. |
   Series: A Lola Wicks mystery; #5
Identifiers: LCCN 2017040953 (print) | LCCN 2017045131 (ebook) | ISBN
   9780738748801 | ISBN 9780738750538 (alk. paper)
Subjects: LCSH: Women journalists—Fiction. | GSAFD: Mystery fiction.
Classification: LCC PS3606.L664 (ebook) | LCC PS3606.L664 U53 2018 (print) |
   DDC 813/.6—dc23
LC record available at https://lccn.loc.gov/2017040953

Midnight Ink
Llewellyn Worldwide Ltd.
2143 Wooddale Drive
Woodbury, MN 55125-2989
www.midnightinkbooks.com

Printed in the United States of America

*For Sean, Kate, and Scott*

# ONE

Lola Wicks slept through her alarm. Again.

"Mom."

Lola cracked an eyelid, an effort roughly equivalent to jerk lifting a deadweight. Light stabbed her. She let the lid drop. Better. With the sun's glare banned, scent intruded. Coffee, once seen as proof of a merciful God. These days, it merely dragged her back into a world she wanted no part of.

"Go away." Was that her voice, that baleful creaking thing?

"Mom."

The single word, cutting through the alarm's insistent beeping, telegraphed a simmering fury that boiled over when Lola's daughter spoke again. "I have to go to school. I made your coffee. Made my own breakfast. Got dressed. I'm leaving. You have to go to work. You can't miss another day. Drink your fucking coffee."

Whoa. Margaret was eight.

Lola struggled to a sitting position and worked on her eyes again, brain striving toward the coherence that would allow an appropriate

1

lecture. But by the time she got her eyes open and her mouth, too, Margaret was gone.

———————

Girl and dog stood alone, fresh snow whitecapping the sea of grass and sagebrush surrounding them. The sky, exhausted from a summer of soaring blue magnificence, had flattened into an ominous gray weight. Wind rushed past, gaining momentum from its charge down the slopes of Montana's Rocky Mountain Front, stirring up a mingled cloud of dust and snow that nearly obscured the school bus laboring up the gravel road.

The girl cast a last glance toward the ranch house, its closed door. For years, a trio had awaited the bus: the girl, her mother, and her father, the border collie frisking far afield, his missing leg no impediment to his harassment of the prairie dogs who popped out of one hole and whistled impertinence as the dog's nose burrowed fruitlessly in another.

But the father, dead these past months, would never wait for the bus with her again. Her mother, sunk in grief and rage, had become unreliable.

Margaret Laurendeau dug her fingers into the dog's silky ruff. He ignored the prairie dogs and plastered himself to her, as if to make up for the missing adults. He would be waiting in this very spot when the bus deposited her in the afternoon.

"Bye, Bub," she said to him as the bus doors sighed open just far enough to admit her reedy frame.

She looked back again at the sepulchral house and mouthed the words. "Bye, Mom."

———————

Margaret's unpardonable cursing had one good effect.

At least on this one morning, Lola's first thought was not of Charlie, her husband of too few years, dead not six months by an ecoterrorist's bomb.

*Dead.*

The finality of the word drummed through Lola's head all day, every day, a metronomic taunt, barely enough space between beats to catch a breath. Dead-dead-dead-dead-dead. Not coming back. Not ever. Her anguish a live thing, squeezing air from her lungs, clawing at her heart, corkscrewing through her gut. Simply to breathe, to stand upright, was a moment-by-moment struggle.

"What?" she said when people spoke to her. "What?"

Their voices reached her from a great distance, distorted; their demands—that she rise every day, dress, care for her daughter, go to work—unreasonable. The only possible response: "But Charlie is dead."

She'd rallied for a time. And then relapsed, worse than before. Now the longing to join him dragged at her, the means everywhere—from the paring knife in the kitchen drawer to the sturdy lead rope dangling from its hook in the horse's shed, just the right length to drape over a rafter.

Only one thing eased the seductive tug toward self-annihilation: the rectangular white pills with the rounded ends that she'd hoarded from her decade-earlier time as a foreign correspondent in Afghanistan. "I'm giving you these in case you get hurt over there, somewhere out in the back of beyond," the doctor had said then. "If you have to use them, be careful. They'll make you dopey. Be sure you're somewhere safe. You won't be able to dodge bullets if you take these things. And they're as addictive as hell. But they'll do the trick."

Lola thought the doctor had been overly cautious about that addictive business. A lifelong insomniac, she took the pills only once every few days, to catch up on the sleep that eluded her even more fiercely after Charlie's death than before. The hours of nighttime wakefulness left her muzzy-headed and fumbling to complete the simplest puff pieces and weather stories at her job as a reporter for the *Magpie Daily Express*, where she'd landed after quitting in protest when her Baltimore newspaper shuttered its foreign bureaus.

So, the occasional pill, suppressing the flare of panic at the realization that each one taken meant one day closer to the end of her stash. Until the next time she reached for the plastic bottle, its contents so much more effective than the sleep meds that had eased her pre-end-of-my-world insomnia. She'd tried those again after Charlie's death, achieving only the lightest of nightmare-bedeviled "rest." But the pain pills! Like being sledgehammered into oblivion. Bliss. Or, more correctly, the numbness that passed for bliss in a world bereft of anything resembling happiness.

She had a sense of Charlie, hovering close, the broad planes of his face askew with worry and disapproval. He'd been a sheriff—the first Indian sheriff in their county—and in his last years had been increasingly preoccupied by pill-poppers and the bastards who fed their habit. The former, as Lola would have reminded him if he'd only given her the chance, lacked the sort of self-control she employed with her own legally prescribed meds. But no matter how quickly she turned, tangles of hair lashing her face as she whipped around to face him, she never caught him. It should have been a comfort, that lingering proximity, but she knew better. Charlie was pissed. Just like Margaret, just like everyone else she knew.

Especially just like Jan, her colleague at the *Express*, her name flashing on the screen of the phone whose buzzing now competed with the alarm. Lola looked at the time. She knew why Jan was calling.

She slammed the alarm off, turned the phone over, and stumbled toward the shower, twisting the "cold" knob and touching the hot not at all. As bad as Margaret's language had been, Jan's was liable to be a lot worse when Lola showed up an hour late for work—again.

———

Two fast-gulped cups of coffee gone cold and a slice of toast later, a barely wakeful Lola steered her truck down Magpie's snow-dusted main drag. To the west, the barrier of mountains mocked her. On the far side of those peaks it would still look like fall, golden leaves clinging to the aspens, the larches standing like burnished brass among the black-green mass of Ponderosa pines.

But in this part of Montana, east of the Continental Divide, fall was a cheat, snow blowing in as early as Labor Day and sometimes even before, harrying late vacationers with stinging pellets of ice. It would be April before streets remained reliably ice-free, June or even July before the final flakes fell.

The brick facade of the *Daily Express* loomed. Lola pulled into an angled parking space reserved for the newspaper's customers, and wished she hadn't. Jan Carpenter shot from the front door, jacket unzipped, head and hands bare. The bank clock next door showed ten on this Friday morning. The clock flipped over to the thermometer. Thirty degrees. In their part of the world, that counted as toasty, especially on such a sunny day. The light caught Jan's coppery hair, its flamelike strands vying with the sparks in her narrowed eyes. Her customary braid was pulled forward over her shoulder, one end in

5

her mouth, subjected to a savage chewing. Lola knew all the signs. She was in trouble. She threw the pickup into reverse. Too late.

Jan smacked the flat of her hand against the window. *Don't even think about it.* The intention, if not the words themselves, clear through the rolled-tight window. She hustled around to the passenger side and climbed in. "Now you can leave."

Lola stared straight ahead. "Where are we going?"

"To Auntie Lena's."

"But that's twenty miles away." Lena lived on the nearby Blackfeet Reservation, "auntie" by virtue of some vague relationship to Charlie that Lola never quite grasped.

"Right. And sitting in this parking space doesn't get us there."

"I've got a story due. I should write that first." Lola was pretty sure she had something or other on her plate, likely a feature overdue by several days, normally a capital offense in her business. Jorkki Harkannen, the taciturn Finn who'd run the paper since Methuselah's infancy and had postponed his retirement while awaiting her return to full productivity, had taken to assigning her "evergreens," stories with no time elements so that they could run whenever she got around to finishing them. She knew she'd pushed the limits of sympathy. "I'll get better soon," she'd promised him. Two months ago. Last week. Yesterday.

"You and I have a different definition of soon." Jorkki had turned his head and pursed his lips. A thin stream of tobacco juice arced unerringly into a brimming coffee can, his signal that she was dismissed.

"You don't have anything due today. You might not have anything due ever again if you don't get your act together." Jan's words banged around the cab.

Lola tried one last forlorn stall tactic. "Why Auntie Lena's then?"

"Just drive. You'll see."

———————

Ten thousand people lived on the Blackfeet Nation, rattling around in, as Lola always reminded people in the occasional freelance piece she did for national publications, an area the size of Delaware. She left it at that, no room in a news site's limited real estate to describe the undulating plains, sculpted by a vast prehistoric ocean that had washed up against the Front's forested lower slopes. The tribe had roamed its breadth until whitemen, arriving soft and pampered from the East, decided they themselves could better manage the area now known as Glacier National Park.

Now, the land once traveled by the tribe attracted millions of tourists and many more millions of dollars each year, nearly every one of which bypassed the pockets of people who lived on its eastern border. But at least the tribe lived on the remnants of its former territory, unlike others who'd been marched hither and yon, dying by the thousands along the way, resettled in alien places due to the superior firepower of the invading whitemen.

Charlie was Blackfeet and so was Margaret, who was born with just enough Indian blood to qualify for the tribal enrollment that conferred some financial benefits and immensely greater emotional ones. Among them, the aunties. They'd swept in after Charlie's death, cooking and cleaning and taking care of Margaret, and Lola too, leading her from bed to bathroom and back again, spooning broth into her mouth in those early days when she thought it might indeed be possible to die of a broken heart.

But that organ lub-dubbed away in her chest, damnably strong, finally compelling her to rise from her bed and go through the motions of life. Which apparently wasn't enough.

"What's this about?" Lola tried again. She drove slowly, steering the truck with exaggerated caution around the sharp curves and steep dips mandated by the rolling prairie, the effects of the pill still clouding her consciousness,

Jan's fingers tattooed the dash. Her foot jammed the floorboards. She, like every other Montana native Lola knew, drove flat-out, passing on curves and damn the road conditions. On a normal day, Lola's driving made Jan crazy. Now, her friend just bit down on her braid, shot Lola a sidelong glance, and deigned not to answer.

The plains flowed by, brittle brown grasses jabbing through the patches of snow. Clouds of steam rose from Angus cattle standing somnolent in the morning sun, their winter coats growing in shaggy. The indifferent majesty of the Front lofted behind them, the land like its people stubbornly resistant to outsiders' notions of taming.

Usually Lola loved the drive to the reservation. On this day, though, her stomach churned under the twin assaults of the coffee's acidity and her anxiety over whatever Jan had in store. Lena's bungalow was a few miles beyond the reservation's main town. Lola slid down a little behind the wheel, trying not to notice the gantlet of curious faces as the truck rolled along the town's main drag. She could imagine the flurry of phone calls and texts that would follow its passage. "She's here with that whitegirl friend of hers. That other girl looked some upset."

A few minutes later, Lola decided the town might have been the easier ordeal.

"One, two, three ... " She counted the vehicles in front of Lena's bungalow. Among them, Josephine DeRoche's pickup, Angela Kills

At Night's fourth-hand Subaru, and the Ford sedan, more rust than paint, still driven—and driven fast—by Alice Kicking Woman, who had to be at least ninety.

"Is this what I think it is?" Lola braked to a stop and turned off the engine. Jan hopped out and came around and opened the driver's side door. She grabbed Lola's forearm, pulling so hard that Lola almost fell from the truck. Jan's tone was triumphant, her smile terrifying.

"Welcome to your intervention."

# TWO

EIGHT CARS. GOD KNOWS how many people per car. The number of aunties was endless, and every last Blackfeet woman of a certain age appeared to have crowded into Lena's bungalow, clutching mugs of Lena's ass-kicking coffee and awaiting the fry bread that Lola deduced would soon appear, given the scent and sizzle of melting lard wafting from the kitchen.

"Is this an intervention or a party?" she whispered to Jan. The women's faces—eyebrows drawn together, arms folded across chests—indicated the former, but the room crackled with the anticipation that accompanied the latter. As was the case with most reservations, the tribe had its own contingent of well-meaning white outsiders trying to help with the alcoholism and addiction that accompanied the stratospheric unemployment in the remote stretches hard by the Canadian border. This time, however, the white person was the problem.

Turnabout was fair play, Lola supposed. She squared her shoulders and faced Alice Kicking Woman, the eldest among the elders in the room, and awaited the inevitable.

Alice sat flanked by Lena and Josephine, whose combined bulk nearly filled Lena's loveseat. Between them Alice looked almost childlike, her head coming only to their shoulders, her feet dangling an inch above Lena's spotless linoleum. Too late, Lola remembered her hiking boots. She bent to undo the laces and struggled out of them, adding them to the pile of knock-off Wellingtons by the front door.

"Look at you." So Josephine had been picked to lead the charge.

A roomful of eyes lasered Lola, assessing a tall woman gone gaunt in her months of grief. Her chestnut hair, at best unruly, could have benefited from a brush or at least a ponytail. She was in her usual jeans and turtleneck, the casual wear customary throughout the region beyond the newly sophisticated cities of Denver and Salt Lake. The aunties wore an array of elastic-waist pants and soft, faded sweatshirts. But their clothing was clean and pressed, the faint scent of starch warring with the aroma of fry bread, while Lola's jeans were on their fourth—fifth?—day, and she'd retrieved the turtleneck from the heap of laundry on the floor beside her too-empty bed. She ran her hands down her sleeves, trying too late to smooth wrinkles.

"What did you make Margaret for breakfast this morning?" Josephine again, more indictment than question.

"Um." Why hadn't she asked Margaret what she'd eaten? Then Lola could have truthfully answered fruit and cereal, same as every morning. But Josephine, the tribe's treasurer, had the precision of a prosecutor, as any council member who'd tried to raid the tribal finances had found.

The women didn't wait for Lola's reply. "When did you leave the house?" That was Lena, mouth hard and tight as a marble.

"I can answer that." Jan sounded entirely too chipper. "She rolled up to the paper just before ten. Work starts at nine."

An unnecessary detail. They all knew good and well when the *Express* opened. Some mornings, Auntie Lena would be waiting at the newspaper's door when Lola walked in, information in hand for an ad touting a reservation crafts fair or school event. She could have placed the ad online or by phone. But she liked the excuse for a trip to Magpie, whose meager shopping options were marginally better than those on the reservation.

"And counseling? Did that help?"

Lola didn't respond. They all knew the answer. Because she hadn't gone. At least, not after that first time, when the counselor suggested that her issues, rooted in a career that sent her careening from one tragedy to the next, had begun well before Charlie's death.

Alice wriggled on the couch, freeing herself of Lena and Josephine, sliding forward until her feet touched the floor. She held out a hand. Josephine boosted her to her feet. Lola stepped back, feeling small even though she towered over Alice.

"How long he been gone?" Alice, as befitting custom, did not utter the name of the dead.

"Five months. A little more." *As if you didn't know.*

"It's time. Past time." She gave Lola a moment to ask, time for what?

Lola didn't bother. Time to pull yourself together. Be a mother to Margaret. Time to do your damn job. She waited for the refrain.

But Alice changed things up. "Time to be yourself again. Your true self. Not ... " Her eyes raked Lola's dishevelment.

Lola jammed her hands into her pockets. One of them had a hole. She poked two fingers into it and spread them, widening the opening, stitches giving way one by one with inaudible pops. She looked up. Caught Alice's glance. She pulled out her hands and clasped them before her, a submissive posture harkening back to a Catholic elementary school, Alice scarier than any Mother Superior. Which was saying something.

"Your little girl, she sees you like this, thinks that's the way to be. Weak." Alice spat the word.

Wordless stirring among the women, who'd experienced a roster of misfortune that relegated Charlie's death to mere routine. Josephine, fending off the occasional death threat from the relatives of corrupt tribal officials who'd ended up in prison as a result of her diligence. Her married granddaughter, Angela, always doing battle on behalf of her son, a two-spirit child whose feminine ways were not nearly so accepted in the white world as they were on the reservation. Lena, whose breast cancer had only recently been declared in remission. And Alice, of an age to have survived most of her immediate relatives, the older ones taken mostly by natural causes, but the younger ones heartbreakingly claimed by drugs and drink and by the fights and car crashes resulting from both. Lola was willing to bet half the women in the room had lost a partner. Alice had outlived three husbands, and, if the relentless reservation rumor mill was true, she was being courted by a possible fourth, a youngster of eighty to whom she now made oblique reference.

"And find yourself another man," she said as Josephine and Lena eased her back down onto the couch. "Doesn't have to be a husband," she said from her throne. "Can just be for good times. Maybe another Indian man. More fun than those skinny whiteboys, break in half you get them in bed."

"Oh, no," Lola said into the chorus of appreciative chuckles. This, she hadn't expected.

"Oh, yes." Alice's head bobbed, showing the razor line of part through hair mostly still black. "Quit holding on to something that's gone."

"How can you—?" Lola couldn't continue. Useless to protest that she hadn't wanted to marry anyone, that Charlie had only managed to change her mind after six years together and Margaret's fifth birthday, that on her darkest nights she viewed his death as punishment for her prolonged aversion to matrimony.

Just as she was about to say something that would have required an apology, Jan stepped forward, an unlikely savior.

"All due respect." Jan nodded to Alice, seeking permission to interrupt an elder with a whitegirl solution. "I agree with everything you say." She continued to address Alice, avoiding Lola's gaze. A moment later, Lola found out why.

———

*Are you out of your mind?*

Lola pressed her lips together as though the words had actually escaped. The women sardined on the loveseat and arrayed on folding chairs around the room straightened with interest.

Angela ducked into the kitchen and emerged with a tray of fry bread, her crew of helpers abandoning their posts at the stove and wedging themselves into the inadequate space in the living room. They'd missed too much of the show already. The women snatched at the tray, blowing on fingers scorched by the hot discs of bread, their eyes never leaving Jan as she outlined her plan.

14

"There's a story assignment. It was my offer, originally. I mean, it was made to me by one of my old professors at the journalism school over in Missoula. He works at a magazine in Salt Lake now. He's got a freelance budget like you wouldn't believe. The story's not heavy lifting, just a feature about adoption. He asked me if I could do it. And, believe me, I want to—"

Lola coughed. She knew Jan well enough to know whatever the size of the paycheck, Jan would no more relish a gooey feel-good story than she herself would. Yet that was exactly what Jan was proposing.

"Anyhow, I think it's just the thing to get Lola here back on her feet. You know her. She's only happy when she's working. Except it seems she's forgotten how to work."

Jan paused, giving the disapproval in the room, which had softened with the emergence of the fry bread, time to reset, harder than before. The reservation's unemployment rate was double the national average, and went higher still in winter when the tourists disappeared. A job, one that paid a living wage and offered benefits besides, was a rare and wonderful thing; to piss one away, as Lola appeared to be doing, was unforgivable. The women shoved the fry bread aside. Glared. A few shook their heads.

Even Jan appeared abashed. She collected herself and soldiered on. "This would get her out of town for a few days, in a new place where people don't know her, won't cut her a break the way we've all been doing. And it pays real money, too. Maybe she can make a donation to the tribe, a little payback for all the help that people here have given her. We'll all have to take care of Margaret for a little longer, but I think it's worth it. And Margaret won't mind."

Margaret loved her time with the aunties as least as much as they enjoyed caring for her. In their presence, she became sunny, helpful, polite. Or so Lola had been told. At home, Margaret was sullen, argumentative, newly reluctant to do formerly enjoyable chores such as brushing burrs from Bub's fur or feeding and riding Spot, their Appaloosa, so long neglected since Charlie's death that he'd gone half wild.

"You do it," she'd snapped at her mother just a day earlier when Lola asked whether Spot had been fed. "You don't do anything else around here."

A roomful of eyes drilled into Lola, as though every woman there could read her thoughts, even though they didn't need to. Margaret's behavior at home was probably fodder for the warp-speed web of gossip that wrapped the reservation, just as Lola's refusal to take Jan up on her offer would be.

Still—"You're kicking me out?"

She rubbed her toe against the linoleum, noting too late that like her pocket, her right sock had a hole in it. No one had to tell her that if she refused the story, the babysitting would come to an end. Not to mention the steady delivery of casseroles—five months' worth and counting—along with the groceries that mysteriously filled her refrigerator, and the kitchen and bathroom that gleamed with cleanings far more effective than her own.

But to leave Margaret! She'd barely survived losing Charlie. In Salt Lake, at least the way Jan had outlined things, she'd be alone, truly alone. Except for her trip to an Arizona prison to confront the man who'd aided the attack that killed her husband, she hadn't left Magpie, let alone Montana, since his death.

"Jan, I appreciate it, I do. But you must need the money."

*No shit*, Jan's face said. But what she said aloud was "Margaret needs you more." And, echoing Alice, "The real you, not this mess you've become." Never one to mince words, Jan.

Josephine took over. "If you don't want to do this—"

Lola turned to her in relief. Under no circumstances did she want to do this.

"—then maybe Margaret comes and lives with one of us for a while. Maybe with someone who has kids. A family."

*I'm her family!* Had she screamed the words? Lola thought she had. But the women sat silent and impassive, judgment rendered. She looked to the door, the windows, any means of escape, and took the only acceptable route.

"Just give me a minute. Please. I need to use the bathroom."

The air behind her went slack. The hum of conversation filled the room, the main business dispensed with, gossip commencing.

No window in the bathroom. What had she been thinking, anyway? Crawl through a window, run across a prairie in full view of everyone in the house, drive away—where? The only true escape, the one she'd already considered. Lola pressed her head against the medicine cabinet's cool mirrored surface and considered breaking it. A single razoring shard, sliced across her wrists, would do the trick. Was there enough time? She imagined the aunties bursting through the door, finding her on the floor, her blood soaking Lena's fluffy lime-green rug. They'd save her, through sheer force of will if nothing else, and make her pay for the rug besides.

But Jan's plan was impossible. For one thing, she was down to the last pain pill that helped her sleep. Maybe she'd find a way to pull through without the pills at home, but in a strange city, away from her child? She was going to have to go back out there and tell everyone no, make them believe that despite all the other times, this time she'd really get it together. Which probably wouldn't work.

Acknowledging as much, Lola lingered a moment more, opening the medicine cabinet and scanning its contents, that old reporter's habit. A toothbrush, toothpaste, floss. Lena's strong white teeth, never subjected to the sugary treats that saw so many rez kids sporting mouths full of metal, were her pride. Jergens face cream. Q-tips. An arthritis rub. And, in one corner, a cluster of pill bottles. Lola's eyes narrowed.

She reached for them so quickly that a couple fell to the floor, fortunately landing on the sound-swallowing rug. Tamoxifen for the cancer itself. Zofran to fight the nausea of chemo. Ambien, the sleep medication that had already proven supremely unhelpful. And yes, finally, a two-year-old prescription, but still—Oxycontin, six tablets left. Lola shook them into her hand and tucked the bottle back behind the others. One a week. She'd been taking her pills two, maybe three times a week, but she could cut back. Make these last long enough to get her through this fresh hell. She emerged from the bathroom, trying unsuccessfully to arrange her face in the memory of a smile as she assembled the lie.

"Look. This is a lot to think about. It's a really good idea"—she tried not to choke on the words—"but I need a day or two to adjust to it." By which she meant, time to come up with an acceptable way to tell them there was no way she'd submit to such bullshit.

Jan looked at Alice. She nodded.

"All right," said Jan. Again, she glanced at Alice. "Two days?"

Alice's lips thinned. "One. What time is it?"

Around the room, women fumbled in pockets and purses for their phones. "About eleven."

"This time tomorrow—real time, not Indian time—you let her know." Alice pursed her lips, pointing them at Jan.

Not Indian time. They weren't screwing around.

A low whisper, barely a sigh, at Lola's ear. She whirled. Nothing. No one. But she'd heard it, a single word:

*Good.*

# THREE

Lola left the newsroom at five that day, something no self-respecting reporter ever did, counting down the hours to the aunties' ultimatum.

Seven hours until midnight. Another eleven until her deadline. Eighteen to come up with a reason not to go to Utah, one that would persuade Alice and the other elders that she'd really turned the corner. Or would. Soon.

She turned off the main road out of Magpie and onto the long gravel lane that led up to the house, scanning the surrounding prairie for the black-and-white streak racing to meet her pickup. No Bub. He must be in the house with Margaret. But when she pulled up, Bub lay on the porch surveying his kingdom, unmoving, not so much as a twitch of his tail. Even Spot, their aging Appaloosa, turned his freckled rump when Lola got out of the truck, finding urgent business on the other side of the corral.

Lola hefted a bag of take-out, stomped up the steps, and waited, willing the dog to leap up as he'd once done, to dance on his hind legs, bracing his forepaws against her, swiping her chin with his tongue between ecstatic yips of greeting. But Bub only stretched his jaws wide in an extravagant yawn. In the corral, Spot lowered himself to his knees, then rolled onto his back, hooves in the air, grunting in the luxury of a roll in the dirt.

Lola knew humans who were less effective at communicating disdain. "To hell with both of you."

She took a second at the door to assume the barely remembered posture of someone with purpose before going inside and offering fulsome thanks—and an extra five bucks—to Ruthie Kicking Woman, Alice's great-grand-something, the high school student who'd been designated Margaret's after-school sitter for the day.

Ruthie shoved a brick-thick book into her bag and scooped some hieroglyphic-covered papers in behind it. "We played a new game today."

"What's that?" Lola directed the question at Margaret. Her daughter was at the table, bent over a spiral notebook, pencil grasped in a white-knuckled fist, attacking the paper so forcefully Lola feared she'd shred it.

"Algebra," Ruthie said when Margaret failed to answer. "She catches on fast."

Lola stopped herself before she made a face. Because despite the fact that it had defeated her in high school, learning algebra was a good thing, right? The kind of thing the aunties would like to know she supported.

She leaned over Margaret, aiming a kiss at her cheek. "Let's see these algebra problems."

Margaret jerked her face out of reach, snatched at the paper, balled it in her fist, and threw it across the room. Ruthie caught her breath and headed for the door.

Lola dropped the take-out bag on the table, extracted foil-wrapped paper plates, and raised her voice, knowing that part of Ruthie's job involved reporting back to the aunties. "Mmm. Meatloaf and mashed potatoes. Nell's special today. And green beans. So we get our vegetables."

Ruthie never would slam the door. But the exaggerated care she took in shutting it conveyed skepticism as effective as any teenage eye roll.

"How about setting the table?" Lola spoke to the top of Margaret's head.

"Don't need to. Nell always puts plastic in."

So that's how it was going to be. Lola pushed one of the plates toward her daughter—along with the predicted plastic utensils—and then went to the sink, ran tap water into two glasses, and returned. She peeled back the foil from the plates. Steam boiled up, wafting a homey scent of warm meat and gravy that filled the space conversation might otherwise have occupied. Margaret, after the first few bites, pushed her food around on her plate, dragging her fork through the mound of mashed potatoes so that the pool of gravy broke free, flowing across the plate in the four precise streams mandated by the tines, puddling against the generous square of meatloaf. Then, in flagrant violation of the rules, she put her plate on the floor and flounced wordlessly away, as Bub dispatched the meatloaf with the same ferocity he'd have turned on a prairie dog if only he could catch one.

"Hey!"

But Margaret, who had no compunction about slamming the door, was already gone. Bub cast a longing look at the closed door. Lola rated only a sidelong gaze, a once-over from his accusing eyes, one brown, one blue, before he heaved an aggrieved sigh and settled himself in a far corner, head on his paws, keeping her in sight but removing himself in a pointed rebuke.

"Fine." Two could play that game. Lola left her own plate on the table and settled herself on the sofa, pen and notebook in hand and a goal in mind—to come up with a rejection of Jan's offer, one that would survive Alice Kicking Woman's gimlet-eyed scrutiny. She'd make bullet points. Memorize them. Practice her delivery. Her pen hovered over the blank page. Movement caught her eye.

Through the window, she saw Margaret perched on the corral fence calling to Spot. The horse who'd so flagrantly ignored Lola not an hour before lifted his head, swiveled his ears forward, and trotted toward Margaret, scattering the chickens scratching around the fence posts. Margaret's flock of intermittently egg-laying hens reveled in their final hours of freedom before being locked away in their coop for the night, safe from prowling foxes and coyotes and, more recently in the region, the grizzly bears increasingly on the move out of the nearby mountains and onto the plains, where to their delight ranches offered up a buffet of fat calves and sheep and even squawking chickens.

As Lola watched, Margaret slid from the fence onto Spot's bare back. She thumped her heels against his flanks. Spot ambled back across the corral. Margaret drummed her feet more insistently, heels a blur. Spot broke into a jolting trot, then a canter, wheeling as he reached the fence, Margaret balancing effortlessly through the turn, reaching back with one hand to whack his rear, Spot in full gallop now, around and around the corral, the girl bent low over his neck, a hand wrapped in his mane, trying to outrun her misery.

The pen fell from Lola's hand. She looked away, lay the notebook aside. Dug in her pocket for one of the pills she'd filched from Lena. Swallowed dry. Her list could wait.

The alarm sounded different, something beyond its usual beep-beep-beep. Which was faint, farther away.

Lola rolled over into space.

When she opened her eyes after the thud, she was on the floor beside the couch, Bub looming above her, his barking nearly drowning out the beeping from the bedroom along with that other sound—an unholy banging—from the front door.

Lola was sure she'd had worse awakenings. Hangovers. Wrong bed, wrong person. This, though. It ranked right up there.

Bub, satisfied her eyes were open, turned his full attention upon the door, dialing up the volume on his barking. Whoever was on the other side responded in kind. The door shook in its frame. *Blam. Blam. Blam.*

Somehow Lola was on her feet, staggering toward the door, skating her tongue across her teeth, scrubbing at her eyes with the heel of her hand.

"What?" She jerked the door open. "Oh. Amanda. Hi."

Amanda Richards took a step back and hugged her clipboard to her chest. "Hey, Lola. Take it easy, Bub. It's just me."

Bub stopped in mid-bark and accorded Amanda a single swish of his feathery tail, an acknowledgment of acquaintance if not actual friendship. Amanda was the region's social worker, stationed at a Department of Public Health and Human Services satellite office in a nearby town, and had worked the occasional case with Charlie. She had her profession's efficient short haircut and indestructible shoes, along with the poker face born of thirty years of walking into unsettling situations.

Something was off today, though. Lola blinked and tried to focus. The suit. That was it. Lola couldn't remember the last time she'd seen someone in Magpie wearing a suit, but Amanda stood before her in a burgundy number, probably something grabbed off the rack at the J. C. Penney store in Great Falls, a little too big, Amanda's hands disappearing into the sleeves, the skirt bagging. And she couldn't be working. It was Saturday.

"You going to a funeral, Amanda?" Lola couldn't think of any recent deaths of note in Magpie, but maybe Amanda had family in one of the outlying towns. Even though nobody really wore suits to funerals. Clean jeans and a pressed shirt usually sufficed.

"Lola, this is business. And it's urgent. May I come in?"

Lola stood aside. "Did we have an interview scheduled? If we did, I'm sorry. I must have spaced it." Her all-purpose excuse these days. She tried to remember why she was supposed to talk with Amanda this time. She occasionally called upon her for quotes to shore up a story, usually about child abuse or neglect, both on the rise apace with a meth problem bedeviling Montana anew after a brief crackdown that had allowed pills to take hold. "Law Enforcement Whack-A-Mole," Charlie had called the cops' always-a-step-behind attempts to keep up with all the ways people tried to escape reality.

"We didn't have an appointment." Amanda stopped in the middle of the room. "Is Margaret here?"

Was she? Amanda's nostrils flared at Lola's hesitation.

Lola rolled the dice. "She's still asleep."

"Lola. It's nearly noon. Where's Margaret?"

Too late, Lola came awake, alertness rushing in like the wind off the Front, icy with imminent danger. The stillness of the house somehow louder than the alarm's beep-beep-beep. Bub stood frozen, hackles lifting. He felt it, too.

Margaret must have gotten herself off to the school's weekend recreation program, this time without bothering to wake her mother. Amanda's gaze swept the room. Too late, Lola saw it as she did— Margaret's paper plate on the floor, licked clean of the previous night's dinner, unlike Lola's, which still sat on the table, the congealed remnants of meatloaf, the gravy's dull skin, potatoes gone yellow and crusted. The water glasses, their rims smeary. A fly, who'd somehow sneaked inside to escape the coming winter, paddled in exhausted circles in one of them.

The beeping alarm, on and on.

Nearly noon, Amanda had said. The alarm had been set for six thirty. Damn. Auntie Lena's pills were *strong*.

Amanda followed the beeping into Lola's bedroom, the sudden silence worse than the alarm. She returned and situated herself at the precarious edge of the sofa, a cautious perch that positioned her to flee if things went south.

The winds of fear howled in Lola's ears, nearly drowning out Amanda's words.

"You'd better sit down."

———————

Lola's hands shook so hard that she punched the wrong setting for Jan's number. She managed to click off, then tried again.

Jan picked up without saying anything. Just waited, the dead air more judgmental than any lecture.

"That story. The one in Utah. It doesn't sound so bad."

"Uh-huh." Disbelief radiated through the ether.

Amanda's words looped through Lola's brain, a backbeat to the dead-dead-dead refrain. *There's been a complaint. Confidential. We've launched an investigation. It's mandatory. I'll need to schedule an appointment to see you and Margaret for an evaluation. Together—and separately, too.*

*Was it you?* Lola wanted to ask Jan now. *Did you call in the complaint?* Because she wouldn't have put it past her friend to force her hand, make her take the assignment. Even Jan might have balked at such drastic action, though. It was one thing for the aunties to talk of taking in Margaret, in the casual way that kids on the rez were fostered by friends and relatives when parents went astray. But to involve the state was to pose the risk that something inexorable would grind into action, that Margaret might be taken away and never returned, might end up with people who despite their outward seemliness would view her as little more than a maid or a nanny for their other children; worse yet, a home where the husband prowled the halls at night, slipping into the room of a girl whose accusations would crumble beneath the weight of his unimpeachable standing in the community.

The aunties' ultimatum had pissed her off. This, though—this was terrifying.

"When can you leave?" Jan thought she was calling her bluff.

"As soon as possible." Lola spoke over the reverberation of the conversation echoing endlessly in her mind.

*An evaluation? Amanda, what does that mean?*

*To determine whether this is a case that justifies removal.*

*Removal? What are you talking about?*

*Please, Lola. You know what it means. The good of the child is paramount.*

Lola clenched the phone and forced the words. "Tomorrow," she told Jan. "Tonight, even."

She hung up and reached for Amanda's business card. Amanda had written her cell on the back along with the appointment information, two days hence at four in the afternoon so as not to interrupt Margaret's school day.

Lola dialed the office line and waited for the voicemail prompt. Amanda was probably still on the road, and with any luck she wouldn't check her messages until Monday.

"Amanda, this is Lola. That appointment. We'll have to cancel. I've got an out-of-town assignment. You can ask Jan. I'll reschedule when I get back."

She clicked the phone off and flung it away.

The hell she would.

# FOUR

Jan had neglected to mention the magazine's name—*Families of Faith*—and that it was a Mormon publication.

"You've got to be kidding me," Lola said when Jan finally got around to it in an "oh-by-the-way" comment as Lola packed her bag. Rather, Jan packed. Lola fetal-positioned herself beneath a quilt, giving minimal direction as Jan tossed things into a duffel.

"Church of Jesus Christ of Latter-day Saints," Jan corrected herself. "LDS for short. Nope, I'm not kidding. Watch out for the Jell-O. Do you have any makeup? Never mind, that was a stupid question. I'll give you some of mine. For God's sake, use it. You'll thank me once you get there. And bring something nice to wear. You'll probably have to interview a bishop or somebody. You've got something stashed in the back of your closet, right? At least a pair of newer jeans? Maybe even a dress?"

Lola's breath caught. Her only dress was black. She'd worn it to Charlie's funeral. She pointed toward the closet, then pulled the quilt over her head as Jan opened the door, revealing the schizophrenic contents. On one side, Lola's clothes hung with no regard to color or season, summer's tank tops dangling crooked next to flannel shirts, all in the muted, stain-disguising colors Lola favored. Running shoes in varying degrees of decrepitude lay with hiking boots in a haphazard mound, evidence that their wearer had simply tugged them off and tossed them into the closet. On the other side, a line of brown uniforms, creased and starched, with the county sheriff's seven-pointed star on the shoulder patch marched down the rod, a decorous inch apart so as to avoid wrinkles. Beyond them hung a few snap-front shirts, jeans folded over hangers, and a lone suit. Charlie had bought it for their wedding, and Lola had refused to see him buried in it. "The uniform," she'd insisted to the undertaker. "He was so proud to wear it."

For years, she'd been afraid that the uniform would get him killed, that some wild-eyed drug courier would take exception to a traffic stop, that Old Man Baggs would go after Charlie when he stepped between Baggs and the wife he was beating again, or that any one of the anonymous trolls resentful over the idea of an Indian as sheriff in a white county would make good on the veiled threats they so frequently posted in the online comments section of every story in the *Express* that contained Charlie's name.

Instead, he'd been on a rare vacation with Lola and Margaret, visiting his brother and sister-in-law in Arizona, when he'd thrown himself in front of a briefcase bomb. Given that he'd been off-duty at the time, the suit would have been more appropriate, which the undertaker suggested in a near-whisper that brought Lola roaring to the surface of the slough into which she'd so deeply sunk.

"No! Don't you touch that suit!" So fierce, the man saw the wisdom of agreeing that of course the uniform was the only logical choice.

How to explain to him that those uniforms, fresh from the dry cleaning that required a weekly forty-mile round trip, smelled only of chemicals and cloth, while daily, sometimes more, she slipped into the closet and buried her face in the wool of the once-worn suit and inhaled her husband's essence? That at night she crawled over to Charlie's side of the bed, clutching his pillow to her face, until weeks after his death when, while she was in the shower, the aunties conspired to whisk the sour sheets into the washer—an act that resulted in a violent outburst whose only victim, thankfully, was a heavy ceramic coffee mug that shattered with the force of an enraged pitch against the kitchen wall?

And how to excuse Jan, who knew these things, as she cast a critical eye on the uniforms and said, almost casually, "You know, if you ever want help packing these up—"

Jan turned, saw Lola's face as it emerged from beneath the quilt. "Never mind. Let's talk about the story. Have you done your backgrounding yet?" In the past, work had always proved an effective diversion for dealing with Lola. Now it served merely as a way to channel her anguish into irritation.

Lola sat up. "What were you thinking, hooking me up with a religious magazine?" Like many reporters, she was a devout skeptic, primarily worshipping deadlines, coffee, the occasional shot of whiskey, and above all being first on a breaking story. At least, those things had been important to her before. She hadn't been first on a story in months.

"I know it sounds bad. But Donovan Munro is a straight-up guy."

"Who?"

"The editor. He was a muckety-muck at the *Salt Lake Trib* until the last round of layoffs. They probably hired three kids right out of J-school with the money they saved by letting him go. Anyhow, he got the last laugh. He's making way more money at the magazine than he ever did at the paper."

Lola thought she'd rather spend the rest of her life asking people if they wanted fries with their burger than working for something called *Families of Faith*, and said as much.

"Well, you're working for them now, aren't you? At least until you get your story done. So lose the attitude—at least with Munro. He's one of the good guys."

*He's an editor*, Lola wanted to say, a term mutually incompatible with good guy. But for once she kept her opinion to herself. Jan was going to stay at the house with Margaret until Lola returned. The aunties would still stop by with food, wisely not trusting Jan's cooking any more than they did Lola's.

Jan, having already stepped in it by suggesting Lola pack up Charlie's clothes, must have decided on a full-on belly flop. She sucked her braid into her mouth, bit down, spat it out. "Alice is right, you know."

"About what?"

"Finding yourself a, uh, distraction. Maybe someone in Salt Lake. Someone you won't have to see again. It's not like you were a nun before he came along." This time, she wisely refrained from uttering Charlie's name.

Lola wisely refrained from punching her. Actually, wisdom had nothing to do with it. No blow could effectively counter the outrage Jan had just heaped upon her. As if she could sleep with anyone else after Charlie. As if she even wanted sex at all. Ignoring, for the moment, all the mornings she woke eager and anticipatory, reaching for Charlie in the split second before reality kicked in, her body's fierce need momentarily trumping grief. And Jan had been tactful with that nun crack. Before Charlie, Lola had been the polar opposite of a nun.

Knowing she'd crossed the line again, Jan changed the subject before Lola's churning thoughts could translate into words that would mandate an apology. "Do you know where you're staying?"

The rage-fueled energy drained from Lola as quickly as it had washed in. She dived back beneath the quilt. Maybe she just wouldn't get up. Then she wouldn't have to go anywhere.

Amanda's words replayed yet again. *Removal. The good of the child.* Amanda had already left five voicemails, the final a warning that she planned to stop by before Lola left town. Lola aimed to be gone for hours by the time Amanda repeated her door-rattling routine.

"Someplace downtown, near the magazine office," she said into a pillow. "They set it up for me. Which reminds me—I need to check and see if it takes dogs."

"You're not bringing Bub."

Anger flashed again, less brightly than before, but enough to send a pillow sailing across the room. "The hell?" Bub had been barely more than a pup when Lola acquired him, and not long after that he'd lost his leg attacking a man intent upon killing her. His devotion to her and to Margaret was so fierce that on the summer days Lola left him at home, reasoning it was too hot for him to wait in the truck while she worked her stories, he lay in a sulk by the front door, refusing to eat or drink until she returned. He'd done double duty each night since Charlie's death, snugging close to Margaret until she fell asleep, then easing from her bed and padding across the hall to Lola's room, positioning himself at her feet, ready to nudge her awake from moaning nightmares.

"It wasn't a question," Jan said. "Bub's not going. You're flying down. They were supposed to send you an email."

Probably afraid she'd go AWOL if she set out on her own. Which of course she'd considered, seizing upon the idea of traveling on and on until she ran out of money and gas, as far as it took to escape the realization that Charlie was dead, her version of Margaret's whipping around the corral on Spot. Better yet, maybe she'd fall asleep at the wheel and never wake up when the pickup careened off the road and into a utility pole or guardrail or the path of an onrushing semi.

Jan broke in before she could object. "Would you really take Bub away from Margaret? First her father and now the dog?" Too polite to add the obvious: that Lola had subtracted herself, too, from the equation of her daughter's life.

As Lola mulled a response to the impossible, Jan pressed her advantage. "The whole idea is that you do this on your own. Get better, I mean. Oh, hey. Before I forget. Somebody said Amanda Richards was in town today. You run into her?"

The room's emotional temperature, already frigid, plummeted. Lola wondered yet again if Jan had been the one to call in the complaint. Of course, the line of suspects for that particular deed could have started at the door of Nell's Café and stretched all the way past the grain elevator.

Jan folded her arms around herself and made a tentative appeal to reason. "You'll be able to finish the story faster without having to worry about stopping to give Bub water or let him pee."

Lola seized upon the conversation's single positive aspect. "Finish the story faster." The mercury crept back up a degree or two. Jan breathed. "If that's what it takes to get this charade over with as soon as possible, then fine. I'll fly. And Bub can stay here." Thinking that if anyone believed her, they were fools.

––––––––

Three in the morning. Lola eased out from under the covers, fully clothed but for her shoes.

Bub muttered low, not quite a growl, but alert to something amiss. She laid her finger across his muzzle. He flattened his ears, but followed in silence as she tiptoed across the living room, shoes in one hand, duffel in the other, timing each hesitant step to the snores emanating from the couch where Lena slept. The auntie had arrived at bedtime, logically pointing out that Lola couldn't very well leave Margaret alone while Jan took her to the airport, could she? No need to point out that she hadn't thought that far ahead. Lola slipped a folded piece of paper from her pocket and put it on the kitchen table—the note she'd written before going to bed. *Changed my mind about flying. I'll drive instead.*

But when she tiptoed onto the porch in sockfeet, duffel in hand, Jan shook herself free of the sleeping bag she'd unrolled beside the kindling box, annoyingly chirpy.

"Time to drive to the airport already? Good on you for being ready early. God, I hate these six-thirty flights." She shook her hair free of its rime of frost and went on about the superior qualities of her new sleeping bag as Lola slung the duffel into the truck's bed with the force of frustration.

She looked back toward the house. Margaret hadn't bothered with "good night" the night before, let alone "goodbye." It was understood that a kiss was out of the question.

Yet at the airport, just before pushing her into the security line, Jan astonished her with a quick, hard hug, backing away fast before Lola could say anything about the tears in her eyes.

# FIVE

LOLA RUBBED THE CONDENSATION from the plane's scratched plastic window and took in the immensity of the lake below.

More than a million people lived in and around Salt Lake City, exceeding the entire population of Montana. *Look at us*, the city's lights commanded as they blinked on against the moonless night fast descending. How grand we are! But the lake dominated, stretching far beyond the knot of humanity at its edge, capturing and holding the flame of the dying day like candlelight in a pewter sconce.

Beyond the lake, mountains circled much of the city, trapping it in a tight bowl. Lola fought a touch of impending claustrophobia. She'd gotten used to the defining boundary of the Front; before it, the beckoning sweep of prairie, offering escape with its ribbons of roads that led on forever.

She handed her copy of the *Salt Lake Tribune* to a passing flight attendant. Jan had told her that even though the Latter-day Saints had long ceased to be the majority population in Salt Lake, they still held sway over the city's power structure. The newspaper's lead story focused on a new church edict that labeled people in gay marriages "apostates" and excluded their children from baptism.

"Taliban," Lola had muttered as she read. Even though she knew things were nowhere near that bad. Spiritual banishment, harsh as it was, didn't compare to the grotesque executions the Taliban imposed upon gay people. She knew the Mormons were hardly alone among faiths in rejecting gays and lesbians. But the strictures applying to their children seemed particularly cruel.

She shut down the iPad she'd ordered as a surprise for Charlie just before his death. He'd never even seen it, but using it still felt like a way to keep him close. She'd been reviewing the notes she'd taken during her conversation with Donovan Munro yesterday, one that had begun badly and ended worse. Her assignment was to interview the Shumway family. Some years earlier, they'd added a ten-year-old boy from Vietnam to their family of five daughters.

"Why adopt, if they already had kids?" she'd asked Munro.

"Guess they wanted someone to carry on the family name, if not the bloodline." There was a clipped, supercilious quality to his voice. Lola pictured him short and rounded, red of face and fierce of mien, befitting the Scottish ancestry apparent in his name.

"It's a trend," he added. "A lot of families around here adopt a foreign child after they've already had a brood of their own."

"But why?"

"That's a question I hope your story will answer."

Lola noted the not-quite rebuke and decided to let it pass. "Why this family? Why"—she checked the name again—"Frank? Wouldn't a baby be more photogenic?" She gave silent thanks that their conversation was by cellphone rather than Skype. The magazine's very name still made her gag. She'd imagined a treacly story, one involving fat brown toddlers nestled in the laps of their new white parents.

"Babies? Why would we do a story on babies? You can't interview them."

Fair enough. Lola told herself she was imagining the sarcasm. "Why this particular kid?"

"Hold on." She heard a conversation, muffled as though Munro had held the phone to his chest. "Okay, I'm back."

"If you're busy— I know it's the weekend."

"I am. From what Jan told me, I didn't figure you'd need this much hand-holding. He's a hockey star. Kind of unusual for a kid from a place with no ice except in the tourists' umbrella drinks. Good details, right? The kind of stuff that make for a good story. All of which you could have found out on your own if you'd bothered to spend five minutes on Google. I'll email you the family's contact info, since I'm guessing you didn't look that up on your own, either."

"I can find it—"

Lola spoke into dead air. She stared at the phone in her hand. *Asshole.* Adding insult to, well, insult, he'd followed up with a text, asking her to meet him at his office at one on Monday. "We can go over your first interview."

It was almost as though he'd known she hadn't arranged it yet. In a fury, she'd dialed Melena Shumway to set it up. They'd agreed on ten a.m. Monday—"Not tomorrow. It's the Sabbath day." Something Lola hadn't considered. It still gave them plenty of time to talk before her meeting downtown with Munro.

"The school will let us keep the kids out for the morning. And I've asked the neighbors over." Melena's voice was soft as a moth's wing, and nearly as soundless. Lola had to strain to hear her. "I hope that's all right. They're our best friends. And their son is Frank's best friend. And Frank and their daughter just got engaged."

"Of course." The more of Frank's friends she could interview in one sitting, the faster she'd be done with her story. Still—engaged? Frank was in high school.

"In some ways, it's a different country down there. Or like going back in time," Jan had said of Salt Lake. Apparently she'd been referring to the fifties.

Lola had tapped out a text to Munro: *Interviewing parents, fiancée, and best friend @ 10 tomorrow.* Maybe, if he knew how extensive the interview would be, he'd cancel their meeting. But there'd been no reply by the time she boarded the plane.

The overhead lights blinked. Things beeped. People winced and cringed at the airline's canned announcement, volume set on ten, about seat backs and tray tables. The ground rose toward the plane, and Lola touched her hand to her hip pocket. The pills she'd grabbed from Lena's medicine cabinet nestled within like a talisman. She'd take one when she got to her motel—the better, she assured herself, to be well-rested for her interview the next morning.

The plane's speakers emitted a sound like tearing cloth. Beneath it, the pilot's announcement that a tailwind had speeded their arrival and their gate wasn't ready. They'd spend a few more minutes in the air before landing. The plane tipped up on one wing, pirouetting away from downtown, nothing but the rippling fabric of lake below, a single boat yanking a thread of wake across it. The plane righted itself at the far end of the lake and headed back toward the airport. Lola pulled away from the window, unsure of what she'd just seen, then pressed her face against it again.

It was still there, a fantastical apparition, a sort of Moorish alcazar at water's edge, all arches and domes, edges dissolving into the gloom. It reminded her, a little, of the old Darul Aman palace in Kabul, or at least what that stately residence must have looked like before decades of war took their toll. A road led to the edifice below, but it was empty of cars. Desert stretched otherwise unbroken from the water's edge. She wondered if mirages could arise from water as well as from sand. She turned to her seatmate to ask about it but the flight attendant stood at their row, rapping seats that had yet to be returned to their upright positions, eyeballing tray tables still mutinously in use.

By the time everyone in Lola's row had been shamed into compliance, the castle was long gone from view.

———

She didn't even bother with dinner, slipping a pill between her lips as soon as the hotel room door closed behind her.

Then she wished she'd given herself a bit of time to appreciate the sort of luxury she hadn't experienced since her days as a foreign correspondent, when the safest hotels in conflict zones like Kabul or Baghdad or Jerusalem—the latter, places she'd worked as a fill-in for vacationing colleagues—were often the most expensive.

The hotel in Salt Lake proper was miles from Camellia, the suburb that the Shumway family called home. More hand-holding, she figured, Munro wanting her downtown, near his own office where he could keep an eye on her. The room was vast, with a faraway glass wall that framed a view of the famed temple, so fiercely spotlit that it glowed, its chalky spires drawing lines of demarcation against the darkness. She thought of the strange palace she'd seen at the far end of the lake, outlines rounded and welcoming in comparison to the temple's emphatic jabbing pinnacles.

She unlaced her boots and kicked them off in deference to the plush carpet. She tiptoed across it, peeking into the bathroom on her way, sighing at the sight of a tub in which she could soak chin-deep, long enough to accommodate her even at her height. She'd save her bath for the following night; she didn't dare take one now, given the efficiency of the pills. Although she thought daily of ways to end her life, none involved the indignity of being discovered naked in a tub.

Out of habit, Lola clicked on the television to a local news station, where talking heads debated the church's new edict on gays. She muted the sound and fell onto the bed, stretching horizontally across it. Maybe because she wasn't going through the same mental checklist that preoccupied her nights at home—Margaret's needs, taking care of the animals, her work assignments—the pill worked even faster than usual, despite a humming vibration in the room that anyone else might have attributed to the heating system. As fiercely as she missed Charlie, she could have done without his constant disapproval. She'd hoped to avoid it here.

"Didn't see you on the plane." She addressed him aloud. "What did you do, fly first class?" The hum intensified. He wasn't amused. Lola wrapped a pillow around her head, the better to escape the pulse of his anger, and let the medication drag her under. Mercifully, Charlie had yet to invade her dreams.

———

Hours later, the buzzing penetrated even her barricade of fabric and foam. It stopped. Began again. Stopped. Then again, each time tugging her a little closer to consciousness. Something familiar about it. Her phone.

She fumbled for it, knocking it from the nightstand. The next time it buzzed, she managed to retrieve it from the floor. The time after that, she read the words on the screen. *Donovan Munro.*

Lola ran a furred tongue around her lips and rubbed at the dried saliva crusting the corners of her mouth. Worked at forming "hello."

An ungodly flow of phrases, most of them unrecognizable, came from the phone. "Hell you doing still in bed?" She got that one.

She sneaked in a question when he paused for breath. "Wha's up?"

"Have you looked at your news feed? Turned on a radio or TV? Checked out a newspaper?" All things that any reporter did immediately upon rising, if not before.

*No, you idiot, because it's the middle of the night.* Sentences formed just fine in Lola's brain, even if she couldn't quite get them out of her mouth. She looked at her bedside clock—nine a.m.—and was glad she'd withheld the indictment. Light strafed the bed through the inch-wide opening in the drapes. She heard a knock two doors down, the creak of a cart, a voice. "Maid service. Would you like your room cleaned?"

"It doesn't matter." Munro had gotten hold of himself. "Get over to the Shumways' house. Right now. Are you all right? You sound sick. Or something."

She tried to ignore the suspicion contained in that "or something." The room tilted. Or maybe it was her head. She lay back on the pillow and concentrated on not moving. He'd called—probably coached by Jan—because he thought she might miss the interview she'd set up with the family. She tried to draw energy from the slight.

"I'm fine. I'm not supposed to meet with them for another hour." Coherence! She congratulated herself, and even hazarded a bit of defiance. "What's the hurry?"

"Sariah Ballard's dead."

"Who?"

"The television. Have you turned it on?"

Lola felt around for the remote, beat the odds by finding it, and then upped the ante by actually hitting the right button. The screen came to life, showing the same local news station she'd watched before she went to bed. An anchorman, face contorted, mouth moving fast. She held the remote to her face, trying to find the volume button. It didn't matter. The view switched to a knot of cop cars and news vans in front of a beige stucco house. A red banner across the bottom of the screen proclaimed *Local Woman Killed*.

"Melena Shumway?" she hazarded into the phone. "I thought you said—"

"I said Sariah Ballard. Get your ass over there. She's the Shumways' next-door neighbor."

Wayward memories tumbled like small hard stones through the mush of Lola's brain and came to rest against an unfortunate outcome. Melena had said something about inviting the neighbors to the interview. The neighbor who was her best friend. Whose son was Frank's best friend. Whose daughter was Frank's fiancée.

She played for time. "If the neighbor is dead, why should I go to the Shumways' house?"

"Because of Frank. Remember him? The subject of your story."

Her brain took another turn around the interior of her head, worse than before. Munro saved her the effort of trying to form her next query.

"Seems he sank a hockey stick into her skull."

# SIX

She kicked into automatic pilot as soon as Munro rang off. The mantra of *get there get there get there*—the first imperative on any breaking story—replaced for a brief blessed time the dead-dead-dead drumbeat in her head.

She wasted precious time figuring out the room's coffeemaker, poured the inadequate results into a go-cup, and hustled to her rental car, logic brightening her morning. Because if her story's subject was charged with murder, the story was deader than—what was the woman's name?—Sariah Ballard. Which was a good thing.

Not that she was glad about Sariah. Lola cast a supplicatory glance over her shoulder, hoping Charlie had caught her half-hearted apology. He'd often accused her of being a little too jazzed about whatever misfortune sent her racing toward the door with phone, notebook, and keys in hand.

"Pot, kettle," she'd retort whenever the call was for him.

Munro, only a few months removed from newspapers, probably operated on the same impulse. She'd go to the scene, then report back. By the time she called him, he would probably have realized he'd wasted both her time and his. She resolved to be gracious, maybe even fake a little regret, when he killed the story.

She hit the horn and swerved around a car backing out of a space in the parking garage. At least she'd programmed the Shumways' Azalea Court address into her phone the previous night. "Take that," she said, as though Munro, with his obvious doubts about her preparedness, could hear her.

She tapped the app and let it steer her through streets and onto the interstate, her gaze pulled upward despite the long-forgotten challenge of driving in traffic, up and up past the sky-piercing spires of the temple and the surrounding office buildings to the peaks of the Wasatch Range to the east, the Oquirrhs to the west, dominating the view from the ground the same way the lake had grabbed her gaze from the air. These mountains were different than the Front, showy peaks rather than a solid wall, lofty and snowcapped. Together with the undrinkable lake they served as a warning that this landscape merely tolerated human intrusion.

"This is the place," Brigham Young famously had said. Lola wondered if he'd been nearsighted.

The city center disappeared behind her, the spread of suburbs funneled between the mountain ranges. She floored it on the highway, speeding past the kind of sprawl she'd nearly forgotten during her time in Montana, whose cities, such as they were, switched abruptly from pavement to prairie. South of Salt Lake proper, shopping center after shopping center had displaced sagebrush. Furniture store, mattress outlet, lamp emporium. Hardware store, garden store, pharmacy. Multiplexes, miniature golf, video game arcades. And, for the hungry, a surfeit of fast food. Burgers, fried chicken, fish. And ice cream. Lots of ice cream.

"Watch out for sweets," Jan had warned her. "Mormons can't have caffeine. They seem to make up for it by overdosing on sugar. More bakeries and ice cream shops and candy shops than you've ever seen in your life."

"Accident ahead. Take next exit," the Directions Bitch chanted. Lola was in the left of four lanes, a solid wall of vehicles between her car and the exit. She managed to ease a single lane to the right before the opportunity flashed past. She could have sworn the Bitch sighed.

Brake lights flashed. A semi-trailer growled through its downshifts in the lane she'd just vacated, almost close enough to touch. To her right, a sports car crept even with her and, with a feint worthy of an NFL running back, air-kissed her front bumper as it slipped ahead of her. Lola raised a hand from the steering wheel and a middle finger from the hand. That much, at least, she remembered from long-ago years of big-city driving.

Ahead, lights flashed red and blue beneath an overpass. She'd be past the accident soon. She looked for a crumpled car, sending a quick plea to the Creator that its occupants had escaped alive; that their families would not find themselves in the same sea of grief that daily threatened to drown her.

But an ambulance sat unmoving among the police cruisers, its lights off. Never a good sign. Lola's car inched closer. A body, covered but not yet bagged, lay in the center lane. But she saw no wrecked cars, nor even the bits of metal and taillight that usually marked a crash scene. The cops and EMTs stood with their heads angled back, looking up at the overpass.

Lola, her instincts honed by long years of covering the worst humanity had to offer, wondered if someone had been pushed. But the high, inward-curving fence that guarded the overpass made it unlikely that anyone with ill intent had heaved someone, even an incapacitated someone, up and over, or that anyone had taken a drunken tumble. A jumper, then.

Envy rose within her, so strong she could taste it, sharp and astringent. Her hands tightened on the wheel. Someone had found the courage she so far lacked. Her longing gaze swept the overpass. She shook her head. Not the right solution for her. The trick would be to make sure it looked like an accident. Charlie, ever the solicitous provider, had made sure both of them had healthy life insurance policies. She couldn't deprive Margaret of that.

As to the emotional effect on her daughter—she punched at the radio buttons, seeking the distraction of an all-news station. Maybe it could tell her what had happened on the highway, and while she was at it, she could get more information on the murder of Sariah Ballard. But the news hour was past and the station had moved on to talk, opinionators yakkity-yakking about the new ruling on gays. A portentous voice issued a stern reminder that Mormons forbade all unmarried sex, gay or straight.

"Good luck with that," she told the radio. She enjoyed a rare laugh before thoughts of sex led to memories of Charlie and their enthusiastic enjoyment of one another that had continued unabated through nearly a decade together. The laugh died on her lips. She turned off the radio.

"Get it while you can," she whispered to all of the unnamed Mormon kids out there, lusting after whatever gender kindled those delicious urges she couldn't imagine feeling again. "Because you never know when something will take it away from you."

---

After the interstate, Camellia was a relief, defined by broad and near-empty expanses of pavement bordering lawns so thickly sodded that they bespoke tyrannical homeowners' associations. Spindly trees and bushes—but certainly no camellias—struggled for purchase in miserly soil more suited to juniper and hackberry. Lola guessed the town and its streets were named by a transplanted Easterner, homesick for the lush, fragrant shrubs and delicate flowering trees that would never truly thrive here, no matter how much compost was applied and money poured into sophisticated drip irrigation systems.

She saw no pedestrians, and didn't expect any. Her years in the West had taught her that most people would rather drive two blocks to pick up a quart of milk than walk, a habit she attributed to ranch childhoods where nothing at all was within walking distance. She took a few deliberate wrong turns, mightily vexing the Directions Bitch, to try to get a feel for the neighborhood before commencing the humiliation of arriving late to a crime scene.

A reporter's notebook lay on the console. She scrawled notes as she drove. *No sidewalks. Nice cars—Am-made, mostly. McMansions? Not quite. But big. Beige, beige, beige.* Quit stereotyping, she lectured herself. Suburbs didn't necessarily mean boring. But she'd bet Camellia was, for understandable reasons. There was the mere fact of its comfortable-verging-on-luxurious presence, a triumphant rebuke to a land that deployed an arsenal of summer heat and winter frigidity. The only vegetation that could withstand both was too bitter for grazing, too scrubby for undoctored lawns.

And yet the inhabitants persevered, descendants of a faith intermittently marked for extermination; tamers of a desert whose largest body of water was not potable; strivers par excellence whose most prominent members included the CEOs of multinational corporations, university presidents, and even a presidential candidate.

But all of that success came with a whiff of suspicion, the taint of polygamist heritage, the accusations of clannishness and secrecy. Suburbs like Camellia stood as a righteous beige bulwark against all of that, testament to barbecues and Little League, grass watered daily and mowed weekly, everything screaming "normal" in protesteth-too-much fashion. Or so it seemed to Lola, who'd spent her adult life in a skeptical occupation that claimed as its motto, "If your mother says she loves you, check it out."

She swung the wheel again, turning onto another street so similar to the one she'd just left that she checked the street sign to make sure she hadn't doubled back on herself. "Recalculating," the Directions Bitch sighed in exasperation.

"All right," she said. "Let's get this over with."

# SEVEN

COP CARS CLOGGED AZALEA Court, along with television vans with satellite dishes cranked high and haphazardly parked vehicles in need of a wash.

Those last, Lola figured, belonged to all of the other reporters who'd beaten her to the scene. She left her rental car a block away, so as not to get caught in snarled traffic should any new development arise that would send the pack of reporters howling after it, and hiked toward the story that everybody else already had.

Not that there was much to see. Yellow crime scene tape surrounded both the Ballard and Shumway houses, fronted by scowling cops who waved away photographers and cameramen venturing too close, mad at being relegated to riding herd on journalists instead of being inside where the real work was happening. The two homes had that just-abandoned look particular to a murder scene, despite the fact that just a few hours earlier, normal life had gone on within each. Until it hadn't.

A small rock sat lonely on the Ballards' walk, at odds with the fastidiousness of the home's landscaping, low bushy shrubs alternating with artfully constructed stone cairns, nothing like the haphazard piles Lola sometimes encountered on hikes in Montana. By contrast, the Shumway lawn next door was a riot of color, late-blooming yarrow and windflower and catmint crowding close to the door and stretching toward the window frames. A black Suburban sat in the driveway. Lola thought she saw a twitch in the drawn-tight drapes there.

More movement, farther down the street, caught her eye. A reporter marched up to a house, knocked on the door, and stood awhile. No response. He moved on to the next house in quest of quotes from a neighbor—futile at this point, Lola knew. The first-arriving reporters would have reached the neighbors before they even were aware Sariah was dead, snagging the quotes that dominated this sort of story: "Shocking." "Such a terrible shame." "Lovely woman." And the inevitable "We never lock our doors here. Now we will."

It wouldn't take long, an hour at most, for the neighbors to tire of the parade of interviews, for their own words to stick in their throats after so many repetitions. They, like the Shumways, would ignore the doorbells, along with the ringtones from phones whose numbers had been obtained from online sites. The smarter ones would flee the neighborhood, to their jobs or to relatives' homes, until the fuss had died down. A very few would continue to open their doors for the sheer satisfaction of slamming them in a reporter's face after a shouted "No comment" or the more pointed "Vulture."

The bright light of late autumn, a last hurrah before winter's descent, threw the scene into high relief. Lola had covered a school shooting on just such a bluebird day. Then a snowstorm had blown in, wet and angry, as though to underscore the obscenity of it all. She glanced at the cloudless sky. For the moment, at least, the gods held their wrath in abeyance.

Lola sidled up to one of the reporters and tried to act as though she knew what was going on. "The boy next door, huh?"

"Looks that way."

She knew that short, don't-bother-me tone. Usually she was the one employing it. She tried again. "A hockey stick. That's cold."

The woman, shorter than Lola, somehow pulled off the feat of looking down her nose. "Yeah. Except that's not what killed her."

Busted. Lola choked out the question that had always provoked disdain when she was on the receiving end. "What'd I miss?"

"Who are you? And who are you with?" Unlike most of the jeans-clad reporters jostling for position, the woman wore a suit, although with the flats that women reporters learned early on would prove an advantage when sprinting toward a breaking story. Lola assessed the suit and guessed the woman covered the court beat, the formality a nod of respect to the attorneys with whom she spoke daily, the same way Lola had worn a headscarf in Afghanistan.

She mumbled her name, hoping the woman would forget it. The last thing she needed was to be embedded in someone's memory as incompetent. Nor did she want to be associated with *Families of Faith* any longer than she had to be. "I'm freelancing," she added. "From out of town." She broke down and resorted to shameless fishing. "What is it? A burglary gone bad?"

"Apparently not. Nothing taken from the house. They're going to hold a press conference with an update. We're just waiting to find out the time. Then we'll head to the police station. Do you know where that is?"

Lola had had about as much embarrassment as she could take. "I'll find it, thanks." She began to edge away.

The woman called after her, taking pity on someone who clearly represented no threat. "She was stabbed."

Lola turned back. "What about the hockey stick?"

The woman shrugged. "It didn't kill her. A single cut did. That's what I heard." She drew a finger across her throat.

Her look challenged Lola to ask where she'd heard it. Lola knew better than to take the bait. As a local, the woman would have her own long-nurtured sources, just as Lola had hers back in Magpie. And she knew that Lola couldn't use the information without confirming it herself. Lola had been on the receiving end of out-of-town reporters trying to get her to give up her sources when the rare big story broke in Magpie. Damned if she'd similarly lower herself with … "What did you say your name was?"

"I didn't say. But it's Anne Peterson. See you at the news conference."

"Doubtful," Lola murmured as she pushed her way out of the mob. She hated news conferences, which she viewed as little more than attempts to control the dissemination of the information that the police, or sheriff's department, or whomever handled such cases in this part of the world would probably post on social media before the conference even started. Everybody who went would have the same story. Lola, never a fan of pack journalism, wasn't about to start practicing it.

Time to go—to Munro's office for the official kiss-off on the story. She reached her rental car and stood there, grasping the door handle. Home meant facing Amanda Richards and her damned appointment. She let go of the handle and kept moving, even as she refused to acknowledge that beyond her apprehension about Amanda Richards lay the compulsion Jan had recognized when she'd thrown the story her way. Lola was no more likely to walk away from a breaking story than she was to get rid of the pills in her pocket.

Just a quick check, she told herself. Then she'd go. She circled back down a street that vaguely paralleled Azalea Court until she came to the house behind the Shumway home, where at this very moment she was supposed to have been well into an interview with the teenage adoptee.

Like the others on the street, this house looked just as emptied out as the homes on Azalea. Lola glanced around and then dashed into the back yard. She pressed herself to the home's wall while scanning the rear of the Shumway house. No crime scene tape there. Or cops. A low fence divided the yards. On the far side of that fence might be the subject every reporter most dreaded—the bereaved family member. Or, in this case, the best friend. The first time, while still in college, that Lola had done such an interview, she'd assumed it would get easier. Nearly two decades later, she knew better. She also knew that the only thing worse than such an interview was not getting one at all.

She tried to remember the vaulting lessons from her high school gym classes, took a running start, and—improbably—soared over the fence.

———

Lola tapped at the back door, readying an explanation if a cop opened it: *I'm a friend. I just wanted to make sure Melena is all right.* She wished she'd thought to stop at a convenience store for a package of cinnamon buns, or better yet, a bouquet. Anything but the damning reporter's notebook in her hand.

No one answered. She shoved the notebook into a back pocket and retrieved a business card to compose a short note on, one that would end with a plea to contact her. *I'm so sorry,* she began. Then she thought to try the door, which should have been a matter of habit.

For the first time, she cursed the pills, the way they fogged her brain. Because, of course, the door was unlocked. She'd yet to meet a person in the West who locked his doors. She'd gotten used to that default trust in a place like Magpie but had wondered if things were different in a city the size of Salt Lake. But then Camellia was a suburb, doing its best to re-create life in Mayberry. She let the card flutter to the ground, opened the door, stepped into a darkened kitchen, and waited for her eyes to focus.

"Hello?" Nothing. Lola raised her voice and tried again.

"In here." A muffled voice, a woman's. Melena's?

Lola skirted yards of marble-topped counters and glass-fronted cabinets, made her way past a breakfast area whose capacity gave lie to the word *nook,* and found her way into the living room, darker still with the drapes drawn against prying camera lenses. A pale gray sofa floated in the gloom like a cumulus cloud, puffy and overly soft. Heaps of throw pillows nearly buried a slight woman tucked into one corner. The woman's arm jerked as though yanked by a puppeteer, the motion dislodging two of the pillows, which landed noiselessly at Lola's feet.

A finger pointed. A voice like smoke wafted toward her. "Shoes."

Lola looked down at the snowy expanse beneath the hiking boots she usually wore. Who—especially with kids—had a white carpet? And who worried about tracking it up at a time like this?

"Sorry, detective. I know it's a bother."

Lola paused in mid-unlacing. Best to keep her boots on, given the extremely likely possibility that the woman might kick her out.

She sank down and down into the sofa and resumed fiddling with her boots as though she intended to remove them. Harder to get rid of someone when the person is sitting right next to you. "Melena?" Her voice rang in the hushed room.

"Nice of you to keep me company after everyone else has gone. So kind." Rote phrases dragged up from somewhere deep in the mind's defenses, albeit in the monotone of shock. Lola, fingers still wound in her bootlaces, sneaked a glance. Even on this, the worst day of her life, Melena Shumway had applied makeup with a practiced hand, had sprayed her graying hair—a sixties-style bouffant pageboy, a roll of curled-under bangs—into stiff submission. But crying had defeated her efforts. Veins mapped the prominent brown eyes; the nose showed red through its powder. Combined with an unfortunate underbite, the effect was that of a rabbit, small, vulnerable, trapped.

Lola lowered her voice to a half-decibel above Melena's. "I'm not a detective. We talked yesterday on the phone. Lola Wicks. Remember?" She deliberately avoided the word *reporter*, something that tended to evoke a visceral response, especially under the circumstances. She hurried on, hoping to distract Melena from the fact of her profession. "What are you doing here all alone? Where is everyone?"

Again, Melena flung out an arm. Another pillow tumbled. "Bryce. My husband. Police station. You're here to meet Frank. He's at the police station, too. Your interview. So sorry."

She spoke with the peculiar hitch between phrases common to people hit with the worst thing in their lives, synapses shorting out under the strain of trying to make sense of the incomprehensible, speech an almost unbearable strain on a system pushed to the point of breakdown.

"I'm here because I heard what happened," Lola said. Which was true. "How can I help?" Translation: *What can I say that will keep you talking?*

Melena caught at her hand in a grip as strong as her voice was insubstantial. Not the defenseless creature she appeared to be, then. Or, more likely, made desperate by grief and fear. "Stay with me."

Lola held herself stiff within the clutch. These moments were the worst, when the grief-stricken sought comfort from the person least able to give it. She fought hard to tamp down her natural sympathy—the woman's best friend was dead and her son accused of murder, for God's sake—and to focus on her neutral role as a reporter.

"About Frank. I wish I could have met him before ..." Before he killed someone? Before he wrecked two families' lives? Lola scrambled to get herself out of a thoughtless sentence. "I wish I could have met him," she backtracked.

"Here. I'll show you." Melena stood, tugging at Lola's hand. Lola struggled from the sofa's enveloping embrace. Melena looked again at her boots. Lola freed her hand from Melena's, freed her feet from the boots, and followed Melena down a long hallway toward the front door.

A photo display lined the walls, a quintet of somber, dark-haired girls stair-stepping in age from childhood to teens and beyond. In the most recent photo, three held babies. "Our girls," said Melena. "College. Married." She pointed to another photo, of a skinny brown boy, head bent, hair hanging over his eyes, face in shadows. "That's Frank when we got him. He was just ten."

*When we got him.* Like something they'd picked up at a store. "May I?" Lola took the photo from the wall and studied it. Frank's outline was indistinct, as though he'd tried to turn away as the shutter clicked. She hung it back on the wall.

Melena straightened it and indicated another. "Look at this one. See how much he's changed?"

The youth towered on hockey skates. Pads exaggerated his shoulders. He thrust the stick before him like a sword and, unlike the image of his younger self, stared directly into the camera, a teasing smile on his face. "I'll turn on the light so that you can see better," Melena offered.

Shadows moved on the other side of the front door's frosted glass pane. Cops. Melena reached for the switch. Lola stopped her hand. "I can see fine." The last thing she needed was for the cops to realize Melena had company.

"Here's one with Kwesi. He's from Ghana. They're best friends. He's Sa—Sa—he's her son." Unable to say Sariah's name.

Frank, his muscular bulk still impressive even without the pads, stood beside a black youth holding a soccer ball.

"It was taken at the annual picnic for adoptive parents. And look!" Melena lifted another photo from its hook and thrust it toward Lola. "That's me and Sariah in high school. We've been friends forever."

Lola looked at the photo and back at Melena. The girls stood with their arms around one another, Sariah facing front, her sweater and pleated skirt failing to disguise curves already generous. Beside her, Melena looked almost boyishly angular, eyes downcast, shoulders hunched, the obligatory plain friend of the pretty girl. Nothing about her suggested the exuberant sort of personality implied by … "Cheerleaders? Really?" Lola couldn't help herself. "Were your husbands cocaptains of the football team?"

Melena's head tipped forward, irony either missed or ignored. "Bryce. My husband. He was. Sa—*hers* was on the ski team. Here they are, hunting." Two men in camo, rifles angled against hips. Between them two deer, gutted, impressive racks nearly scraping the garage rafter from which they hung.

She replaced the photo on the wall and handed Lola another. "Here's a better one, all of us together. Me and Bryce, Galon and…" Her voice disappeared.

Lola held the photo close to her face. Even in miniature and one-dimensional, Sariah dominated, again standing a step closer to the viewer than anyone else in the photo, assaulting the camera with a megawatt smile. Still, Sariah's husband gave her a run for her money in the look-at-me department. Galon Ballard had the shoulders-back posture, careful hair, and cleft chin of a catalogue model. No one would have mistaken him and Sariah for siblings, but cousins wouldn't have been a stretch. The men stood between their wives, Galon's head thrown back, evidently laughing at something the photographer had said. Bryce bristled beside him, thick hair barely tamed by a brush cut, jawline shaded by the beard threatening to break through, brows a single black slash. He was nearly as tall as Galon but with the meaty shoulders of the football player he'd been, and a body that had filled out to match them. As in the earlier photo, Melena hung a little behind Sariah, almost a shadow. Lola wondered if Donovan Munro had picked the wrong couple for his magazine's feature. Which didn't matter now.

Melena replaced the photo and leaned against Lola, who wrapped a reluctant arm around her and worked at saying something solicitous. "Can I fix you some tea? Coffee?" Too late, she remembered that caffeine was on the LDS forbidden list.

Melena politely ignored her gaffe. "I just want to sit down."

Lola steered her back toward the living room, away from the front door and the unnerving proximity to the police. Her arm brushed a piece of wood affixed to the wall. Three pieces, actually, two uprights and a bar across the top in a sort of pi shape, the wood smooth and silvery, two deep hollows worn in the crossbar.

"What's this?"

"Ah." Melena's face, frozen with the prolonged effort of keeping her panic under control, thawed a degree. "It's the shafts and crossbar from my family's handcart." She fitted her hands into the crossbar's hollows. "It took months. Two of their children died. But their faith was strong. They made it."

What was a handcart? What took months? And—dead children? Lola wanted to ask. She glanced behind her, toward the front door, cops lurking on the other side. The handcart, whatever it was, could wait.

Once again imprisoned within the sofa, she went for direct. Almost. Melena wouldn't be ready yet, if she ever was, to hear words like *kill* and *murder* and *arrested*. "What happened? I just heard that Sariah ... "

"Oh, it was awful. Bryce found her."

"Bryce? Not her husband? Or kids?"

Melena batted some of the throw pillows out of her way. "Galon and Kwesi were at a soccer tournament. They just got back a little while ago. They're at the police station."

Lola rubbed at her arms, trying to smooth away the sudden gooseflesh. Reporters and cops alike knew the most basic guideline. When a woman is killed, look to the husband. And if the husband's ruled out, check for a lover. Bryce, right next door, who "found" Sariah?

But why on earth had Frank been arrested so quickly? Because of the hockey stick? Something so obviously connected to the boy as to easily have been a plant.

Lola had been silent too long, her thoughts lurching around in the realm of the obvious. "What about—" She couldn't remember, if she'd ever known it, the name of Sariah's daughter, to whom Frank apparently was engaged. Still, she couldn't bring herself to use the word *fiancée* about a high school student. "What about your son's girlfriend?"

Melena blanched and cringed away. Lola scooted a safe distance down the couch, awaiting a terrible pronouncement.

Melena's voice rose in a wail. "Everyone will find out."

Lola couldn't help herself. "Everyone already knows," she said. "Your lawn is crawling with reporters." Hoping that the disparaging twist that accompanied *reporters* would somehow separate her in Melena's mind from the mob.

Melena shrank still further into herself. "This is going to ruin the family. Both families."

Well, yes. Murder had a way of doing that. Lola waited.

"I can't believe it. Tynslee was—they both were—raised to be pure. I never once suspected this. No one ever even saw them alone together." A long shudder ran through Melena's body, so intense that Lola felt it even through the overstuffed cushions.

She thought she was beginning to understand what, beyond murder, Melena so dreaded people knowing. "She was, ah, involved, with Frank?"

Melena bent double, pressing her face against her knees. "Involved. Yes. Disgusting!"

Melena hadn't specified the timing. Lola suggested a possibility. "If she and Frank were together last night, you don't have anything to worry about. He couldn't have done it. The police will question him and then let him go. And no one will have to know anything. They'll just say there wasn't enough evidence to hold him."

Another mood seesaw, to moist-eyed hope. "Do you really think so? Oh, that would be wonderful. I mean"—the shame of it all still front and center—"under the circumstances." Ignoring Lola's fumbling attempt to find out whether the young people had been together when Sariah was killed.

"Mmm." Even if Frank's alibi were to be firmly established, the police would then look to the next logical suspects, and nothing about that would be wonderful. Lola wondered when Melena would realize that. "Where is Tynslee now?"

"She's at my sister's house. Bryce's idea. The press won't think to bother her there."

Lola silently thanked her for bringing up Bryce. "Melena, how did he find Sariah?"

"Rex woke him up."

Lola tried to place Rex among the Shumways' brood—she'd seen only girls in the photos—and failed. "Rex?"

"Sa—her dog. The whole family's, I guess, but he worshipped her. Bryce said he got up early and went outside to get the newspaper." Lola took a brief moment to be thankful the Ballards still got a daily newspaper. "He saw Rex running around on the street. So he caught him and brought him back to their house and put him inside."

"Because the house was unlocked." Of course it was. Lola wondered why Bryce hadn't simply deposited Rex inside, closed the door behind him, and gone home. Why he'd instead followed the dog in and walked the length of the hallway and up the stairs—the Ballard home looked to be a variation of the Shumways'—and into the bedroom.

Bryce, in the hallway photo, posing next to the gutted deer. The precision involved to remove the organs without piercing intestines and ruining the meat. Whoever killed Sariah must have sliced an artery, sending blood pumping in great spurts across the bedding, the carpet. Done it so silently as to not alert the daughter down the hall.

"I just don't get it," she said aloud.

"Get what?"

"Why they arrested Frank so fast."

Melena clutched a pillow to her chest. "They warned me. They warned me."

Heavy footsteps sounded outside. Cops. Probably coming back to ask Melena the same sorts of questions she herself was asking.

Lola forgot that she hated touchy-feely. She reached for Melena's hand and tugged, unwinding the woman until she again faced her. "Melena, who warned you? Warned you of what?"

"Not to adopt. A foreigner. Especially an older child, and a boy besides."

The knock boomed throughout the house, three sharp raps, a pause, then a fourth.

Melena lifted herself from the sofa. Lola pulled her back. "Melena. You were saying."

Melena gulped air. Her voice gained strength, the words nearly running together. "So many of our friends had adopted. Look at Kwesi. He was a mess when Sariah got him. Scrawny, some sort of skin infection. Screaming nightmares. Bryce said she was a saint, taking that on. Frank, though. You should have seen him in that orphanage. Oh, Lola. He was such a beautiful boy."

# EIGHT

ADOPTION DAY WAS SUPPOSED to be the best day of your life, the day you left behind the watery soups, pee-smelling bedding, and mildewed walls of the Kind and Caring Home in Hanoi, hand-in-hand with your new yellow-haired parents, these Americans who lost the war but nonetheless returned like conquering heroes.

For Le Cong Trang and his sister, Mai, it was the worst.

In *Thang Ba*, Month Three, of 2005, Trang was not quite eleven years old, and Mai was twelve. They'd spent two years at the Kind and Caring Home, plucked from the spoked streets of the Old City by people who supposedly mirrored the home's name but who in reality rubbed hands together in glee at the exorbitant fees commanded from barren foreigners. Among the street rats the home's operatives were well known and ranked only a half-step below the police and Fat Fingers—Hanoi's number-one pimp, specialty, prepubescence—among those to be avoided. Worse yet, the home was rumored to be in league with Fat Fingers, assessing upon arrival whether a plump and comely boy, or that rarest of all commodities on the streets, a near-teenage virgin, was worth more to them as an American couple's shiniest prized possession or as Fat Fingers' sale of the month.

Mai had been ten, then, nearly of an age to be traded to Fat Fingers when she was dragged squalling away from a display of dolls where she'd lingered too long, eyes avid, oblivious to the approach of Old Quang, the home's "sweeper" who doubled as a scout for Fat Fingers. But in those days Mai was a shrunken, hunched thing, with a swollen eye that leaked pus and blisters about her mouth from eating food snatched hot from streetside braziers. Trang, who crept from his stairwell hiding place when he saw his sister captured, was considered the more obvious prospect, with his sleepy round eyes and plush mouth. An assessing gaze—and Old Quang had honed lecherous discernment to a lethal edge—could see the beautiful youth he'd become. But he was so little, and everything had its boundaries, even the depravities sought by sunburnt tourists with overstuffed billfolds.

Who could have predicted the way Mai's body would straighten and fill out on the laughable portions that passed as meals in the home? Or that her arrival would coincide with a rare visit from a physician, who prescribed the antibiotics that cleared up her eye, although for the rest of her life she would employ the sidelong gaze she'd developed during the worst of the infection. By the time a new crop of Americans swept through the home on one of its regularly sponsored "volunteer opportunities" for the guilt-ridden, she and Trang were desperate. Neither needed a mirror to tell them that their time was short. Already Old Quang had run his calloused hand across Trang's soft cheeks, had tugged Mai's damnably wavy hair free of its demure bun and leered at the way it fell over her shoulders. Mai wondered aloud how much he would get for selling them. The Americans were their last hope.

But this batch was like all the others, gravitating toward the youngest, scooping the rare babies ("stolen from their mothers' arms!" Trang wanted to shout) from their cribs, or wrapping their arms around startled toddlers. "That one." Mai elbowed Trang, pointing to a three-year-old decked out for the day in a western-style dress complete with ruffled pinafore. "Her mother sold her to Old Quang last week. Her husband left her and she has five others at home."

She and Trang hung back along the perimeter of the concrete courtyard, which had been hastily decorated for the occasion with tall vases holding branches of pearly sura flowers and delicate peach blossoms. Miss Hoang, the home's director—"the human abacus," Mai called her—passed with mincing steps dictated by a too-tight *ao dai* of shimmering rose silk that clung to the rolls circling her torso. "She gets fat from the money she makes off of us," Mai grumbled as Miss Hoang stopped near the couple fawning over the three-year-old.

"At least she looks out for us," Trang said. It was true. Whenever Miss Hoang saw Fat Fingers slinking around, she chased him away with shouts and curses, once with a broom. She did everything possible to make sure those in her charge went home with new parents. Yes, she profited, but to the best of her ability, she kept her charges safe.

"Oh, you musn't take her from us. She is so dear," Miss Hoang cried now, hiding a relieved smile as the woman's arms tightened around the little girl.

"We should have been caught when we were younger," Mai said. "We'd have had a chance. No one wants older children. Only the babies."

"And nobody wants *bui doi*." Trang slung the phrase with abandon, anxious to rob it of the power that had relegated first their mother and then the two of them to the streets. *Bui doi*, dust of life, the derogatory term applied to children of Vietnamese women and American soldiers.

Which they weren't, technically, Mai reminded him of that now, as she always did. They were a generation removed, their mother the one to rightfully receive the insult. Trang remembered her barely, the cascading curls, her skin the color of *ca phe sua da*, the black-black coffee lightened and thickened with condensed milk and sipped in comfort by the fashionable who populated the Old City's fan-cooled outdoor cafes.

Their grandmother had never told them what happened to their mother, but she didn't need to. There were others like her, plenty, thinking they'd be safer in the north where the people hadn't mixed with the Americans, but one look was all it took and people knew. A child like that could never hope to have a normal life, to marry well or even poorly, and for the girls there was only one line of work, one that led inevitably from prostitution to drugs, and no one ever recovered from that. The grandmother who'd raised them, whose unwise pregnancy had resulted in the doomed daughter and now the doomed grandchildren, had died not long after their mother had disappeared. Hence the streets, the home.

Mai pinched his arm, bringing him back to the present. "They can't tell we're *bui doi*." She nodded toward another couple who'd entered the courtyard. No pale magazine Americans these two, the man huge and dark, the woman so slight as to nearly disappear beside him. "Smile." The flat of Mai's hand struck Trang's back. He lurched forward. "Go to them. Hurry, before Sad Linh makes her move."

Sad Linh was a girl of seven whose special talent involved attaching herself to the leg of the nearest American and wailing as though her heart had shattered as her victim tried to pull away. "You see how she loves you! You must not leave without her," Miss Hoang would say, so far to no avail.

Mai and Trang had unsuccessfully endured several of the "volunteer opportunities" that were little more than cattle calls to match aspiring parents with suitable children, and had formed opinions of Americans as a result. They were fat, they sweated and smelled bad, they shouted when they spoke, and they smiled and smiled and smiled. These two flashed their teeth when Trang sidled up to them, but their cold eyes lacked a corresponding gleam.

The man, though. An ease about him, an approachability despite his intimidating size. A light flared in his eyes, an indrawn breath of empathy as Trang drew near. Trang made the sort of split-second judgment that had ensured his survival on the streets for so many years: whom to trust, when to run. *This one. He'll understand.* The man, as if divining his thoughts, nodded. Trang would need to woo the woman. He turned to her, made his voice soft, his features worshipful. "Kind lady," he breathed. "Beautiful." He inclined his head toward the man. "Lucky huh-band." His tongue struggled with the unfamiliar S-sound of English.

And that was all it took.

"Oh, honey." The woman crouched before him, held out her arms.

"What's your name, buddy?" The man stuck out his hand. Trang shook it with two hard pumps, the way he'd learned. The woman still clutched his left hand. She looked a plea toward her husband. "Bryce, look. He's probably just Kwesi's age. He'd have a friend from the very start." Her eyes shifted. She dropped Trang's hand and touched her husband's arm.

"Honey?"

Trang followed her gaze to Mai.

# NINE

THE POLICE OFFICER AT the door wasn't alone.

A large, shambling man stood beside him, in khakis and a windbreaker barely disguising what looked like a pajama top, feet stuck sockless into loafers. Lola barely recognized him as the husband in the family photographs. Dark stubble charcoaled his jaw. He rubbed it as he apologized to Melena in a bass rumble. "I forgot my keys. Everything was so crazy this morning."

"Where's Frank?" Melena pushed past Lola, all quivering intensity.

"They're still talking with him."

"Without you?" Lola, struggling into her boots, stopped. Surely someone had called a lawyer.

The trio—husband, wife, and cop—turned as one to her, Bryce stopping mid-sentence. "He's eighteen. An adult …" He looked at Lola with dull acceptance, probably assuming, as had Melena, that she was another detective.

The cop knew better. "I didn't see you come in." Hard-eyed, perhaps with instincts worthy of Charlie, who'd always called Lola on her bullshit.

"I came in the back door. I didn't realize it was a problem. I won't do it again. I'm a friend of Melena's. Lola." All in a rush, counting on shock and surprise to forestall questions or objections. And it worked, at least with Bryce, who nodded dumbly.

The cop, though. He wasn't buying it, not exactly, but also looked as though he didn't want to deal with any new challenges in an already complicated day. "Come in the front way from now on. At least until this dies down. I'll walk you to your car. Most of the press is gone, but there might be a few still hanging around. No one should have to deal with that."

Lola took him up on his offer, eager to get him out of the house before Melena remembered that their "friendship" was only of fifteen minutes' duration and realized that Lola was one of the reporters so disparaged by the cop. But she didn't see any other reporters at all. They'd trotted off like sheep to the news conference while her brief talk with Melena had given her information that none of them had, spurring her old competitive urge.

But to what end? She was off the hook. Her original story was deader than Sariah Ballard. She could go back home, where she really, truly would pull herself together and be a better mother to Margaret, a better friend to Jan and the aunties, and a better employee at the *Express*. She could tell Jorkki to put her back on news, show him that, as demonstrated this very morning, she still had the old moves. She might filch a few more pills—Lena wasn't the only person she knew who'd battled cancer—to get her through the difficulty of the first few days back. Then she'd quit the pills cold. As to Amanda, she'd figure out a way to deal with her. Later.

Lola glanced at her phone. Not yet noon. She'd call Munro to confirm that their meeting was canceled, check out of her hotel, and head for the airport. Even if she had to wait for the last plane out, she'd be home before midnight.

She tapped Munro's number into her phone.

He answered before the first ring ended. "Wicks. What have you got?"

Muscle memory, she thought, Munro falling back into his old newspaper ways, just as she herself had when confronted by the crime scene.

And she couldn't help herself, responding in kind, offering him the information that was chum to the prowling shark that defined any editor. "The hockey stick didn't kill her. Her throat was cut." She hoped he wouldn't ask her source. Another reporter's word was no good; the only sources that counted, your own.

"What else?"

"The next-door neighbor found her." Which Munro probably already knew. It was the sort of thing that would have come out in the news conference, was likely already heading the home pages of every news outlet in town. "And get this—it's possible the victim's daughter spent at least part of the night with Frank. So I don't understand why he's the suspect."

"Wonder how that'll fly with our readers."

"Wait—what?"

He'd spoken as though the story she'd been assigned to do hadn't just gone straight to hell.

She tried a reminder. "For your purposes, I guess it doesn't matter. This isn't a piece for a family magazine anymore. I don't know how this works. When a story falls through, there's a kill fee or something, right? I'm happy if you cover the hotel and the rescheduling fee for the flight." Anything, Lola thought, to get her out of there.

"What are you talking about?"

Lola had the unwelcome sensation of grasping at straws. Once again, she stated the obvious, speaking slowly, telling the fool on the other end of the phone what he surely already knew. "There's no story now. No more fluffy feel-good feature. Not with the subject being the main suspect in a murder. I mean, sure, it's a story. For a real news organization. Just not for a magazine like yours."

She steered the car into the hotel's parking garage. The phone mercifully went dead. She was already back in the room, collecting the contents of her Dopp kit, when it rang again.

"Why in the name of God would you think this isn't a story?"

"Because—"

Apparently the question had been rhetorical because he talked right over her. Lola kicked the nightstand.

"I don't know what you think this is, but I was hired to make *Families of Faith* a quality product, one that takes a hard look at things affecting the church. You probably don't know this because you appear not to have done a spot of prep work, but as I mentioned before—you do remember me mentioning it, right?—foreign adoption is big in LDS families. Very big. So when something like this happens, it's going to rock the whole community. I want you to stay on this. Run your butt all over town. Report it just like you would a daily. Go to the news conferences"—Lola groaned—"the court appearances, stuff like that, but go deep, too. Maybe it won't make it into print, but it'll give you the background you need. We'll figure out what the story has turned into as we go along. Think the parents will talk to you?"

Again, Lola switched into automatic pilot, blaming it on the need to redeem herself. "Probably, given that the mom already has." She savored the silence of surprise.

"That's something. Get back to her. And get that girlfriend, the one with the sleepover. And teachers, coaches, the whole nine yards, whatever it takes. Speaking of which, I know this means spending more time here. Don't worry about it. We'll foot the bill. Just get everything you can. You know the drill. At least, I think you do. Prove it to me. Meanwhile, the last I checked, we still have a meeting at one. It's"—a pause; Lola imagined Munro to be the sort who would still wear a watch—"almost twelve thirty. See you soon."

Someday, Lola thought as she threw her phone across the room, he was going to catch her saying "asshole" before he hung up.

# TEN

*FAMILIES OF FAITH* WAS the first surprise.

Lola was used to the raffish atmosphere of a newsroom, an echoing open space populated by reporters with phones at their ears and fingers pounding keyboards nonstop, desks awash with stained coffee cups, pens run dry, and the newspapers and documents that the digital age had failed to vanquish.

But *Families of Faith*, which took up the fourth floor of a downtown Salt Lake office building, had a vestibule worthy of a law office, all dark wood and gilt-edged portraits of somber men, brass plates identifying them as past editors. No women, Lola noticed. She searched the plates for Munro's name. Nothing. Maybe editors didn't rate the wall until they'd retired or moved on.

The desk assigned the office manager—also male, according to the nameplate—was bigger than Jorkki's back at the *Express*. It was vacant. The clock stood at five past one. Maybe the manager was on a lunch break, also a departure from a newsroom, where meals were afterthoughts, consumed if at all at desks or in cars between assignments.

Lola sat in the vestibule, one foot tapping silently on the carpet, waiting for the manager's emergence and trying to imagine what it would be like to work cooped up in such a plush cage.

A photo of the resplendent temple just a few blocks away dominated another wall. Which reminded her: the pieces of wood displayed in Melena's hallway. She'd said something about a handcart. And faith. Lola pulled out her phone and went to Google.

As usual, a few moments told her more than she needed to know. Mormons fleeing murderous opposition in Illinois headed by the tens of thousands for Brigham Young's proclaimed haven in what would become Utah. A few hundred, unable to afford the luxury of a jolting Conestoga wagon and the sturdy oxen to pull it, piled hundreds of pounds of belongings into rough handcarts and shoved and pulled them across the desert. On foot. For more than a thousand miles. In some groups, more than one in four died.

Lola thought of the barren expanse that had unfolded for mile after unpopulated mile beneath the airplane that had whisked her to Salt Lake. Tried to imagine crossing it on foot, especially as a woman, already exhausted from too-frequent childbearing, only to see those children wither and die during the pitiless Darwinian trek. Hard people, the survivors. No wonder Melena's family had held on to the remnant of the cart.

Her research used up all of five minutes. She waited another five. "Hello?" she called into dead air.

Somewhere down a long hallway, a door sounded. The office manager loped so purposefully into the vestibule that his chin-length sandy hair swung back from his face. The navy blazer worn by every junior staffer Lola had ever known flapped behind him. His tie hung askew. He raised an inquiring eyebrow.

"I have an appointment with Donovan Munro."

He turned on his heel and beckoned her to follow, still moving at a good clip. Closed doors passed in a blur. The hallway dead-ended in a door with a frosted glass pane that proclaimed *EDITOR* in etched gold letters. Beneath the pane, a brass plate read *Donovan Munro*. Lola's escort opened the door and stood aside.

Somewhere in that room was a desk, its presence signaled mainly by stacks of paper even taller than the stalagmites of documents rising at precarious angles from the floor. A heap atop a tall file cabinet reached nearly to the ceiling, and the mess on the windowsill partially obscured what otherwise would have been a precisely framed view of the temple's Oz-worthy spires.

The chair in front of the desk held yet another Leaning Tower of Paper, rivaling the rest. Lola knew better than to touch it. If Munro's system was anything like hers, the slightest change could wreak havoc when it came to finding a crucial document. Munro's chair, like that of the office manager, stood vacant. He'd been so insistent that she be prompt, and now he was the one who was late. Fine. She'd take anything that would give her an advantage. She turned to her escort to ask when to expect Munro.

But he stepped around her and dropped into the chair behind the desk.

"You must be Lola Wicks." He held out his hand. "Donovan Munro."

———

Lola's jaw hung somewhere just above her toes. With some effort, she closed her mouth. Words emerged. "No way."

Munro's hand, his fingers long and tapered, hung empty in the air. He started to pull it back. "You're not Lola Wicks?"

"Yes, I'm Lola." She did some quick calculations as she took his hand. Munro had been one of Jan's instructors in college, and then spent some time as an editor at the *Salt Lake Tribune*, so he'd be pushing forty. This man didn't look close to that. Had Jan said professor? Maybe she'd meant teaching assistant. Lola had little enough respect for the best of editors. Despite what Jan had told her, she doubted Munro fell into that category.

He dropped her hand and leaned back in his chair. A rakish mustache curved toward his chin, giving him the look of a Western movie gunslinger—or a seventies lounge lizard. A grin spread beneath it.

"You're not … " she began.

"Not what?"

*Not the stumpy bearded elder I'd expected.* A yawn, the combined result of the previous night's pill and the inability of the hotel's weak coffee to combat its effects, ambushed her.

"Are you all right? You seem a little—I don't know." He canted farther back still, the chair now tilted at a dangerous angle, threatening to upend its occupant as well as a paper skyscraper behind it. "Worse for the wear."

*And you're even more rude in person than you are on the phone.* Which left her free to respond in kind. "Other than not seeing the point of this story, I'm fine."

His own jaw-drop rivaled hers of moments earlier. Except that he recovered faster. "No point? No point? Boy kills girlfriend's mother—at least, that's how it looks at this point. Sex and death. Two of the three subjects guaranteed to grab readers. Dig up a money angle and we've got ourselves a trifecta."

"Getting the story you're talking about could take a while." Lola dredged up a kind of generosity she hadn't known she possessed. "It would make more sense for someone here to do it. I could hand off what I've gotten so far." She hoped Munro wouldn't dime her out to Jan, who'd be quick to inform him that never once in her life had Lola Wicks willingly turned over a story to another reporter.

She slouched against the wall, waiting for him to invite her to sit. Munro leaned forward. His chair descended onto all four legs with a thump. "Let's talk about what this story could be."

Lola knew this trick. Suck her in, make her part of the process. Maybe it had worked with younger reporters. Or students. People who were Jan's age. Lola folded her arms across her chest as he spoke.

"How old was this kid—Frank, right?—when they adopted him? Remind me."

Trying to trap her, thinking she didn't know. Not an hour ago, she'd stood in Melena's darkened hallway. She felt again the weight of the framed photo in her hand and saw the image of the child, blurred in his attempt to escape the camera's scrutiny.

"Ten." So there.

"Anything about that strike you as odd?" Munro spoke very slowly, as though addressing someone who didn't understand English.

Insult received, thought Lola. She fought another yawn. "Isn't that a little old for adoption?"

"Just so. You're talking about a fully formed kid. You're a mom, right? How old is your—what do you have, a son or a daughter?"

"Daughter. Eight. What the heck does she have to do with this?" Lola congratulated herself for the restraint of *heck*. Mentally she threw some stronger words toward Jan, who apparently had briefed Munro on her family situation.

"What if something happened to you? What if she were orphaned? Adopted by another family, in another country, another culture? How would she handle that?"

Lola came away from the wall. Her hands fell to her sides. Munro rattled on. "Even if they were the nicest people in the world, it would be tough, both for her and for the people who adopt her. Especially at first."

"No."

"No, what? You can't imagine it?"

Lola shook her head. Even though, thanks to Amanda Richards, she could imagine it, in a way that made her breath come short, catching in her chest. *Removal.* She coughed, trying to clear the constriction in her throat.

"Now take that experience and multiply it by dozens, maybe hundreds, of families around Salt Lake. A lot of these kids are older when they're adopted. They're under tremendous pressure to conform to this new culture. But if they do—" He held out his hands, palms up, inviting her to continue.

Playing along helped sideline the specter of Amanda. "It means giving up some essential part of themselves. Their home. Their families. Everything they knew before."

She thought of Margaret, with her white mother, her Indian father. Raised off-reservation, going to a white school, but with near-daily exposure to the Blackfeet Nation and its mix of familial love and taken-for-granted poverty. Margaret was still young enough that she seemed oblivious to the differences. But what about later? Would she be angry about them? Feel forced to choose sides? And if so, which side would she choose?

"It's got to scare those adoptive families to death, wondering if they might be rejected someday. And now here we are, maybe looking at the ultimate rejection—murder. Think that might be a story?"

For a moment, she was almost grateful to Munro for the way his clumsy attempt at manipulation, the hackneyed story idea, derailed her runaway thoughts. She envisioned a dreary round of interviews with families who'd adopted, every last one of them handing her a version of "So sorry, such a terrible thing. Thank heavens our own Frank/Kwesi/Maria/Katya is so well-adjusted. It could never happen in our family." A rookie could do that story. She started to say as much, but Munro beat her to the punch.

"Not the story you'd write." It wasn't even a question.

"It's the story everyone will write."

"Fair enough. But what's the story no one else will write?"

Lola expected him to launch that tired mantra: *Zig where the others zag.* Or was it the other way around? But he just waited.

"Whomever"—Lola tried to infuse the single word with *not me*—"writes this should stick with this particular family. Whatever went wrong here is probably the sort of thing that could happen in any family. It's not like a teenager has never killed a parent before. On some gut level, people know that. They'll read every word."

"But everyone will be writing about this particular family as this thing winds through the court system. Our next deadline is weeks out. How do we make our story different?"

"By focusing on what you just pointed out." Lola, secure in the knowledge that she was moments from handing the story back to him, let slip a bit of magnanimity. "The whole culture clash. How it exacerbates tensions. Can these sorts of adoptions, especially with older kids, ever really work? Actually"—she pulled a bit of useful information out of her ass—"I know an adoption lawyer here in Salt Lake. She'd be the perfect person to give perspective on the story. She's a Navajo woman who was taken from her mother and adopted by the Mormons. They used to do that, you know." Lola hoped he didn't. It would be nice to turn the tables.

But Munro nodded as though it were a familiar story. Which, maybe in this part of the world, it was. Still, Lola was proud of her Hail Mary move. She'd come to know of Loretta Begay in Arizona through her mother, who was an elder she'd befriended before Charlie's death. She and Loretta's mother, Betty Begay, had kept in sporadic touch.

Lola buffed her bona fides. "She could speak to the whole different culture, different skin color thing."

She studied Munro with narrowed eyes as he shuffled through some papers. Cheekbones dominated a thin face. He glanced up, meeting her eyes in a gaze so direct that she glanced away. His were hazel. BC—Before Charlie—she'd have thought him bedworthy, if only for a single night, one that preferably involved as little talking as possible. She'd had a long-standing policy of not getting romantically involved with anyone better-looking than she was—and on her best days, she rated herself a seven. Munro was a solid nine. Cut the hair, lose the 'stache, he'd be an easy ten. And, even though she'd never broken the rule about not sleeping with a supervisor, after another five minutes Munro wasn't going to be her supervisor anymore.

*Get laid*, Alice and Jan had advised, albeit more tactfully. But Lola's years with Charlie had transformed her into a confirmed monogamist. She did a gut check, both seeking and fearing the incandescent flicker of lust that at one point in her life invariably meant she'd lead someone off to bed before he'd entirely realized what was happening. Now, though, she felt nothing—other than a wash of relief at the realization. *Not happening, Jan. Your suggestion respectfully declined, Alice.*

She scanned Munro's desk. The only photo was of a young boy. No sign of a wife. She checked his hand. No ring. Probably the boy's mom had realized early what a jerk she'd married. Lola dusted her

hands, trying to rid herself of unwelcome thoughts, the gesture a hold-
over from long-ago assignments to the Middle East. *Hallas!* people
would say. Enough! Conversation over!

As apparently it was. Munro mined one of the piles, threatening
an order-wrecking tumble, and emerged with a folded pamphlet.

"Give that lawyer a call. The sooner you can set something up,
the better."

Lola backed toward the door. "I thought we agreed"—even
though she knew they'd done no such thing—"that you'd hand this
off to someone else. Someone who can take the time. I'll pass the
lawyer's name along. I've got to get back to Montana."

Munro made his own sort of *hallas* motion, the paper snapping
in his hand. "Do you see anyone else standing in front of me? That
boy has his initial court appearance Wednesday. They announced it
at the news conference—which I guess you chose not to attend. Get
what you can in the next day or so. Go to court. Call your adoption
lawyer friend yourself. And talk to as many people who are close to
the family as possible. Start with that girlfriend." He held out the
pamphlet. "This might help with some other contacts."

"What is it?"

"Maybe you could read it and find out."

Lola silently congratulated Munro's runaway wife on her great
good sense, even as she shook open the leaflet. "A hockey schedule?"

"For Frank Shumway's team. Go to one of the games. There's one
on Friday. If nothing else, it'll make for some nice color. I know, I
know." He held up a hand to forestall any response. "You'd already
planned on going to the game. Right?"

On Friday? Lola hadn't planned on being in Salt Lake at all at the
end of the week, let alone at a hockey game. On the other hand, she
supposed she couldn't turn up back in Montana too soon without

risking whatever was left of her credibility with the aunties and Jan. And she could avoid Amanda, whose texts had already started to stack up in her phone. So she would do these first few interviews and then hand her notes over to the dimwit behind the desk, not giving him a choice about assigning the story to someone else.

She stuffed the pamphlet in her pocket and turned to go.

"Don't forget to check in. Daily. More than," he called behind her.

In a long history of hostile encounters with editors, she thought as she stalked from his office, this ranked high on the list. She headed down the street toward her hotel, trying to distract herself with the nugget that had snagged her attention amid his string of insults and orders.

Frank would be in court Wednesday. The police must have found something that justified filing charges against him despite the tryst with his girlfriend, and even though Bryce had been the one to find Sariah.

None of it, thought Lola, made any sense at all. A feeling that had been AWOL since Charlie's death reasserted itself as she thought of the coming court appearance:

Anticipation.

# ELEVEN

"IT LOOKS LIKE I'M going to be here a little longer."

Lola delivered the news to Jan instead of Margaret, who'd handed off the phone as soon as she heard her mother's voice.

"Good. That's really good."

Usually, Lola liked Jan's lack of ambiguity. No need for gamesmanship, for guessing at what she really meant. But on this day, she would have welcomed some tact. "Good? Does that mean you're glad I'm not coming home right away?"

"That's exactly what it means."

Margaret's voice sounded in the background, calling to Bub. Probably trying to teach him some new tricks. She'd schooled her chickens in a circus array of stunts but had less success with Bub. A border collie, he was smart enough to learn whatever she was trying to teach him, which also meant he was smart enough to realize it wasn't in his best interest to become a performer.

Lola sat in her hotel room with its king-size bed and thick, yielding carpet and bathroom all to herself and pictured the house in

Montana. This time of year, with its honeyed last-of-autumn days alternating with early snow and the resulting mud, the kitchen's worn linoleum would likely be gritty with Bub's pawprints. Margaret's schoolbooks would litter the kitchen table in a fakery designed to indicate that she'd paid attention to her homework. If one of the aunties had dropped by with a casserole, the kitchen would smell good. If not, Jan would be boiling water for something instant.

Lola had backed off from a fight with Munro, but with Jan, she didn't have to respect niceties. "Why in the name of God is it good that I'm not coming home? First you say I'm not paying enough attention to Margaret. Now you want me to stay away from her."

"Hold on." Jan's voice grew faint as she directed it away from the phone. "Miss Margaret Laurendeau, don't you even think of trying to make Bub carry a chicken around in his mouth. The chicken'll bite him, and then he'll bite the chicken, and how do you think that's going to end up?"

Words that could have come out of Lola's own mouth. And would have, if she were there with her daughter. A feeling grown too familiar jabbed at her. Maybe she'd have put a stop to Margaret's shenanigans if she were there. Or maybe she'd be "napping" in the bedroom, sleeping off the effects of her most recent pill.

Jan didn't know about the pills, but she knew what the last few months had been like. Her words sped through the phone like slaps, hitting all of Lola's sore spots. "Damn straight I want you away from her, at least until you can ditch the zombie routine. Look, you're depressed. I get it. And you've got good reason. Unfortunately, you can't afford to be. I know you. The one thing that'll snap you out of it is work. And it looks like you're going to be working your butt off for the next couple of weeks."

"You talked to Munro."

"Yep."

Lola cursed under her breath. At least, she thought she did.

"What was that? What do you think of him, anyway? Great guy, huh? Really old-school."

"He's keeping me busy."

Jan's laugh rang out. "You mean he's riding you. Excellent. That's just what you need."

"What I need is to talk to Margaret." Lola forced the words through gritted teeth.

Jan set the phone down with a thunk. Lola heard a prolonged negotiation, too far from the phone for her to catch the words. The next voice that reached her was Jan's.

"She's pretty busy right now. Why don't you try again tonight?" At least Jan had the grace to sound abashed.

Lola knew she wasn't helping her own cause, but she acted on her first impulse and hung up without responding.

---

*Talk with the girlfriend*, Munro had said.

The next morning, Lola dug around in her brain for the name of Frank's fiancée—Tina, Lindsey, something like that—certainty lost amid the other, more urgent, details. She pulled out her iPad and searched engagement announcements on the *Salt Lake Tribune*'s site. Nothing. She googled "Sariah Ballard." Surely anything about Sariah would mention her children. Stories about the killing filled the screen. Most mentioned that Sariah had a husband and children. None mentioned their names. Lola went prospecting through her gray matter again.

Melena had pointed out Sariah and her husband in the photo of the two couples. Gay-something. Gaylord? But a search for Gaylord Ballard came up blank. In more than a decade of reporting, Lola had amassed a reserve of Hail Marys. She called upon another one now, googling "Boys' Names" and searching through a pastel-blue website for names starting with G, looking for one that snagged her memory.

"Yes!" She punched the air. Galon.

There he was, all over Google. No question of a mix-up with some other Galon Ballard. The same square jaw and Chiclets grin she'd seen in the hallway photos dominated the ones online. Galon the church leader. A decades-younger Galon in college, on the slopes, low to the ground, mere inches between his skis, a fan of snow as he carved a turn. Galon in group shots for any number of civic organizations. And—more air punches—the entire Ballard family at, wouldn't you know, the annual picnic for adoptive families.

A tall blond girl, her pulled-back hair accentuating a thin face, clasped hands with her adopted brother, Kwesi. Tynslee, Frank's girlfriend. Fiancée, Lola corrected herself. Now that she had the name, she had only to find the girl.

Galon Ballard had taken Tynslee to Melena's sister's house, Melena had said. Lola wished she'd thought to ask Melena her sister's name. She pounded at her tablet's tiny keyboard, keystrokes heavy with purpose, giving herself ten minutes of googling to find the sister.

It didn't even take five. Bryce and Melena's wedding announcement lived online, informing her that the bride's only sister had served as maid of honor. From there, it was another few clicks to get to the maid-of-honor's own wedding announcement, and thus her husband's name, and from there, Lola turned away from the laptop and to that most retro of search engines, the hotel's telephone book, betting that Melena and her extended family were the types to hang onto their landlines.

She'd bet right.

She fed the sister's address to the Directions Bitch and tossed a finger toward Donovan Munro on her way out the door.

———

Getting to the sister's house was the easy part. But as Lola sat in the car across the street, staring at another paragon of the American dream—this one even had a picket fence—she realized she'd forgotten a key element: how to get to Tynslee alone, away from the gaggle of relatives drawn by the guilty excitement of tragedy. She couldn't risk calling the landline. The aunt or another relative might answer, and almost certainly would want to know who was calling. A hulking black Suburban sat at the curb. Melena or Bryce—or maybe both—were there, too. She needed Tynslee's cell number.

She slid down in the seat and went back to Google. She prayed that Tynslee's name would come up in some sort of activity that required a phone number. Photos flashed past, Tynslee at various track meets, not the sorts of things that would be accompanied by a phone number. Still, Lola's finger hovered over them. Gone was the demure girl of the adoptive families picnic. In the posed photos, she stood fierce and focused, jaw set, with the careless beauty of girls who have yet to realize their power. Lola swiped through more: Tynslee breaking the tape at the finish line, thighs and calves a mass of flexed muscle, propelling her far ahead of her hapless opponents.

The captions told her Tynslee was a statewide champion. She'd broken records. Scholarships must have been dangled. And Tynslee was going to give that up to be a wife at eighteen, almost certainly a mother by nineteen or twenty? Lola shook her head and forced herself to concentrate on her search.

Within moments, the journalism gods winked, flashing a number attached to a story about a Meals on Wheels program. Evidently Tynslee was a do-gooder when she wasn't breaking records in the 800- and 1500-meter events. Lola dialed fast.

It rang. And rang. And rang. And picked up on the fourth ring. "Ballard residence," said a recorded voice. The family landline. Lola imagined it ringing in the empty house, the evidence crews done with their work, nothing left now but for a practical-minded family member to call the sort of specialized cleaning crew who'd polish the granite countertops free of the circles left by the cops' coffee mugs, replace the bloodstained bedroom carpet with its pieces cut out and sealed in evidence bags, buy a new mattress to replace the one on which Sariah had breathed her agonized last.

Lola went back to Google. Again, a number, a different one. Tynslee also was a contact for a local mentoring program involving disadvantaged teens. Lola looked skyward, although she was never sure that was the right direction for the journalism gods. More likely, they lurked in a bar. Wherever they were, this time she got a full smile when she called.

"Hello?" A choked voice, barely more than a whisper. "Who's this?"

Lola tucked the phone between ear and shoulder, crossed the fingers on both hands, and wriggled her toes inside her boots in an attempt to cross them, too. "Lola Wicks." Normally she'd avoid revealing herself as a reporter until they'd exchanged at least a few sentences, enough to establish even a tenuous bond, one that would make it harder for the girl to hang up on her. But she made a leap of logic that the girl would find the magazine's name reassuring. "I was supposed to interview you yesterday at Frank's house for *Families of Faith*."

"Wait a minute." Lola heard people talking in the background, then the sound of a door closing. Silence. "The interview got canceled. I'm sorry that nobody told you."

Falling back on civility in the midst of grief. Tynslee operated far better on automatic pilot than Lola had when Charlie died.

"I know what happened," Lola said, and varnished the words with her own belated courtesy. "I'm so sorry."

"What do you want?"

Tiptoe, Lola warned herself. Don't go stomping into this one. "Mostly, I just wanted to know how you're doing."

She held the phone away as sobs assaulted her. When the sounds began to resemble words, she put the phone to her ear again.

"He didn't kill Mom, Miss Wicks! You have to believe me!"

Lola pitched her voice as low and reassuring as possible, trying to hide her eagerness. "I want to believe you. That's why I'm calling you. Because you know the real story. Can we meet somewhere?"

---

No matter where Lola suggested getting together, Tynslee came back with a veto.

"You don't understand." Her sobs had subsided. "If I get caught talking to you, to anyone, I'm dead. They won't even let the police talk to me alone. Because—because—"

Lola decided to save her the agony. "I know about you and Frank. Not only that you're engaged. That you're … " What was the word she'd used with Melena? "Involved. No judgment here. None at all."

But Tynslee wailed afresh. Lola had forgotten the intensity of a teenage girl's emotions. First love. First sex. Had her own youthful romances been so fraught with drama? Just in time, she checked an impulse to speak sharply to Tynslee, to shock her into composure. Teenage romances, hell. Look how she'd fallen apart over Charlie's death.

She glanced up and down the street, worried that if she lingered too long it would attract the neighbors' attention. After all, how long would it take other reporters—the local ones, anyone, the ones who had a cousin who knew someone, who knew someone else who'd know where the Ballards had decamped—to show up? The street ended in the inevitable cul-de-sac, but instead of a semicircle of houses, a park stretched into the distance.

"Tynslee. Tynslee. Listen to me. Is your dog there with you? What's his name?"

"Rex. Yes, he's here. We couldn't leave him alone in the house with Mom." Another strangled sob.

Lola countered emotion with logic. "He'll be upset, too. Dogs know when things are wrong. And he's out of his element, in a different house, surrounded by too many people. He needs a walk. You take him. Meet me in the park at the end of the street."

# TWELVE

LOLA COULDN'T BELIEVE IT worked.

By the time she'd driven to another block and parked the car in a less conspicuous spot, and then jogged back, Tynslee and an aging German shepherd, stiff in the hips but with the alert gaze of a youngster, paced near a stand of trees.

Lola tried to catch her breath as she approached. Before Charlie—everything in her life these days seemed to have a Before Charlie component—she'd been a runner, nothing to brag about in terms of speed or distance, but she'd found it a fine way to unwind from the stress of a daily deadline. But running, too, had fallen away since Charlie's death. The two-block jog left her winded, with a stitch drawing fingernails down her side.

Between ragged breaths, she studied Tynslee. Without the dog, she'd barely have recognized the golden girl of the photos. Her hair hung loose and unwashed, and weeping had turned her face into a Rorschach of blotches. Even in Magpie, Montana, casual wear had come to be defined by yoga pants and leotard tops, but Tynslee's slender form swam in an open jacket that revealed a baggy T-shirt with a spaghetti-strap top pulled over it and shapeless sweatpants. She dropped the leash and threw herself sobbing into Lola's arms.

Lola stepped on the free end of the leash, lest Rex be inclined to escape. But he sidled in close, hackles rising, in a warning that clearly telegraphed *I think you're probably okay, but don't try any funny stuff. Because I will rip you to shreds.*

Lola stroked Tynslee's hair and spoke soothingly, as much to Rex as to the girl. She led Tynslee to a bench and eased her onto it. "I know this is hard. Really hard. But it might be better if you can stop crying. People will stare. Someone might recognize you. Another reporter, say, who'll want to take your photo and put it in the newspaper."

Tynslee's sobs choked off on a gasp. "Would they really do that?"

"Believe it. And tomorrow they're all going to be at Frank's initial court appearance"—Lola neglected to mention that she'd be there, too—"writing stories about the charges against him. So if you know something that would help him, you need to tell someone." *Someone like me.*

"I can't." The pink patches on Tynslee's face went scarlet. Another watery eruption seemed imminent.

Only Lola's grip kept the girl from sliding from the bench to the ground. She'd been worried about Tynslee weeping aloud, attracting attention. Now she feared Tynslee would faint. Sixteen years old, she thought. Mother dead, boyfriend in jail with a murder charge in the offing. And being outed as having sex with her boyfriend to boot. Lola gathered that for a Mormon girl, the implications were monumental, so much as to be on par with the shattering losses she'd suffered only the day before.

As for the loss of Tynslee's mother, Lola thought her own bereavement seemed clean, almost pure, by comparison. What if the person who'd killed Charlie had been someone she'd cared for? How would she handle the loss of trust as well as love? And if someone she'd loved had killed Charlie, would she have been able to accept that person's guilt? Or would she, like Tynslee, insist upon innocence even in the face of a plausible motive? She needed to calm the girl.

"Let's talk about something else. That'll help you settle down." But what? Lola had never been good at small talk. "This is the first time I've been to Salt Lake. The lake—it's really big."

"The largest salt lake in the Western Hemisphere." Tynslee's automatic response had the sound of something memorized since elementary school.

"I saw something strange when I flew in. Like a castle, at the edge of the lake."

Tynslee nodded through a hiccup. "SaltAir. It's an old resort. They use it for concerts now. I'm not allowed to go to them, though."

"Why not? It was pretty."

Tynslee lifted a shoulder. "Maybe from the air. Up close, it's pretty decrepit. My parents think people do drugs there."

Drugs. The fear of every middle-class parent. Followed closely by sex, although Lola guessed most parents didn't want to know about their kids having sex, as long as nobody got pregnant. The warnings about drugs, though, started in kindergarten and intensified by the year. Already she was getting pop-up ads on her iPad about drug-testing kits for parents, the internet having somehow divined that she was the mother of a child approaching middle school age.

"I take it you don't use drugs."

"Of course not."

Lola's remark had had the intended result. Tynslee straightened, eyes flashing indignation.

"But you and Frank ... Tynslee, you're his best alibi. If he was with you all night, then he couldn't have killed your mother. And if you tell the police that, the information that you were together never has to come out in public. They can just say simply that he has a credible alibi and let him go."

"Trang."

"What?"

"His name is Trang. And I'm no alibi. I wish I were. But I'm not."

Trang? No, Melena definitely had called him Frank. As had the newspaper stories to which Munro had directed her for background. Lola filed the discrepancy away for future reference and concentrated on the more pressing matter. "You really can't give him an alibi?"

"I didn't go to him that night. I couldn't. We got caught. We had to stop."

"In his bed?" Lola's own teenage escapades had taken place in the safety, if not the comfort, of cars. She tried to imagine her parents, to whom like all teenagers she'd assigned utter asexuality, walking in on her and a boyfriend. Even now, from the comfortable remove of adulthood, her face burned at the thought. She stared at some nearby tennis courts where a doubles game had begun, the ball thunking back and forth, a background of incongruous normalcy to the scenario of shame and death.

"No. His dad ran into me one night going home, crossing the lawn."

Bryce, outside again in the middle of the night.

"What did he say?"

Tynslee shook her head. "He didn't have to say anything."

A ball went wild and bounced toward them. Rex yanked the leash from Lola's hand and leapt after it, tail wagging as he presented it to one of the players. "Great dog you've got there." The man waved his appreciation. Rex bounded back to them and, satisfied that Lola posed no threat, dropped his head into her lap and rolled soulful eyes her way. Lola ran her hand over his head and dug her fingers against the sweet spot at the base of an ear. He groaned his appreciation. Longing for Bub knifed through her.

With some difficulty, she returned her attention to Tynslee. "What happened after he saw you that time?"

"Nothing. He just looked at me and shook his head and said, 'You, too? Guess I was wrong.'"

"You, too? What does that mean?" That Bryce had been trysting with Sariah? Just as Tynslee was sneaking around with Frank?

A thought that had apparently never occurred to Tynslee. The girl ducked her head and hitched a shoulder. Her glance slid toward Lola, then away. "That I was just like those other girls, I guess. Gentiles."

"Gentiles?"

Tynslee's lips twitched in something that, under any other circumstances, might have been a smile. "It's what Mormons call everyone else."

"So the Shumways are the only ones who know?"

"I wish." All traces of a smile vanished. "Mrs. Shumway must have told my mom, because Trang said she came over to his house and yelled at his mom later that day."

"Yelled what?"

"Kind of what you'd expect. 'It's time to make this right.'" The shoulder lifted again, higher than before. "So we got engaged."

That last word a rising wail. Lola sat on her hand to keep from clapping it across Tynslee's mouth. She tried a verbal slap instead.

"You don't want to marry him."

"It's not that." Tynslee's gaze drifted sideways again, met Lola's, kept going. "I love him!"

Lola's bullshit meter pinged. Tynslee was trying to convince her of something, maybe something beyond her boyfriend's alleged innocence.

The back-and-forth thunk of the tennis ball halted. Lola didn't dare look toward the courts. She tried again to lead Tynslee back into conversation.

"What about Frank? Trang." Dancing around the conclusion the police already may have reached. A reluctant boyfriend, looking for a way out, too scared to say as much to an insistent parent, coming to the logically illogical conclusion that the only escape lay in murder.

The girl wrapped her arms around herself and rocked to the faltering rhythm of her words. "He wanted to get married as much as I did. But we couldn't have a wedding because of … what we'd done. And that's not the worst of it."

Tynslee knuckled a fist into eyes gone startlingly clear. Lola tried to ignore the relentless BS meter, flashing on full alert now, and concentrated on what the girl had said. Being forced into a marriage at age eighteen was bad enough. "What's worse?"

"He couldn't go on his mission."

Even Lola knew that LDS youths were required to serve two-year missions after graduating high school. "Why not?" she asked.

Tynslee's look was withering, worthy of Donovan Munro. Lola began to wish she'd done a lot more homework.

"You have to be pure." Tynslee spat the word, the same one Melena had used. "For the temple wedding and the mission, both."

"Pure? Does that mean what I think it means?"

"Exactly. But if you're married, you can't go on a mission. And that mission meant everything to him. The church just started a mission in Vietnam and he wanted to go there. We all tried to tell him that probably wouldn't happen—the church chooses where you go. But he wouldn't listen. Nothing was going to stop him. He was desperate."

Desperate enough to kill someone who got in his way?

Tynslee answered Lola's unspoken question. "That's why he never would have killed Mom. She was on our side."

"On your side? What does that mean?"

Tynslee swiped at her damp face with the back of her hand, took the leash from Lola, and stood. "I've got to get home. They'll be worried."

"Wait. You haven't told me why he couldn't have killed her. And why your mom was on your side. And what she was on your side about."

"I want to. Believe me. But I can't. I promised him. You just have to believe me. Miss Wicks, I've lost my mother. I can't lose him, too."

God help her, she did believe the girl, Lola thought. She didn't know why. Because if anything, Tynslee had provided even more ballast to anchor the narrative that Frank killed Sariah. The nagging feeling that something was off, that somehow Tynslee was playing her, remained. But Tynslee had wrenched the story from herself word by agonized word, with none of the ease of a practiced liar.

"Tynslee!" Lola ran after her, rounding a turn that took her back toward the house. A couple walking across the street stopped to stare. Lola could bet that within minutes, Tynslee's aunt and uncle would know that a strange woman had pursued their niece down the street.

Lola slowed to a rapid walk and hissed to Tynslee, a few steps ahead, "I respect your promise to Frank. But is there someone else I could talk to, someone else who knows why he couldn't have killed her?"

"No!" Tynslee shrieked. "Leave me alone!"

The woman across the street conferred with her husband, and reached for her cellphone. Lola turned on her heel and headed back to the park, sprinting for her car as soon as she was out of sight.

———

Lola fled the neighborhood, hoping the couple wouldn't remember what she looked like, wouldn't pass that information along to police.

Her biggest liability in pursuing the story—her near-total unfamiliarity with Salt Lake and its environs—was also her strongest advantage. She didn't want her anonymity blown quite so quickly. It wasn't until she was back in the car, confounding the Directions Bitch with one impulsive turn after another, designed to foil any pursuit, that she relaxed enough to consider her next move.

She had to talk to Kwesi. From what Melena had said, the two boys were at least as close as Frank and Tynslee, albeit in different ways. But Kwesi was in the house with his sister, likewise mourning the loss of his mother and arrest of his best friend. Lola had taken her one shot at that household for the day. She'd go to Frank's court appearance the next day, and then maybe try Kwesi afterward. With the barest plan in place, she finally gave in and let the Directions Bitch steer her back to the hotel and the sweet relief of the waiting pill.

She patted her pocket. Then again. Took a hand off the steering wheel and contorted herself to dig inside it. Her finger poked through a hole. The pills were gone.

# THIRTEEN

LOLA DROVE BACK AND forth, back and forth, on a grid of extra-wide streets and extra-long blocks that managed to be both simple and bewildering at once, their names an odd jumble of numbers and directions—streets with North and South in their names, even though they ran east and west? Two sets of numbers and directions designating a single building? Really?—changing altogether if the street in question took the slightest bend.

It didn't matter. She wasn't looking for a specific address, but a kind of neighborhood. Jan had described Salt Lake as the squeakiest-clean city in the country. At the time, Lola accused her of exaggeration, and of the added insult of falling back on cliché. Now she feared Jan had been right. She'd yet to see a scrap of trash on the streets and the sidewalks were nearly empty of pedestrians, let alone the kind she sought: a disreputable, shifty-eyed sort. The kind of person who might sell pills.

Her hands slipped on the steering wheel. Lola told herself her sweaty palms had everything to do with wandering in a new place, and in no way were a sign of incipient, let alone full-blown, addiction. She could quit the pills. Would quit, in fact, once she was safe at home again. But here, dealing with the stress of a strange city, it would be foolish not to seek a little solace. She shoved aside memories of her time in Kabul, where she'd managed without pills in a place where seemingly every other person carried an AK-47 and every few weeks brought the news of another reporter's death. She passed a convention center—no people at all outside—took a turn, and then another. And let a long breath escape.

———

A park stretched before her, filling one of Salt Lake's super-size blocks, at first glance so green and inviting as to explain the crowds.

A longer look told a different story. The throngs were male, poorly dressed, and lacking in purpose—at least the sort of purpose typically found in parks. No one jogged or even speed-walked on the paths. No one played tennis, volleyball, or basketball, despite the inviting courts. The people lounging on the grass could be mistaken for picnickers until one noticed the preponderance of brown paper bags with bottles poking from them and the utter absence of food. Every city, even Kabul with its burgeoning population of heroin addicts, had someplace where the down-and-out congregated. Lola found it reassuring that Salt Lake, too, grappled with normalcy.

She parked the rental car and waded in. The trick, she thought as she shook her head at repeated requests for change—holding her breath against the fug of unwashed bodies, alcohol fumes, and even the occasional whiff of weed—would be to avoid the rummies and find the pill-poppers, and then hope that the latter were dealers, too.

So far, except for her guilt-inducing foray into Alice's medicine cabinet, her stash had been acquired legally. Lola had no idea how to go about buying drugs on the street. She strode through the park, trying to look like she knew what she was doing. The older guys were probably alcoholics and therefore useless to her. But the older guys predominated. She heard the sound of wheels on concrete and whipped around, not fast enough to catch the skateboarder as he zoomed past. Damn. He might have been a prospect.

Lola cast an eye skyward, assessing how much time she had before dark. Not enough. She had handled her fair share of sketchy situations, but thought that even in Utah, a park full of vagrants after nightfall probably wasn't the safest place. On the other hand, the thought of spending a night alone and teeth-grindingly awake in the hotel room was unbearable. She'd make one more circuit.

This time, nobody bothered hitting her up for change. Maybe they thought she was a tourist from one of the nearby upscale hotels, oblivious to her surroundings as she logged some mandatory steps on her fitness tracker before erasing the day's gains in a steakhouse. A few blocks away, high on the hill that marked the city center, lights glowed golden within the office buildings. Spotlights around the temple cast bright beams against a cobalt sky.

She quickened her pace. Maybe it was time to give up on the park. Buy a bottle of something on the way home, although she didn't enjoy getting drunk and hated a hangover. Besides, she was pretty sure she remembered Jan saying that even though Salt Lake had relaxed its straitlaced ways mightily in order to accommodate the 2002 Winter Olympics, buying alcohol could still be a tricky proposition. In the deepening gloom, Lola couldn't quite see the golden statue of the Angel Moroni—thanks to Google, she knew his name—that topped the temple, but she glowered in his direction.

"This is all your fault," she muttered. In Baltimore, where she'd lived for so many years, it would have taken her all of about five minutes to find pills, despite her inexperience in procuring them.

A voice floated her way.

"Need a hit?

———

The youth's face shone thin and pale beneath a black watch cap. A hank of sandy hair had escaped, flopping over his forehead.

"Well?" The boy shuffled his feet.

Lola glanced around. No one near them. Still, she stepped off the path and under a tree. Bad move, maybe. In the dark, no one could see their transaction. Nor could anyone see if he decided to rob her. She edged back toward the path, close enough to leap into the light if necessary, and tried to sound tough. "What you got?"

"Pills, a little weed." His voice shook.

He was as least as nervous as she. Not necessarily a good sign. Jumpy people were prone to panicked violence. The quicker she completed this transaction, the better. "Oxycontin?"

The watch cap moved from side to side. "Vikes."

"Vibes?"

"Vikings, Vees, Vitamin V."

Lola shook her head. So much for her knowledgeable pose.

"Come on. Vicodin. That work for you?"

Lola remembered a lazy dreaminess from a long-ago wisdom tooth extraction, not the knockout punch of Oxy but pleasant none-theless. "It'll have to. How much?"

"Uh, five bucks apiece."

Lola had stashed a hundred dollars in her pocket before venturing into the park. She hadn't expected the pills to be so cheap. "How many you got?"

The youth backed farther into the shadows. "How much you looking for?"

She calculated. What if she didn't like it? She didn't want to be stuck with a bunch of useless pills. On the other hand, having a substantial stash would obviate the need to raid Auntie Lena's medicine cabinet again when she got home, erasing the crawly feeling of guilt.

"Twenty."

"Holy shit. That's all I've got. I mean, sure. Here." The boy shoved a baggie toward her. Lola reached for it.

"Hey. Aren't you forgetting something?" He rubbed the fingers of his free hand together.

Lola extracted five twenties from her pocket. He snatched them away at least as eagerly as she grabbed the bag from his hand.

# FOURTEEN

EVEN AS SHE REACHED for the phone, Lola knew it was early, well before she'd set her phone alarm to go off. She wondered how long it had been ringing. It kept on, barely a few seconds' pause for the kick to voicemail before the person calling hit redial. She looked at the screen. "Oh, no. Not again." Donovan Munro.

"Do you always sound this bad when you wake up?"

"You didn't wake me up." Lola sat up in bed and hung on to the end table until the room righted itself. Vicodin had changed since her teens. Or maybe because the painkiller wasn't wasting energy fighting actual physical pain, it had gone straight to her brain. Whatever the reason, she'd floated away into a blessedly dreamless sleep. That is, if she didn't count Munro's call as a nightmare.

"If this is how you sound when you're awake, we've got trouble. I was just calling to make sure you're set to go to the kid's initial court appearance. I thought maybe I was being overly attentive, but I'm glad I called. I hope you don't sound like this when you interview people today."

Asshole. She was going to have to come up with a new expletive for Munro. This one was wearing thin.

"The hearing's not until ten." She had plenty of time.

Munro disabused her of that notion. "It's rush hour. And court will be crowded and you don't know anybody. Best to go early and scope things out, put names with faces."

The sort of thing he might have said to a young inexperienced reporter or, back in the day, a student like Jan.

Her thumb slid toward the "off" icon.

"Wait. What'd you find out yesterday? Anything that's not in the papers? Our next deadline's not for three weeks, but if you've got good stuff, we can post it online. At least, we can if you verify it. Not anything like that throat-cutting thing you strung me along with yesterday."

Still a newspaperman, she thought. He may have been trapped in the magazine's cushy cage, but at least he retained his get-it-first instincts. "Actually—" She started to tell him about her conversation with Tynslee when a beeping noise on his end interrupted her.

"That's the publisher. I've got to go. Listen, come by after the hearing and tell me about it. Better yet, come by my house later. I'm bogged down all day but I do Family Home Evening with my son on Wednesdays because his mom has him on Mondays, so I can't stay here late. We'll have pizza."

Lola stared at the phone that had gone silent in her hand. Was Donovan Munro hitting on her? But no, his little boy would be there. Her phone flashed back to its home screen, the time prominently displayed. Eight thirty. Plenty of time for a shower and a stroll to the courthouse. Then she checked the distance on her phone. A mile. Once, she'd have jogged over without breaking a sweat. Now she decided to drive, which would give her time for a second cup of coffee before she left.

Lola put Donovan Munro out of her mind and headed for the shower.

---

He had warned her about rush-hour traffic. Lola thought of rush hour in terms of the freeway and not at all within the city center.

But a solid, unmoving line of cars confronted her when she pulled the car out of the hotel's garage, not a single driver inclined to let her edge into a lane. Lola waited as the cars inched past through two turns of a light before long-dormant skills acquired in Baltimore reasserted themselves and she simply accelerated, forcing a motorist to hit the brakes and let her into the lane, or risk being struck by the crazy woman in the rental car.

Reality quashed her moment of triumph as the minutes on the car's clock flipped past. She could have walked to the courthouse and back twice over in the time it took her to drive there. And, once there, she confronted the utter lack of parking spaces, a problem exacerbated by the TV vans taking up more than their share. Parking was never an issue in Magpie or on the Blackfeet Reservation or at most of the other places her job at the *Daily Express* sent her. She wasted still more time creeping along the blocks surrounding the modern courthouse, whose architectural excesses included a rounded entrance that looked like nothing so much as a multi-story R2-D2.

By the time she finally gave up on finding an empty space and opted for a parking garage, taking an extra minute to adjust to the reality of the eight-dollar fee, it was a quarter to ten. She trotted the three blocks back to the courthouse, yet again cursing herself for abandoning her running routine, and shouted a question about the courtroom's location to a man standing outside the door.

He laughed. "Just follow the crowd. Can't miss it."

As soon as she entered the building, Lola heard the purposeful hum that accompanied any press gaggle. She endured the metal detector and slipped through the courtroom door just as the bailiff began to pull it shut. The benches were full. Television cameras on tall tripods lined the wall. The bailiff touched her arm. "Full up," he whispered. "You'll have to wait in the hall."

The bailiff was dreaming if he thought Lola Wicks was going to miss the action. She stepped into the back row and lowered herself toward someone's lap. "Hey!" Lola's butt inched down. The person inched aside. Murmurs of outrage rumbled along the row. Lola shoehorned herself sideways into what felt like a hand's width of space and avoided the bailiff's eyes. She was in.

She'd wait awhile to pull out her iPad. People were mad enough at her already. Let them think, at least for a few minutes, that she was a grieving relative or at least a nosy neighbor.

She glanced around the courtroom, taking stock. Most of the reporters, including Anne Peterson, the woman she'd met at the crime scene, were in the front row, tweeting away on their phones. The Shumways filled an entire bench; across the aisle, the Ballard presence was touchingly sparse. Galon Ballard sat between Kwesi and Tynslee, clasping his daughter's hand, whatever strain caused by her nighttime trysts dissolved by their mutual grief.

Galon, the Person Statistically Most Likely to Have Killed Sariah, had been immediately cleared by police by virtue of being, as Melena had already told her, a hundred miles away. Lola scrolled through her phone to the affidavit she'd downloaded after paying the fee required by the state's public records system. In laconic legalese, it laid out the scanty but damning evidence against Frank—the hockey stick, his prints the only ones on it. No mention of the knife or whatever sharp object had killed her.

Galon had the weathered skin of someone who'd spent weekends since boyhood on the ski slopes, but his cheeks were pink from a recent shave and the blond sweep of his hair freshly gelled. He turned to whisper something in Tynslee's ear and Lola saw the cleft in his chin that she'd noticed in the photograph. He and Sariah must have made such a postcard couple. Lola wondered uncharitably if the inevitable next wife would also lend the image of a matched set.

Tynslee's appearance was an improvement from the previous day, if only by virtue of having exchanged her sweats for a school-worthy skirt and blouse. But her blouse was buttoned up wrong, and her hair lay lank around her shoulders. She slumped against her father. Beside her, Kwesi, the only person of color in the courtroom, was a contrast in straight-backed, narrow-eyed attentiveness.

Lola shifted her gaze to the opposite side of the courtroom. The Shumways, naturally enough, looked as though they'd rather be anywhere else. But a first-year law student could have told them the obvious: it was important for the accused's family to show up in force, to let the world know that someone from such a loving, supportive environment could not possibly have committed such a brutal crime. The couple's daughters, outfitted in yards of flowered rayon that added years and pounds to their appearance, clutched babies and shushed fidgety toddlers.

Melena was absent, a regrettable lapse in courtroom etiquette. Still, the appearance of a distraught mother, one possibly prone to hysterics, was to nobody's advantage. Melena would be forgiven this

111

early absence. Later proceedings would be a different story. Lola had seen more than one mother swaying glassy-eyed on a courtroom bench, her necessary presence enabled by tranquilizers.

Bryce glared at his lap. At one point, he turned toward the Ballards. Galon dipped his perfect chin in acknowledgment of his best friend's presence. Bryce's expression softened so abruptly that Lola feared he would burst into tears.

"All rise!"

Lola bobbed in her seat, afraid that if she stood up all the way, the bench would fill in behind her when everyone sat down. It was time to take out her iPad.

———

The judge, with the hunched shoulders, forward-thrust head, and darting eyes of a raptor, swept into the courtroom, black robes billowing. He climbed up behind the bench and perched on his stool, banging his gavel twice. "Be seated."

Lola wedged herself back into her keyhole, claiming a bit more space and ignoring the resentment wafting down the row. The judge waited until the room had settled itself, then nodded toward the lawyers sitting at different tables. "Mr. Kimball? Mr. Hulet? Are we ready?"

Lola scratched down an approximation of the names. The nice thing about working for a magazine instead of a newspaper, she thought, was that she could look up the spellings later. A newspaper would expect her to be tweeting and posting updates throughout the appearance, and woe to her if she got a detail wrong. The wrath of the internet would rain down upon her. Her phone dinged with an alert. Behind her, the bailiff ostentatiously cleared his throat. She silenced her phone and glanced at the text.

*Give us something ASAP that we can pop online. Add a line at the end saying a full story will appear in the mag's next issue.* Munro.

Hell and damnation. Lola reminded herself to buttonhole Anne Peterson after Frank's court appearance was over. Maybe Peterson would take pity on her and give her the lawyers' full names. A side door creaked open. A sigh gusted through the room.

Frank shuffled in, awkward in plastic sandals and ankle chains, an armed jail guard on either side. His pants were jail-issue orange, but instead of the usual tunic, he wore a ridged Cordura vest imposed upon inmates deemed a suicide risk. But he didn't have the hopeless, desperate look of others Lola had seen subjected to the garments, instead turning and subjecting the room to a curious scrutiny. He was smart enough not to smile, but his gaze lingered on the Shumways and stopped again on Kwesi and Tynslee. He lifted his head in a sort of salute. Kwesi nodded back. Tynslee gasped and turned her face into her father's broad shoulder.

The judge rapped his gavel. "I know this is a difficult day for everyone, but please restrain yourselves. Further outbursts will result in removal from the courtroom."

Frank's glance stopped a final time, with a jolt so palpable that those watching twisted in their seats to see who'd caught his attention. Lola suppressed a gasp of her own. Without the knit watch cap, the floppy forelock was even more pronounced. She was almost certain it was the same youth who'd sold her the Vicodin. Bold move for a felon, showing up in a courthouse. Of course, buying the pills made her a felon, too. A long look passed between the two boys, their faces unreadable.

Frank's lawyer touched his shoulder, urging his focus forward. Vicodin Boy, belatedly aware of the stares focused his way, withdrew into an oversize sweatshirt and pulled its hood up around his face. Lola was sure he hadn't seen her. Still, she was relieved when the lawyers introduced themselves: the district attorney, Andrew Kimball—the head guy; no assistants for a crime of such magnitude, Lola noted—and Robert Hulet, a public defender. There. Now she had the names, if not the spellings.

But a more urgent question dominated. It was two days after the arrest, and the Shumways hadn't yet obtained an attorney for Frank? It wasn't unusual for a public defender to take the initial appearance, but surely the Shumways had the resources to hire their own attorney for their son ... and just as surely, a city the size of Salt Lake had a stable of hotshot lawyers who'd jump at the chance to be involved in such a prominent case, not to mention the billable hours it would entail.

"Today we're going to outline the very serious charges against you," the judge began.

"I didn't do anything," Frank interrupted. "So you don't need to charge me."

*Slam.* The gavel hit the bench so hard it nearly bounced back into the judge's face.

"We will have no more of that! Mr. Hulet, please instruct your client as to decorum."

The public defender leaned over and spoke urgently into Frank's ear. "But I didn't—" Frank began.

"Not now." The public defender made a slicing motion with his hand.

The charges of murder, felony assault, and breaking and entering were read, along with the potential penalties they carried. At the words "life in prison, or death," the room stirred as one. The judge raised his gavel. The room resumed its hush.

The prosecutor stood and adjusted a three-piece suit. Lola braced herself for some grandstanding. It was not uncommon for a big-city prosecutor to position himself as a state's next attorney general, and from there, governor. Or maybe a state Supreme Court seat. Politicians rarely went wrong by proclaiming themselves to be tough on crime. A murder trial was a gift wrapped in shiny paper and a big opportunistic bow.

Kimball outlined the crime scene in brief but pointed detail. The slash across the throat. "Almost surgical, your honor. Nearly decapitated." Lola no longer had to worry about finding a source for that particular detail. The knife that had inflicted the fatal wound was missing, however. Unlike the hockey stick: "Sunk an inch into the skull. Unimaginable force. Clearly the work of a very strong person." He stared at Frank, letting his gaze linger on the well-defined biceps revealed by the vest.

Frank sat, impassive, following the proceeding as though all of the suits were talking about someone else.

"Also very much to the point, Your Honor, Le Cong Trang Shumway is foreign-born—"

The public defender rose. "With all due respect, *Frank* Shumway is a US citizen."

"—and, until this vicious crime, was hoping to travel in just a few weeks to his home country for his mission," Kimball continued, unperturbed. No mention of the pending wedding that had canceled the mission. And Tynslee had said it was unlikely Frank would be assigned to Vietnam, anyway.

The public defender seemed unaware of that particular detail, also. "On a mission! A church mission! And there was no guarantee he'd go out of the country. There are plenty of missions within the United States. As you know."

The gavel banged, followed by a lecture about interruptions.

The prosecutor let the silence that followed the lecture linger, milking the moment before intoning, "I'd respectfully request that no bail be imposed. Or, if you must, bail of one million dollars."

*Crack.* This time, the gavel anticipated the shocked gasps.

The public defender rose for his own predictable arguments: no previous record, good grades in school, outstanding athlete, supportive family. At that last, the judge looked toward Bryce, who managed a wan nod.

"Under the circumstances, Your Honor, there's no reason not to release him on his own recognizance," Hulet finished.

Bryce blanched.

Lola tried to imagine how she'd feel if Margaret had been accused of such a crime, then sent back home to await trial. Would she fiercely defend her child against such an outrageous charge, damn the evidence? Or would she bring her home but sleep with door locked and dresser shoved against it? A silly exercise. Margaret would never do such a thing. Lola reminded herself that nearly every parent whose child stood accused of anything from shoplifting to outright terrorism had likely felt the same way.

A final bounce of the gavel. "No bail. This proceeding is concluded."

Frank shuffled to his feet and turned toward the spectators, searching the space where Tynslee and Kwesi had been. But their father was already hustling them toward the door, a protective arm around them, shielding them from the television cameras swinging their way. He didn't give them a chance to look back.

———

Outside the courtroom, reporters mobbed the district attorney.

Lola dodged from one side of the horde to the other, looking for someone she didn't see. Finally, she spotted the public defender heading alone down a side hallway, ignored by reporters seeking the DA's quotable bombast.

He turned a corner. Lola didn't dare call attention to herself. She forced her legs into what she hoped resembled a leisurely stride, breaking into a run the minute she rounded the corner. "Mister... Mister...?" What the hell was his name? Whatever it was, he turned.

"I'm Lola Wicks. With *Families of Faith*." She mumbled that part. "I just have a few questions. Starting with the spelling of your name."

"J-o-h-n S-m-i-t-h."

Lola leaned back on her heels. "Cute. But seriously."

"Sorry. It's been a long couple of days. Bob H-u-l-e-t." Lola scratched a line across some scrawls in her notebook. She'd written it as *Hewlett*. Which is why you always, always asked.

Hulet removed the kind of round wire-frame glasses that everyone else had abandoned years ago in favor of faux tortoiseshell in retro shapes. Although Lola guessed the wire frames were retro now. He held the glasses up to the light. Even she could see the smudges.

"Here." He thrust an armload of files at her. Lola took them as he polished the glasses on his tie. "I don't talk to the press. So, as long as you spell my name right, we're good." He put the glasses back on and reached for the files.

Lola took a step back. "I don't need to quote you on this. I just want to know something. Why you?"

"Give me those." He reached for the files.

Lola took another step back. "It's off the record." She had a long-standing rule of never offering an off-the-record conversation in advance. But in this case, it didn't seem to matter. Hulet wasn't going to give her anything anyway.

His arms dropped to his side. "Why me? You mean because without a private attorney this kid doesn't have a prayer of a chance? I've got news for you. He doesn't have a prayer of a chance anyway. Even though he didn't do it. Remember, you said you wouldn't quote me. So don't."

"How do you know he didn't do it?"

"I've been at this awhile. Just like you, apparently. Do you think he did it?"

People were always trying to get reporters to take sides, and reacted badly to any protestations that it was unethical. Lola told the truth. "Every time I've tried to guess which way a case would go, I've been wrong. Same with elections. I just wait for the outcome."

Hulet muttered something. Lola handed him the files, pretending she hadn't heard the word *coward*. He started to walk away, then turned back. "That business about the mission. I don't know where Kimball got that information—and it bothers me, it bothers me greatly, that the prosecution had it and I didn't—but you're obviously not from here, so you probably don't know this. He might have wanted to go to Vietnam, but it was extremely unlikely he'd have been posted there. People don't get a choice about things like that."

Exactly what Tynslee had said. Questions, so many, ricocheted around Lola's brain.

She took a shot with one of them. "Just one more thing. Have his parents been to see him? Either of them? Both? Anyone from the family? Or anyone else?"

"That's more than one thing." Hulet reached for a door. "No. Nobody." The door closed just short of a slam.

———

Lola pecked at the iPad's keyboard, typing up a quick summary of the court proceedings—with Hulet's name correctly spelled—and emailed it to Munro.

No response. But a few minutes later, when she checked *Families of Faith's* website, the story was there. She drove slowly back to the hotel, mentally compiling a list of questions that, no matter her reluctance for the initial topic, she attributed to her own hardwired instinct for story.

*How could Bryce and Melena let a terrified teenager sit in jail for more than twenty-four hours without visiting him? Or trying to get him a lawyer?*

"Easy." She answered her own question out of habit. "He's accused of killing one of their best friends. And seducing her daughter." Although, as Lola knew from personal experience, daughters were quite capable of doing the seducing.

*What had Bryce Shumway been doing outside in the middle of the night when he caught Tynslee sneaking home from his son's bedroom?*

"Again, easy. Anything. Maybe he's a secret smoker. An insomniac. Had a bad dream. A fight with his wife." Lola thought of all the reasons she'd gotten up in the middle of the night. She'd never gone outside, though. The Montana prairie—alive with rattlesnakes in the summer, subjected to Arctic blasts in the winter—didn't invite nighttime meanderings. But she couldn't rule out the possibility of an affair with Sariah—lovely in a way poor Melena had never been, and with the added attraction of proximity—lending a plausible explanation for Bryce's "You, too?" comment to Tynslee.

*Why did Tynslee seem so sure about Frank's innocence, yet reluctant to share more information?*

"Also easy. She's in shock. And she's a teenage girl, which means everything that happens in the world is about her. Maybe she's still fixated on being caught having sex. She can only process one big thing at a time. And her boyfriend being accused of killing her mother—that's more than an adult could handle, let alone a teenager. Also, being a teenage girl, she was probably locked in some kind of combat with her mother even before the sex thing came up. Maybe even wished her dead. Now this. No wonder she's in shock."

Lola's car idled at a traffic light. She glanced over at the next car. The driver peered at her, watching her animated conversation with herself. She grabbed her cellphone and held it to her ear, pretending.

The light changed and she hit the gas, propelled by another thought. Tynslee had said their impending marriage would interfere Frank's mission; that the thought made him "desperate." Again, the obvious questions, especially given that he'd hoped, no matter how improbably, to go to the country of his birth. *Desperate enough to kill? And might Tynslee, out of some misguided loyalty, have helped him?*

Lola's imagination plunged deeper, darker still. Tynslee had seemed so sure that Frank hadn't killed her mother. Was it possible that the girl herself had? She wouldn't be the first child to kill a parent over thwarted love. But then, why the hockey stick that so clearly implicated her boyfriend?

Even if Frank hadn't killed Sariah, whoever did kill her wanted Frank to take the blame. Lola's next job would be to come up with a list of possibilities. To give to Munro, so that he could hand it over to the reporter who replaced her, of course. But first, there was the unpleasant prospect of dinner with Munro.

# FIFTEEN

LOLA HEADED FOR MUNRO's house, rehearsing her get-out-of-the-story speech, pausing occasionally for interruptions by the officious tones of the Directions Bitch.

Munro lived within the city, his neighborhood streets bedeviled by Salt Lake City's bewildering street numbering system but a relief after the deliberate meandering of all the Courts and Circles and Ways in Camellia. A small business district featured coffeehouses, bookshops, and boutiques. People sat at sidewalk tables, in jackets but determined to take advantage of the kind of evening they wouldn't see again until spring. Lola had lived so long in Magpie, with its lone cafe reliably fronted by a row of muddy pickups and a convenience store for faster fare, that she'd forgotten how a big city, beyond the inconveniences of crowds and traffic and parking, also offered its share of enticements.

The car before her stopped, maneuvering itself into the sole empty parking space in front a bookstore. Tall windows on either side of the store's door gave a view of crammed shelves and end tables high with enticing stacks. Lola drew a deep breath, imagining the pleasurable musty scent that invariably greeted her in such stores, the seductive wandering past the shelves, a finger trailing over the spines. This one. No, this. And this. Lola's trips to Great Falls or Helena or Missoula were rare, but in each city, bookstore owners greeted her by name. Charlie swore the cash registers ka-chinged in delight at the very sight of her.

*Charlie.* Lola yanked at the wheel, cutting around the car trying to park, cursing an oncoming vehicle. Inside it, three faces—child, mother, and goddamn father—turned to stare. For once, Lola welcomed the flat, unemotional voice of the Directions Bitch.

"Turn left here. In two blocks, your destination will be on the right."

Away from the business district, older homes predominated, brick bungalows and small Tudors. Lola lingered in the rental car after finding Munro's house, once more going over her ironclad reasons for ditching the story.

The door opened. Light flooded the front steps. Munro's voice reached her even through the closed car window.

"Are you going to sit there all night? Because I'm not toting your pizza out to you."

---

The house was a surprise, with its commodious leather sofas and chairs, worn Persian rugs, and just enough clutter to make Lola feel at home. She'd figured on the dorm room decor of the divorced dads she'd known.

"This is a lot nicer than I expected." Someday, she thought, I'll learn not to say the first thing that comes to my mind.

Munro pushed his hair back from his face. "My wife—my ex-wife—moved into her new husband's place over by the university. Worked out great for me, house-wise."

"I didn't think Mormons got divorced."

"They don't. But exceptions are made when one makes the mistake of marrying a Gentile and then comes to her senses and leaves him for a Mormon."

So Munro had been dumped. Probably a whole new experience for him. Unfortunately, it didn't appear to have humbled him.

The kitchen table was much like his desk, two spaces cleared amid a scattering of newspapers. With a sigh of envy, Lola noted the *New York Times*, which had yet to bestow home delivery upon Montana. Munro cleared away a third place and handed Lola three plates.

"Silverware's in there." He pointed to a drawer. "Napkins in the one below it. What are you drinking? Water? Juice? Beer? No wine, I'm afraid. I've got some of the hard stuff somewhere, too, if that's your preference."

Lola raised her eyebrows. "Booze? Really?"

"I didn't have it in the house when Bevany was here. Out of respect. The minute she left, the beer came back. Don't ever let anybody tell you divorce is all bad."

*Marriage is better.* Something that, pre-Charlie, Lola never could have imagined herself saying. The words caught in her throat. She spoke around them. "A beer would be fine."

He reached into the fridge. "This is the real thing. Hard to get anything but near-beer in Utah. Anytime someone visits from out of state, I ask them to bring full-strength brews. If you'd been driving instead of flying, I'd have put in an order. Damned if I'm going to support the crazy alcohol laws they've got here by shopping in the state stores."

Lola refrained from reminding him that he'd been the one who'd insisted she fly. She licked her lips at the hiss and fizz of opened bottle and dealt the napkins to their places.

"Glass?"

She shook her head and nearly grabbed the bottle from his hand, eager for a quick buzz. Throughout her career, she'd avoided unwelcome assignments with the wiliness of the professional she was, but she'd never backed out of a story once she started one. Especially not a story as good as this one had improbably turned into. She needed all the fortification she could get.

Munro looked at the table, raised an eyebrow, and retrieved knives and forks from the drawer. He stepped to the kitchen door. "Malachi! Dinner!"

Lola took a breath and prepared to launch into her spiel as Munro removed a pizza box from a warm oven. The plan was to hit him with her decision just before his son walked into the kitchen. She figured he wouldn't dare rebuke her in front of the boy, and that the meal that followed would take the edge off his anger.

She tilted the beer high. Swallowed long. They didn't call it liquid courage for nothing. "This story. With all the changes, it's going to take a long time. Given the kind of story you want, I really think it's best for you to pull me off it now, and hand it over to someone else, just like I suggested before. You know, to do the story justice."

Footsteps on the stairs. Lola congratulated herself on her timing.

Munro's lips thinned. He made an abrupt movement. His hair swung free. He looked beyond her.

"Malachi, this is Miss Wicks. Miss Wicks, my son Malachi."

Lola turned and stooped, holding out her hand at toddler height. Found herself looking at thighs. She straightened. Her hand fell to her side.

"Hey, Miss Wicks," said the youth who'd sold her the pills in the park.

# SIXTEEN

THE MEAL BEGAN, AND continued, in silence.

Lola folded her piece of pizza over on itself and raised it to her mouth. Munro and Malachi paused with knives and forks poised.

"I grew up eating it this way." She took a defiant bite and chewed longer than necessary, the better to avoid talking.

Forks scraped two plates. Three jaws thoughtfully worked over bite after bite. Munro set his crust aside. Longing for Bub stabbed at Lola. The crust was his favorite, his reward for sitting apart from them while they ate, without overt begging, although his beseeching gaze from across the room was practically audible.

"Lola—Miss Wicks—is from Montana."

"Oh, yeah?" Without the knit watch cap, Malachi's hair fell free like his father's. A little shorter, though, probably in deference to some school rule. Or, Lola thought, more likely his mother's rule, given that she was LDS.

But maybe, just maybe, she was wrong about it being Malachi. In fact, probably. It had been dark the night she bought the pills. The courtroom had been so crowded. It couldn't possibly be the same boy. Lola retrieved a new piece of pizza from the box that Munro had put in the middle of the table and rued an overactive imagination.

"How do you like Salt Lake, Miss Wicks? Seeing the sights?" Was the voice the same? She couldn't remember. Again, the odds were against it. The guy in the park had been scared.

"She's here to work. Or, she was." Munro stabbed a piece of pepperoni with his fork.

Lola flinched. He wasn't going to make this easy. "I haven't had much time for sightseeing."

Malachi slouched in his chair, all elbows and knees and too-big feet, not yet grown into his body, features still so soft as to be almost pretty. No way a kid like him could work the park. That crowd there would eat him alive.

"Even just driving around you must have seen some things, Miss Wicks." The boy bit his lip, seeming almost abashed at his own nerve in speaking up. None of his father's arrogance. Lola hoped he stayed that way.

"Like Pioneer Park. A really big park, right downtown. You've probably seen that. Right, Miss Wicks?"

Lola choked on her pizza. Munro pounded her back. "You okay?"

"Yeah." Malachi leaned across the table, face all concern but eyes gleaming malice. "Are you all right? Are you, Miss Wicks?"

She didn't answer but sent him an unmistakable response with her eyes. *Go to hell, kid.*

————

"Actually," she said when she'd recovered, "I did see the park. At least I think I did. What's with that place? Such a beautiful park, but so many rough-looking people there."

"Just homeless, more likely," Munro said. "Didn't you notice the streets around it?"

Lola braced herself for another comment on her inadequate powers of observation.

Munro answered his own question. "Soup kitchens. And shelters. There's a cluster of them down there. Say what you want about the Mormons, they take care of people like nobody else. Salt Lake has some of the most progressive homeless shelters in the country. The rumor is that cops in the surrounding states buy their winos bus tickets and ship them our way. Other cities look to us when it comes to dealing with their own homeless issues."

"Not all of them seemed homeless." Lola shot Malachi a look. "It must attract drug dealers, too." Two could play this game.

"And junkies," Malachi said. "Even if they're from out of town, they seem to find their way there." Check and mate.

He shoved his chair back from the table. "May I be excused? I'm going to the library. Study group."

"Is that what they call it?" Lola murmured as he passed. She thought he slammed the door on his way out. But the front door was heavy oak. Maybe that was the way it always sounded.

"Nice kid," she said, trying to postpone the inevitable. "What grade is he in?"

"He's a senior. Just like Frank Shumway."

Lola had hoped to avoid the topic of the story for at least a little longer. "I guess he doesn't know him. Different school districts and all, what with Frank living in the burbs."

"Different districts, but same hockey team."

Something Munro might have mentioned sooner. That explained Malachi's attendance at Frank's court appearance. The boys must be friends. Munro's next words, though, made Lola wonder exactly why his son had gone to the hearing.

"Actually, he knows Frank pretty well. Frank beat him out for first string. Malachi plays center, too. He was sure he had that spot, but he said Frank skated like a maniac in the tryouts. Man." A look crossed Munro's face, equal parts pain and frustration. Anger, too; a look Lola was all too familiar with, summed up in a single word: *kids*. "Malachi was some kind of pissed off. Came home, threw his stick against the wall"—Munro pointed to a scar next to the refrigerator—"said he wasn't going to play hockey anymore. Guess he'll get that spot now."

How badly had Malachi wanted that spot? Badly enough to kill—and to set his rival up to take the fall? Preposterous.

Except it wasn't. There was that case, Texas, someplace like that, where a girl had killed a cheerleading rival. Kids had massacred other kids at Columbine and blamed their plan on bullying. And a California college student had driven down a street shooting people because he'd felt rejected by women.

Would Malachi have been capable of bashing Sariah Ballard's brains in with a hockey stick? Not just any hockey stick, but his rival's?

Improbable? Sure.

But impossible? No way.

She already knew that Malachi was capable of dealing drugs in a park full of older and presumably tougher types. What else was he capable of? What about his life had pushed him into crime? His parents' divorce?

And why hadn't Munro been asking the same questions? Or— Lola took an intense interest in her pizza, examining the half-eaten slice before her as though the answer lay beneath what appeared to be a canned mushroom—maybe he had. Maybe that's why he was so insistent that she pursue the story. Because he couldn't bear to be the one who found the answers himself. Or ... or ...

What if he'd pushed her toward the story, thinking she wasn't capable of getting it? That way, he could persuade himself that he'd looked into it. And that, when she abandoned the story—as he knew she wanted to—he could tell himself he'd tried, and could stop worrying about any possibility of his son's involvement.

"Wow." Not just an asshole, but a manipulative one.

"Wow, what?"

"Nothing. Can I have another beer? And, uh, maybe a glass this time?"

Stupid. Who asked for a glass on the second beer? But she needed a couple of seconds to think. Munro had known she'd do a half-assed job. Maybe even counted on it. Her indignation, flaring so hot a moment earlier, receded to a bright ember of shame. Beer wasn't going to do the trick.

"Actually, never mind on the beer. You said something about the hard stuff."

Munro raised an eyebrow. "Scotch okay?"

It wasn't her favorite. "Sure."

He rummaged in a cabinet. "Ice?"

"God, no. Just a splash of water."

He handed Lola a glass with a generous amount of amber liquid and dropped back into his chair. "So, you want out of the story."

There it was. Her out. On the proverbial silver platter.

Handed to her because he knew she'd take it. More subtle than his son's taunts, but with the same assumption that she wouldn't push back.

A rushing sound in her ears. *You're a giant pain in the ass when you're on a story. Always made me happy I wasn't the story. Fun to watch, though.*

She forced herself not to turn, not to swat at Charlie the way she always had when he teased her.

She could show this asshole Munro that she was capable of chasing down the story, even if it led right to his solid-oak front door. Which would serve him right. Then go back to Montana able to reassure Jan she was back in the saddle. Lola took a sip. And then another. Whatever was in the glass was fast changing her opinion of Scotch. She held up the glass, tilting it, watching the whisky slid up one side, then the other.

"What is this stuff, anyway?"

"Lagavulin. I decided I'd gone way too many years not drinking to waste my time on anything but the best."

Bitter father. Bitter son.

Lola swirled the magical stuff in her mouth, letting it warm her. She stretched her lips and showed all of her teeth, willing him to see it as a smile.

"Out of the story? Not necessarily. But let's talk about how long I'll have to stay."

# SEVENTEEN

"Library, my ass."

Lola spoke over the haughty tones of the Directions Bitch, who was steering her back toward Pioneer Park, where she hoped to find Malachi and quiz the crap out of him. She'd used that lame library excuse during her own high school years. Luckily, her mother had never picked up on the scent of weed that clung to her clothing after her own supposed study sessions. More likely she'd chosen to ignore it.

Now that Lola herself was a mother, she appreciated the wisdom of choosing one's battles. She had never cut classes, pulled down A's and a few B's in school, didn't get pregnant, and avoided the principal's radar. Her rebelliousness was of the furtive variety. At best, she hoped for the same from Margaret, although given her daughter's confrontational manner, she doubted she'd be so fortunate.

The Directions Bitch claimed her attention. "Your destination is on the right."

The first time she'd gone to the park, it was twilight. Now it was full dark, and the garish floodlights illuminating its deserted pathways with slashes of white only intensified the surrounding blackness. She strode toward the spot where she'd first met Malachi, trying to ignore the deeper shadows moving beneath the trees, the hushed voices there, the gurgling bottles.

Rounding a corner near a small building housing the toilets, she came upon two men in the shelter of the entrance, faces close, bodies entwined, words of love amid the gasps.

"We shouldn't—"

"Shut up. I had to see you—"

"I know. But what are we going to do?"

"This. We're going to do this."

"Oh. *Oh.*"

Not a casual hookup, apparently. Or maybe an encounter with someone skilled at reading his clients' emotional as well as physical desires, and reaping the benefits in cash.

Lola's money was on the former. *I had to see you.* No matter the danger posed by a church that had ramped up its stance against anything it considered unnatural. Even love. She lingered in the shadows, unable to look away, a voyeuristic flare, a stab of envy for the eroticism that had fled her life. No. It hadn't fled. Charlie's killer had stolen it from her.

*Charlie.* So close she could hear him breathing, harsh, urgent. She spun toward the sound, reaching, aching to pull him close—and saw only a man in a parka mere steps behind her, cap pulled low over his face, melting into the shrubbery. *Jesus.* In her moment of distraction, she'd allowed a pervert to creep right up on her.

Charlie, closer still, his worry palpable as her own.

"Sorry, sorry," she mumbled to him as she took another path, fleeing both love and its twisted variation, keeping an eye peeled for the latter. But the creeper in the parka had vanished, probably because of the person now approaching. A cop.

"Jesus." Aloud this time.

"That's how you use the Lord's name?"

Great. Even the cops were LDS. "You scared me."

"You should be scared. You must not be from here. This is no place to be looking for business. These guys are only interested in what they can pour down their throats or stick in their arms. And don't get me started on the degenerates."

The cop had the smooth skin and self-righteousness of the young. Lola wondered how long he'd been on the beat, how long it would take him to acquire the seen-it-all weariness that on his worst days had even affected Charlie.

He folded his arms across his chest, apparently awaiting some sort of explanation.

"Exactly what kind of business do you think I'm in?" Lola stepped around a large stick that lay across the path and stood beneath one of the lights so that he could take a good long look at the jeans and turtleneck (clean, at least) she'd donned for her dinner with Munro. "Do you honestly think I'm a hooker?"

He had the grace to look embarrassed. "Whatever brings you here, it's not a good place to be."

Lola huffed, trying to approximate outrage. "I was just trying to get some exercise. I saw the park from my hotel. It looked nice." She jogged a little in place, hoping he wouldn't notice how even that slight exertion left her short of breath. And who went for a run in jeans?

"Which hotel?"

So he wasn't as callow as he looked. Lola tried to remember the various hotels she'd passed. Damned if she'd tell him the right one. She recalled a giant M. "The Marriott." Moments ticked past. She had to get rid of him.

"Speaking of degenerates—" She paused. Was she really about to do this shameful thing? "Over by the restrooms. I saw—you know. Two men." Charlie bellowed his rage, so loud Lola wondered at the cop's failure to hear it.

The cop's head snapped up, his own anger flashing across his face. "I'm sorry you had to see that. I'll take care of it right now. Oh, and the Marriott? It's that way." He jabbed a thumb to her left. "You should probably go back there. This park isn't safe—as, unfortunately, you've seen. Next time you want exercise, stick to the streets around your hotel."

Lola jogged backward a few steps. "Appreciate that. Thanks." She turned and headed where he'd pointed, looking back over her shoulder. He marched away, straight down the middle of the path. Lola hoped the gay couple was long gone.

As soon as the cop was out of sight, she ducked onto a path that cut into the heart of the park. She ventured a few more steps before reason prevailed. She could no longer see the main walkway. This track was narrower than the other, overhung with tree branches that probably made for pleasant shade during the day, but now rendered the darkness complete. Better to return tomorrow, maybe right after school let out, and find Malachi then.

She turned. A low voice hailed her from the darkness, devoid of the eagerness that might have warned her.

"Are you lost?"

She hesitated, just long enough to be puzzled at the swish of the stick that caught her behind the knees, knocking her off her feet, realization too late, coming even as the hand covered her mouth, stifling her scream.

———

Her attacker fell atop her, pressing something sharp to her throat.

Lola grabbed at his arms, which were clad in something slick and puffy. A parka. The creeper. He'd found her. She managed to wrestle the knife hand away from her neck. He was a wiry bastard but strong, writhing atop her now, spreading his arms wide, trying to break her grip. The woolen cap scraped at her face. She smelled aftershave and hair product. She opened her mouth, searching for purchase. Clamped her teeth on an earlobe. Tasted blood.

A hand jerked free. A fist landed against her jaw. Oh, thank God. Not the knife hand.

"Hel—!"

A shoulder ground into her face, cutting off her cry for help.

*Charlie*, Lola screamed into it. *Charlie*.

The knife hand went back, breaking her grip. She tried to roll away, but sharp knees pinned her down. From the corner of her eye, she glimpsed something shiny, flashing high.

"Hey! What's going on?"

A scramble and her tormenter was gone, vanishing into the trees. She could breathe. But her scream was spent, escaping only in a choking sob.

———

A man loomed above her, a mere silhouette against the shadows. Lola scuttled backward, scream rising anew.

"Whoa, whoa." He raised his hands and moved into the light. Layers of hard-used clothing—not a parka—wrapped his body. The grime on his face and hands probably provided extra protection from the elements. His eyes were bloodshot, his voice slurred. "Not trying to hurt you. But somebody did. You okay?"

*No. I'm not okay.* But couldn't make the words come out.

"You're bleeding." He touched a finger to his stubbled chin.

Lola brought her hand to her own face. Her fingers came away dark and wet. The ear. She'd must have bitten it bloody. Good. Then there'd be DNA. Guys who jumped women usually had a history.

"I'm fine. I have to go. And, um, thank you."

She should have offered something more tangible, money for booze. But she had to find that cop. She staggered toward the main path, knees gone rubbery with the fear that follows adrenaline. The path stretched long and empty before her. She forced her legs into a jolting run. She went back over the attack, trying to fasten down the facts. It wasn't unusual, she knew, for assault victims to be scattered in their recollections, especially immediately after a crime, something defense attorneys often used to undermine them in court—if a case even got that far. Prosecutors sometimes took that natural response as proof a victim was changing her story, and might deem the case unworthy of pursuing.

*Not this guy. He's going down.* Even as her footsteps slowed.

The cop would wonder why she'd lingered in the park. He'd remember that she told him she was registered at the Marriott. He'd check it out. Not only would she need an excuse as to why she was still in the park, she'd also need one for why she'd lied about her hotel.

He'd want a description of the man who'd attacked her. But it was pitch-black under the trees. She'd never seen his face. All she knew was a parka—she couldn't even remember the color, only something light. Blue? Green? Yellow?—and a cap with a face-obscuring brim. That she'd seen him just a few minutes earlier. That he smelled good, of something old-fashioned—bay rum?—unlike the park's typical denizens. Maybe some suburbanite who drove into the city to get his twisted jollies. Because it had to be the creeper. The way the man ground against her had been somewhat sexual, even though—her mind snagged on a detail—she hadn't detected the expected hardness. Nothing added up.

The trail jogged to the left. Far ahead, before yet another bend, nearing the restrooms, she finally saw the cop. She lifted her hand. Started to hail him. Stopped.

He'd bring her back to the police station for questioning. It could take hours and, in the end, they might not believe her. They'd ask what she'd been doing in the park. Would they search her? Probably not. No reason, no warrant. But the pills—wary of losing them again, she'd divided her stash in half, some back in the hotel room, the rest in a pocket, a different one, one with no holes, where they rubbed guilt into her thigh. What if, somehow, they found them?

The cop rounded the far turn. Lola's arm fell to her side. Better to go back to her car. There, within the safety of locked doors, she could think clearly. Decide what to do.

She'd only gone a few steps when a man's gargling howl ripped the darkness wide open.

———

Lola spun toward the sound, fumbling for her phone as she ran, hardwired to get a photo of whatever had happened, forgetting for the moment that even if it was a story, it wasn't her story. Shoot first,

139

ask later, was her motto when it came to photos. You could delete a useless image, but you could never recapture one you'd missed.

A slight figure, also moving fast, stepped out onto the path beside her, so close that she put out a hand to keep from crashing into him. They locked eyes, the recognition such a shock that Lola stumbled. He grabbed her arm to steady her. She jerked away.

"Malachi?"

"Miss Wicks?"

A quick scan. No parka, no cap, just the usual hoodie. "What are you doing here?"

"What happened to you? You're bleeding."

Running again, both of them, Lola lengthening her stride to keep up with him.

"I heard—" They rounded the bend and nearly fell into one another in their haste to stop.

The cop lay in the middle of the path, sprawled on his back, arms flung out, hands opening and closing as though trying to grasp the life rushing from his body. Eyes wide, staring unblinking into the cruel streetlight above. Blood burbled from the gash across his neck.

Lola and Malachi exchanged a last long look. Then, as though they'd reached some unspoken agreement, they turned and sprinted like hell in different directions.

# EIGHTEEN

THE CAR, THE MAZE of streets, the hotel.

Lola must have negotiated them all, because she was back in her room, desk dragged away from the wall and shoved against the door as though someone might have followed her from the park, intent upon doing unto her what he'd done to the cop.

Her phone lay where she'd flung it, blinking accusation from atop the bed, the screen showing 911. She'd gotten as far as punching in the numbers. But there'd been no fourth tap. Her finger had hovered repeatedly over the green "call" icon—nearly giving in to the impulse to tap it as she ran through the park toward the street, again in the safety of the locked car, even while driving far too fast through the city. At which point, she knew it was already too late. Someone else would have discovered the wounded officer, would either have called 911 himself or prevailed upon another of the park denizens to do so.

That person, the one who'd done the right thing, would have to describe how he'd found the cop. Would be grilled to within an inch of his life about every detail surrounding the discovery. The time. What he'd been doing there. Whether he'd seen anyone else.

A woman, maybe. Someone obviously not a park regular. Running away.

She raised a clenched hand as though to strike herself. Slowed the motion and bit down on her knuckles instead. She should have called 911 right away. Taken her chances. Because the only thing worse than being hit with the same questions now facing whomever had reported the cop's assault was being asked the most important one: why didn't you report this the second you saw it?

She paced the room from the foot of the bed to the door and back, three long strides each way, a new rationalization with every turn.

Because the cop was already dead, maybe, or almost there. I couldn't help him.

Turn.

Because no matter what, I'd seem suspicious.

Turn.

Because I didn't see anyone or notice anything that would help an investigation, anyway.

Turn.

Except Malachi.

A single slow step.

But he seemed as surprised as I.

Step.

Something else is going on.

Step.

Because...

And there it was, the thing the cops wouldn't put together, not at this point anyway, and especially not without talking to her. And maybe not even then.

Two people attacked within the space of a week in a state notable for its low crime rate. Two throats slashed. No obvious connection between them.

But minutes before the cop's death, and only yards away, someone had simulated—the more she thought about, the more certain she was of the fakery—a sexual assault on her. Had held a knife, or whatever sharp thing it was, to her own throat.

What if?

A question that, until smothered in the fog of grief following Charlie's death, had lurked insistently at the forefront of her reporter's brain, the propelling force of every story.

What if the attacks—lethal in Sariah's case and maybe the cop's, and potentially in her own—were somehow connected?

That humming in the room again, Charlie someplace close. Sense of a shadow. By now, she knew better. Still, she turned. Nothing.

She froze, holding her breath, trying to divine the message. Disapproval? Because just as she was above all a reporter, Charlie was a cop, blue brotherhood and all that. He'd come thundering back from the grave if she withheld information that could lead to a cop's attacker.

Or, just maybe, he'd urge her on, knowing after all their years together that to stand in the way of her pursuit of a story was to be bulldozed without a backward glance. Especially one that might lead to an answer about who'd gone after that cop.

"I can't go to the police. Not yet," she argued aloud, as though Charlie stood before her barely containing the frustration he clearly felt, but rarely expressed, when she chased an improbable lead.

The police probably would label as unlikely her theory that the assaults were somehow related. She walked to the sink, pulled her sweater away from her neck, and examined her throat in the mirror.

A scratch, nothing more. Saved by the turtleneck. Which wouldn't have saved her at all had the vagrant not wandered past when he did.

She turned the hot-water tap on high, peeled the wrapper away from the oval of soap whose stamp proclaimed it hand-milled, whatever that was. Lathered her hands. Washed the blood away from her chin, evidence swirling down the drain. She raised her head and stared at the woman in the mirror, peering past her, searching the reflection of the room behind her for someone who wasn't there.

"I have to do it this way," she told Charlie. "I have to find out myself."

# NINETEEN

An hour later, exhausted by a prolonged argument with someone who wasn't there, an immense weariness pinned her to the bed.
Lola rolled onto the floor, willing the fall to jolt energy back into her
bones. No dice.

She crawled the few feet into the bathroom, reached for the sink,
hauled herself up, retrieved one of her newly purchased pills from
her Dopp kit, placed it on her tongue, and headed back into the too-
big, too-empty bed.

*Make decisions.*

The words came unbidden, almost as though Charlie were in the
room. In his role as sheriff, he occasionally got pulled into search
and rescue operations—tourists unprepared for Montana's mercurial weather changes, hunters who got lost in the excitement of
tracking an elk, kids separated from their parents on a group outing.
Most of those people survived. Some didn't.

The difference, Charlie said, came down to two things: a healthy
dose of luck and a person's own actions. "The ones who panic almost

never make it. You can see where they've wandered all over the place instead of staying in one spot where somebody could find them. They lose body heat. They hyperventilate and get lightheaded and can't think straight."

"And the ones who do?"

"They make decisions. They don't let their fears spiral out of control. They say, 'First, I'll do this one thing. Then I'll do one more thing. Then I'll do the next thing.' They make one small decision after another, rather than looking at the whole overwhelming picture, which is what makes people lose their damn minds and do stupid things."

Lola was on the verge of losing her own damn mind. Thoughts skittered around in her brain like drops of water flicked into a cast-iron pan over a high flame.

A bitter taste fizzed against her tongue. The pill. She'd forgotten about it. She spat it into her palm. There. That was one decision. She needed to be clear-headed for whatever came next. Which was to talk with Malachi, a need grown even more urgent after the attack on the cop. Another decision.

She didn't dare go back to the park to find him. Decision number three—an easy one.

School, maybe. Linger outside, wait for him after classes. She tapped her iPad and googled high schools in Salt Lake, relief in the familiar moves. Malachi probably went to the school closest to his neighborhood. She reached for her notebook and pen, ready to jot down an address. A photo flashed on the laptop screen. She groaned. Once again, she'd forgotten the implications of working in a big city. Salt Lake's high schools, whether the crenellated stone piles dating to the previous century or low-slung modern varieties, were huge. No matter which school was his, each offered a wealth of doors from which Malachi might leave. He might drive his own car, or ride with friends. He might take a school bus or a city bus or ride his bike or walk. Her chances of "accidentally" bumping into him at school were minuscule.

She shoved the notebook away from her. A folded pamphlet peeked from its pages. She pulled it out. Raised it to her lips for a big fat kiss. It was the hockey schedule that Donovan Munro had pushed upon her. Malachi would almost certainly be at the Friday night game, claiming what he'd imagined to be his rightful spot as center in Frank's absence.

The journalism gods had delivered up Tynslee. Lola beseeched them yet again. "Let Malachi be there—and let him talk to me—and I promise I won't call his dad an asshole anymore. Not to his face and not even behind his back."

There. She'd made her decisions. She rewarded herself with the pill, partially dissolved, warm from her palm, and lay back. *Oh, Charlie.* Her agony—kept at bay for a few hours thanks to the distraction of assault, both her own and that of the police officer—fell upon her with a great hunger, so savage that it hurt to breathe. She willed the pill to work faster. Which it did, finally, just enough.

It was like low tide, she thought, harkening to the Chesapeake Bay excursions of her Maryland childhood. The waves still pounded the shore, but farther away each time, leaving the sand smooth and firm, the sort of surface you could trust, not like the churning, sucking shoals that would be stirred up when the tide rolled back in again. Lola's breaths came long and shallow. Her eyelids drooped.

The phone buzzed in her ear.

"Damn Munro." She hoped she hadn't clicked the "on" button while she was still speaking. At least she hadn't called him an asshole.

She congratulated herself for keeping her promise to the journalism gods.

"What? Maybe I have the wrong number?"

Not Munro. A female voice. Lola held the phone before her face. The numbers and letters blurred and danced. She wasn't sure she believed what they were trying to tell her.

"Tynslee?"

"Miss Wicks. Are you all right? You sound funny. Did I wake you?"

"I'm fine." Lola sought safety in the lie. "Just sleepy."

"I'm so sorry. I'll call back later."

"No! No! I wasn't really asleep. Just dozing." She waited, both for Tynslee to declare intention and because she didn't trust her voice.

"I thought about what you said. About how maybe you could help me."

"Yes?" That much, at least, sounded okay.

"Is there any way we could talk again? Someplace that wouldn't be obvious?"

Lola still had a bit longer to think before the pill fully kicked in. The journalism gods took stock and stared it down.

"Of course. Think you could handle a hockey game?"

---

She regretted the words almost as soon as they came out of her mouth. Of course Tynslee couldn't face a hockey game. Her boyfriend had been the team's star. Not to mention the fact that she had yet to bury her mother. How would it look if she showed up for a night of lighthearted fun? Lola mumbled as much, along with an apology. But Tynslee cut her off.

"You're right. Even if I could go to the game, I don't want to. But I need to get out of this house. I'll ask my dad. Maybe I can meet you outside the game."

Lola looked at the phone and thought that surely the gods were setting her up for some sort of spectacular fall. She stuttered something about the funeral.

"It's tomorrow. The game's not until the day after. You're coming to the funeral, right?"

Damn straight Lola was going to the funeral, one of the richest sources of material for any reporter writing about a newsworthy death, especially if the death in question was the sort of thing resulting in "no comments" and firmly closed doors. No matter how tight-lipped people became at the sight of a reporter, they blabbed at length in eulogies, oblivious to the person in the back row surreptitiously taking notes. Lola reminded herself to thank Jan for urging her to bring a dress, and for the fact that the dress in question was black.

The one she'd worn to Charlie's funeral.

She pushed the thought away with a quick mental apology to Charlie. He, better than anyone, had understood her single-mindedness when it came to work.

"And please stay afterward. Someone's going to have to help us eat all of those funeral potatoes. Wait—"

Lola heard a man's voice.

"I have to go." Tynslee clicked off.

Lola tossed the phone in the air and caught it, a quick celebration that an invitation by a family member—not just any family member but the daughter of the deceased—had just assured her of entree to the gathering of family and friends after the funeral itself. She'd almost certainly have it all to herself, other reporters probably barred.

For that split second, she forgot about Charlie. She forgot about the man in the park. She forgot about the poor cop. She forgot about everything other than the fact that, even if only for a little while, she was going to wholly own the story. And then the pill, its effects held at bay by her momentary elation, asserted itself and dragged her under.

# TWENTY

LOLA'S DRESS WAS A wrap number for which Jan had made a three-hour round trip to Great Falls so that Lola could be presentable at her own husband's funeral.

Knowing too well Lola's wardrobe, Jan had also picked up a pair of black flats. Which Lola had forgotten to bring to Salt Lake. She stood in front of the hotel room's mirror in her dress and her hiking boots and tried to tell herself that no one was going to look at her feet. And then reminded herself that on this of all days, she needed to blend in.

Hence, the stop at Payless on the way to the funeral for a cheap pair of pumps that pinched her toes and, despite their reasonably low heels, challenged a balance long accustomed to sturdy Vibram soles. With a nod to the certainty that showing up at a funeral with a bookbag slung over her shoulder would not make her fit in with the nice Mormon ladies, she also picked up a purse, just big enough for her phone and iPad and notebook, a couple of pens, and the wad of Kleenex she'd grabbed from the box in the hotel.

Her hair, its usual disheveled chestnut snarl, was beyond redemption. Knots snagged her fingers when she ran them through it. Lola pulled it back into a ponytail, then folded it over on itself and wrapped the elastic around it once again, hoping it looked like a chignon, knowing it didn't. She'd smeared on Jan's makeup, then removed most of it when she tried to blot away the streaks with a tissue. The eyeliner defeated her, and she spent more time washing off the crooked black lines than she did applying them in the first place, scrubbing hard at the dark smudges beneath her eyes until she realized the liner was long gone. She swiped blush across her cheeks, drew the line at lipstick, and called it good.

Charlie would have smiled if he'd seen her in pumps and carrying a purse, grinned at any attempt to tame her hair, and laughed aloud at the makeup. He'd always said he appreciated the extra room in the medicine cabinet that cosmetics would otherwise have occupied. Her heart clenched at the thought, then loosened, a bit of lightness in the memory, the first such sensation since his death. She shut it down fast, her ever-present pain a way of keeping him close.

She scanned her phone as the scowling Payless clerk complied with her request to snip the price tag from the purse and replace the pumps in the box with her worse-for-the-wear boots. Stories about the officer's assault—he'd held on through the night, kept alive by beeping machines and the magic potions flowing through IV lines—dominated the Salt Lake news sites. Lola swiped through them, searching for any damning mention of witnesses. But each time the word appeared, it was preceded by what on this day were the most beautiful two letters of the alphabet, *N* and *O*.

She tried to temper her momentary gratitude with the knowledge that within the half-hour she'd watch two families still dazed from the first smashing blows of bereavement. They didn't know yet that the pummeling would continue, a hail of near-knockout punches that mercilessly stopped just short of delivering the unconsciousness that would have been infinitely preferable.

She pulled into a parking lot full of shiny SUVs and minivans and sedans, every one of which would have looked out of place back home in Magpie, and edged into the throngs pressing their way into the community center where Sariah Ballard would make her last public appearance.

---

If there was a hell, Lola told herself about halfway through Sariah's service, she herself would surely go there because of the murderous thoughts taking aim at the funeral's officiant.

The notebook squirreled away in her fake-leather purse for some surreptitious jottings during the eulogies stayed blank. Nor was there any need to click her phone's recording app in hopes of capturing a few words. Lola turned Munro's condescending words upon herself: if only she'd spent five minutes on Google before going to the service, she'd have realized that the Latter-day Saints saw funerals—which welcomed the unchurched—as ideal opportunities for proselytizing. She heard barely a word about Sariah, and far too much about the wonders that awaited if she joined the church.

At least she didn't have a daily deadline, with a demand to write a story despite the fact that the funeral yielded exactly zero new information. For whatever reason, Munro hadn't requested anything for the website. And she wasn't like the photographers and television journalists who'd been met at the door with a firm "no cameras, no reporters" as Lola slipped past in her respectable black mufti. She didn't recognize any of them from the pack in front of Sariah's house

153

or in the courtroom. Many were younger. The B team, she thought, pressed into service as editors and news directors threw their most experienced reporters at the story about the cop.

It wasn't as though they'd missed anything by being banned from the service. The very few words spoken about Sariah were the sort of generic pap—"faithful wife, loving mother, devoted to the Lord"— that told Lola nothing at all about the woman.

She shifted in her seat, trying to peer through the gaps in the crowd toward the front rows, noting that family members sat behind church leaders. It was a repeat of the courtroom scene, with Galon Ballard flanked by Tynslee and Kwesi, and the lineup of Shumways across the aisle. As in the courtroom, Tynslee appeared near-catatonic, sitting motionless, eyes at half-mast. Kwesi turned this way and that, his gaze scanning the congregation. Statistically, most murder victims died at the hands of someone they knew. It wasn't unreasonable to think—if Frank indeed were innocent—that Sariah's killer sat among the mourners, which explained the presence along the room's back walls of several broad-shouldered men sweeping the room with hard stares. Only the most naive would fail to recognize them as cops. Exhaustion shrouded their faces, skin gray, eyes hollow. They'd have been up all night, either on bedside vigil with their colleague or trying to find his assailant. The funeral detail must have felt an insult. Under the circumstances.

Their eyes flicked toward the Shumways, who stared holes in the floor, Melena bending almost double in her effort to make herself invisible. Lola wondered what it felt like to have the gaze of the entire congregation upon you, trying to figure out what you'd done to produce a murderer.

———

Lola guessed the Shumways wouldn't attend the reception afterward, and she was right.

They were nowhere to be seen among the procession of casserole-bearing mourners marching into the church building's multipurpose room. This time, Lola had thought ahead, stopping at a supermarket for a tray of crudités from the deli section. She fetched it from the car and joined the crowd, looking enough like everyone else that even the cop who'd encountered her with Melena that first morning took no note as she hurried inside, gaze averted.

Just inside, Galon Ballard stood but two feet away, surrounded by mourners. Lola wanted to take his arm, pull him from the crowd, and get him someplace quiet where she could pepper him with questions, probably the same ones the cops had already asked him ad nauseam, along with some tactful enquiries about Sariah's friendship with the Shumways, especially with Bryce Shumway.

He turned to her. "And you are?"

She felt the press of new arrivals behind her, the curious glances that must have mirrored the look on Galon's face. A scent teased her nostrils, a niggling memory, something unpleasant, even though it was in itself inoffensive.

"Just looking for a place to put this down. Don't worry, I'll find it. Oh, and I'm so sorry for your loss. Sariah was a lovely woman."

She glided away, to the long tables stretching along the walls of the room. The tray Lola held looked pitifully inadequate compared to the rows of robust casseroles there. At least half featured the gleaming gold of melted cheese atop sliced potatoes, crushed potato chips floating like sailboats atop the cheese, a dish so loaded with starches and fat and salt it might have tempted Lola on any other day. The sheer volume, though, left her slightly nauseated.

The only variation in color, besides her sad offering of carrots and broccoli and cherry tomatoes, was at the other end of the counter, where Technicolor Jell-O molds shimmered and shook each time another casserole made its ponderous landing. Lola set her tray down beside them, briefly relieved to be freed from her prop before realizing it had served as protection of sorts. Now, with her hands free, she had nothing else to do other than mingle with people she didn't know, which might force her to explain herself, something she didn't dare do truthfully for fear of a fast escort to the door.

She craved coffee, but there'd be none here. Pitchers of juice and punch presented themselves. Lola poured some of the latter and wandered into the crowd, holding her cup to her lips like a shield, hoping no one would try to talk with her. She saw Kwesi across the room, at the center of a knot of scrubbed and combed teenagers. No sign of Tynslee. Bits of conversation eddied about her, most of it of the "so sad" variety. Occasionally, though, something stood out.

" … knew when Melena adopted that boy. What was she thinking?" "I suppose the wedding is off." "What wedding?" "Oh, you didn't know?"

Lola sidled closer. She slid her phone from her purse and pretended to check it. As if on cue, Tynslee materialized beside her. Damn. Lola wanted to talk with the girl, but she also wanted to continue eavesdropping. She cast a regretful look at the group of women beside her, all of whom looked completely at ease in their dresses and pumps and nylons (an indignity that, even for the sake of a funeral, Lola had refused), real leather bags dangling from their shoulders.

Tynslee tugged her away. A familiar scent caught Lola's attention as they made their way through the room. She breathed deep but it was gone, replaced by a mix of warring perfumes and warm potatoes.

"Is this really the best place to talk?" she asked. Tynslee had positioned them at the back of the room next to the Jell-O molds, their innards spangled with bright bits of canned fruit and snowflakes of marshmallow. One, green, contained shrimp, curled within like pink fetuses. If Charlie had lived, would they have had another baby? Lola looked away.

"I haven't asked my dad about the game yet."

"Of course not. This isn't the time. Will Kwesi be there, too?"

Lola held her breath. A two-fer was probably too much to hope for.

"Maybe. Probably. He went to all of Frank's games. Some of the guys on the team are talking about wearing armbands with Frank's number in support."

Lola figured that idea wouldn't fly once adults got wind of it. The team's loyalty was admirable, as was the concept of innocent before proven guilty. But the coaches would look down the road, realizing how badly it would reflect on the team if Frank turned out to be Sariah's killer.

She gave a noncommittal nod, the staple response in all difficult conversations.

"You said we could talk outside the rink," Tynslee said. "Is that still all right? No one will see us there. They'll all be inside watching the game."

"And you can't just talk with me now? We could take a walk outside. Or you could call me later—"

The air around them changed, taking on weight and substance. Heads turned. Mouths fell open. Beneath the weight of its makeshift chignon, the back of Lola's neck prickled.

A path through the throng opened as Melena Shumway, the mother of the youth accused of murdering her best friend, entered the room with yet another batch of potatoes in her hand.

157

Melena stopped before Tynslee. Woman and teenager; guilty party—
at least by association—and bereaved.

Lola stepped back. Utter silence reigned.

"I won't stay."

Lola, standing so close, strained to hear Melena's next words.

"I just wanted to do … something. To bring this." The casserole
joined the others. Relieved of their burden, Melena's arms fell to her
side. Tynslee raised hers. Extended them. Melena fell into the girl's
embrace.

A sibilance in the room, the mingled hisses of caught breath, of
whispered disbelief. People pressed toward the kitchen, wanting to
see for themselves the scene whose description had zinged among
them like the shock of too many feet rubbing against a wool carpet,
almost pleasurable in its unexpectedness. A panting avidity permeated the room. The Jell-O molds shivered atop their chilly beds of
iceberg lettuce.

Time to go, Lola thought. There'd be no talking with Tynslee
now. As soon as Melena left, the girl would be mobbed, unseemly
curiosity masked as concern. Best to slip out, wait for Melena, try to
talk with her again.

Lola murmured her way toward the door. "Excuse me. Excuse
me." A final time, that scent. She dared a few quick glances as she
made for the door but saw nothing that explained it. The crowd was
too thick.

Only when she was free of the church did it hit her. Aftershave.
The same bay rum that her father had worn. As had her assailant in
the park.

Lots of men wore bay rum. Lola forced herself to walk slowly toward her car, listening for Melena's steps behind her. Even though she knew that bay rum had gone out of style years if not decades earlier, this was a conservative crowd. It wasn't inconceivable that men all over Salt Lake doused themselves in it before setting out to do whatever it was they did each day.

Still, she couldn't shake the feeling that she'd just been in the same room with the man who'd attacked her not twenty-four hours earlier.

# TWENTY-ONE

"Miss Wicks? Lola? Is that you?"

Maybe she'd just brushed elbows with her assailant. Maybe not. But there was no doubt that Melena now stood beside her in the parking lot.

Lola filed away the hint as to her attacker's identity and wrenched her focus toward the mother of the accused murderer. She cast a glance at the crowded church annex behind them, where mourners no doubt stood at the windows, waiting to see what Melena would do next—and wondering about the stranger Melena was talking to.

"Melena. How nice to see you again. I'd love to visit for a while. But not here. Maybe someplace with a little more privacy."

"I'd like that, too. I think the entire Relief Society is in there."

As before, Lola had to strain to hear her. She took a few steps, forcing Melena to walk with her, anything to get away from the watchers at the window. The sooner they separated, the better. "Why don't we meet at Starbucks? Isn't there one just off the interstate?" Then mentally berated herself. When was she going to remember that the Mormons were strong enough to eschew the most necessary substance on earth?

She started to apologize, but Melena stopped her. "It's all right. They have orange juice. Other kinds, too. We'll see you there."

We?

She arrived to see Melena and Bryce together at a table rendered inadequate by Bryce's bulk. Lola faked a cough, an excuse to cover her face, hiding the leap of elation that surely showed there. An unexpected bonus, Bryce. He must have lingered in the church while Melena took her casserole to the gathering afterward. Smart man. She'd have to up her game if she was going to deal with him, too.

A water bottle poked its head from Bryce's fist. A scone the size of a saucer and shiny with glaze sat before Melena. Lola put in her order for a latte and returned to the table, extending a wary hand to Bryce. He looked like the kind of guy who went in for the finger-crush. He was.

"We met at the house the other day, just for a minute. We were supposed to meet under happier circumstances. For the magazine story." She flexed her fingers under the table. Nothing seemed broken. "I'm so sorry about all of this."

"No need to apologize." The rumbling voice so mild as to take the sting out of the words. Brown eyes beneath beetled brows. Tired. Kind. And brimming with the same anguish that was her own daily companion.

"Oh, honey. I didn't want to do this in front of everybody else." Melena stuck her finger in her mouth, then reached across the table and rubbed at Lola's cheeks, hen-clucking in sympathy. Her own makeup was perfect, her hair brushed forward and shellacked into place, obscuring half her face. "Those hotel room mirrors." She withdrew her hand, fingertips pink and powdery with Jan's blush. "They just aren't worth a darn, are they?"

She blotted her fingers on a napkin and redirected her attention to the scone, nibbling at it in a way that made Lola think yet again of a rabbit. "Want some? I can cut it."

Lola waved away the offer. "How can you eat something like that and stay so tiny?" Start with innocuous chitchat, the same kind of happy talk buzzing at the tables around them, words uttered by people whose proximity to murder was enviously remote. Besides, you never went wrong terming a woman the opposite of fat.

"I work out a lot." Melena patted her upper arm, sheathed in navy rayon. Lola pictured one of those women-only gyms, rows of pink, two-pound dumbbells. A pool, with hourly water aerobics. A place designed more for socializing than strength training. Melena's next words confirmed it. "I went every day with—" She held a napkin to her mouth as she struggled to swallow the bite of scone.

"It will be a while before you can say her name," Lola said. With Charlie's death, the Indian prohibition against speaking the names of the departed made sudden sense. Why force people to do the impossible? So practical, compared to the stiff-upper-lip nonsense that permeated white society.

"You've lost someone."

It was Lola's turn to go speechless. "My husband," she managed at last.

"When?"

Her throat hot and thick, she held up a hand, fingers extended.

"Five years?"

She shook her head.

"Five months? Oh, no. I'm so sorry." It was Melena's turn to offer the rote apology, one Lola had heard too often in the last months, flung like a plea by anyone who knew about Charlie, with its unspoken addendum *please let's not talk about it because it's all so awkward and painful.* She'd been grateful, then, to the aunties, their brisk acknowledgment of the sort of routine tragedy that permeated their lives, forgoing condolences, telling her instead about the old Blackfeet custom of chopping off one's hair, even a finger at the first knuckle, a visible symbol of grief, substituting—if only briefly—physical pain for mental. Lola thought it made perfect sense, and for weeks had cast longing glances at the hatchet in its kindling box on the front porch.

She felt Melena's knowing gaze upon her and sensed she was being drawn into an unwelcome sisterhood.

"Cancer?"

"No." If she told Melena that Charlie, too, was murdered, she'd never get out of the conversation. Redirect, she told herself, the emotional equivalent of the Directions Bitch.

She turned to Bryce, the man who'd found Sariah, delivered to her this day by the frightening generosity of the journalism gods. At some point, there'd be a reckoning. "How are you holding up?" she asked. "I can't imagine."

She left it at that, the open-ended invitation for him to remove the need for imagining. To tell her exactly what it had been like.

He passed a broad hand across his face. Said something behind it … "so much blood."

"You don't have to talk about it if it's too hard." Melena. Damn her.

Lola tried to muscle past Melena's roadblock. "You saw the dog. Rex, yes? You put him back in the house. And?"

"And we called the stake president right away." Melena again.

"You *what?*" The shock so palpable she was afraid Charlie had spoken past her. Redirection went to hell.

Melena started to repeat herself.

Lola stopped her. "Not 911?"

"Of course not."

Of course not? *It's a different country down there*, Jan had said. But this felt like an alternate universe.

"I was so afraid for Bryce. The shock of what he'd seen. And then Tynslee just down the hall. He thought she'd probably been murdered, too. A sight he couldn't bear to face. And even if the killer had left her alone, if she was just asleep, can you imagine the effect on her—woken up by police in her bedroom, being told her mother was dead? Murdered? She'd never recover."

She may never recover anyway, Lola thought, even as she herself tried to recover from the shock of the information Melena had so blithely delivered. "So you called the—who?" Trying the words herself, seeing if they made any more sense coming out of her own mouth. They didn't.

"The stake president," Melena said. "A church leader. I called him. Bryce was in no shape to call anyone." She slid a glance Lola's way. That look, the one universal to women burdened with the messiness of reality, forced into practicality by the actions of men. "It was wonderful. The leaders were on our doorstep within—what would you say, Bryce? Fifteen minutes? Twenty?"

A nod. Not the talkative type, Bryce. Alas.

Twenty minutes. Every twitch forward of the minute hand a gift to the killer.

"Then what?" Lola feared the worst. She got it.

"We went next door with them. They went to Sariah's room first, to make sure she was really dead. That Bryce hadn't mistaken what he'd seen."

Bryce shook his head, glaring down at the tabletop, now littered with crumbs from the scone. There'd been no mistake.

"The police," he said. "I was a suspect at first."

Of course he was. No reason he couldn't have grabbed his son's hockey stick on the way out the door, heading across the lawn to kill his neighbor.

"But they ruled him out." Melena now. "His fingerprints weren't anywhere in that room. Just the family's and—and—on the hockey stick"—Lola nodded, saving her the agony of saying her son's name, of mentally placing him in that gruesome tableau—"and the church leaders' fingerprints, of course."

"I didn't go in," Bryce said. "I didn't need to see more than I'd already seen through the door."

Oh, why the hell not, Lola almost said. Join the crowd trampling over the evidence, moving things around, adding their fingerprints to those already in the room, maybe obliterating those earlier ones altogether, trashing a perfectly good crime scene. As Melena laid it out, Lola sensed Charlie nearby, almost an electrical jolt, fury sizzling in the air around them. For once, they were in sync.

# TWENTY-TWO

LOLA TRIED TO KEEP her questions to a minimum, fearful of slowing the gush of words.

Still. "What time was it?" Barely more than a whisper.

"Four thirty? Five?" Melena looked to her husband for confirmation. He continued his silent communion with the tabletop, nodding down at it.

Lola could see it. At that hour, it would have been cold, maybe even a touch of frost—she'd check the date against the weather charts later—the mornings a reminder that winter lurked. Camellia was far enough from the city center that its streetlights would have been no match for the sky's black depths, the stars outshining the artificial light below in a final blaze before being vanquished by the lurking sun. The hush would have been absolute, as only a doors-locked, shades-drawn suburb could be, the well-watered lawns muffling nocturnal prowling—of scavengers like coyotes and raccoons, who'd learned fast that human-populated places provided far better forage than wilderness—and of the killer.

The church leaders' car doors would have echoed like shots as they slammed shut behind the contingent arriving at Melena and Bryce's home, lingering a moment before their purposeful march toward whatever awaited them at the house next door.

Already, Lola wondered at the narrative. Melena, of course, hadn't been in the bedroom. Hadn't seen the hockey stick. But Bryce had; he must have understood the implications, must have known that he and Melena and the leaders were possibly leaving the killer behind in their own home, giving him the chance to escape were he so inclined.

She sat on her hands to keep from pounding the table, bit her lip to hold back the question demanding to be shouted.

Melena's glanced flitted again and again toward Bryce as she spoke. His head bobbed obediently, confirming her recitation.

"We stopped outside the bedroom." Postponing by seconds the ordeal that awaited. Bryce and Melena waited in the hall until the leaders emerged, faces gleaming pale even in the darkened hallway.

"You should have seen them. Their eyes."

Lola didn't care about their eyes. Her teeth gnawed her lip raw. What about their feet? Had they stepped in blood? Tracked it around? Smeared it across other, more damning, footprints? She choked back a yelp as the air around her sparked and crackled, Charlie behind her again, leaning over her shoulder, his presence so vivid that she put up her hand to grasp his for support. Closed her fingers around air.

The men looked toward Tynslee's room. Conferred briefly, chose one. That man stiffened his back. Walked the length of the hallway. Cracked the door. Saw the sleeping girl within. His shoulders slumped in relief. He turned to Melena, crooked a finger. Women's work, this.

They all converged on the front step, Melena with an arm around the girl whose voice climbed in panic, tearing great rents in the still night air. "What's going on? Where's Mom?"

"I told her that there'd been some sort of accident. That an ambulance would be coming for her mother."

So, no blood then, at least not out into the hallway. The killer must have been lucky—or very, very careful—to have avoided the arterial spray.

*It's messy*, Charlie had always said about murder. *Like you wouldn't believe. It's a wonder anyone ever gets away with it.* On his watch, no one had. Of course, thought Lola, he'd never had to deal with the equivalent of a parade through any of his crime scenes.

"Then what?" Again in a whisper, so soft that Bryce gave no sign of having heard.

"We called the police."

About damn time.

"We didn't know how Frank would react. What he might do."

He'd have heard the church leaders arrive, Lola thought, maybe even have peeked from his bedroom window to see the procession enter the house next door and emerge with Tynslee. Had to know what awaited. Had he feigned sleep? Or greeted them defiantly? Assuming he was the killer. But what if he wasn't? What was he to make of the scene unfolding in the yard below? And when confronted by police, accused of murder?

"I was too afraid to go into our house, especially with Tynslee. So we waited outside for the police. Someone brought a blanket for Tynslee."

And again, Lola could see it, the huddle on the sidewalk, Tynslee shaking in cold and shock and bewilderment.

"The police were good enough not to use sirens. But the whole neighborhood saw."

She could see it, too, the forest of flashing lights outside the house, several cars called as a matter of protocol on something of this magnitude, an ambulance, too, useless though it would be. The cops, more arriving by the moment, their dark uniforms blending with the night, moving in a single mass toward the group on the sidewalk, pulling apart to flow around them, one group into Sariah's house to begin the grim task of collecting evidence—whatever was left of it—another into Melena's, emerging with Frank, his hair standing up in sleep-sculpted cowlicks, still in his pajamas. And handcuffs.

Twisting in the officers' grip toward Tynslee as she screamed and sobbed his name. Bryce stepping in to help Melena hold her back. It took both of them.

"That poor girl. That poor girl."

———

Bryce cleared his throat. Looked at his watch.

Melena went from a shell-shocked almost-witness-to-murder to a concerned wife, the transformation so fast and complete as to leave Lola blinking.

"Goodness. I've rattled on far too long. Sweetheart, I know it's just after the funeral, but you need to at least stop by the office. It's been days. Getting back into a routine will help. Lola can give me a ride home, right?"

Lola nodded. Bryce stood and held out his hand. She touched his fingertips with hers, the Indian way, and then snatched her hand back before he could inflict further damage.

"Pleasure," he said. Even though it hadn't been. And he'd said nothing useful. Somehow, sometime, she'd have to get him alone.

Meanwhile, she had Melena to herself.

"The church leaders…" She made an intuitive leap. "Are they telling you—advising you, I mean—how to handle this? Is that why you haven't gotten a lawyer for Frank yet?"

Melena nodded. "They'll find just the right person. In the meantime, we're to stay away. It's hard. Especially for Bryce. Fathers and sons, you know."

Lola didn't know about men and their sons and now she never would. The conversation kept turning back on her own situation. She had to put a stop to it.

"Is that why you adopted? Because you only had daughters?" *Only*. For God's sake.

Melena held her orange juice in both hands and bent her head to sip from it. "It was the right thing to do."

Then, before Lola could question the concept, Melena added, "And Sariah had just gotten Kwesi."

There it was again. *Gotten*. Like something she'd pointed to on a store shelf: *I'll take one of those*. And no mention of Galon. As though Sariah had arrived home one afternoon after a shopping trip: *Look what I got today, honey*.

Judgment tightened Lola's vocal cords. She cleared her throat and veered into safer territory, trying for small talk, never her strong suit. "I never got to meet you properly, the way I would have at the interview. We'd have had more time to get to know one another. You could have shown me—" What, exactly? "Your beautiful house." Lola saw it again, the suburban box, maximum space, minimum style but for that riot of flowers surrounding it, in contrast to the severity of the stone cairns next door. "Your flowers. They're lovely."

"Oh, that. Bryce does all of that."

So much for gardening. Lola tried again. "What do you do?"

"Do?"

"Your job." Lola's foot in her mouth again, all the way up to her knee. The woman had five children of her own, and then another. And this was Utah. She had just stomped squarely on the steaming heap of mutual disdain between stay-at-home moms and the career variety.

Melena straightened. Lifted her chin. "I'm a mother," she pronounced, with none of the condescension Lola had expected. "And a wife."

Motherhood as work, sure. Lola got that. In fact, after she'd had Margaret, she'd started referring to each day at the newspaper as her eight hour—or nine, or ten—vacation. But wife? Lola never thought of her marriage to Charlie as a job. It just *was*.

She took a guess. "Sariah, too?"

"Of course. Even though she only has"—something shifted in her face, that mental reminder again—"*had* two kids."

"Is that why they adopted? Because Tynslee was their only child? Or"—Lola almost choked on the phrase—"also because it was the right thing?"

Melena gave no sign of detecting her aversion to the phrase. "A little of both, probably. She and Galon were so in love. Like a fairy tale. And then they had their golden princess. Tynslee. They just wanted to share their happiness. Bryce and I always said they were the only couple as happy as we were."

171

Clang! One a scale of zero to ten, Lola's bullshit meter hit twelve. In her experience, people who felt the need to proclaim themselves happy rarely were. A point she'd often argued with Charlie, bringing the inevitable retort: "Or sometimes things are exactly as they seem."

"Are you?" she said now to Melena. "Are you and Bryce happy?"

She held her breath. She'd crossed the line, both of courtesy and journalistic strategy. It did no good to piss off someone so soon into a conversation, especially in circumstances so fraught. Melena might never talk with her again.

But the gaze Melena turned upon her was wide-eyed, guileless. "Of course. Weren't you?"

Well played. Lola fought an urge to touch her coffee cup to Melena's juice glass in a kind of acknowledgment.

Melena swallowed the last of her juice. "I should go. Did you see the way everyone was looking at me? They'll be calling, stopping by. Pretending they care about how I'm holding up. I wonder who will be the first to ask about Frank?"

Dispelling with a few vinegary sentences the initial impression of a personality as beige as her neighborhood. Not the simple housewife she appeared, not at all, Lola thought as she steered the rental car back into Camellia, the streets so familiar by now she barely needed the orders from the Directions Bitch, supplemented by Melena's far more palatable guidance. Lola wondered what it cost the woman to maintain that docile, whispery facade.

Melena clasped her hand before getting out of the car. "Thank you."

For what? "Good luck" was the only response she could manage. And, self-servingly, "I hope we'll talk again."

"Count on it."

Lola held her face very still, hoping the relief didn't show.

Melena turned toward the house. Then back again. "Five months?"

Lola's breath caught. She managed a nod.

"It hurts that long?"

Lola dragged the words from the bottomless hiding place of truth. "It hurts forever."

# TWENTY-THREE

Twice now, Melena had used the word *got* about Kwesi and Frank. Maybe that's how adoptive parents talked about their children. But the word remained an annoying mosquito whine at Lola's ear, drilling under her skin no matter how often she brushed it away. She had other things to do, like talk to Malachi again, and try to talk to Kwesi. But the hockey game was still a day away. She checked her phone for updates about the cop—still in critical condition, still no witnesses—and called Loretta Begay.

"Stoddard, Higbee, and Begay Law," a secretary chirped. Or maybe it wasn't a secretary, Lola thought, remembering how she'd mistaken Munro for a receptionist. She'd spoken with Loretta on the phone a few times after Charlie's death, mostly to inquire about the health of her mother, Betty, and wasn't sure she'd recall her voice.

As soon as the call was transferred, it came back to her, the barest trace of an accent, the clue to the fact that Loretta had spoken Diné before she learned English, and still spoke it during her trips home to the Navajo Nation.

"Lola! How nice to hear from you. Are you in town? Your timing is perfect. I've just cleared the decks so I can go back to Arizona and spend a couple of weeks with Mom. I leave tomorrow morning. Do you have time for a cup of coffee?"

Lola had gulped down three cups while talking with Melena, on top of what she'd drunk before the funeral. So much coffee sloshing around inside her that she feared a single pill would be inadequate to the task of knocking her senseless that evening. But, affecting enthusiasm, she gave the Directions Bitch the address of yet another Starbucks where, to her surprise, Loretta ordered a smoothie.

"Too late in the day for caffeine?" Lola asked. "We could have gone for a glass of wine instead." She preferred whisky, maybe even some of that fancy Scotch Munro had served her, but figured wine was more socially acceptable. She paid for Loretta's smoothie and her own latte—confronted with coffee, she couldn't force herself to order something more sensible—and joined the lawyer at a corner table, flipping her notebook open to a blank page and testing two pens before she found one with ink. She'd long ago learned that taking notes by hand was less intimidating, and reserved recordings for the most important interviews.

"I don't drink wine, either."

"Oh." Lola kicked herself. She kept forgetting the Mormon prohibitions. "So you stayed with the church even after … ?"

Loretta stirred her smoothie with a long spoon. She appeared to have come straight from her office, still armored in suit, hair pulled back into a *tsiiyéél*, the traditional yarn-bound bun at her nape that her law office colleagues probably took for some new hairstyling trend. Tiny button earrings of turquoise gave another nod to her identity. She'd mastered makeup long ago, an unnecessary layer of foundation atop her smooth brown skin, translucent gloss highlighting a generous mouth, clear lacquer on her nails, all of it projecting an impervious surface no doubt necessary in the emotionally fraught field that was her specialty.

"It's the faith I was raised with," she said. "By my parents."

"Your parents." Lola knew that despite Loretta's forced removal to a white family at an early age, she and Betty were close. She'd figured that meant Loretta had broken with the LDS family that took her in. Apparently not.

"I hate to reduce it to a cliché, but it's complicated. I love my white parents. They didn't treat me any differently than their biological kids. Even better, they did their best to teach me about my heritage, at least what little they knew. I'm lucky. My birth father died when I was just a baby, but I have three wonderful parents. The human heart has an amazing capacity for love—if you let it in."

Lola told herself there was no reason to take Loretta's remark personally, that Loretta had no way of knowing how she'd let Charlie's love in and how that had turned out. She stared into her latte until Loretta sighed and resumed talking.

"Remember, my adoptive parents believed, because that's what they were told, that taking me was part of God's plan. And there were so many of us. The Indian Placement Program didn't officially end until 2000."

Lola tried to remember what she knew about the program. "Kids removed from their families and legally adopted out to white couples."

"Early on, that's how it worked. Later, the Mormons moved away from legal adoptions to something more like foster care. But even with legal adoption, my mother was always part of my life." She grinned. "Can you imagine her letting something like a whiteman's law get in her way?"

Lola smiled with her. Both on and off the Navajo Reservation, people respected unto the point of fear the ninety pounds of fury that was Betty Begay when crossed. "Then why'd she let you go?"

She expected a flash of anger, or even regret. But Loretta radiated empathy. "You have to understand. Things on the reservation were so bad then, worse even than now. No plumbing or electricity, it goes without saying. Not that that was a problem. We'd always done fine living the old way, without those things. But when they came and killed our animals"—Lola nodded her understanding of the 1930s government edict that saw eighty percent of Navajo sheep herds slaughtered—"it took years to recover. Some people nearly starved. With the placement program, people knew their children would get enough to eat. An education. Was there pressure? Sure."

*Please, Lola. It's for her own good.*

"But try to imagine your Margaret hungry, cold. How far would you go to help her? Would you let her go?"

*Removal.*

"Not that far," Lola nearly snapped, her words directed at Amanda Richards back in Magpie. "Never."

Except that, in effect, she *had* let Margaret go—albeit with a push from Amanda Richards—turning her over to the aunties and Jan even before coming to Utah. She wondered how much Loretta knew about her current situation. Loretta had helped care for Charlie's niece, Juliana, who lived with her father on the Navajo Reservation. Margaret and Juliana remained in touch, intermittently emailing and Skyping.

Lola's pen wobbled in her hand. A jagged line of ink trailed across the page of her notebook. The caffeine was catching up with her. She put down the pen, wrapped her hands around the warm ceramic mug, and willed Loretta to keep talking.

"A lot of us in the placement program stayed with our LDS families during the school year and came home in the summer. Some kids opted out early. They missed their real families too much, or they didn't like their LDS families. And others liked their LDS families too much, maybe. Or the transition back became too difficult. Anyway, they never came back to the reservation."

At least the Navajo adoptees had been within a day's drive of their families. But an ocean lay between Utah and Kwesi's home of Ghana, and Frank hailed from the other side of the world.

"What about the children the LDS families adopt now?" Lola asked. "The ones from Africa, Asia. It's not so easy for them to go home if things don't work out."

"Impossible," Loretta agreed. "Which, if you think about it, makes these types of adoptions more attractive. Cut a young child off completely from everything he knows, immerse him in a new culture—it makes for a tough adjustment at first, but probably a tighter bond in the long run. They're totally dependent on their new families, even more than they would have been on their own. Memories fade. They forget their parents, their brothers and sisters."

"Wait a minute. They're not orphans?"

A corner of Loretta's mouth twisted down. "Surely you're not that naive."

Lola's hands tightened around the mug. "No."

She'd seen it time and again in Afghanistan, orphanages full of kids placed there by parents who preferred to give up their children rather than see them starve or fall prey to the myriad ills that stalked that country—the shootings, the bombings, the trafficking. "She's safe there," one woman had told her, lingering across the street from the crumbling walls of the orphanage, only marginally more sound than the hovels surrounding it. The arms that had cradled her toddler only moments before dangled empty. "Maybe she'll go with a rich family." She turned upon Lola, eyes blazing hope and anguish. "You take her? Bring her to America?"

Lola had backed away, the very notion unimaginable. Her? A child? Margaret was still years in the future, mentally inconceivable. She dragged herself back to the present. "Do they ever reconnect with their families?"

Loretta pushed away the smoothie as though she'd swallowed a bit of fruit gone rotten. "It's rare. I don't hear much about it, and I would, given my line of work. I've only handled one case. It was awful."

In Lola's experience, lawyers rarely spoke so frankly. Cases were *complex. Time-consuming.* At worst, *challenging.*

*Awful,* though. That was new territory.

"How so?"

"It was years ago. He was Bosnian. You remember that war. It was chaos. Dad was killed, rape was epidemic. Mom set out on foot with all four kids, trying to get to safety. One of the boys got separated somehow. It took her years, but Mom finally tracked him down to a family here, and—get this—she wanted her son back. Imagine. A mother thinking her own child belonged with her."

Beneath the foundation so expertly matched to her skin, Loretta's face had gone gray. Lola guessed what came next. "His family here didn't want to give him up."

"No. They took it to court. He was only three when they got him." That word again.

"They thought he wouldn't remember his mother. That it would traumatize him to go off with strangers."

Lola took another guess. "You represented them. The adoptive parents."

Loretta held up her hands, palms as empty as the expression on her face. "It's my job. I'm good at it."

Lola felt sick. "You won."

Loretta picked up the smoothie, sipped, and set it down, leaving a petal of lipstick near the rim of the glass. "Thank God, not entirely. He went back to Mom, but we got a shared custody situation, a lot like divorced families have. Two weekends a month with the adoptive parents. Both families are here in Salt Lake. He's grown now, on good terms with all of them. But he found a job in New York. Can you blame him for moving across the country?"

"Did he remember her? His mother? When she found him all those years later?"

Loretta turned her head away and touched her napkin to her eyes. "Yes."

First Melena's heartache, now that mother's. Lola gave Loretta a moment to compose herself.

"What about with an older child? Say, ten. How would adoption affect her? Or him, of course. For example."

"Like Frank Shumway. For example."

Loretta, like her mother, was two steps ahead. She swirled the spoon through what was left in the glass. Her eyes met Lola's with the sort of directness that bespoke her years in the white world. "This is off the record."

Lola snapped her notebook closed.

"There are always exceptions. I've handled some cases like that, seen some wonderful success stories. But a ten-year-old, one who almost certainly has family back home? So much can go wrong."

She stopped there. Left unspoken the obvious.

Like murder. About as wrong as it gets.

# TWENTY-FOUR

LOLA DAWDLED OUTSIDE THE hockey rink and hit Tynslee's phone number one more time. No sign of the girl, and she wasn't answering her phone.

People pushed past her into the rink. Lola searched their faces, sniffed the air. No one she knew. And not a whiff of bay rum. For years, the rare occasions she'd smelled the classic aftershave had brought a wistful smile, along with memories of her father. She wondered if she'd ever have that same warm association again. After Charlie's death, she'd switched from Ivory soap to whatever brand was on sale in Magpie's small supermarket, or at Teeple's on the reservation—anything that didn't smell like Charlie, scent too powerful a trigger.

But nothing could erase the aroma of sage on the morning breeze, the whiff of vanilla from the trunks of the Ponderosa pines, the wetted dust in the rare rainstorm—all things that Charlie had loved and often remarked upon.

Maybe she and Margaret should move to some anonymous locale, a place like Salt Lake, where the very air was scrubbed free of painful association, smelling only of exhaust and concrete and plastic, the sorts of things nobody would fall in love with. Lola tamped the thought down as soon as it arose. The aunties, simultaneously so stern and affectionate, would turn murderous if she tried to move Margaret away. And Jan—she'd lead the charge.

Another group of people shouldered past. Every time the doors opened, sound and icy air assaulted her. She'd already switched to a parka in Montana, but had switched back to a light jacket for the Utah trip after checking the forecast and finding considerably warmer predictions for Salt Lake. The parka and its puffy warmth were back in Magpie. Lola shoved her hands into her pockets and followed the crowd inside.

This time, with Donovan Munro's taunts about research and her lack thereof echoing in her head, she'd gone online to check out the team before heading to the game. The Wolverines were the ones in black, their namesake mascot snarling from a white circle in the center of their jerseys. Lola was glad she'd memorized Malachi's number—82—because towering atop their skates, their gangly bodies bulked up by layers of protective padding, helmets hiding their faces, the boys all looked alike.

The Wolverines were up against a crosstown rival, the Polar Bears, whose white jerseys made them blend in with the sheet of blinding alabaster ice. The two teams were fighting for the lead spot in the league, and Lola had a hard time finding a place to sit among the press of parents cheering on their children. She spotted Munro a few rows away and cursed herself for her own idiocy. His son was playing. Of course he'd be there. She skulked to a different section of the bleachers, her caution unnecessary given the noise level at the rink, grateful

183

when she spotted an unlikely opening in one of the front rows near the Wolverines' box. Too late, she realized why no one wanted to sit near the youth who occupied the middle of the space.

It was Kwesi, so beset by mourning that no one could possibly know what to say to him, especially in the light-hearted environs of a game, and so they avoided him, sliding away on the bleachers, contenting themselves with casting sidelong glances his way. Only a soccer ball sat beside him.

Lola took a seat beside him and angled herself away, bending her head over her phone as she searched for any updates on the condition of the cop. Nothing new. She told herself that was good, even though she knew that every day he lingered in critical condition was a day weaker, the same machines that kept him alive also a constant stress on his struggling body.

She sneaked a glance at Kwesi. Much as she wanted to talk with him, this wasn't the way she'd have chosen. Too soon, too public. She would wait until after the game, then corner him in some out-of-the-way place.

Her jacket had a hood. She pulled it tight around her head, as much for warmth as disguise, and blew on her fingers. The air in the rink hovered just above freezing. It had a sharp, clean tang. Ice crystals sequined the air as the players cut and swerved across the rink, skates hissing as they carved arabesques into its surface. It looked tense and thrilling and impossible to follow, at least for Lola. Around her, people pounded mittened hands together and yelled whenever Something Important happened. The scoreboard stood 0-0.

Lola looked for 82. He glided ahead of the others, moving the puck up the rink with short, protective strokes. Someone caught up with him and slammed him into the boards just below where Lola sat. The bleachers shook. "They got that little fairy good," said someone near her.

Fairy? Lola hadn't heard that term since high school. Was it still an epithet? Maybe, especially given the controversy over the church's stance on gay teens, it had regained currency, questioning a boy's sexuality being the surest path to insult just as "slut" had never lost its currency when applied to girls.

Malachi hopped to his feet and looked into the stands, raising his fist in a defiant "I'm okay" sign. A few desultory claps sounded. Lola sensed movement beside her and saw Kwesi raising his own fist in a return salute.

She tried not to stare. Kwesi and Frank had been best friends. And Malachi hated Frank—at least, that's what Munro had hinted. But Kwesi and Malachi appeared to be on good terms, an impression strengthened when Malachi was sent to the penalty box for some incomprehensible infraction. Kwesi scooted down to the boards. Malachi leaned around the edge of the penalty box. The two spoke for a few moments. Among the spectators, heads craned, everyone else almost as curious as Lola. Kwesi turned away from the box and climbed back to his seat. People suddenly became fixated on the game.

What the hell. "Hey," said Lola.

Kwesi turned, and she saw herself as he probably saw her, a middle-age woman, a stranger, not part of the hockey crowd given her inadequate clothing.

Wariness shaded his eyes. "Do I know you?"

Fortunately, for all his years in his adopted country, Kwesi had yet to acquire a loud American voice.

"I know Tynslee," Lola said, beneath cheers for yet another inexplicable advantage, albeit short of a goal, gained by the Wolverines. She jerked her head at the exit. "Talk?" she mouthed.

She didn't wait for an answer but excuse-me'd her way down the row, sure that her ploy would fail, that she'd wait outside for a boy who'd never show. A welcome warmth hit her as she slipped through the door. She shook her head free of the hood and opened her jacket. Other than a solitary smoker in the shadows, his back to her, the area around the door was deserted. She edged away from the smoker and resolutely ignored the door when she heard it open. It won't be him, she told herself.

It was.

---

Kwesi stood a few feet from her, not looking at her, the soccer ball tucked under one arm. For all anyone who might be watching could tell, they were two strangers thawing out before heading back into the rink.

"Lola Wicks," she introduced herself. "I'm a reporter."

The ball thudded to the ground.

"But I'm not writing a story right now," she hurried to add. "I'm just trying to figure out what's going on here."

"That makes two of us." The words floated toward her, weightless as an exhalation.

Good. Now all she had to do was keep him talking.

"I have to say, I was a little surprised to see you here, so soon after your mother's funeral."

"My dad thought it would be good for me to get out, spend some time with my friends." Kwesi rolled the ball off one ankle, spinning it upward, catching it in his hand.

Lola hoped Galon Ballard would never find out that Kwesi's friends had been too uncomfortable to sit with him at the game. "What about your sister? Doesn't she need time with friends, too?"

He dropped the ball again and began dribbling, jogging in circles around her. Lola forced herself to stand still.

"She told me about you," he called from somewhere behind her. "She's not coming."

She did? Lola wondered exactly what Tynslee had said. "Why not?"

He circled back to stand in front of her, the ball once again in his hands, jiggling it with a boy's energy but looking at her with the eyes of someone who'd been forced to assume a man's burdens in the past few days. "Because we told her not to."

"We?"

"Me and Malachi."

So that exchange in the stands had been just what it looked like. They were friends. Or maybe something more sinister. Maybe Kwesi was in on Malachi's pill business. Possibilities caromed off the walls of Lola's skull, thoughts coming so hard and fast her head ached. What about Frank? Was he part of it? If *it* even existed, she reminded herself. But if it did ... maybe Sariah had somehow found out the boys were dealing. Threatened to ground them, tell all their parents, even go to the cops. Would they have felt she had to be stopped? By, as the saying went, any means necessary?

Kwesi stood before her, eyes hooded, face a mask. Unmoving. Waiting.

"Tynslee said you might know something that could help me. Do you know what she was talking about?"

"Yeah."

"And?"

"That you should get out of here."

Lola almost laughed. "That's not going to happen. Just talk with me. I won't write anything without your permission." Generally, she never offered such assurances. But they were still kids, even if she was beginning to suspect that, as with most teens, these were hardly the innocents their parents prayed they were.

Kwesi's prolonged sigh implied infinite patience, a brick wall to Lola's urgent, probing curiosity. "You've been to Afghanistan."

"How did you know?"

He didn't bother to answer. Five minutes—more like thirty seconds—on Google. Not only had he learned about her from Tynslee, he'd done some homework on his own, more effort than Lola would have expected from someone his age, especially someone caught up in the firestorm of grief and anger following the murder of his mother.

"You know what those places are like," he said. "I was only five when I was adopted. Way younger than Frank was. I'd been with my parents for five years before the Shumways brought him home. I've forgotten a lot what it was like at home. Not everything, though. So when I say you should get out of here, you should listen to me. I come from a place where people end up dead if they don't get out in time. Same as Afghanistan. So go away. For your own sake, go away."

He turned away. The door slammed.

Lola glared at it. "Not a chance."

---

"Well, that's encouraging."

Lola whirled. Donovan Munro stood behind her, a lit cigarette dangling from his fingers.

Her heart gave a couple of deep bass beats. "You scared the crap out of me. When did you come out here? And what's encouraging?"

He grinned. Another whack of that internal drum, with a long, trailing vibration. She reminded herself that she didn't like smokers. Again, she flashed to Before Charlie, when a smile like that, one with a hint of challenge, would have moved her to acquisitive action. She made another gut check. No last bang on the drum. No heat. Maybe someday, her libido would flare back to life. But it wouldn't be on Munro's account.

"It's encouraging that you appear to have no intention of backing off. You've been doing everything possible to weasel out of this story. I'd expected—how'd they phrase it?" He pulled a printout from his pocket and read aloud. "'I pity anyone who tries to keep Lola Wicks from getting a story. She'll roll right over him like a bulldozer.' Bulldozer, hell. You've been more like—oh, I don't know. A unicycle. Wobbling away from things as fast as you can go on one wheel." He stuck the cigarette between his lips and grinned around it.

"Give me that." Lola snatched at the paper in his hand. He'd found an old profile of her, written after she'd won an award for an investigation into a campaign finance scheme that had exposed a white gubernatorial candidate posing as an Indian.

"Gladly. I'd advise you to read it. Let me know if you recognize that woman. And don't tell me. Show me."

Lola crumpled the paper and tossed it away.

Munro picked it up. "We don't litter here. Maybe you've noticed. Although noticing things doesn't appear to be your strong suit. Maybe you should hold on to this. Remind yourself of who you are."

Lola's eyes flashed a *shut up* warning.

Munro apparently missed the message. "Anyhow, what'd the kid say to you?"

Kwesi's over-the-top phrase came back to Lola: *people end up dead*. She shook her head. "Just some typical teenage drama." She pointed to the cigarette. "What's up with that? Pretty sure you're not supposed to be doing that here. I've never seen as many *No Smoking* signs as I've seen in this city."

He took an exaggerated drag and sent a slipstream of smoke her way. "Maybe I break the rules sometimes. Just like you—" He waved the crumpled printout at her. "Excuse me. Like you used to."

*Asshole.* It arose unbidden. Only way to deal with someone who hit you was to hit back. "So what's the deal with Malachi and Kwesi?" she asked. "Are they friends?"

Munro's face tightened as he gave an unconvincing shrug. "Dunno. Malachi doesn't have many friends. And the few he has, I can't keep straight. Speaking of Malachi, I'd better get back in there."

He left Lola standing with her mouth agape. "You shouldn't smoke," she called after him. Then muttered her way to her car. "Can't keep them straight, my ass." In the few days she'd been in Utah, Kwesi's was the only black face she'd seen. Not something that anyone, especially Munro, with the heightened observation of a journalist, was likely to forget.

Such thoughts occupied her mind for a five full minutes, possibly the longest she'd yet gone before remembering again that Charlie was dead.

# TWENTY-FIVE

LOLA WOKE TO THE sound of the wind blustering off the Front, picking up steam as it hit prairie, rolling east with nothing to stop it.

Most people hated it. All those old stories about pioneer women losing their minds. Not-so-old stories, too. A few years earlier, the EMTs being occupied with a fourteen-year-old who'd taken a car joyriding and ended up accordioned against a tree, it had been up to Charlie to wrestle Ada Karlsson into his cruiser and drive her all the way down to Great Falls where they could better handle psych cases. Ada wailed and hollered the entire sixty-mile trip, trying—as the frantic neighbor who'd called Charlie had told him—to out-scream the wind.

*Charlie.* At least, as the awareness of a new day asserted itself, he hadn't been her first thought. Her chest tightened. Was this how she'd lose him forever? Being distracted by the sound of the wind, the need for coffee, a thousand different things pushing themselves into her consciousness until Charlie receded into some faraway niche, relegated to the bottom of an endless to-be-remembered list?

"Damn wind." Maybe it was making her crazy, too. It sounded different today, deeper, more of a growl than a shriek.

A car horn sounded. Then another. The backhand slap of reality. She wasn't in their bedroom in Magpie, but a hotel room in Utah. It wasn't the wind, but the sound of traffic.

And Charlie was still dead.

---

*It's encouraging that you appear to have no intention of backing off.*

Munro's words echoed their challenge. Fake challenge, she reminded herself. Maybe.

Of course, real or fake, she still had every intention of backing off. Eventually. If nothing else, Loretta Begay had already confirmed the story's original angle, the problems inherent in adopting older children, especially from a different culture. Dog Bites Man. Stop the presses.

And if she found something more? The possibility simmered beneath her grief, pinprick bubbles of ideas and plausibilities rising to the surface. She pushed the thought away even as the bubbles rose faster, grew larger. She took a mental spoon to them, stirred them down.

The strange symbiosis among Kwesi and Malachi and Frank— maybe they *were* druggies, playing at being badasses with Kwesi's "people end up dead" warning. Maybe they weren't. Either way, for sure it wasn't a story Munro would want.

And Tynslee, now-I'll-talk-to-you-now-I-won't Tynslee? A teenage girl, mercurial? Stop the presses yet again.

An hour earlier, Lola had feared the slow, incremental loss of Charlie. Now he was back full force, the room rumbling with censure, nearly audible, the traffic noises relegated to the background.

*Go away,* she almost said. Even though a judgmental Charlie was preferable to no Charlie at all. She closed her eyes so that she could see him better, the scowl that suited his square features, the narrowed eyes, the pursed mouth, lips pointing in the Indian way.

Pointing at what?

She'd missed something obvious. The accusing lips thrust forward insistently.

What? What?

The room fell silent. The lips relaxed. Lola nearly laughed at her own dimwittedness. The rumble receded.

Not what. *Who.*

She had to talk with Frank.

———

Back when Lola was a baby reporter, jailhouse interviews were easy. You dropped in, jawed with the guards, showed an ID, and scooted through the metal detector.

No more. Now there were permissions to be gained, visiting days to be observed. Lola decided to chance ignoring the former and checked the latter on the jail's website. The journalism gods, so generous as of late, continued benevolent. Frank's jail pod actually had Saturday visiting hours. Lola dreaded the day when the gods demanded their inevitable payback.

"But not just yet," she pleaded as she signed the request to visit Frank Shumway. Please let the public defender not have given Frank the standard speech about not talking to the press. Please let the local reporters be exactly as young and green as they appeared, not thinking to make this same obvious move, and the more seasoned ones distracted by the assault on the police officer. And pleaseoh-please, she added as the guard made the laconic pronouncement that the inmate would see her, please let Frank talk.

———

He didn't, not at first. Just sat in the plastic chair, arms crossed on the ledge in front of him, making no move to lift the phone receiver on his side of the bulletproof Plexiglas cloudy with scratches.

Lola picked up her own receiver and pointed to his, trying not to breathe too deeply the stench of mingled rage and despair that permeated every jail and prison she'd ever been in. He reached for it, never taking his eyes from hers, the same curious, attentive expression he'd worn in the courtroom.

She introduced herself, name only, skipping over for the moment the inconvenient fact of her profession. "Am I the first person who's come to see you?"

He shook his head. "My lawyer. Are you my new one? He said that sometimes they change lawyers."

Sometimes? More like change, change, and change again. If Utah's public defender system ran true to form, its lawyers burned out faster than a wildfire moving across the prairie. A case of any length might involve multiple shift changes. And if no one bothered to procure a private attorney for him...

Lola wasn't sure how Utah's public defender laws worked, but she wondered whether someone might be able to make the case that, as an eighteen-year-old adult, especially one about to get married and be on his own, Frank could legally be declared indigent. She could find out about that later. For now, he was expecting an answer.

"I'm a reporter," she said, as always moving fast to get past the instinctive resistance, throwing out something innocuous for distraction. "Please—what should I call you? Your name is Frank in all of the newspaper stories, but Tynslee called you Trang."

"Because it's my *name*." Emphasis added for the idiot adult who faced him through the glass. "*Obviously*."

"Of course, of course. How stupid of me." Granting him the upper hand, not pursuing the *ob*vious question of the different identities—the original name, the one from home, for those closest to his heart; the other name, bestowed upon arrival in this strange place, used by parents, teachers, anyone at an emotional arm's length. And what of it? Didn't all teenagers assume split personalities as they navigated their various worlds?

"I've already talked to Kwesi." Whose parents had thought his name was just fine, who'd never had to morph into Ken or Kevin. No use mentioning that Kwesi had been disinclined to converse. "And Tynslee. She thinks you didn't do it."

Frank's shoulders slumped. The skin beneath his eyes shaded from brown to nearly black. Jail, with its clanging and shouting and constant sizzling fear, was no place to get a good night's sleep, and he'd been there for several nights now. But those eyes themselves were clear, his gaze direct. "That's because I didn't. How much longer before they let me out?"

Oh, you poor clueless kid. Even if the church leaders finally came through on their pledge to find a defense attorney, one who could talk the judge into setting bail, the amount would probably be prohibitive—in the house-mortgaging realm—and the negotiations would take a while, anyway.

"It's a long process." Surely his public defender had explained as much. Or his parents.

"But I have to get out of here. I'm supposed to go to Vietnam."

"I thought you couldn't go now. I mean, even before … this. Because you aren't—" Lola stopped, uncharacteristically embarrassed.

Frank wasn't. "Pure?" He shrugged. "Just because I can't go on my mission anymore doesn't mean I can't go on my own. In a way, it's even better. This way, I can be sure to go to Vietnam. That's what I wanted do."

"What about Tynslee? Weren't you going to get married?" Lola tried not to think about all the times she'd left Charlie in pursuit of a story, heedless as to his concerns.

Trang raised his chin. He didn't smile, not exactly, but his face softened. "Tynslee wants me to go. She knows how important it is to me."

"Why is it so important? Please. Knowing this might help." She already knew. But she needed to tell it in his own words. "I want to share the real story."

"There's no real story. I didn't do it. That's all."

Lola looked at the heavy receiver in her hand. She wondered if Frank knew that jailhouse interviews were recorded. Still, she had to ask. "Do you have any idea who did do it?"

"No." A beat too late. "I wish I did."

That pause, with its clumsy follow-up, could mean anything. Probably not anything good, though. Either he did have an idea, or he was trying to cover his own guilt.

Lola wondered how best to bring up Bryce. "I saw your parents. Your dad—he's seems like he's having a pretty rough time." *Duh.* She'd just one-upped Trang in the clumsy department.

No hesitation at all this time, though. "You saw Dad? Is he okay? I mean—how can he be? But still. Did he ask about me? Is he coming to see me?"

Even as her cynical reporter's heart broke a little at the sight of the boy's eagerness to see the father who'd withdrawn when most needed, her vigilant reporter's brain made a quick notation: whatever suspicions Trang might harbor about who killed Sariah, they weren't focused on Bryce.

"He didn't say," she replied. If the boy didn't know about the church leaders' advice to his parents to stay away, she wasn't going to be the one to tell him. She hurried to a more agreeable subject. Frank had given no hint that he was upset at the prospect of his impending marriage, but she had to be sure. "About you and your"—she still couldn't bring herself to say *fiancée*—"sweetheart."

"What about us?" Another palpable leap of feeling, the intensity so raw she looked away.

"Is it real? Is it love?"

The hard plastic receiver clattered onto the metal table. A guard started down the row toward them. Trang rose.

"We're done here," he mouthed.

Lola sat stupidly, looking at Frank's retreating back, until the guard touched her shoulder.

"Ma'am? Did you hear what he said? You're done."

# TWENTY-SIX

THE REAL STORY.

He couldn't imagine sharing that with anyone, let alone a stranger.

Even though it was hardly unique. You heard about these things. At school, kids who were technical virgins whispered precise instructions on how far one could go while still qualifying for a temple wedding.

Trang did all of those things. And then he did more.

In theory, it was nearly impossible. The Mormons, knowing in the ways of lust, had tried to prepare for every contingency. Mostly, when it came to teens, the idea—in addition to endless readings and talks on the value of purity—was to keep couples from being alone together. Hence, so many group activities that Trang, who like everyone else he knew had grown up in a house full of siblings, sought moments alone with the craving of an addict. At least he had the benefit of being the only boy in a house full of sisters, thus rating a room of his own.

Blissfully alone at night, he explored his body and learned. And learned still more in that most old-fashioned of ways, the library, full of information and besides, a place to soothe the concerns of suspicious parents, who merely waved gaily as he and his friends—safety in groups—set out on their near-daily trips.

Kwesi and Tynslee were a constant, forming a trio with Trang ever since he had arrived next door and gravitated naturally to Kwesi, a boy who barely remembered the time before his own adoption and guided his new friend through this bewildering world where copious amounts of soap and water, and rigorous adherence to schedules, held tyrannical sway. At first, Trang's stomach rebelled at the nauseating hunks of meat sitting in pools of their own blood on his plate, at the mealy potatoes, the mushy vegetables. Rice, when it made its rare appearance, came in amounts that would have left a toddler hungry, and noodles—that staple, even in the Kind and Caring Home—not the silky rice variety of his childhood but fat and floury, drowned in a thick red tomato sauce.

Later, when he'd mastered English and, more important, the strange American way of relating to friends by slinging insults rather than showing respect, he would tease Kwesi and Tynslee. "Your mother, she tried to kill me. Feeding me those terrible things whenever she invited me in." He swung from a crossbar on their backyard swing set that had stood mostly unused for years now. Malachi, who by this time had rounded out their group to a foursome, folded himself on the glider and sailed to and fro, his knees almost touching his chin. Tynslee and Kwesi pumped high on the swings in an echo of their childhood contests.

Tynslee still wore her hair in braids then. She soared from the swing and hit the ground, sticking the landing with barely a bobble. She flicked the braids back over her shoulders and squared off. "She was trying to fatten you up. You were so skinny we thought you'd break."

"Stick boy!" "Skeleton!" A chorus of hoots, the inevitable rough-housing, all four of them tussling like puppies. A grab at his midsection, bared where his shirt had ridden up. "Whatever she did, it worked. You might try to pass this off as muscle, but I'm pretty sure it's fat."

"Hey. Hands off! Forbidden flesh, remember?" He dropped to the ground, in his confusion not hearing the gibes that followed.

That's probably when it began, the touch of skin on skin. A sudden new awareness. Glances, once casual, now caught and held, slid down. Each noticing. Looking away when caught. At first. Hands following eyes, any excuse to touch.

"Here, hold this book for me, will you?" Fingers twining in the exchange.

"Ugh. My shoulder itches. I can't reach it. Can you?" A scratch that became a quick caress.

Which was about as far as it could go in a back yard, the sheltered lee of the library's back door. So: hikes, the others obligingly trekking ahead of the couple as they stepped off the trail. Hands beneath shirts, sliding down into pants. *Oh.* But quickly, quickly. Salt Lake was a city of outdoors enthusiasts. The trails were packed, a veritable freeway, jammed with youth groups and their chaperones. You never knew when a church leader would come around a corner and catch you with your shirt hiked high, your belt undone, body yearning for more.

Finally, inevitably, the daring suggestion: a middle-of-the-night bedroom tryst. All it required was silence.

"You're crazy." His first response.

It took him about a half-second to get to "Really?"

And so it was done, that first night brief, both of them trembling in fear and excitement. "Careful. The sheets." Bodies slick with sweat, scent of sex, gasps stifled.

"I've got to go."

"Not yet." Clasping one another close. "Do you remember what people said to my parents when they brought me home?"

Teeth flashed in a smile. "Yeah. 'I thought you were getting a girl.'"

A last, lingering kiss.

"So glad they didn't."

Was it love?

Yes.

And fear.

# TWENTY-SEVEN

THE DRIVE BACK TO the hotel was just long enough to fan the flicker of energy and indignation stirred by the previous day's hockey game and its small revelations, which joined the brighter flame of curiosity roused by the brief visit with Trang. Lola dropped her bookbag just inside the door and went to the bathroom to retrieve her pills, on this night more from habit than intent.

She counted them out, making a mental list as she plunked each pill onto the counter. Call Tynslee and get her to explain herself. Maybe, if the girl continued to avoid her phone, she would lurk in Melena's sister's neighborhood in hopes of intercepting Tynslee as she walked Rex, or, if she was going to school again, on her way home. As for school, she could go to Tynslee and Kwesi's high school and talk to kids there on the pretext of interviewing people about the murder, eventually bringing the conversation around to Trang and Kwesi and Malachi, too, even though he went to a different school. If any or all of the three were involved in some sort of drug dealing, everyone in the high school would know, even if teachers and cops didn't.

Meanwhile, she hadn't even tried to talk to Galon, Sariah's husband, and still the odds-on the most likely suspect even though he'd been gone that night. Galon wouldn't be the first man to hire someone to kill his wife. Maybe it was time to try to talk with him.

The pills sat in their silent row, bereft of their usual pull. This night wouldn't be one of permanent darkness. She had too much to figure out. Lola swept the pills back into their baggie and replaced it in the Dopp kit, stalling before her daily call to Margaret. She ran tepid water in the sink, tossed in the previous day's bra and underwear, and scrubbed at them with the soap, an old habit left over from her foreign correspondent days, when she'd traveled for weeks on end with only two changes of clothes. She rinsed them out, rolled them tight in a towel to wring out excess moisture, and tossed them over the shower curtain rod. So much for that particular delaying tactic.

She picked up the newspaper from its place near the door. She'd kicked it aside on her way out of the room that morning. Now she sat at the desk and studied its pages as though she'd face a quiz on whatever passed as news in Salt Lake.

The cop's attack. That would have been news anywhere, and the paper played it with the usual package of stories, the main one on the so-far-futile search for his assailant and the knife that nearly killed him, plus sidebars on the cop himself (young, married, sweet-faced wife and adorable kids, of course) and on the history of cop killings and attacks—enviably few—in Salt Lake. Lola's hands grew damp as she re-read the main story. But despite her searching for coded meaning in the scripted comments from police, nothing indicated they had even a hint of a suspect, despite the roundup and intensive questioning of the park's habitués, most of them too drunk, drug-addled, or mentally ill to be of much use. She whispered a belated prayer of thanks that the officer's condition, dire though it remained, had not worsened and had even showed slight improvement.

Another story stopped her. *"Highway Suicide."* The jumper whose covered body she'd seen on the interstate her first day. A kid, it turned out. Gay. Kicked out of his home by parents who'd taken the church teachings one step too far. *"We tried to help him. But he wouldn't change."* The predictably anguished quotes from local advocacy organizations, issuing a public plea for the church to rethink its stance. *"He's the fourth so far this year. This goes beyond policy. It's life and death. Of our children!"*

Lola had envied the anonymous leaper's strength in making the choice that had so far eluded her. But this was different. For all practical purposes, when the boy had struggled up and over that high, inwardly curving fence, he hadn't made a choice at all. It was almost as though he'd been pushed, propelled over the fence by the strength of the church's disapproval.

Lola put the paper aside. Time to call Margaret. She reached for her phone, but pulled her hand back, empty. She couldn't face another rejection from her daughter, more hectoring from Jan. The damn phone buzzed anyway.

Munro. Again.

"Jesus Christ. Don't you ever take time off?" This time, Lola didn't care that he could hear her.

"We tend not to take the Lord's name in vain around here. Not that I mind. But someone else might. It's a good thing to get in the habit of not cussing. Although you don't seem to care about offending people."

Something new in his voice, a tautness beyond his usual sarcasm. Lola decided not to remind him of his own lapses into impressive

204

invective, all of which so far had been directed at her. "I don't. What do you want?"

"I need to talk to you about something. Two somethings."

Talk *to* you. Not *with* you. "Goddammit."

He cleared his throat.

"I mean, hell." That probably wasn't acceptable, either. "Oh, for God's—gosh—sake. What is it?"

"I'd prefer we do this in person."

She'd had more than enough of Donovan Munro for a while. "How about noon tomorrow?" She really wanted to sleep in.

"How about now?"

"Now?" It was nine o'clock. "I was getting ready for bed. Making an early night of it. Seems crazy to head out at this hour."

"You don't have to go anywhere. I'm in the lobby. Which room is yours?"

"I'll come down."

"I'll come up." He hung up before she could object.

Lola darted into the bathroom, yanked her dripping undergarments from the shower curtain rod, and tossed them into the closet just as Donovan Munro rapped on her door.

---

Bed? Or chair?

There was a reason Lola avoided hotel room interviews. The presence of a bed shot professionalism all to hell.

Munro pushed past her into the room. Lola inhaled. Not bay rum. More like just plain rum. Something alcoholic, anyway, mixed with the scent of tobacco, not unpleasant. She grabbed the chair for herself and left the bed to him. But instead of perching at the edge of the bed as she would have done, he propped the pillows against the headboard and leaned against them, stretching his long legs—shoes still on—across the spread. Lola comforted herself with the thought that anyone so relaxed couldn't possibly have come with bad news.

Donovan's first words smashed that theory. "The story's dead."

Lola sat back and awaited relief. She waited some more. Something entirely different gnawed at her innards, a feeling she associated only with her shortcomings as a mother, a wife, a friend. But never, despite her recent slacking, as a reporter. Failure. She'd never blown a big story, and this one, no matter that it had begun light as a leaf, had gained considerable heft.

She started to apologize. Munro held up his hand. Only then did she notice its barely perceptible trembling, the whiteness around his tightened lips, the way one foot bounced against the spread. He wasn't simply upset or—again, she inhaled—lit. The man was furious. Lola hitched her chair back a few inches as he hurled words her way.

"'Serious journalism,' they said. 'Dig deep,' they said. 'Give our readers some meat,' they said. What a load of horseshit."

Until then, Lola hadn't realized she was holding her breath. Munro was livid, but she wasn't the cause. She hadn't failed.

"Thank God," she said. And, at his look, fumbled through a recovery. "That at least you know what you're dealing with."

"You mind?" He dug in the pocket of the blazer he'd thrown down beside him and extracted a flask.

Lola shook her head. There was a long gurgle.

"You?"

She hitched the chair forward and took it, albeit with a considerably shorter swallow. Whatever was going on, she needed her wits about her. Donovan took the flask back and helped himself to more.

"It's not like everyone didn't warn me."

By "everyone," Lola assumed he meant others at his former newspaper.

"But what was I supposed to do? Bevany and I had just split up. I'd agreed to buy her out of the house. And the magazine pays real money. By God, does it pay."

Lola followed his train of thought to its logical conclusion. "But now you want to quit. And you can't. For all of those very good reasons."

Glug.

"Steady there," said Lola, even as he passed the flask back to her. She took another sip, noting as she did that the flask was only about half full. She hoped it had been partially empty when he started. She guessed it hadn't.

"There's no shame in supporting yourself and your son. At least you ended up with a decent job when you got laid off. Most don't."

They sat silent a moment. Lola knew he was thinking, as was she, of all the former reporters they knew who were either collecting unemployment or scratching and scraping at marginal jobs.

"But most didn't sell their souls."

"There's that." Better not to do journalism at all than to do crap journalism.

Glug.

His head lolled back against the pillows. Lola considered the fact that he was fast becoming drunk. She tried to get him back on track.

"They killed the story?"

Munro made an attempt at straightening. "There'll be a kill fee, of course." He named it.

"Holy hell." Lola couldn't contain her surprise.

"I insisted they pay you the full fee, just as though you'd done the story. It was the least I could do."

Lola leaned over and took the flask back, drinking deeper this time. "Much appreciated." It really was the best of all scenarios. She could go home to Margaret. Make another stab at acceptable parenting. If it didn't work out, well, she had enough pills now for the easy out. Still, the wriggle of disappointment persisted.

"What happens to that kid? Trang? I mean, Frank."

Munro listed to one side. "What always happens. You know the drill. Especially without a good lawyer."

She did. A private lawyer would file motion after motion, tying up the case for months while searching for the shreds of evidence that might win an acquittal, or at least a reduced charge, for Trang. But while the overburdened public defender would do his best, he'd be no match for a better-funded prosecutor, especially one bent on making his political bones.

Donovan held the flask over his open mouth. "Damn. Almost gone. Guess that's my signal to get gone, too. I've done what I came here for."

Lola swore under her breath. The man was clearly incapable of driving safely. She forced a brightness she in no way felt into her voice. "How about I make you some coffee first?"

She busied herself with the room's miniature coffeemaker to forestall a "no." She filled it with water and dumped both packets of coffee into the filter. Maybe extra-strong would sober him up extra-fast. She called to him over her shoulder. "You said you had two somethings you wanted to talk to me about."

"Oh. Yeah. That."

Lola waited. When he failed to continue, she poured a cup of inky brew and turned. His eyes were closed.

"Munro!"

He jerked upright. "What?"

"What else did you have to tell me?"

"Are you a junkie?"

"Excuse me?"

"Got a call. Said you were a pill-popper. Are you? 'Cause that would explain a lot."

Malachi. That little shit. Lola thought that her last order of business before leaving Salt Lake might be to wring the brat's neck.

"Who said?"

"Dunno. Anonymous call."

Lola thought of all the times he'd greeted her by name on the phone before she'd even announced herself. "No calls are anonymous anymore."

"This was one. *Caller unknown*, it said."

The kid was selling drugs. He was probably acquainted with burners. She wondered how Malachi had managed to disguise his voice to the extent that his own father didn't recognize it. Maybe he'd gotten Kwesi to make the call.

"So? Are you? A pill-popper?"

He'd slumped again, lower this time. The coffee sat ignored on the nightstand.

"Pot calling the kettle black, I'd say." Echoing her favorite retort to Charlie. "You're plastered."

"You didn't answer the question."

He had her there. Maybe he wasn't as drunk as she'd thought. Maybe he could drive home after all.

A snore interrupted her thoughts. Munro toppled from the pillows onto the spread, where he lay, eyes closed, mouth agape.

She raised her foot and nudged him. "Hey." Another snore.

She picked up the coffee cup and took a swig. "Gahhhh!" Still, it did its job, doing brief, triumphant battle with the Scotch she'd sipped. She needed to think.

The story was dead. But the jerk who'd called Munro, trying to discredit her, would have had no way of knowing that. She cast a longing look through the open bathroom door to her Dopp kit on the counter. At least for this night, even a single pill, let alone the whole batch, would not be an option.

She put her hands on Munro's shoulders and rolled his sorry carcass to one side of the bed, giving thanks that it was a king, thereby ensuring an arm's length of space between them when she gingerly tucked in her fully clothed self on the far side of the bed.

# TWENTY-EIGHT

LOLA SLEPT LONG AND hard, her first truly deep slumber in months without the nudge of a pill.

She spooned close with Charlie, pulling his arm around her. His erection pressed against her hips. She rubbed against it and moved his hand to her breast and sighed in pleasure. Scratch of stubble against her neck, lips to her ear.

"This is embarrassing."

Lola bounded from the bed and across the room in a single giant step. "What. The. Hell."

"Hey." Donovan sat up and hooked his hair behind his ears. "No harm, no foul. It's not like I'm your editor anymore. So there's no conflict of interest."

Conflict of interest? That was his first concern?

"There's no interest, period! Christ."

Donovan swung his long legs over the bed and stood and stretched. His shirt, wrinkled and untucked, rode up over an admirably flat belly. Lola, after a second, looked away.

"The lady doth protest too much. But under the circumstances, I don't blame you. This isn't my ideal scenario either. No candlelight, no wine, just straight into the sack."

"Stop that. Nothing happened."

"You sure?" His grin ended in a wince. He brushed past Lola and went into the bathroom. Lola squirmed at the sound of a long and prodigious piss, followed by vigorous splashing at the sink.

He stood in the bathroom doorway, hair damp. "That's better. It's been a while since I've done that to myself. I forgot about cottonmouth. Not to mention what it does to my head. Got any aspirin?"

"In my Dopp kit." Anything to get him out, Lola thought, before she remembered that the pills she'd bought from Malachi were in the kit. "Actually, I don't think I have any aspirin—" she started.

"Yeah, you do. Found 'em," Donovan said after a pause. He came out of the bathroom rattling the travel-size container as proof, wincing again at the sound. He shook four into his hand. "Cheers. How about I buy you breakfast? It's the thing to do, right?" Entirely too nonchalant.

"Nothing happened. So there's nothing to do." Lola spoke through gritted teeth, hoping the unspoken message *just go* would get through to him. And it did, although maybe, given his jaunty wave as she closed the door behind him, he'd missed the bile that accompanied her words.

She shivered, a reaction she refused to attribute to emotion. After thumbing the room's thermostat upward she hurried to straighten the bed, erasing all signs of his presence, hoping that Charlie, always hovering, hadn't seen, and trying very, very hard to forget the warmth of Donovan's hand on her breast.

———

An hour later, Lola remained motionless where she'd fallen back onto the bed, drained of her previous night's hunger for the story, not to mention her traitorous craving for the warm body—apparently any warm body would do—so briefly next to hers.

She hadn't drunk nearly as much as Munro the night before, but she had the sensation of spinning down into a dark hole, deeper and deeper. She clutched the sides of the bed as though to stop herself. A great weight tugged at her limbs. Her grip on the comforter loosened. Pain—held briefly at bay by her unexpected interest in the story—came clawing back at her heart, carving new channels through that shredded organ. Her vision blurred and blackened around the edges.

Somewhere, it was light. Margaret was there. Jan and the aunties. The ranch. Peaks and prairie and open sky. Life. All of it beyond reach.

Last night, she'd assessed her options for pursuing the story. Now, she confronted a different checklist.

The story, dead.

Margaret, more distant by the day.

Friends, openly contemptuous.

Amanda Richards, with her clinical, assessing gaze and her clipboard, ready to effect Margaret's *removal*.

And Charlie—not only gone, but she apparently couldn't even be faithful to his memory.

The swirling feeling stopped with a physical jolt. Bottom. She raised her head an inch from the mattress. No spinning. She eased one leg to the floor, then the next. Headed for the bathroom.

She upended her Dopp kit. There, amid the jumble of the deodorant stick, the little containers of lotion and baby powder, the Band-Aids, and the makeup that Jan had provided, were the pills. Beckoning.

Lola flipped the pleated paper cover from one of the glasses by the sink, ran water into it, lowered the lid on the toilet seat, and sat while she ran through the familiar pros and cons one last time.

Margaret, of course, topped the list. But really, wouldn't her daughter be better off without her? Look at all the fun she was having with Jan in charge, more than she'd seen in months. And it wasn't as though she'd be left alone. The aunties would look out for her, accustomed as they were to taking in the children of too many others who'd succumbed to alcohol and drugs, or had died in car accidents or been killed by raging husbands or boyfriends—all the legions of ills besetting a people who persisted and triumphed despite them. That last thought gave Lola a twinge of guilt. Margaret might be better off without her, but she'd remember Lola as just another mother who'd let her child down.

Jan—the closest thing to a best friend she'd had since her friend Mary Alice was murdered years earlier, a crime that had brought Lola to Montana—would miss her. For a while, anyway. Jan was younger, ambitious. Inevitably she'd get a job offer that would take her up and out of Montana. Lola would fade into memory.

Bub. Whenever Lola thought she couldn't hurt any worse, some new form of pain stabbed her. She bent double against the fresh assault. How many times had the phrase "he's just a dog" been thrown her way? He'd saved her life, literally, more than once, and then, just before the bombing that killed Charlie, she'd saved his. Who knew if a dog could miss someone?

Her thoughts meandered to childhood tales of dogs like Greyfriars Bobby and, more recently, to Shep, the dog beloved in Montana for his habit of waiting—for five and a half years, until his death—at the Fort Benton railroad tracks for the return of the train that had taken away his master's coffin.

Yes. Bub would miss her. Another black mark against Lola in the afterlife.

Raised Catholic, Lola had abandoned her faith with alacrity, starting with the minute the nuns of her childhood had outlined its exclusivity. She'd seen no reason her Presbyterian cousins should be doomed to hell, although the latter was a place whose possibility was tougher to shed.

If hell indeed existed—and Lola's suspicions that it did yet lingered—she knew where she'd end up, a vague and secret fear barely alleviated by airy, out-loud protestations that at least she'd be among friends.

But Charlie wouldn't be there. And if there was any sort of afterlife, he'd be so angry that he'd be the first to shove her downward into the flaming pit, or whatever it was. (Lola secretly suspected a newsroom populated only with editors.) He'd hate her for what she was about to do. On the other hand, there was his oft-repeated rule: "In a crisis, make decisions." Well, she was making this one.

She took a defiant swig and picked a few pills out of the pile. After all, it was Charlie's fault. If he hadn't stepped in front of that bomb to protect his brother, he'd still be alive and none of this would be necessary.

She brought the pills to her lips. Gulped more water. Tossed the pills into her mouth. Swallowed.

The phone, the merciless fucking phone, rang.

# TWENTY-NINE

"GODDAMMIT, MUNRO. LEAVE ME alone."

This time, Lola didn't care whether he heard her. But it wasn't Munro. In fact, she didn't recognize the number. Maybe that rotten kid Malachi had gotten himself another burner. One of the pills had caught in her throat. She gulped more water and choked it down.

"Miss Wicks?"

"Tynslee?" Lola knew the voice. Or at least she thought she did. The girl must have some kind of radar. It was the second time Tynslee had called her after she'd downed pills. Except before, it had been a single tablet. This time, the multiple dose would get to her faster. She wanted to hear what Tynslee had to say but needed to get off the phone before the girl realized something was wrong.

At least Tynslee seemed to be in a rush, too.

"I'm on my aunt's phone. I'm afraid they're checking mine." Her words were whispered, hurried.

"We were supposed to meet at the hockey game," Lola said. She spoke slowly, with care, her senses already beginning to blur.

"I know. The guys wouldn't let me come."

"The guys?"

"Kwesi and Malachi."

"Malachi, too?"

"He was helping us raise money so that Trang could go to Vietnam."

Vietnam, again. Trang was obsessed. "Why?"

Tynslee misunderstood the question Lola hadn't been able to fully articulate. "Because he didn't have enough money for a ticket. We were all pitching in to help him. Malachi had already gotten a few hundred dollars. He wouldn't tell us how."

Lola was pretty sure she knew how. Was she to think better of Malachi because his pill pushing had a higher purpose? She banged a hand against her head, trying to shake the words loose. "Why was he going to Vietnam?"

"That's what I wanted to talk to you about. But the guys said it would be too dangerous."

Lola leaned her head against the sink. Sleep tugged at her. "Dangerous, why?"

"Because if the person who killed Mom found out … "

Even in her fogged state, Lola could supply the end to the sentence. They were afraid someone would kill Tynslee, too. Just as Kwesi had warned Lola that she herself could be killed.

More drama, she thought. But the words wouldn't come. She made a great effort until she found some new ones. One last try. She spoke very slowly and carefully. "Tynslee, why was it so important for Trang to get to Vietnam?"

Tynslee lowered her voice further still. Lola could hardly hear the answers to the fumbling questions she put to the girl.

Taking a long breath, Tynslee wrapped things up. "So you see, Miss Wicks, why he couldn't have killed my mother. Like I said, she wasn't stopping him from going. He was going to go anyway."

Lola was still trying to process what Tynslee had just told her. "A sister?"

Loretta Begay's words came back to her. *Surely you're not that naive.* "Yes."

"Not a mother? Other siblings? Cousins?"

"No. No one. His grandfather was black. An American soldier. All the other relatives cut them off. So you see why he had to go back. He had to find her. She was all he had."

"Why doesn't he just tell the police here about her? They might be able to help him find her. They might even want to talk to her themselves."

Tynslee's sigh went on forever. "Because even if they found her, she couldn't help them."

Lola swayed on the toilet seat. She grabbed the sink for balance and slid to the floor. There. Better. Her head lolled against the toilet.

"Why not?"

"Because she's dead."

———

The next time she looked at the phone, the screen was black. She must have rung off. Or maybe Tynslee did.

The bathroom was warm. Her thoughts swirled hazily, riding the currents of warm air pumping from the vent. Like a spring chinook on the Front, she thought. She loved those, the way a balmy wind would kick the mercury upward, melting snow before it, clearing patches of prairie, sometimes even coaxing a deluded blossom or two from a tightly curled bud. She missed the Front. She was tired of asphalt, tired of cars, tired of too many people she didn't know. She wanted to boost Margaret in front of her on Spot and ride up into the trees, as far as they could go before the snow got too deep, Bub streaking ahead of them, his mission to spook every single creature whose scent ghosted his way, Charlie leading the way on a borrowed horse. Charlie. A final, wrenching eddy of memory. Then, focus.

Tynslee had called. Why?

Right. To tell her the big secret. Which turned out to be a dead sister. A live sister—now, that would have been something. Would have explained Trang's compulsion to go to Vietnam. Loretta Begay had talked about the gravitational pull of forcibly abandoned family.

But if the sister was gone? Long gone, according to Tynslee.

"He found out not long after getting here," she'd whispered into the phone. "For some reason, her trip got held up. She was supposed to come join him a few weeks later. But his parents got a letter from the orphanage in Hanoi."

Again, the memory of the orphanage in Afghanistan, the scabbed faces, the filthy hands, the wracking coughs spraying microbes through the two- and three-to-a-cot dormitories. No surprise that the sister had died.

"He said he didn't talk for a week after they told him, and then he never talked about her again."

Until he'd told her. "And you told Malachi and Kwesi."

"We needed help once his mission was out of the question. We had to get him there. He had to find out what happened to her. To pay his respects at her grave."

Lola knew exactly what had happened to Charlie; had been in the room, knocked across it by the force of the blast that killed him, came to with ears ringing so loud as to obliterate all sound, including that of her own voice screaming Charlie's name.

But what if she hadn't known?

What if strangers—as Melena and Bryce must still have been to Trang at that point—had come to her one day and told her simply that Charlie was dead? No how, no why. Just...gone. Wouldn't she have done everything in her power to find out what had happened to him? If, for no other reason, than to be able to picture his final moments on earth, to visit the place he'd died, to run her hands over the same bit of ground he'd touched before he left her life forever. Hadn't she gone back to Arizona after Charlie's death not just to demand explanations from a conspirator in the bombing plot, but—she'd never told anyone this—to drive alone to the school where the bombing had occurred, to stand outside the new wing being built to replace the one destroyed, to scoop up a bit of sand blackened by ash, touch her lips to its rough grains?

Now, Trang would never be able to have even that cold bit of solace.

He'd sit in that jail cell until the trial that would see him convicted on circumstantial evidence, and then he'd be moved to the state prison that would house him for the rest of his life.

Given his youth, he'd probably not get the death penalty. Although that wasn't a sure bet. Skillful prosecutors would play on the jury's barely submerged fears—of teenagers, of boys, of brown skin—so subtly that the jurors themselves wouldn't understand the last-minute hesitation that caused them to abandon mercy and cast their vote for the most severe penalty possible.

No matter what, years of appeals and legal maneuvering would follow the verdict. Years of not knowing what had happened to his sister—and Trang would never be able to go to Vietnam to find out.

Lola thought of all the impossible stories she'd chased over the years. Of the ways people had tried to keep her from getting those stories, ranging from garden-variety lies to actual physical assault, resistance that only spurred her on.

She thought again of the Afghan woman she'd met outside the orphanage, making the ultimate sacrifice by giving up her child to a better life. That had happened more than a decade ago, a decade during which the woman must have wondered, every single day, about her child's fate. Because she would have no way of knowing what had happened to her child, and no one would find out for her.

Lola hadn't helped her.

But she could help Trang.

She reached for the edge of the sink. Pulled herself to her feet. Her arm rose. Her hand hung in front of her face. She extended a forefinger. Put her other hand to her elbow and guided the finger toward her mouth, down her throat. Gagged. Nothing came up. Two fingers, farther still. Remembered, just in time, to flip up the toilet seat and bend over the bowl.

The pills came up in a vile knot, partially dissolved, but still. Lola refilled the glass with water and drank it down. It came back up, too. Good. She drank another glass. That one stayed down. She drank another, and then another, determined to flush whatever remained of the pills from her system. When she stopped drinking water, she made coffee, considering and rejecting a different possibility with each cup.

She could contact the US Embassy in Hanoi. No—their only interest was in American citizens, not long-dead Vietnamese children.

She could contact orphanages directly, either online or by phone. A better route, for sure, if not for the barriers of distance and language, not the mention the paucity of information on her end.

She sloshed more coffee from the pot into the inadequate Styrofoam cup, the caffeine zinging through her veins, pushing blood to her brain, lighting up the obvious answer, Charlie nodding support as she remembered what she already knew.

You didn't get stories by sitting on your ass working phones and the internet. You got them by going there.

Lola gulped the last of the coffee, crushed the cup in her hand, and threw it toward the trash can. She missed. No matter. The pills might still be messing with her coordination, but they'd loosed their hold on her mind.

She traded the bathroom for the desk, wary of the bed, which might lull her back into dangerous sleep and—more to the point—whose spread still bore the lingering tobacco scent of Munro. She fired up the iPad and fumbled her way past several typos to a travel site. A few clicks and she'd spent nearly enough to erase the substantial kill fee that Munro had promised.

She turned to the phone.

"Why are you calling in the middle of the day?" Jan, as usual, answered without the courtesy of a hello. "Are you all right?"

Lola registered the fear in her friend's voice and thought back to what she'd nearly done. How it would have hurt Jan. How much more it would have hurt Margaret, an unbearable burden of pain in addition to the one already suffered with the loss of her father. How it would have given Amanda Richards the excuse she needed for *removal*, possibly to strangers, white strangers, no guarantee Margaret would end up in the familiar embrace of the aunties.

"I'm fine. Or, I'm going to be. I just wanted you to know that I'll be out of touch for a few days."

"Why? What the hell is going on?" A pause. When Jan next spoke, suspicion had chased the concern from her voice. "Are you going into rehab or something?"

"No. For God's sake. Actually, a little like that. Chasing a story."

Maybe it was a story. The odds were against it. But Lola had based an entire career on Hail Marys, learning through repeated lessons to trust her gut even when logic argued otherwise.

"You mean you're back?" The soaring hope in Jan's words pierced Lola anew.

"Not yet. But working on it."

She hung up. She had one more call to make. But in the end, again aflame with the embarrassment of waking up beside him, she one-fingered a text to Munro.

*Story not dead. Details later. Going to Vietnam.*

---

Lola retained a few habits from her foreign correspondent days, a few things she always traveled with even if she were just making a Costco run to Helena in her truck. A headlamp, for the inevitable power outages. Old-school notebooks and pens, for same. And her passport, because you never knew when you'd have to jump from one country to another.

Because she'd had to get so many last-minute visas, she'd bookmarked a site that specialized in them. She hadn't visited it in years, but it popped right up when she clicked. She lingered a little over her old haunts—Pakistan, Afghanistan, and the cluster of warring nations in the Middle East, all the places whose colorful stamps had populated her ragged passport, expired now. She was embarrassed by her new one, sitting unused for the two years she'd had it, its pages stiff and blank. This trip would at least give it a little character.

Things on the visa-approval front had gotten faster in the interim, she saw to her relief. A few more clicks, and another drain of her credit card, assured her of a visa to Vietnam in a few hours, just before her flight was scheduled to leave.

She'd go straight to the airport, using the wait to conduct as much research as possible based on the shreds of information Tynslee had given her. With luck, her body would recover from the combined abuse of Munro's alcohol and the bits of pill that she hadn't managed to expel from her system. She still had half the pills that she'd bought from Malachi. She pocketed one—after making sure the pocket didn't have any holes—to take after she'd boarded so as to sleep through the thirteen-hour flight, a coping mechanism she retained from her days in Afghanistan.

The one thing she wouldn't do was turn her phone back on.

If she was going to get better, truly better, she'd have to do it without interference from Jan or Munro or anyone else, well-meaning or otherwise. Lola hefted her duffel and wondered how long she'd be able to resist the temptation to check her messages. She lay her key cards on the desk, dropped the phone in the trash can, and headed for the door. Stopped. All of her contacts were in that phone. Photos of Margaret and Bub. Making a break was one thing; completely erasing the past, another.

She went back to the trash can, popped out the phone's SIM card, sealed it into a hotel stationery envelope, and slipped it into her hiking boot beside her ankle, a spot unlikely to damage it, a favorite place to stash cash back in her foreign correspondent days. She left the phone in the trash and let the door slam shut behind her locking out of the possibility of retrieving her link to everything that had come before.

# THIRTY

It had been a very long while since Lola had traveled overseas.

She'd nearly forgotten the sense of anticipation that accompanied a trip to a new country, always to the drumbeat of story-story-story. She'd also forgotten the security-line drill. Long gone was her collection of slip-on shoes. She cursed beneath her breath as she bent to untie her hiking boots, tucking the envelope with the SIM card into her bookbag, all too aware of the impatient rustlings of those in the line backing up behind her.

"Got all your liquids out of this?" A TSA operative held up her Dopp kit.

"Um." Jan had packed her bag for the flight to Salt Lake, but Lola had since mingled her liquids with everything else in the Dopp kit.

"Didn't you read all the signs? We like people to be prepared. Makes things move faster."

A man slammed his roller bag onto the belt behind Lola's duffel and pointedly dropped a baggie full of travel-sized plastic bottles beside it.

"Let me help you with this," the guard sighed. He pulled lotion and toothpaste and shampoo from Lola's kit and dropped them into a basket. "What about these?" The baggie with the pills dangled from his hand. "Where's the bottle they came in? Do you have the prescription for them?"

"Um." Lola seemed to have misplaced her words along with her travel smarts.

The man behind her coughed. Loud. "I'm going to miss another flight," said someone else.

The baggie swung. "You need these, or can I toss them?"

"Toss," Lola managed to say.

"Thank God," said the man behind her.

As Lola hurried to retrieve her goods, she could have sworn she saw Charlie out of the corner of her eye, smiling in approval.

———

At least she still had the single pill in her pocket, which—employed for newly benign purposes—responded graciously. The flight attendant had to shake her awake in Seoul, where she spent a layover just long enough to make her think that maybe Jan had had a point about paying attention to one's wardrobe.

Lola's years-ago travels had involved frequent layovers in the Dubai airport, where the women travelers, while stylish, had been scarved and robed. But Seoul Incheon was populated by aggressively fashionable women, surefooted in impossible heels, faces masks of impeccable makeup, hair coiffed in swingy styles that somehow looked capable of falling back into place even if tossed about by the gale-force winds of Montana. Lola touched a hand to the tangled mess on her head. She swung on her heel and marched back to a salon she'd seen near a restaurant where she'd eaten lunch.

The stylist spoke little English. Lola mimed what she wanted, making scissors of her fingers, holding them close to her head. When the woman hesitated, Lola took the plastic smock from her hands and fastened it around her own neck. She pointed to the woman's shears, then back to head, and held her fingers an inch apart.

The stylist shook her head.

Lola took her arm and turned her around, facing the window that looked out onto the concourse. She indicated a passing man, his hair moussed into short spikes.

"Like that."

The woman's sigh nearly keened. Her lamentations continued as she sluiced hot water across Lola's head, rubbed in the shampoo and then the conditioner, and then treated Lola's scalp to a massage just short of painful. She toweled Lola's hair and started to work at the curls with a wide-toothed comb. She called to a colleague, a woman with an edgy asymmetric bob, one side barely grazing her ear, the other dipping below her chin.

The stylist touched her hand to her colleague's hair and smiled hopefully. One last try. "That. We can straighten." She pointed to a medieval-looking hair press, apparently capable of subduing even Lola's curls. "Yes?"

"No." Lola leaned forward, took the shears from the counter, and whacked off a foot-long length of hair.

The women stared, their lipsticked mouths perfect O's of shock.

Lola handed her stylist the shears. "I've started it. You do the rest."

———

While Lola had spent years in Afghanistan and elsewhere in Central Asia, along with stints in the Middle East and Africa, Vietnam marked her first foray into Asia proper. A single step outside the airport brought home the difference.

Afghanistan had been hot, summertime temperatures routinely climbing beyond one hundred, with barely enough electricity to power her laptop, let alone a luxury like air conditioning. But at least it was the same sort of oven-dry heat that defined a high plains summer in Montana. Pakistan was more humid, or so she'd thought at the time.

Five minutes in Hanoi, and Lola revised everything she'd ever thought about humidity. She thought of all the clichés—sauna, wet washcloth, dog's breath—and rejected them as inadequate. She'd had the foresight to switch from a turtleneck to a T-shirt before leaving, but had donned a long-sleeved shirt over it against the plane's glacial frigidity. By the time she peeled out of it, dark patches of sweat festooned the tee beneath. Her jeans plastered themselves against her legs. Her feet, braising in their boots, wept for mercy. Every pore in her body seemed to have sprung a leak.

She paid for the extravagance of a cab rather than take a bus from the airport to her hotel, craving a bit of near-solitude in which to form initial impressions—and also so that she could quiz the cabdriver, inevitably a font of information, about orphanages. Because she had no idea which orphanage she was looking for.

But she forgot that quest for a moment of unabashed gawking at the city that stretched before her. She'd known better than to expect another Afghanistan, with its villages that seemed frozen in ancient times—their mud homes, their communal wells, their women and children threshing wheat by hand in utter absence of anything signaling modernity. She'd thought Vietnam might be more like Pakistan, rushing toward the future and into the past with equal speed, a schizo-phrenic mix resulting in a nuclear power that saw more than a thou-sand honor killings each year.

But, at least at first glimpse, Hanoi was rocketing forward at warp speed, its skyline dominated by construction cranes, with none of the hand labor and rickety tree-trunk scaffolding that char-acterized building projects in Pakistan. Lola cracked the cab's win-dow, sniffing for the evocative scent of wood smoke and dung that characterized so many of the places she'd worked. But all she got was a lungful of exhaust and a sharp glance in the rearview mirror from the driver. He cleared his throat. She raised the window.

"Vacation, miss?"

Right. She needed to find that orphanage. *I don't know*, Tynslee had said when Lola had asked its name. *He always said it in Viet-namese. He said it meant something like nice. Or gentle.*

Two words. Along with the photo of Trang, slightly out of regis-ter, that she'd clipped from the newspaper and Xeroxed. Now that she was actually in Hanoi, in this taxi islanded by a sea of darting motorbikes, panic gnawed at her. An indistinct photo, a confound-ing name for the orphanage. She'd just spent more money than she cared to think about on a fool's errand. And even if she found out what had happened to the sister, how could that possibly help Trang, other than give him peace of mind about her fate, a small bit of com-fort during the long years of prison likely facing him?

Pain sliced across her forehead. Goose bumps rose on her arms. Sweat congealed. "Could you please turn down the air conditioning?"

Another look in the rearview mirror. Surely it was the first time a white foreigner had ever made such a request. Lola wrapped her arms around her torso and spoke past chattering teeth. Maybe she'd picked up a bug on the plane. "I'm looking for an orphanage."

"Orphanage?" the cabdriver said. "You adopt baby, miss? I can take you." He shot her an assessing glance in the rearview mirror. If he could guide her to the orphanage that provided the baby of her dreams, a large tip likely awaited.

"Trying to find one." She rubbed her forehead with fingers gone icy. "Not a baby. A boy."

The driver's face changed.

"For your husband, maybe? Or, for—" He tapped his heart and whipped the cab to the curb, motorbikes whisking out of its way like a school of fish at the approach of a shark. He turned and spat imprecations in a mix of Vietnamese and English, words indecipherable but their meaning clear. Lola was to immediately remove herself from his cab and catch the first plane back to the United States.

"No, no, no! Wait." Panic momentarily displaced the headache. She held up one hand and fished through her bookbag with the other, emerging with the sheaf of copies she'd made of the grainy newspaper photo. "This boy. He is fine. He is not sick. He ... "

She couldn't think of the words, or even the gestures, to convey that she wasn't after what the man so obviously and needlessly feared—that she was in search of a soft young boy to satisfy her husband's unnatural urges, or, even worse, a boy with a healthy beating heart or other organs that would replace whatever was failing in her own child. In the research she'd done while waiting for a plane, Lola had read that Vietnam had sharply curtailed adoptions based on false reports that people were acquiring foreign children solely to harvest their organs for transplants into ailing American children.

"He is fine," she said again. Even though he wasn't.

He looked at her, and then at the photo. "This boy," he repeated.

"In America now," Lola said. "From here. But which orphanage?"

He took a handful of the images. "I find?"

She nodded.

"How much?"

Lola had almost forgotten this part, too. At least she'd had the presence of mind to withdraw nearly all of the cash in her checking account before leaving. She barely stopped herself from pulling out a hundred. The twenty she extended brought an insulted snort and more invective. Negotiations commenced. They settled on a hundred per day, with a bonus if he actually located the right orphanage.

Her chill fled, replaced by heat so intense that for a moment she wondered whether she'd been struck by an early hot flash. Her stomach churned. She'd definitely been bitten by the plane's microbes. If, indeed, microbes bit. Great. Now she was going woozy.

The cabdriver cleared his throat, awaiting her final answer.

"Three days. No more." Lola imagined he'd take every last one of those days whether he found anything or not. But at least she could limit the financial damage.

# THIRTY-ONE

LOLA WANTED TO ACCOMPANY the cabdriver on his search. But he managed to convey, with frowns and a series of choppy hand gestures, that her presence would only increase the difficulty and—here, he rubbed his fingers together in a gesture universally understood—the expense.

He held out his phone. "Your number," he said, indicating that she should enter it.

Lola held out her hands. "No phone."

There was a long moment while he digested this incomprehensible bit of news. "You get," he said finally. He scrawled something and handed her the scrap of paper. "You go here." He took her first hundred dollars, gave her his card, and dropped her off at a hotel, leaving with a firm "Tomorrow morning."

"Goodbye, Benjamin," Lola called, behind him, to what was almost certainly her wasted bill, before entering the miraculously air-conditioned lobby. A few minutes later she was bolting into her room, barely stopping to peel off her sticky clothes on her way toward a shower and a nap, determined to sleep off whatever ailed her.

Four ibuprofen and two hours of sleep later, the pain was bearable—just—and replaced by restlessness. She'd long ago learned the wisdom of using fixers in unfamiliar places and cultures. She needed to stay out of the cabbie's way and let him do his job. But it didn't make the waiting any easier. She retrieved the paper he'd given her. A word jumped out at her. *Pho.* A restaurant, then. Lola could never keep straight whether you were supposed to feed a cold and starve a fever, or the other way around, and generally operated on the theory that food would settle her stomach. She showed the woman at the front desk her piece of paper and received directions. Maybe, she told herself as she headed outside, the humidity hadn't really been that bad.

It was. A mere half-block's walk erased the cooling effects of the shower and air conditioning. Lola gave thanks that the new T-shirt she'd donned was black. Yes, it would absorb more heat, but at least it looked the same soaked as dry. Likewise with her jeans, although she gave serious thought to picking up a skirt at one of the market stalls. Other than for the funerals—first Charlie's and then Sariah's—she couldn't remember the last time she'd worn a skirt. But she didn't want to look as miserable as the European and American tourists prowling the spaghetti-swirl of streets in the Old Quarter, faces pink and moist as canned hams. She started to cross the street to avoid them. She wasn't a tourist.

Half a block away, a light turned green. A phalanx of motorbikes buzzed toward her, filling the width of the street, some jumping the curb and zooming along the sidewalk. Lola leapt back.

"Just go. And once you've started, don't stop." The accent was British. It belonged to a man whose professorial mien reminded her of her father, but for his full khaki regalia, more pockets and snaps and loops on his shirt and pants than anyone could possible use. And, in the annoying way of the British, he wasn't sweating. As Lola watched, he stepped into the street and, as advised, kept moving, the wave of motorbikes parting to admit him and then flowing together as soon as they'd passed. Lola held her breath and followed suit, emerging on the other side of the street miraculously unscathed, though the bikes passed so close that any exaggerated movement— an extra-long stride, a wave of her arm—would have brought her into contact.

Her benefactor had paused beside a beer parlor—*Bia*, it advertised phonetically—and Lola thought to offer to buy him a beer in thanks, maybe pick his brain about Hanoi. But as she watched, a woman a fraction of his age approached him. They spoke briefly, then he took her arm and disappeared into a building next door.

Oh. That old story.

She looked around for the restaurant; saw none. Double-checked the street sign. Then laughed at herself. Different marks over the O in *pho* were apparently all that separated the signature dish from a place name. She couldn't pronounce the street's name, but for all practical purposes it translated to Cellphone Street, since one store after another sold nothing but cellphones.

It reminded her of the markets in Kabul, with all the tinsmith stalls clustered together, the same with the fabric shops and spice stalls. How did one choose? In this case, she picked the closest, emerging twenty minutes later with the Vietnamese equivalent of a burner phone, an accomplishment that gave her an inordinate sense of pride. She'd get a new iPhone when she got home and put the SIM card in that. In the meantime, the SIM card was back inside her boot, high on her ankle, far removed from the increasingly swampy soles.

A few blocks' exploration brought her to what she dubbed Shoe Street, one that delivered the knockoff designer sandals that promised relief for her traumatized feet. Making decisions. Taking action. "See, Charlie?" she said, trusting that he was nearby, floating above the crowds and motorbikes, a calm and—finally—approving presence amid the chaos.

---

Lola took a more direct route back to her hotel, flush with both the heat and her accomplishments.

Overcome with both guilt and common sense, she'd texted her new number to Jan, then found a restaurant, lowered herself without falling onto one of the tiny plastic stools on the sidewalk outside, and slurped pho without spilling it all over herself. The tang of the fish sauce, the delicate rice noodles, awoke her long-dormant hunger, and when she finished her bowl, she had to stop herself from ordering another. Charlie would like this, she thought. Then braced herself against a renewed onslaught of grief.

It came, but not with the thunderbolt of fury she'd come to expect, scorching her with pain. This was more of a mist, almost soothing, but with a bittersweet tinge. Charlie had often expressed envy of the exotic places she'd seen, had wondered aloud if she missed her old itinerant life. She always countered that life in Montana had been an improvement in so many ways, imposing the stability, along with the resulting friendships and family, lacking during her years in Kabul.

And while she sometimes—often—missed the big stories she'd pursued there and the sense of purpose that came with the clichéd-but-true chronicling of the first draft of history, she'd almost imperceptibly succumbed to the security of her new life. It took the bombing in Arizona to remind her what she'd learned during those years of reporting from war zones: that security was always an illusion; that it could dissolve in a moment on the whim of a terrorist, the election of a presentable-seeming madman, or even a natural disaster.

Now, in this new place, wholly removed from her life with Charlie, Lola vowed that she would never again forget. She hadn't yet figured out how to live with this renewed awareness in a way that wouldn't terrify Margaret but that would, to the extent possible, keep her daughter safe. But she could tilt against the world's basic unfairness by figuring out whatever it was that had seen a Vietnamese orphan falsely—maybe—accused of murder.

She paid for her meal and marched back toward her hotel, energized by her own thoughts, until the sting of salt in her eyes woke her to the reality of the sweat sluicing down her face and drenching her clothing anew, worse than could be accounted for by the humidity. The pho, so good going down, threatened an unpleasant reemergence. Lola slowed her pace, fanned at her neck with damp, shaking hands, and congratulated herself again on the haircut that probably accounted for a five-degree cooling factor. She couldn't wait to get back to the hotel and exchange her boots for her new sandals. And hit the ibuprofen again. Goddamn that guy at the airport who'd taken her pain pills, anyhow.

She stepped into her hotel's air-conditioned lobby, so overcome with relief at the refrigerated air surrounding her that it took a moment for her to notice the desk clerk's frantic gestures, to realize that the pair of policemen at the desk were there for her, and to understand that the forceful words they directed her way meant that she was under arrest.

# THIRTY-TWO

"Your room," said one of the officers. "You take us there now. We search."

He took her arm. She pulled away. "Search for what? Do you have a warrant?"

Oh, silly American. Such ignorance might have been expected from a tourist, not from her. Lola knew that people who complained about the American criminal justice system had plenty of justification, but sometimes, just once in a while, she wished the naysayers could see what she'd seen in those faraway places where notions of "justice" made an overlong jail stay while awaiting trial, or aggressive racial profiling, look almost quaintly gentle in comparison to middle-of-the-night disappearances, confessions achieved by electric shock and near-drownings, and executions barely disguised as suicides.

But the members of the Vietnam People's Public Security, in their green uniforms with the scarlet epaulets, didn't even respond to her ridiculous questions, brushing past her toward the sardine tin that masqueraded as an elevator. There were four of them. Lola considered what the ride to the fourth floor might be like, all of them pressed against one another. "I'll walk."

"We walk, too." They trooped up the stairs with her, two in front, two behind, making Lola glad she'd never gotten around to getting that skirt. By the time they reached her fourth-floor room, she was sweating—again. They weren't. She fumbled around in her pockets for her key, but the lead officer opened the door with one furnished by the manager. When Lola tried to accompany him inside, he held up a peremptory hand. "You stay."

She watched from the hall, helpless, as the men tossed the room with quick, practiced motions, yanking the sheets, coverlet, and mattress pad from the bed, upending the mattress, and running their hands around it seeking openings. Satisfied, they flung the bedding into a corner and dropped the mattress back into place, dumping the contents of the drawers, her duffel, and her Dopp kit upon it. They ran their hands beneath the dressers, the end tables, the sink. They lifted the lid from the toilet and peered inside. An officer held out his hand for her bookbag. When she hesitated, he jerked it from her shoulder, unzipped its various pockets, and shook it out over the desk. Her new sandals tumbled out. She prayed they wouldn't make her remove her boots, her SIM card within rubbing against her ankle.

Maids, drawn by the commotion, gathered behind her, whispering among themselves. The bellboys soon joined them. Lola felt sorry for the desk clerk, deprived by her duties of the spectacle. When other guests began to congregate, she lost her patience.

"What are you looking for?"

The officer who appeared to be in charge whirled to face her. "The pills. Where are they?"

"I have no pills." A deep and abiding affection for the TSA officer in Salt Lake permeated her very bones.

"You have." He radiated certainty.

"I do not." Lola pulled herself to her full height and glared down at him.

"You come."

Down the stairs again, this time with the entourage from the hallway in tow. The others crowded into the hotel's small lobby, disappointment glazing their features as the police hustled the source of their entertainment into a car and drove her away as the journalism gods, having extracted their fee for all the favors they'd bestowed, laughed and laughed.

———————

The building was small, the room shabby. Lola figured it for a satellite office. That meant she probably wasn't in too much trouble. Yet.

The man before her watched in silence. Lola knew this part. Charlie, in his role as sheriff, employed it with great success with first-time miscreants. "Keep quiet long enough, and they'll tell you everything before you ask a single question." It also worked well when Margaret went astray of the house rules. And Lola herself used it all the time in interviews.

On the other hand. The fringe of hair that showed beneath the man's peaked cap was shot through with silver. Fine lines fanned out from his eyes, the corners of his mouth. His neck sagged over his stiff collar. He was older than she was, maybe nearing sixty, serving out his final years in an easy posting. But his age meant he'd seen the conflict they called the American War. And he'd been on the winning side. His definition of "interview" was probably a lot different that hers. Rougher. Almost certainly, he could out-wait her.

A window unit chugged behind the officer, steadily dripping water into a plastic basin set beneath it. The room was not stifling. Nor was it cool. Lola wanted her hotel room, with its cold shower and icy air conditioning. Maybe it was the thought of the AC, but another chill swept through her. Best to get this part over with. She jumped in.

"Why am I here?"

"You sell drugs."

More verdict than question, delivered in the same casual tone in which he might have said, *You are American.*

"I do not." Damn. Lola had already broken a cardinal rule. Never get defensive. Always attack. "Where is your proof?"

He pushed a form across the desk toward her. In Vietnamese. Lola pushed it back. "You know I can't read this."

"We received a telephone call. That a drug dealer with your name would be arriving here. That you would bring pills with you. Do you know what the penalty is for smuggling drugs into our country?" His English careful, precise.

Lola again pictured the TSA agent who'd so blithely tossed the baggie of pills into the trash. She'd thought she would never love again after Charlie, but at that moment, she was pretty sure that what she felt for the anonymous agent was close.

"I am not a drug dealer. I did not smuggle drugs into your country. Did you find any drugs?"

"No. Maybe you have sold them already."

"I have not. Because I did not smuggle drugs. Who made this telephone call?"

"We do not reveal this."

Not that he needed to. Malachi. Just like he'd made the anonymous call to Munro—at least, she'd assumed it had been Malachi—calling her a pill-popper. Only Munro knew she was in Vietnam. He must have said something to Malachi. Like father, like son. Or maybe the other way around. Both equally untrustworthy.

Lola vowed that when she got back, immediately after tracking down the TSA agent and planting a big wet kiss on his startled mouth, she'd find Malachi and … and … she'd figure that part out later. What she didn't understand was Malachi's motive. If the only reason he'd been selling drugs was to raise money so his friend could go to Vietnam, why was he so determined to stop her from going? Maybe his drug dealing went beyond helping a friend. Maybe the reason he'd raised so much money—beyond Lola's contribution to his coffers—was that he already had a business going, one that she'd inadvertently stumbled across.

It had been no small feat to get his message through to a local police precinct in a foreign country. Would someone who went through that much effort also be capable of killing?

Lola thought of Munro, of the expression of love and pain that crossed his face when he looked at his son. Quashed the flash of empathy. Munro was almost certainly the reason Malachi knew where she was, and hence the reason she was in this fix.

She exhaled. She'd deal with Munro and Malachi later. First she'd have to get through this nonsense. But it wasn't nonsense. Vietnam was good and sick of Americans both using and dealing drugs in their country, and its penalties reflected that. A hefty bribe could make a weed charge disappear, but heroin possession could bring a life sentence or even the death penalty. She wondered where pills landed on the scale.

"I do not have drugs. I have not sold drugs." Damn. Defensive again.

"Then why are you here?"

She grasped at the most slender of straws. "I'm a journalist. I'm working on a story."

She held her breath and counted. One ... two ... Maybe he wouldn't ...

No, he was reaching for her passport. Leafing through it until he found her visa. Reading it back to her.

"Tourist visa. Not press visa." Entering the country under false pretenses wasn't as bad as being a drug dealer. But it wasn't good.

Lola had no choice but to tell the truth, as confusing and even suspicious as it sounded. "May I?" She pointed to her book bag, waiting for permission before searching its jumbled contents. She found one of the copies of Trang's photo and smoothed it upon the desk. "It's a story on this boy."

"You look for him?"

"No." This was the hard part. If it didn't even make sense to her, she had no hope of explaining it to this man. She did her best. "He is a man now. Almost. He lives in the United States. He was born here. Adopted. I want to try to find the orphanage."

His eyes narrowed. He stood. Leaned across the desk, his face level with hers.

"There is no story. You want to adopt another baby. Maybe you're sick. Need a new heart. Or liver. You Americans drink too much."

Lola stopped worrying about looking defensive. "No, no, no! I don't want to adopt a baby. I have my own child. This boy. He is in trouble. I'm trying to help him."

He straightened but remained standing. "What kind of trouble? Is he a drug dealer?"

"No. Enough with the drug dealer bullshit—wait. I'm so sorry. I didn't mean that the way it sounded. But his trouble is so much worse. They think he killed someone. An American woman."

The officer sucked his cheeks in, no doubt imagining a sex crime. A brown man, a white woman, the sort of scenario that in America always went badly for the brown man. He sat. Lola breathed easier.

"How does finding this orphanage help?"

Even she didn't fully understand the dead sister business. No way would the cops bite. She spread out her hands. "I don't know. Only that it was very important for him to return to it. I think maybe someone was trying to prevent him from coming here." She wished she could take back the damning "I think." As a reporter, she had no business having an opinion. And she wasn't even sure she thought Trang was innocent. But a lot of other people thought he was. She said as much.

"His friends—his American friends—believe he did not kill anyone. They are so sure."

"What orphanage?"

"I don't know that, either. The Nice and Gentle Orphanage. Something like that."

So far, the man had maintained an admirable poker face. Now disgust and disbelief showed through. "You do drugs."

Square One.

"I do not do drugs." Drugs were needles, scarred forearms, scary neighborhoods.

"You do. You are junkie. You need fix." He pointed to her goose-flesh-pimpled arms.

"No." But—the nausea. The shakes. The chills. Withdrawal? She hadn't taken that many pills, though. And she hadn't taken them that often. This was just a garden-variety traveler's virus. It had to be.

"You sell drugs."

She shoved away a memory of Pioneer Park. "I have sold no drugs." He hadn't said anything about buying them.

"How do we know this?"

"I can account for my movements since arriving." At least, she hoped she could. With some trepidation, she handed over the cabdriver's card, hoping that he didn't have any illegal business going on on the side. Even if he didn't, a visit from the authorities, especially cops interested in prosecuting a foreigner, would make his life uncomfortable at best. She gave him her new cellphone, free of any calls but for the text to Jan, along with the receipt for the phone's purchase, damp and crumpled from her pocket, thankful that it had a time stamp.

"That's all I've done since getting here. I took a cab ride. Bought a phone. Some sandals. Pho." She extracted the other receipts, saved by force of habit from her expense-account days as a foreign correspondent.

"You could have sold the pills on the way to buy these thing."

Of course she could have. But she chose to disagree. "How? Your men are everywhere in the Old City." She thought it a safe assumption that plainclothes cops prowled the most popular tourist districts, on the lookout for tourists seeking mischief as well as to protect the more clueless ones from themselves, or from those eager to prey upon them. Not only had Vietnam won the war, but it was busy accumulating as much *dong* as possible from the former invaders. Safety was an important ally.

The officer picked up the telephone on his desk and snapped an order. Two underlings materialized. "Take her," he said.

At the entrance to what appeared to be the Vietnamese version of an interview room, Lola stopped. She'd learned a few things over the years. "Wait," she said. She pointed to a door with the international symbol, a stick woman in a skirt. "Mind if I use that first?"

# THIRTY-THREE

HOURS LATER, LOLA WAS glad she'd opted for the bathroom. She'd wished she'd also asked for something to drink, and—her queasiness having abated—a snack. And maybe something to read. She missed her phone, the old one, the distraction of her Scrabble app. She wished she hadn't been so quick to toss it.

She suppressed an urge to pace, to fidget. Surely she was under observation. She slouched, propped her chin on her fist, and closed her eyes, willing herself to doze. She hoped at least to give the impression of catnapping, of intense boredom, of anything but the anxiety plucking at her nerves like a harpist on crack.

She thought of all the bad movies she'd seen about Americans moldering in foreign prisons. Worse yet, she thought of the reality that too many of her colleagues in the foreign press corps had experienced—whipped, sexually assaulted, imprisoned for months, sometimes years. She wondered how long it would be before Jan panicked and started making inquiries. And then, exactly how concerned the US Embassy might be about a journalist who'd blatantly ignored the regulations of the host country by traveling on the tourist visa. Her thoughts chased themselves around in circles until she finally did drop off, waking with a start when the door swung inward.

The captain—or whatever his rank—entered first, followed a pair of police officers and the cabdriver, his face knotted in fear, with two more officers behind him.

"Oh, no." Lola leapt to her feet. "This man did nothing but drive me around. He's done nothing wrong. You must release him."

"I tell them," the driver said. "I tell them, 'No drugs. She only want this boy.'" He clutched a copy of the photo, stained and crumpled, in his shaking hand.

"No, not the boy…" Lola wished, far too late, she'd found a driver more fluent in English, one who might better have understood what she sought even if she didn't entirely understand it herself.

"But we find no boy."

"No," she tried again. "I wasn't looking for the boy." She stopped. She didn't know what she was looking for. Only that she'd be sure—maybe—when she found it. But now she wasn't going to find anything.

"No boy," the driver repeated. "Just—"

He moved aside, revealing the person behind him.

"Just girl."

———

She stood, Hanoi-chic in slim black jeans and heels and a white tailored blouse, cheap and a little worn but clean. Lola guessed they were her best clothes. The girl's gaze flitted among the policemen and lingered on the captain. She raised a shaking hand and patted a strand of wavy hair back into place.

Lola broke the silence. "You're from the orphanage?" Too young to be the director. Maybe an assistant director, or a secretary. But someone who might be able to explain what was going on, assuming the driver and police had found the right orphanage. Lola wondered if she spoke English.

"Yes." So soft as to be almost inaudible.

"The orphanage that is called—" Lola prompted.

"The Kind and Caring Home."

Nice Home. Gentle Home. Tynslee had been close. The young woman seemed near tears. Lola understood how a visit to a police station could be intimidating, even in the United States where at least lip service was paid to protecting people's rights. She proceeded gently.

"You work there?"

"Y-y-yes."

"You know about this boy?"

By now, the photo of Trang was so creased and smeared that his features were nearly obscured. But the woman gazed upon it with such intensity that no answer was needed. Lola stepped to her side and put a steadying hand upon her arm.

"What can you tell me about him?"

"He is my brother."

She burst into tears.

———

It took some moments, along with the offering of several handkerchiefs (apparently all the cops carried them) and a cup of tea, to calm her to the point where she could speak.

The cup rattled back into its saucer. The girl, seated now, with Lola in a chair opposite her, reached and took Lola's hands in both her own. Fresh tears carved new tracks in her careful makeup. Her mascara had long gone to hell. "Please," she said, "tell me when my brother died."

Lola forgot her dislike of hugging. She came around the table and drew the young woman into her arms. "Oh, you poor child. He's alive. Your brother, Trang. He's alive."

The tears came harder, and lasted longer this time. Fresh handkerchiefs appeared. Lola imagined a file drawer somewhere in the police station filled with neat stacks of folded, starched cotton squares. The woman finally freed herself from Lola's embrace and gave her a damp smile.

"Alive? Truly? You have seen him?"

"Yes. I'll tell you all about it. But first, I suppose I had better learn your name."

———————

The group decamped to the captain's office. When Mai calmed further, she explained that the appearance of the cabdriver bearing Trang's photo had led her to only one conclusion—that her brother had died in America before the reunion of which she'd dreamed for so many years.

Lola asked the captain if the geriatric computer at his desk had internet access, and if she could do a quick search. There, with Mai alternately laughing and crying beside her, she clicked fast past all the reproductions of Trang's booking photo posted on every media outlet in Salt Lake and several beyond, and pulled up images of

Trang in his hockey uniform, at the picnic for adoptees, at various school functions.

"So tall! So handsome! But what is this?" She lingered over a Facebook photo of Trang and Tynslee.

"That is the girl he will marry."

"Marry? This girl? My brother? Are you sure?"

"Yes. They marry young in Utah. A state—um, a place in the western United States." Lola sought for ways to describe Utah, and gave up. No way to get across in words the vast, empty aridity of the land to someone who'd known nothing but this country where moisture saturated the air, where "alone," other than maybe a few moments in a bathroom, remained an alien concept.

"Now you see," she told the captain. "I wasn't here to sell drugs or to buy them. You know my hotel. You've got my phone. Please return it. Take the number so you have another way to find me if you need to talk to me again."

He scowled, but he copied the number from the burner phone and handed it over.

The charge was nearly gone, low-battery light blinking red, just enough juice for Lola to note the chain of incoming calls, all from the same number.

*Jan.*

*Jan.*

*Jan.*

The phone blinked a final red warning, then went black.

# THIRTY-FOUR

"WHAT THE HELL, LOLA? Vietnam? The police? Are you all right? What have you done? What am I supposed to tell Margaret?" Despite the eleven-hour time difference that put Lola's call at three in the morning Montana time, Jan was fully awake.

The police, after calling Jan, had finally released Lola, apparently convinced—almost—that she wasn't a drug dealer. Mai was to join her later at the hotel, after returning to the orphanage to explain her absence. The cabdriver had deposited Lola at the hotel door, still so shaken by his experience with the police that he almost waved away the bonus she pressed upon him for finding the orphanage and Mai.

She'd hurried past the front desk, ignoring the clerk, face bright with questions, and pretended not to see the way the rest of the staff found excuses to linger in doorways as she passed. Safe in her room, she turned the air conditioner up to high, plugged her phone into its charger, swept her overturned belongings from the bed, and fell onto it, calling Jan as soon as the phone beeped back to life.

Something caught in her throat at Jan's trademark blend of worry and accusation. It escaped in peals of laughter. She drew her knees up to her chest and flung out her arms and let it rock through her, even as she thought God, how long has it been?

"Lola? Lola? What's wrong with you? Because nothing about this is funny."

Lola pressed a hand to her chest, willing her mirth back inside. Her friend was right, she knew. And she herself heard the edge of hysteria in her guffaws. But after so long, it felt so good! She thought of the pressure from the aunties, from Jan, to have sex again. But really, laughter was almost as good. Better, even, under the circumstances.

"I know. It's not. But everything's fine, Jan. It's really fine. You won't believe this."

Just like the laughter, the story came out in a rush, the impulsive decision to fly to Vietnam without even knowing exactly what she was looking for—"following your gut, just like you used to do," Jan interjected with satisfaction—or even where to look.

"How did the police get involved?" Early on in their friendship, Lola had styled herself a mentor to Jan. Now, as her friend homed in on the weak link in her story, she wondered if she'd done her job too well.

"Something the cabdriver said, maybe." Lola hurried on to the part about Mai before Jan could probe the unspoken "maybe not" part of that particular equation.

"It's unbelievable. Trang—Frank—thought his sister was dead. And when she saw the police, and they asked her about him, she thought *he* was. It's a great story, the kind of happy story that stupid magazine loves."

Jan's voice muffled in the familiar way that meant she'd bitten down on her braid. "No, it's not. Because that kid is still in jail, looking at Murder One."

Any laughter remaining in Lola's lungs fled with her next breath. "Right. There's that. There's something else, too."

*Pfft.*

Lola wondered if Jan had any braid left.

"What else?"

"I don't know what any of it means. Trang wanted to come over here, presumably to find out what had happened to his sister, given that he thought she was dead. I get that. And maybe somebody wanted to keep him from coming here. That's why whoever killed Sariah, if someone else did kill her"—the old reporter's caution against assuming anything kicked in—"that person tried to make it look like Trang did it."

Jan took up her train of thought, whacking the ball back at her in their familiar ping-pong routine of talking through stories, each playing devil's advocate to the other, finding the holes, figuring out how to fill them in. "Because getting someone arrested for homicide is a surefire way to keep him from going anywhere."

"But what's that leave us with?" Lola answered her own question. "Nothing. From the very beginning, not one thing about this has made sense."

Defeat, Lola's boon companion these last few months, crept back in, surveyed the room, and did a victory dance. The old heaviness returned to her limbs.

"No. There is something."

Lola's eyelids drooped. The day at the police station, along with the effects of the virus or whatever it was—yet again, she refused to consider withdrawal—plus the jet lag, had left her exhausted. She longed for sleep. "What's that?"

"Family. After all these years, this kid has a family. Since he can't go there, bring that girl back here. Get them together. Who knows what will come up? And speaking of family..."

Lola was tired, so tired. "What's that?" she murmured.

"Someone wants to talk to you."

Lola bolted upright. Defeat took a tumble.

"Mommy?"

"Margaret!"

"Mommy, are you all right? Aunt Jan was worried about you. I know, because I listened when I wasn't supposed to. Don't be mad. Mommy, I'm glad you're all right because I have to tell you about school. And basketball. I'm a forward. Do you know what that is? Did you ever play basketball? Were you any good? I'll bet you weren't as good as I am."

Lola didn't know why her daughter had decided to speak to her again. Maybe the time away had served its purpose. Maybe Margaret, no longer confronted daily with her mother's emotional collapse, had reverted to memories of better times. Whatever. The why didn't matter. Just her daughter's voice, full of life. *Life.*

As Margaret chattered on and on, Lola did a dance of her own around the room, pausing every so often to give Defeat another kick in the ass.

# THIRTY-FIVE

LOLA COACHED MAI THROUGH the interminable process of getting a visa, the necessarily vague responses. For starters, the standard reason—visiting a relative—was to be avoided, given that the relative was in jail.

They agreed on a story that involved Mai visiting the University of Utah as a prospective student. "They'll want proof," Mai protested when Lola first suggested it.

So Lola spent a few minutes on the internet, falling back on a skill she'd acquired as a foreign correspondent when every dipshit official in every sweltering, flyblown office required a letter from a supervisor certifying her as an official representative of her newspaper. In her first forays overseas, Lola's supply of such letters had proven pitifully inadequate, and so with her editor's blessing she'd become an adept forger, blithely running off copies on the ancient one-sheet-at-a-time Xerox machines operating from market stalls. No one ever questioned the gray, tissue-paper quality of those letters as opposed to the sturdy and blindingly white sheets of American stationery upon which the original letters had been printed.

Now, she found a PDF of a University of Utah press release, downloaded the letterhead, and crafted beneath it a letter of invitation from a fictional university provost, telling herself that if no such person existed, it wasn't really forgery. The letter went into some detail about the English-language classes Mai would be required to take before she began her intended course of study in … Lola looked a question to the girl.

Mai lifted one hand and made her fingers fly over the right side of an imaginary keyboard. "The money numbers. Miss Hoang shows me. What do you call it?"

"Accounting," said Lola. "Smart choice. You'll have a job," she added, lest Mai had caught her tone. Lola filed her expense reports months late rather than deal with the math involved. If someone had ever suggested a career in accounting, she'd probably have punched the person. She added "CPA prep" to the letter and printed it out at the hotel's business center, praying that no one would test the phone number or email address on her newly created stationery. No one did.

Visa obtained, there was the expense of another last-minute plane ticket, gobbling up whatever was left of her kill fee and putting her credit card decidedly beyond the point where she'd be able to dispense with the bill in a single payment.

Then, the endurance contest of the three separate flights, the added nightmare of middle seats in the middle section on the longest, Lola's head rolling against the backrest in her half-sleep, craving the pills with an intensity that rivaled her grief over Charlie, aware of Mai rigid and wakeful beside her, nerves humming in anticipation of seeing her brother. Occasionally, when Lola's eyes fluttered half-open, a tentative hand would land on her arm, accompanied by the question, "You're sure? You're truly sure it's him?"

Lola wasn't sure at all. All she knew was that Trang once had a sister. That he believed her dead. And that even so, he'd been intent upon visiting her grave. "It was important for him to honor her," Tynslee had said in that befogged conversation when she'd revealed the existence of Mai—albeit, a Mai believed dead. "He didn't even know the anniversary of her death. And there's a big holiday where everyone is supposed to visit the graves. I forget what it's called."

"Tet," Lola supplied, marveling at how quickly the word had passed from the national consciousness.

She had replayed the conversation with Tynslee into infinity. It looped through her head yet again, along with memories of her visit with Trang, as she twisted in half-sleep in the torture device masquerading as an airplane seat. Whenever she closed her eyes, she saw his guileless mien, the trusting belief in his own innocence, and the accompanying belief that a simple "but I didn't do it" would convince a judge and lawyers who'd heard the same protest several times a day for years on end.

Lola tried to remember the impulse that had propelled her to Vietnam. What had she hoped to find? The sister's grave, proof that if one story was true, it would somehow make Trang more believable? And how would the miraculous discovery of a living, breathing sister affect things—if at all?

She shuffled the facts in her mind like a mismatched deck of cards, but no matter how many times she laid them out, she came up with a bad hand, one that only got worse.

Orphanages were full of children with dead siblings, certainly not as many as during the war, but poverty still took a significant toll. The photo she'd brought was so indistinct. Maybe Mai, aching for her own brother, was simply mistaken about the boy in the photo. Or—a darker possibility, one that a journalist's natural skepticism demanded Lola consider—maybe there was no brother at all. Maybe Mai just saw an opportunity to come to the United States and grabbed it with both hands. Maybe she'd disappear as soon as they deplaned.

With that possibility in mind, Lola kept a watchful eye on the girl through Baggage Claim and Customs, trailed her into the ladies' room, and insisted that Mai accompany her to the rental car counter. She brought Mai with her into the lobby when she checked into a motel—not the luxurious accommodations that *Families of Faith* had provided, but a suburban mid-range chain that was easier on her overstressed credit card. She hovered outside the bathroom door while Mai took a shower and skipped her own desperately needed ablutions, settling for a Navy shower at the sink and a change of clothes as Mai averted her eyes.

And, after far too much time, finally the drive to the jail, Mai's fingernails digging long scratches in the rental car's vinyl seats. Breath held as the guard scrutinized their identification, released in an audible whoosh when he waved Mai through.

He held up his hand to Lola. "One at a time," he said.

Mai didn't even look back, just hurried after her escort in the tiny, tripping steps mandated by her high heels.

"Five minutes," Lola told herself. If Mai were quick to return, then her worst-case scenario would be realized. Trang wasn't the right boy after all. Lola would have spent—her brain refused to calculate the exact amount of money, only that a comma was involved—all of her remaining cash, and more she didn't have, on a fool's errand.

But five minutes passed, and then ten, and at fifteen minutes, Lola slumped in her chair and closed her eyes, trying to imagine the reunion between brother and sister and whether it might mean anything at all in the case against Trang.

# THIRTY-SIX

THEY'D BEEN CHILDREN WHEN last together. Now they stood on opposite sides of the Plexiglas window, the slight young woman dressed in clothing fashionable for Hanoi—fitted blouse, miniskirt, teetering heels, heavy makeup around the eyes whose sadness belied her youth—but just short of scandalous in Salt Lake; the youth grown man-size, his muscled frame testament to the American faith in bountiful servings of meat, potatoes, and vitamins.

She waited for him to recognize her. Watched his lips form her name. Watched the tears, even as she herself began to weep, prevent the word.

———

"What happened?"

The inevitable question.

"Someone paid Miss Hoang to keep me behind." Mai spat the words.

"Even more than the American Mother and Father paid to adopt us?"

A slow nod.

His eyes grew wide. "But why? Why separate us?" Even as he asked, he feared the answer, the one he'd assumed for all these years. There was more money to be made in the kickback from Fat Fingers, who would auction Mai off to the highest bidder, than from the adoption. He called down curses upon Miss Hoang.

"No. Miss Hoang, she cried and cried when she told me. And she let me stay on at the orphanage, keeping me away from Old Quang, giving me a job there so I wouldn't have to leave when I turned fourteen. It was her way of apologizing. But she said, 'What am I to do? This money will help so many children.' When I learned how to use a computer, I tried at the internet cafes, searching for you. But I did not know American Mother and Father's names, and I did not know your new name, and Miss Hoang would not tell me. 'You must accept,' she said. But I never accepted. I knew that someday I would find you."

The corners of Mai's mouth tilted in a sad smile. "But I did not think that when I finally did, it would be here. This"—she looked around the visiting room—"this thing they accuse you of. I do not believe it. It is not possible."

Trang lifted a hand from the glass and waved it, as though shaking off a bit of dust, something meaningless. "It's not. I didn't do it."

"Then, who? And why?"

"I don't know." His shoulders sagged. His eyes, so alive at the sight of her, went dead again.

Mai's eyes narrowed. "Listen. Maybe this is nothing. But maybe not. Do you remember the day American Father was sick? The day before we were to go to America? That day started as so much fun!" Even now, Mai clapped her hands at the memory.

———————

"Bryce—Dad—is sick today. So we'll make this a special time. Just us girls," American Mother said when she arrived to pick up Mai, who felt almost ashamed as she skipped out of the home without her brother. She had worn her best *ao dai*, her only silk one, a many-times hand-me-down nearly too small for her, frayed about the hems but a lovely jade-green, the color of new beginnings. She'd brushed out her hair so that it trailed over her shoulder, knowing the Americans were unaware of the shame its waves represented, and tucked a *hoa dao*, a peach blossom, behind her ear. The flower was purloined from one of the arrangements whose appearance coincided with the arrival of the Americans, and its presence in Mai's hair would not have gone unnoticed.

She would pay, later, another child's wrist flicking in a casual backhand as she passed, a hiss trailing her. "Thief girl. Maybe Fat Fingers finds you before the Americans take you home." Soon, though, there would be no more slaps, no pinching and twisting of the soft skin of the inner arm where the bruises wouldn't show. No more chasing a few individual noodles through watery broth, no never-quite-dry mattresses.

She led American Mother to the Old City's main attraction, Hoan Kiem Lake, both of them twirling the matching paper parasols her new mother had bought to keep the sun from unattractively darkening their skin. Mai was too polite—and besides, she did not yet have the English words—to let her new mother know of the mistake involved in choosing parasols of white, the color of death.

"We went to the cafe overlooking the Turtle Tower. You know the one."

Trang did, and his heart swelled at the memory. Cafes and restaurants lined the east side of the lake. There, wealthy people and tourists took in the centuries-old view that gave the lie to the high rises beyond. The small concrete pagoda, topped with twisting dragons rearing their heads from its tile roof, took its name from the golden turtle who had demanded a magic sword from an emperor. Mai and Trang had spent countless hours skulking around the lake's edges, trying to catch sight of the soft-shelled turtles that occasionally poked their heads above its placid waters. They had to be careful, though. Waiters who spotted the pair when they approached cafe patrons with sad faces raised, beseeching hands extended, drove them away with shouts and kicks.

But no one chased Mai away on this day. Her small brown hand clasped firmly in her benefactor's white one, she sauntered past the waiter in her new pink dress with the scratchy petticoats, almost disappointed when his glance slid past her, seeking instead the ruffians who would disturb those seeking only to sip their sugary concoctions in peace.

"Anything you like," American Mother said.

Mai liked *sinh to bo*, the rich avocado drink that was a dessert in itself, and she also liked a slice of chocolate cake with coffee ice cream. She was surprised when American Mother ordered only a croissant, waving away the waiter's suggestion of *ca phe sua da*, the iced coffee syrupy with condensed milk that most tourists drank by the gallon.

"The ice, it is safe," the waiter assured her.

But American Mother shook her head, explaining to Mai that her faith did not permit her to drink coffee, or tea, or even soda pop.

Mai, who had envisioned Coca-Cola with every meal in her new American home, slid this unwelcome bit of information into the mental file, along with uncomfortable shoes and starched, stiff clothing. When the croissant arrived, American Mother only nibbled at it.

"Why?" Mai asked, unable to fashion the entire sentence in English. Why, with so many delectable things, not partake? Especially when, as with all Americans, money was no object?

American Mother put her hands to her waist, nearly as tiny as that of the average Vietnamese woman. Mai and Trang had already commented on this difference. It was taken for granted that Americans were fat, lumbering through the Old Quarter burdened by their high, hard stomachs and wobbly butts. But not American Mother.

"I work hard at this," American Mother said. "I watch everything I eat."

Mai didn't understand. One just ate—and if one was a former street rat, one ate as much as one could, whenever one could. But she nodded as though the woman's words made sense, and agreed again as American Mother commented approvingly of the legions of women and others taking their morning exercise at the lake, doing vigorous aerobics to the beat of a boom box despite the ascending mercury heartlessly burning off the mists that lent such a mysterious and picturesque air to the Turtle Tower.

Later, in the full heat of the day, the cake and ice cream and avocado commingled uneasily in her stomach as she stretched to reach the pedals on the swan boat that bobbed on the much larger West Lake, their next stop after Hoan Kiem. She tried not to notice the curious looks from people toward this pair disporting themselves on the lake beneath their funeral parasols.

Wavelets struck at the boat in whispery slaps, nearly obscuring American Mother's question. "How old are you really, Mai?"

Mai didn't know the English word, but held out her other hand, fingers spread. Five. And again. And, finally, thumb and forefinger. Twelve.

"Are you sure? Do you ... have you ... do you have blood yet?" American Mother gestured toward her lap.

Mai grasped her meaning. "No. Not woman."

"Oh, Mai. You are more of a woman than you know. You are going to be a great beauty."

She looked so sad when she said it, her weak chin trembling, her awareness of her own plainness nakedly apparent. Mai hunched her shoulders and drew her arms protectively forward, obscuring the damnable buds on her chest, her still-childish body nearly a match for American Mother's own. She searched for English words to force American Mother's attention away from her and toward the russet tower rising high above the lake.

"Tran Quoc Pagoda," Mai announced. "Very old. Very important. Very beauty."

She herself looked beyond the pagoda and scanned the shore, wondering if American Mother might later buy her one of the trinkets from the stalls set up to woo tourists. The lakefront promenade was nearly deserted at this hour, when most foreigners retreated to their air-conditioned hotels. Except for one man, so impossibly familiar that Mai had to look twice to ascertain that it was indeed American Father, supposedly too ill to accompany them on their outing.

He must be feeling better, she told herself. Maybe he was looking for them. She started to raise her hand in a wave. His head jerked. He'd seen her, and immediately looked away. Mai lowered her hand. He turned toward the woman approaching him; a girl, really, not much older than Mai herself, head tilted, walking with an exaggerated sway. She put her hand on his arm.

American Mother lay the parasol aside and shaded her eyes. The boat took a lurching turn, American Mother's left foot jammed against a pedal. Her glance skated toward Mai. She'd seen her husband. And she wondered if Mai had seen him, too.

Mai made the sort of split-second decision that had helped her survive the streets, until it hadn't.

"This lake," she said, pointing to the far shore, away from the problematic presence of American Father and whatever he was up to. "Biggest in Hanoi."

She chanced a quick glance over her shoulder, just long enough to see American Father shake his head, to see the woman move away. But an American man, walking alone? There would be another woman, and another beyond that. Boys, too. Officially, Vietnam was communist, but among the demimonde, capitalism ruled.

"Those houses." Apartment buildings lined the lake, walls of glass to take in the views. "Very rich people." Talking, talking, trying to reassure American Mother that her attention was elsewhere.

Was American Mother's face a little redder, her lips drawn a little tighter? Maybe. But, as Mai reminded herself, all white foreigners suffered terribly in the heat. And American Mother seemed absorbed by the columnar pagoda rising eleven levels into the sky, the boat rocking gently on the water, floating farther and farther away from the husband who clearly wasn't sick at all.

———

She said nothing of the day's events when she returned that evening to the Kind and Caring Home. Why torment Trang with descriptions of the treats he hadn't shared?

Instead, she insisted they practice their English as they packed the things American Mother and Father had bought them, soft tracksuits for Trang, frilly dresses for Mai. And shoes! Trang got the puffy sneakers he'd long craved, the Nike knockoffs he recognized from the Hang Dau shoe stalls in the Old City, but poor Mai saw her feet stuffed into stiff shiny shoes of fake patent leather that scraped blisters into her heels and toes. She consoled herself with the thought that Miss Hoang would likely claim the clothes and the awful shoes before they left for America, and also with Trang's assurances that real American shoes were probably far more comfortable than the look-alikes.

"Tomorrow," he reminded her. They chanted the strange English words together. "Thank you." "Please." Which came out like "Plea," both of them unable to twist their tongues around the damnable hissing consonant at the end, so unlike the gentle vowel sounds that ended Vietnamese words. "I love you," though. That was easy. And, most thrilling, "Mom." "Dad." They were ready.

Morning brought Miss Hoang. "They're waiting in the taxi." Something different about her, features more pinched, steps shorter and choppier than usual. She held out her hands for their new clothes, the shiny books with their smooth thick pages, and whatever candies they'd yet to consume. "American airplanes—they allow only one small bag."

Mai shoved the horrible shoes toward her and tried to look as though she was sorry to give them up.

Miss Hoang jerked her chin toward Trang. "You. I must speak to you alone. In my office."

Trang followed her. But at her office door, she turned and put the flat of her hand to his back, ushering him toward Kind and Caring Home's front door. And outside, onto the street, where his new mother waited beside a taxi. She opened the back door and stood aside, then slid in beside him. She closed the door. "Dad is still sick. At the hotel. We'll pick him up."

The driver turned the key in the ignition. The sea of motorbikes parted and flowed around them as the taxi slid into traffic.

"Wait!" Trang screamed. "Wait for Mai!"

His new mother spoke through tears, crying so hard Trang could barely understand the words. "There was a problem. A last-minute thing. Miss Hoang just told me about it. Mai cannot come. Not now. Just you. Oh, Frank, I am so sorry. We'll work it out from America. We'll bring her home as soon as possible." She reached to hug him.

He pulled back, comprehending only that the taxi was moving farther and farther from the Kind and Caring Home without his sister. He tried to open the taxi door but the lock would not give. He beat the windows with his fists, begging for help from the passing motorbikes. People averted their eyes and gunned their engines, speeding away from the unseemly spectacle as he screamed and screamed for the sister left behind.

———

Mai and Trang twisted in their chairs, eyeballing the camera, whispering in bursts of Vietnamese, interspersed with enough English to keep the guard at bay.

"I have missed you so much, my brother." In stilted, proper English. Then, quickly, "Was he sick when you went to the airport?"

"No. No more than when you saw him at West Lake."

"They left me on purpose. And they told you I was dead. But why?"

The guard scowled their way. Mai raised her voice and said, again in English, "I will be here two weeks only on this trip." And, nearly beneath her breath in Vietnamese, "My coming here. He knows I saw him that day. Looking for a woman."

"Two weeks," Trang said in the same loud voice. "After so many years apart, it is not much time." He coughed and spoke below it. "Not him. He is not like that."

Mai pursed her lips. No need to say anything, to point out that all men were like that. "I know what I saw."

"No. It is not so. I cannot believe it."

Mai rapped at the glass. The guard shook his head. She ignored him, the older sister, taking charge, demanding attention. "And now you cannot believe"—she waved her hand, taking in the odious visiting station, the guard, the orange jumpsuit—"this, this catastrophe. Brother, you must open your eyes."

He closed them instead. "Why did you not tell me, that day?"

Again, the pursed lips. A foreigner, even American Father, chasing women? It would have been like telling him that the sun had come up in the morning, that the rains poured down in the afternoon. She sat wordless.

Trang squeezed his eyes tighter shut still, trying to come to grips with this new reality. When he finally spoke, it was from a place of great pain. But his eyes were open again, clear of the doubt that had clouded them. "That is why they told me you were dead. That is why they told me I'd never get the mission I wanted to Vietnam, and why I couldn't be permitted to go back, even to find your grave. Because ... "

"Because?"

"Because if I found you, found you alive, you would tell me. It would—"

They were back to their childhood, each divining the other's thoughts, Mai now finishing her brother's sentence.

"It would ruin him."

# THIRTY-SEVEN

MAI REMAINED STUBBORNLY SILENT on most of the walk across the prison parking lot, but unleashed a torrent of words as Lola unlocked the car door.

Lola understood only "American Father." She started the car and turned on the heat. The sun still shone bright, but the temperature was dropping almost imperceptibly. The Wasatch and Oquirrh sported meringue swirls of new snow, and the last few leaves hurried to let go of the trees before a shredding wind could tear them rudely away.

"American Father? Do you mean Bryce?"

Mai sagged, seemingly held up only by her seat belt, and dropped her face into her hands.

Lola pressed her for details. But the girl shook her head, repeating only that she had information that might help her brother, that it had to do with the American Father and that she would tell Lola after she'd slept.

"I never told my brother. I should have. This"—she looked toward the jail, an institutional rectangle of beige stone—"all my fault."

"Never told him what?"

Mai shook her head.

Lola tried again. "Is it something that could free him?"

"Maybe." Mai, heavy-lidded and nearly incoherent from the combination of jet lag and emotion, scrubbed at her eyes.

Lola gave up. At the motel, she made another attempt, thinking food might revive the girl. She picked up a plasticized sheet featuring take-out menus from nearby restaurants and waved it. "You must be starved. I know I am. I can order something for us to eat."

"Later, maybe. Now I sleep. And sleep and sleep and sleep." A smile flitted across Mai's face. "And dream about my brother!" She sat on the bed, thin arms enfolding her thin body.

Lola showed her how to work the thermostat and asked for her phone. Before leaving Hanoi, she'd bought Mai a burner phone like her own, one that would work in the States. She programmed her new cell number into it. During the layover at Seoul Incheon, while Mai wisely took advantage of one of the sleeping lounges so thoughtfully provided, Lola had procured a new iPhone for herself and popped in her old SIM card, another bit of proof to Charlie and everyone else that she was rejoining the working world.

And rejoining it with true eagerness, not the initial reluctance of her forced trip to Utah. Her thoughts fizzed with the possibilities raised by two words Mai had uttered: *American Father*. She needed the butt-kicking of fresh air and caffeine to focus them, though.

"I have to go out for a bit. If you wake up and you need me—if you can't sleep, or you're hungry or if you need anything, anything at all—call me." Mai nodded, but Lola remembered the automatic politesse of people in more courteous cultures. "I'm serious."

But Mai was already asleep, fully clothed but for the shoes she'd kicked off upon entering the room. Lola tiptoed to the closet, took an extra blanket from the shelf, and tucked it around her. Asleep, with the anxiety and confusion of the last few days finally smoothed from her features, Mai looked her real age, not the older, worldly woman she pretended to be. Lola wondered how she'd survived the years after her brother's departure, then pushed the likely possibilities from her mind. She had more important things to think about.

*Bryce.* All along, Lola had wondered about the possibility of an affair, impermissible for a church leader, between Bryce and Sariah. What had Tynslee said? That one day Sariah had screamed to her best friend that it was time to make things right.

Lola could see it: Melena in shock, thinking Sariah was enraged over the news of their children's affair. Bryce silent beside her, wondering about the deeper message. Afraid to even meet Sariah's eyes, knowing too well her longing to break free of the sham of her marriage, to find open happiness with him. After all, it happened all the time in other places. People got divorced, remarried. Even the LDS church allowed divorce. But the social cost was dear.

For sure, Bryce—maybe she'd let him fall too far down her list of suspects?—wouldn't be to first man to kill rather than face revelation of his tawdry secret. Lola's thoughts flew back to the night Tynslee had described, the girl tiptoeing home across the dew-damp lawn after her tryst with Trang, meeting Bryce possibly returning from a liaison of his own. The quick insistence that the young couple marry, the sort of holier-than-thou move common to secret sinners.

And it might have explained his objections to Trang's wish for a mission in Vietnam, even though it was an unlikely possibility, anyway. Maybe Mai had seen something else while Bryce and Melena were there those many years ago—an argument between them, Sariah's name bandied about, something Mai wouldn't have understood at the time but would come to comprehend all too well after only a little while in America. Better to tell Trang his sister had died than risk her joining the family, figuring things out. Saying something.

She wondered if Melena—with her rhapsodizing over her beautiful boy, her happy, happy marriage—knew. Maybe deep down. Probably. But likely not in a way that she'd admit even to herself, let alone anyone else.

Well, she'd have to learn about it now. Lola pictured the small, fragile woman in the concrete box of a police interview room, dwarfed by men in uniform, hearing the unthinkable under unbearable circumstances. Realizing, unavoidably, that her husband had betrayed her. And that she, by believing the scenario he'd created, had betrayed her son by believing him guilty of murder.

She tried not to think of what her revelation would mean to Melena's life. Marriage ended, public stigma—the reality that might have driven Bryce to kill Sariah rather than have their secret revealed—along with the extra shame of a son who might not forgive her. How would Melena face the world? And how, as a stay-at-home mother accustomed to a comfortable suburban existence, would she support herself?

Lola felt a twinge of guilt. She'd let Charlie's death nearly break her. But compared to the enormity of what Melena was about to face, her own grief seemed almost manageable. Yet she was about to push Melena into the abyss. Even if she hadn't known for sure about Mai's existence, she'd been the one to track her down, to uncover the impossible truth—that she was alive. The least she could do was tell Melena herself. And maybe, just maybe, Melena would reveal something, a shred of information that might have seemed meaningless before, that could definitively tie her husband to Sariah's murder, and thus exonerate her son.

A low growl of disapproval.

"I'm not stupid," she told Charlie. She knew the dangers. Melena might be one of those wives—those spouses, she reminded herself, since men were as susceptible as women to the self-deception that enabled some marriages—who'd rather not know. Who might choose to disbelieve. Who might warn Bryce, help him escape, even flee with him.

"Don't worry," she added. "As soon as I've talked to her, I'll call the police so that they can set up an interview with Mai."

But the rumble only intensified, Charlie having heard far too many such assurances during their too-brief time together.

She dawdled, dreading the task ahead, tapping out a text to Munro in a few seconds' worth of procrastination. *Killer possibly ID'd*—the sort of shameless, as-yet-unverified hype one sent to an editor in the hope of sending one's own story leapfrogging over the offerings of other, equally ambitious (maybe not *quite* equally) reporters.

She watched the screen for a reply. Nothing. Which left her thoughts free to return to Melena. Surely, all those women … what had Melena called them? The Relief Society. Surely they would live up to their name, would surround her, wrap her in comfort and caring and probably supply enough casseroles to fill a gigantic suburban freezer. Or would they?

Not my problem, she lectured herself. Charlie's palpable disapproval ebbed. He was a compassionate man within the limits of the law, but he'd always welcomed the black-and-white nature of those limits. "You're the one who worries about the nuances," he told her. "Save them for your stories. Me, the story ends with ninety miles per hour in a fifty zone. Or somebody blowing three times the legal breath limit. Or the guy standing over his dead wife with a face full of scratches and his fists all bloody."

"Tough talk," Lola would tease, not bothering to remind him of how he'd found empathy aplenty when a family with six kids took an elk out of season, or when a teenager who'd be the first in her family to graduate got stopped with an open container in her car. "Pour that damn thing out," he might say. And then he'd stop by the girl's house on the way home to rat her out to her grandmother, who'd be tougher on the girl than the law would ever be.

Lola lingered with her memories, willing Charlie closer. But all she felt was a sharp sensation in the small of her back—a virtual nudge to get on with it, that a killer was out there and she was on the verge of getting the information to put him away, so what was she doing sitting on her ass?

# THIRTY-EIGHT

MELENA, WHEN SHE ANSWERED the door, looked nearly as sleep-deprived as Mai, eyes sunken, lines like tensile threads from mouth to chin, tugging her lips downward.

"Lola? What happened to your hair?"

Lola wondered why the obvious required explanation. "I cut it."

"You certainly did." Melena's characteristic courtesy reasserted itself. "I wondered where you'd gone. Come in out of the cold." She peered past Lola. "They say it might snow tonight."

Lola hadn't heard the forecast, but she'd already noted the lowering sky that hastened sunset, the tang of moisture on the tongue. Inside, it was darker still, drapes drawn and safety-pinned shut although the media scrum had long since decamped. At least, most of them. Lola handed Melena a business card that had been stuck in the door. Anne Peterson. The same trick she herself had used. Anne Peterson was developing some chops.

She wondered if Anne had thought to visit the jail. Hoped that, if she did, Trang wouldn't tell her about Mai. She'd have to talk to

Trang and Mai about the need, a little longer, for secrecy. Just enough time for her to deliver Bryce to the cops and to write a story.

Melena let the card drop. It fluttered down onto a pile of others, most apparently from Anne. Melena didn't seem to care. Lola wondered why Bryce hadn't picked them up. Maybe he didn't care either. Because, as she had begun to think now, he had bigger things on his mind.

The air inside the house smelled stale. Lola resisted the temptation to pull open the drapes, lift a window despite the cold, let the chill sweep the rooms free of despair. She flicked a switch, flooding the entryway with light. Melena stepped back, into the shadows of the hall. Lola followed, closing the door behind her.

"Something to drink?" Melena offered automatically. "I'm afraid I can't offer you coffee, though. I know you like it."

"Nothing, thanks. I grabbed some coffee on the way over." Lola took a breath. "Melena, I've got some news." She'd decided to lead with the discovery of Mai, with the fact that Trang probably wasn't guilty, and save the *why* for the end of the conversation. Give Melena a few minutes of relief before clobbering her with the real reason for her visit.

"Good news," she added. But the atmosphere in the house had already seeped into her. Her words sounded brittle, false.

Melena, wordless, led the way into the living room and waited until Lola sank into the depths of the sofa before taking a chair. There would be no repeat of her earlier hugs, something that made Lola both glad and a little uneasy.

"You won't believe this."

"Try me. Because I never would have believed my best friend would be murdered. I never would have believed my son killed her. I never would have believed . . . well, a lot of things." Voice still nearly inaudible but with an edge, words emerging from thinned lips. Melena apparently had moved beyond the initial shock of grief and had planted herself squarely in the anger phase.

"Is Bryce here?" His presence would change the equation. If he was around, she'd need to get Melena alone somehow. Lola had taken some foolish risks in her life, but even she knew better than to confront a possible killer on his own turf.

Maybe Melena meant to laugh. At the sound, whatever it was, Lola jumped.

"Bryce? He hasn't been here for days. He's staying with one of our daughters."

Smart on his part, Lola thought. Better for Bryce to remove himself to the unquestioning love of a daughter. Still.

"Why aren't you with them? Or why isn't someone staying here with you?"

Melena shook her head so forcefully, a few strands escaped her sprayed coif. "I want to be alone. It's better."

"You may change your mind when you hear this," Lola said. "You said that you wondered where I'd gone. I went to Vietnam."

"What?" Melena's voice shrilled through the dim room. Lola hadn't thought her capable of such volume. "Why?"

"He—Frank—seemed so determined to go. And also, so insistent that he was innocent. It was just a hunch, really. I thought that maybe whatever I might find there would cast some light on his case. I didn't have any solid information, just the name of the orphanage, and I wasn't even sure of that."

"How did you get the name? I'm not even sure I remember it. It's been so long."

Lola didn't want to give up Tynslee. Couldn't, anyway. Officially, she and the girl had never talked. She hurried the conversation along, ignoring Melena's question.

"I just asked about orphanages. Somehow I found the right place." She decided to gloss over the cabdriver's part in finding it. "And—you won't believe this. His sister, the one they told you was dead? She's alive."

"Alive?"

Even in the dim light, Lola could see the shock that rendered Melena incapable of anything beyond simple repetition.

"It gets better," Lola said. "She's here."

"*Here?*"

"Yes, here. In Salt Lake. She's at my motel. I think she knows something. Maybe it's even something that could free Frank."

Melena pressed a hand to her heart. "Free him? How? What?"

Now, thought Lola, bracing herself. This is where the hug comes in. She forced herself from the sofa and took a step toward the chair where Melena sat rooted—and froze at the sound of an opening door.

"Melena? Who's here?"

"In here, sweetheart. It's Lola. The reporter. You remember her. You won't believe what she's come to tell us."

———

Get out. Get out. *Get out.*

Lola didn't need Charlie's urging.

"I, ah—." Any excuse. Anything at all. Just get the hell out of there. No telling what he'd do if he knew that Mai were alive. That she'd talked to Mai. He'd think that Mai had told her whatever it was that made the girl think her brother was innocent. His motivation for killing Sariah. Lola slid a shaking hand into her pocket and clutched her new iPhone. What were the chances that she'd actually be able to hit 911 if he made a move toward her? That the police would get there in time?

And Melena, looking cluelessly at her husband with eyes brimming with emotion? What might he do to her?

"I don't believe I've had the pleasure." Another voice, male, its owner still in the hallway.

Lola's breath escaped. However Bryce might be tempted to react, the presence of a witness would likely deter him. Indeed, as Bryce crossed the room to shake her hand—the one she pulled from her pocket, reluctantly releasing her phone—he looked much the same as when they'd met in the Starbucks: sorrowful, shuffling, stooped beneath the burden of his grief. *Feigned* grief, probably, she reminded herself.

"Miss Wicks. Good to see you again." The words automatic, accompanied by a quirk of the lips that acknowledged the inadequacy of etiquette under such circumstances.

Yet again, Lola fought her gut reaction: this man hasn't killed anyone.

Shoes thudded against the hallway floor. A man padded across the living room's snowy carpet in sockfeet.

"Galon needs to get some things from the house. They still haven't moved back in. He didn't want to go in alone. I said I'd help him. Have you two met?" Bryce, still in monotone good-host mode, turned her way again.

Recognition lit Galon's eyes. "After the funeral. But we were never properly introduced."

He reached for her hand and held it a moment, bending over it, a courtly, old-fashioned move, charming but for the familiar fragrance wafting toward her, one that stirred a schizophrenic recall of her father at his shaving mirror—and more recently, of herself helpless on the ground in Pioneer Park as an unknown assailant forced a knife toward her throat:

The scent of bay rum.

# THIRTY-NINE

LOLA DROVE WITH THE windows open, hoping the cold would slap some sense into her.

But nothing made sense.

She'd gone to Melena's thinking Bryce had killed Sariah, and left with her suspicions fixated on Galon. But why would he kill his wife? And try to put the blame on Trang? And then, why the attack in the park? Somehow, unwittingly, she must have stumbled across something that pointed toward him. What?

Her head ached, bewilderment and exhaustion bubbling in a toxic brew. She longed for the motel, a bed, the relief of sleep. Maybe, upon waking, all would become clear. Even though she was pretty sure it wouldn't. Besides, Mai was waiting in the room, would turn toward her with those too-old eyes that went young and hopeful whenever she spoke of her brother. Lola couldn't face the prospect of watching the darkness cloud them again, herself the cause.

Her phone vibrated, a welcome distraction. For the first time in history, she thought as she checked the screen, she was glad to hear from Donovan Munro.

*At the house*, he texted. *Can't wait to hear.*

Lola's brief burst of enthusiasm faded. When she'd thought Bryce was the killer, she'd also assumed that after her visit to Melena, she would be able to present Munro—and, as she'd reassured Charlie, the police—with evidence.

Maybe, she thought, Galon had found out about the affair. And, as fearful of the stain of divorce as Bryce, had arranged to have his cheating wife killed, punishing his best friend for his betrayal and neatly freeing himself to remarry someone far more suitable.

But was she too quick to switch her fixation from Bryce to Galon based on an instant's whiff of aftershave? She needed to consider all the possibilities. What about Malachi and his pill pushing, and the repeated anonymous phone calls about her own habit? Maybe Galon ran some sort of ring, with a bunch of teenage minions doing the dirty work. Could be that story about raising money to help Trang get to Vietnam was just a smokescreen.

"Get a grip," she muttered before Charlie could beat her to the punch. The most obvious solution was almost always the right one, and she'd strayed very far from obvious. Which brought her back to Bryce. It didn't get more obvious than the lover. But if Bryce killed Sariah, why did Galon attack her in the park?

In any event, at least she'd taken the precaution of warning Melena not to say anything.

"Lola's brought us the most interesting news," Melena had started to say. Stopped when Lola shook her head.

"I'm, uh, going back to Montana," she'd said in answer to Bryce's unspoken question. Had that been relief on his face? On Galon's?

She'd added some embroidery, quickly stitching what she hoped was a reassuring design. "Obviously, there's no story, at least not the one I planned to write. You've been so kind to talk with me, given everything you're going through. I wish you the best of luck."

Backing toward the door as she spoke. Melena following, walking with her to the car, taking Lola's arm against the buffeting wind that had arisen just in the short while she'd been in the house. A hug, Lola forcing her arms up and around the smaller woman. "Melena, I wouldn't say anything about Mai to anyone just yet. I probably shouldn't even have told you. It seems cruel to get everyone's hopes up about Frank."

A Hail Mary if ever there was one.

Melena dropped her arms, stepped back, locked Lola's gaze in her own, more intense even than the hug. "You're so right. Between us." She raised her hand and drew a line down her chest. Crossed it, the childhood promise. "But I can't wait to hear more. Maybe we can catch up tomorrow. You'll bring Mai, won't you? To think that she's alive! She could have been with us all this time." Her breath caught. "Well. No use looking back." She shook her head and thrust her little chin forward, and Lola caught a glimpse of the kind of women who walked away from all the comforts they had known to follow their husbands on foot across a desert.

"Best to focus on what it could mean now," she continued. "For Frank. For all of us. Your hotel is downtown, right? I think there's a café in the lobby. We could meet there."

"I'm actually a couple of miles from there now, at the motel just off the interstate. I think there's a Starbucks a block or two away."

Tomorrow. That would give her time to think. Under the circumstances, a gift. No way was she going to bring Mai. But she would probably have more questions, this time with far greater detail, for

Melena. She'd make an excuse in the morning as to why the girl hadn't joined them.

"I know that place. Ten o'clock?"

Perfect.

———

Lola flipped her phone over, too late to avoid seeing Munro's guilt-inducing text. *On your way?*

The problem with pimping a story before it was nailed down was the possibility that said story would go straight to hell. This one was headed for perdition. Better to present Munro with her suspicions that his son might be involved, if only tangentially, with Sariah's murder. *Let's talk about Malachi too*, she texted back. That ought to distract him.

She checked the time. Barely an hour since she'd left Mai in the room. Spending some time with Munro would let the girl sleep a little longer before she returned to quiz her about whatever it was she knew about the man she called American Father.

But first, more procrastination. Lola pulled over and scrolled through her phone, checking on the condition of the cop who'd been attacked in the park. "Off the ventilator! Charlie, did you hear that?"

And the cop wasn't talking, not yet, which was also good news. At some point, he would remember the tourist he'd encountered earlier in the park, the one he'd mistakenly accused of prostitution. Maybe. Sometimes the drugs they gave people caused a sort of amnesia, hell for investigating officers, but for Lola's purposes, it would be a godsend.

Next up, Jan. This time calling rather than texting. Her fingers could never keep up with Jan's rapid-fire questions.

"Looks like I'll be coming home soon. Really."

"What about the story?" Jan's priorities were nothing if not predictable.

She had to fake it. Any hint that the story had disintegrated yet again and Jan, that traitor, would be on the phone with Munro before Lola was halfway to his house. "It's good. Strong." She rattled on. The story would play out over weeks, though. The reunion with Mai was an important element, but whether it affected Trang's case remained to be seen. She'd try to persuade Munro to let her write a wrap-up piece down the road, something she could do in Magpie. In the meantime, though, "I just want to see Margaret."

Saying it made it so. All those months she'd avoided her daughter, ostensibly sunk in grief. Not ostensibly. Truly. Grief shaded by something even darker, the inescapable fact that to resume her old routine with Margaret—the unthinking daily drill of school and chores and meals and bathtime and before-sleep reading—would be to acknowledge Charlie's absence. Her stubborn immersion in mourning, while keeping Charlie close, had locked Margaret out. Now it hit her what she'd missed: Margaret's burbling laugh at Bub's ongoing battle with the flock of chickens, her fiery defiance when confronted with the most reasonable request—yes, she had to wash behind her ears; yes, she had to pick up her clothes from the floor and put them in the hamper; yes, she had to feed the horse *right now*. Lola directed mental apologies to her daughter.

Jan pushed her advantage. "Then you'd better get your butt home before she changes her mind about wanting to see you."

Lola forgot about Bryce, forgot about Galon, forgot about Malachi. She was halfway to Munro's house before she identified the lightness in her chest as happiness.

A follow-up text from Jan as she pulled up to Munro's house afforded her a final few seconds of delay.

*The aunties are going full fry bread. You've been warned.*

Lola groaned. The private reunion she'd envisioned with her daughter would have to wait. The aunties had other plans, ones that probably involved half the reservation, enough food to end world hunger, and of course a fry bread production line in Lena's kitchen. Much as she hated being the center of attention, her mouth watered at the thought of the puffed pieces of bread, fresh off the griddle, hot enough to burn the tongue, the shake of powdered sugar—so bad, with its delivery of lard and white flour and sugar, but oh, so good.

Almost as good as sex. Again, the hackneyed comparison arose unbidden. Where had that come from? Lola told herself she was delirious from lack of sleep. Mai had been the smart one, insisting upon rest and recovery.

She looked toward Munro's arched oak door, flanked by lights that cast a welcoming golden glow across the steps, and ordered herself to get it over with. When she rang the bell, Malachi answered.

"What are you doing here?" she asked. More accusation than question.

"I live here. Why are *you* here? What happened to your hair?"

Like father, like son, Lola thought. Could be she was doing them both a favor. Maybe forcing them to face up to harsh facts would temper that attitude. Except that Malachi's demeanor didn't match the challenge of his words. He hung back, shoulders hunched, his slight body swallowed up within baggy pants and a sweatshirt that hung nearly to his knees.

"Wicks!"

Munro appeared in the doorway. He grasped her hand and pulled her in, talking too loud, too fast.

"Great to see you. Can't wait to hear about your trip. Sounds like we've got a lot to talk about. Come on into the kitchen. Sorry, but it's pizza again. Neither of us has quite figured out cooking yet. Nice haircut, by the way. What'd you use, hedge clippers?"

Lola wasn't sure who followed him more reluctantly—herself or Malachi. They shuffled along behind Munro, leaping apart as if burned when they accidentally brushed elbows. The last time she'd seen him, other than on the ice at the hockey game, they'd been fleeing the sight of the wounded cop, a memory that seemed to have weighed at least as heavily on Malachi as it had upon her. The kitchen's bright lighting, wholly unwelcome, drew attention to the shadows beneath his eyes, the red lines radiating across the whites.

Munro pulled plates from the cupboard and loaded each with two slices of pizza. He poured two beers, one for Lola and one for himself. "Sorry, Malachi," he said. "Water for you."

He sat, one foot jiggling so fiercely the table shivered. "Eat up."

Lola took an obedient bite. The pizza, pepperoni this time instead of mushroom, tasted of cardboard.

Munro waited until he'd finished his first slice and was halfway through the second before he finally asked. "You said you wanted to talk about Malachi. So, I thought he should be here. What's this about?"

He hadn't asked about the story at all. Which meant his concern about his son ran deep. Lola thought of the occasional messages from Margaret's school, noncommittal voicemails that left her with palms sweating and heart racing. Even though they almost always turned out to be something innocuous, a form she'd forgotten to fill out or a request to take a shift for a room parent who'd had to cancel.

291

Room parenting, by the way, being one of Lola's least favorite activities, although she was always so relieved at the bland nature of the request that she agreed.

"Yeah." Malachi picked a piece of pepperoni from his pie, dropped it into his mouth, and spoke around it. "What's this about?"

Like he really wanted to know. Lola took a long swallow of beer.

"Spit it out." This was the Munro she knew, irritation flashing across his face.

Lola pushed a bit of crust around on her plate. "I'd hoped to talk with you in private."

Donovan rose, retrieved the Scotch from the cupboard, and poured himself a healthy slug. He held the bottle out to Lola. She resisted an urge to drink directly from it and shook her head.

"Say it."

Malachi's glance was unreadable. Start with the easy stuff, Lola told herself. Even if she implicated herself in the process.

"Your son, ah, I think he has a drug problem."

"Look who's fucking talking." Malachi's voice skidded high and broke.

Munro's knuckles whitened around the glass of Scotch. He'd brought the bottle to the table with him. Lola remembered the way he showed up at her motel room, already drunk, and the way he'd kept drinking, hard. As to what else had happened in that room— she reddened. No need to think of that now. Or ever again.

"What are you—each of you—talking about?"

———

"He sells pills in Pioneer Park."

"She buys them!"

They spoke nearly at once, Malachi's accusation coming a beat behind Lola's.

"Whoa." Munro held up his hands. "One at a time. Malachi, what were you doing in Pioneer Park?"

"He was selling pills. Like I just said."

"Pills that you were buying." Their glares clashed like swords, each of them seeing in the other's eyes the knowledge of what had happened to the cop, the secret they shared, never to be revealed despite their dueling accusations. Something in the set of his jaw, the defiant fold of the arms, reminded Lola of Margaret. Dear Lord. Was this what she was in for?

"Wicks." Munro dealt first with the less personal of the two problems facing him. "I got a phone call about this. And I saw pills in your Dopp kit—" He broke off and glanced toward his son, who fortunately seemed too sunk in his own misery to grasp the implications of his father's having been in the same space as Lola's Dopp kit. "Do you have a problem?"

"The phone call to you was the least of it. And no, I don't have a problem. Those pills you saw—I just use them to sleep. Anyway, I got rid of them." Only a slight deviation from the truth. No matter how it had happened, she no longer had the pills.

"What do you mean, the phone call to me was the least of it?" Munro seemed to have forgotten his query to Malachi about Pioneer Park. Malachi sat back in his chair and watched Lola stew.

"Somebody tried the same shit while I was in Vietnam. Except that this time, I almost ended up in jail." She turned to Malachi. "What's your beef with me? Because it's almost like you don't want me around. Not around here, and definitely not in Hanoi." Lola took a breath and went for broke. "Maybe because I was asking too many questions about how Sariah Ballard died."

293

She expected an immediate denial, another high-voiced protest. Malachi's struggle to control his voice was obvious. "You think I had something to do with that?"

"Jesus Christ." This from the man who had warned her about her language. Donovan's glass jumped when his fist hit the table. "This has gone way too far. Are you seriously accusing my son of murder?"

"It *has* gone too far," said Lola. "I should have said something about this a long time ago. And I'm not accusing. I'm asking. I think he knows something about it. Let him answer."

"I'm not a murderer," Malachi blurted. "I'm gay."

# FORTY

LOLA STARED FROM SON to father.

Father stared at son.

Son, at the table.

No one spoke. Lola reached for the bottle, swallowed, waded in. "What does being gay have to do with drugs in the park?"

"Everything. Everything." Malachi's voice had gone from high-pitched adolescent embarrassment to barely audible.

"Wait." Munro found his own voice. "This is a real thing? The drugs?"

"It's not what you think," Malachi said, even as Lola spoke over him.

"It's a real thing, all right. But for him, not for me."

Munro gained some equilibrium. He took the bottle back from Lola. "Best to be sober for this. You go first."

"I saw him selling drugs in the park." Truth, albeit highly edited.

"To her! She bought them!"

"Wicks?"

Lola fought an urge to slump in her chair, tuck her chin to her chest, and cross her arms, mirroring Malachi's pose. "I use them to help me sleep, like I just said. I, uh, lost my prescription. Rather than go through the hassle of calling my doctor and finding a pharmacy, I thought I'd buy a few to tide me over while I was here."

"Vikes to sleep? That's a good one." Moral superiority straightened Malachi's spine. "And—a few? Try twenty."

"Vikes?"

"It's what he calls Vicodin. I mean—" Too late. Redirect, redirect! "How do drugs have anything to do with being gay?"

"Wait." Again, Munro tried to play catch-up with the barrage of new information. "You're really gay?"

Malachi nearly disappeared back into his sweatshirt with a mumble that mimicked assent.

Munro's sigh was longer than any of the previous questions. He slid his chair around the table, put his hands on his son's shoulders, and turned Malachi to face him. "First things first. I love you. Gay, straight, it's immaterial. I love you. Got that?"

Lola would have preferred violent sobs to the silence of Malachi's tears. He drew several long, shuddering breaths.

"Mom doesn't. She kicked me out."

"*What?* Where's my goddamn phone? I'm going to call her right now." Munro stood and patted his pockets.

"No. Dad, no!" Malachi pulled him back down. "She felt like she didn't have a choice. That new rule."

Donovan delivered an opinion of the church with such intensity and length that Lola and Malachi exchanged fearful glances. He finally broke off with a dazed look.

"When did this happen?"

"About a month ago."

"A month? Why didn't you say something?"

Malachi's look told him why. He'd already lost one parent. Like Margaret. Except Margaret hadn't had a choice. Malachi's mother had made the incomprehensible decision to excise her son from her life.

Munro visibly gathered himself. "All those nights I thought you were staying at your mom's house. Where were you?"

"Friends, mostly. And—" His glance slid away.

Lola knew that look. So, apparently, did Donovan. "And?"

"And what?"

The tactic reminded her of Margaret, who often lobbed questions right back at Lola, possibly in hopes of sidetracking her mother or wearing her down, neither of which ever happened. Reading Munro's expression, Lola could have told Malachi to save his breath. But maybe the technique had worked with his mom. Until it hadn't.

"Where did you stay when you weren't with your friends?"

A mumble, from even deeper within the sweatshirt than before.

"I didn't catch that." Munro's tone had gone from loving to icy. She felt a reluctant flash of sympathy for Malachi, the youth so apparently determined to destroy her.

"Motels."

*"Motels?"*

Lola wished Munro would quit talking in italics, as annoying when spoken as they were in print.

"Motels where?"

Lola was unfamiliar with the neighborhoods Malachi named. Munro wasn't. "Those places are nothing but drug dens. And speaking of drugs—"

Malachi's face was white. "They were in the medicine cabinet at Mom's. They've been there for years. I sold them to help Trang get to Vietnam. And to pay for the motels. I don't use them. I never have. I promise."

"I believe you." Lola was shocked to hear her own voice enter the fray. She remembered the way Malachi's hand shook as he'd handed her the baggie of pills, his jitters as pronounced as her own. She'd attributed it to being in need of a fix. But if that had been the case, he had the means at hand to satisfy a jones. He just wanted money. "But here's what I don't understand," she added.

Malachi turned to her, seemingly relieved to be out from under his father's interrogation.

"Why'd you keep trying to dime me out? To your dad and then to the police in Hanoi?"

Malachi's bafflement appeared as unfeigned as his earlier anguish. "What are you talking about?"

"Yes, Lola. What are you talking about?"

Lola rubbed a hand over her spiky new cut. "I don't care that you're gay. And I'm glad that you're not using. But it doesn't erase the fact that you tried to stop me from pursuing a story. Why?"

Both shook their heads, identical wags. "I didn't call anybody," Malachi said.

"He didn't." Munro tucked his hair behind his ears, that irritating teenage-girl gesture. "I don't know about this Vietnam business, but I know my own son's voice. The person who called me about you wasn't him."

———

Something teased at the edge's of Lola's brain, something she needed to ask. It slipped away. She stalled for time, trying to coax it back. "Are you sure?"

"I'm sure," Malachi said. "It wasn't me. Why would it be? Telling on you would only get me in trouble. And I wouldn't begin to know how to call Vietnam. So it doesn't matter."

"Oh, bullshit," Lola said, even though she half believed him. "You know how to use the internet, right?"

"It doesn't matter." Munro echoed his son.

Yes, it did, Lola thought. It mattered very much to her. Had the cabdriver not found Mai, she might be sitting in a jail cell in Hanoi, not knowing when or how she was going to see Margaret again, a removal at least as ominous as the one sketched by Amanda Richards.

At the thought of her daughter, her heart lurched. She recognized the same emotion on Munro's face as he took his son's hand. "Getting kicked out of the house, skulking around Pioneer Park selling drugs to dangerous people—"

"Hey!"

Munro ignored Lola's protest. "Staying in fleabag motels. This last month must have been hell for you. Why'd you tell your mother and not me?"

"I didn't tell her." Yet again, Malachi receded turtle-like into his hood. He slid his hand from Munro's grasp and tucked it back into the pouch.

"How did she find out?"

A long pause. The hood rustled.

"Come again?

"We got caught."

A long, quivering silence.

"*We?*"

"Me and … "

"It doesn't matter who," Munro started to say. Too late.

"Me and Trang."

———

The gasp Lola heard was her own.

Munro's own reaction came in slow motion.

"Your mom. Caught you. With Frank? How?"

Lola watched him struggle to accept the same images flashing through her own mind: his son embracing another boy, leaping apart at the sight of Bevany.

Wrong image.

"My computer."

Of course. These days, the downfall of anyone with a secret. And especially for gay kids, a double-edged sword—on the one hand giving them a way to find community, to discover the answers to all their never-ask-aloud questions, but on the other offering a quick reveal to a prying parent. Lola vowed that when she finally allowed Margaret her own computer, she would never look at it. Never, ever. Her fingers twitched. She forced herself not to cross them and tried to get a grasp on the subject at hand.

"Back up. You and Frank are gay?"

"Yeah. Trang, Dad. That's his name. We are." A bit of defiance now, along with some palpable relief that things were out in the open, that he could finally say the forbidden thing.

"I don't get it."

"Oh come on, Lola. Even where you live, there must be some gay kids." Munro, the old sarcasm roaring back.

She rolled her eyes at him. "No shit. Bisexual, too. Like Trang apparently is."

"No, he's not!" Malachi's head, powered by outrage, emerged from the sweatshirt. "He's never liked girls. He's always known. Just like me." He chanced an abashed glance at his father.

Lola felt the satisfaction of spite as she pricked at his certainty. She wasn't entirely sure she believed that he hadn't made those calls. "Trang got caught with Tynslee, too. You didn't know that I knew about that, right? The question is, did you know?"

"He wasn't with her. Not like that."

"Yes, he was. She told me so herself."

"It was all an act. We were afraid Trang's mom would throw him out, too. We knew Mom had told her. So Tynslee and Trang went to her and said that Trang's mom was confused, that she and Trang were actually the ones fooling around. And it helped that Tynslee really had been caught sneaking out of his house at night. She'd gone over there to talk about what to do."

"Now I'm confused," said Lola. "Why would you do any of that?"

"Because as bad as it is to have sex before you're married, it's even worse if you're gay. And we knew that no matter what Mom saw, she'd be happy with any other story."

"But she's not," Munro said. "Because you're still living on the streets. Or couches, or wherever. You sleep here from now on. Got that?"

Malachi nodded grateful assent before his face clouded anew. "You're right, she's not. She said she'd believe it when Tynslee and Frank walked down the aisle. Not until."

"Sounds like her," Munro muttered. The Scotch reclaimed his attention.

Bevany sounded like a right proper bitch. "So you all were going to go ahead with this sham marriage."

Malachi lifted a thin shoulder. "If we had to. Trang and I would be able to keep seeing each other. Just like—" He stopped.

"Like people used to do? News flash, those days are long gone."

"Not here, they're not. They … never mind."

Lola thought that if she hadn't cut her hair, she'd now be chomping on the ends, à la Jan, out of sheer frustration. "Never mind? Fine for you and Trang to keep things on the down-low, although why you'd want to is beyond me."

"Try living here for five minutes and you'll know why. Everything here revolves around the church. If you're not part of it, you've got no life at all."

"So go someplace else." During all her years bouncing around the country and the world, Lola had never understood people who tied themselves to one place. And then came Magpie. An image of the Front arose, the perfect triangle of Sinopah rising above Two Medicine Lake, the heart-catching dominance of Ninahstako. Chief Mountain. She'd hated being told to leave it, even for what was supposed to have been just a few days in Salt Lake. What if someone told her she had to remove herself forever?

Still. "You were willing to sentence a young girl, your friend, to a lifetime of lying, too. What if someday she met someone and fell in love? What was she supposed to do then?"

"She said that from what she'd seen of marriage, she never wanted to get married. Besides, we figured that the longer the engagement went on, the more Mom would be able to persuade herself that she'd made some sort of mistake. That maybe she hadn't seen what she thought she had, and that I could come home. We didn't stop to think what it would mean to his mission. He was so sure he could talk the church leaders into sending him to Vietnam."

"So everybody knew about this. "Lola held up her hand and counted on her fingers. "Your mother. Trang. Tynslee. Melena— Mrs. Shumway. Maybe even Mr. Shumway." Which left the obvious question.

How much had Sariah known?

# FORTY-ONE

Munro and his son had a lot to talk about, Lola said as she retreated from the house, scattering excuses like confetti.

Munro called after her. Wasn't there something about the story she wanted to tell him? Something important?

"It'll keep."

She glanced back into the house before she closed the door behind her. Munro had pulled his chair beside his son's and sat with his arm around Malachi, their heads together. They spoke in low voices. A laugh—Munro's—punctuated the conversation. Lola's heart cracked. When was the last time she'd hugged Margaret close? Laughed with her?

She thought again of the inevitable party that awaited her return to Magpie. Maybe it would be a good thing, giving her and Margaret time to get used to being around each other again before they had to face the hard work of figuring out how to be alone together.

But first, she had to make sense of the incomprehensible. She'd gotten lucky twice—with the invitation to meet Melena the next morning, and now with Malachi's revelation that distracted Munro from his focus on the story. Probably too much to hope for that Mai would still be asleep when she got back to the motel, affording her more precious time to puzzle over this latest bit of information and whether it fit anywhere in the larger picture.

Despite what she'd learned about Malachi and Trang, she'd discovered nothing about Bryce that might support her theory about Bryce and Sariah. And certainly nothing to back up her own recent certainty that Galon was somehow involved. As to the revelation of Malachi's involvement with Trang, the police were likely to treat it as giving further credence to the belief that Trang as the killer, raging at being forced to marry Tynslee, even if all the kids stated that this particular deal with the devil was voluntary.

Still, she'd press Mai. Find out whatever it was she knew—or thought she knew—about Bryce. And whatever it was, she'd pass it along to Munro. Let him deal with it, whatever *it* was at this point.

"Because by then, I'll be on my way home." To Bub this time, instead of Charlie, as though he were perched as usual on the seat beside her, nose to the window she reflexively lowered a little whenever she started the car. Another tug at her overworked heartstrings. She missed the dog nearly as much as she missed her daughter. She'd developed the secret habit of kissing him almost on the mouth, letting her lips graze the soft hairs of his muzzle, something he tolerated, barely, with an air of wounded dignity. When she got home, she wouldn't care who saw it. She'd embarrass the dog in front of everyone.

———

Lola tiptoed down the motel hallway and swiped her key card in the door.

It swung open on an empty room.

Mai's bed was barely mussed, just a depression in the spread, the blanket Lola had lain over her tossed aside. Lola crossed to the bathroom. The door stood open. Just to be sure, she flipped on the light and pulled the shower curtain aside. The tub was empty and dry. She fought a rising panic. Maybe Mai had been curious about this new place and had gone for a walk. Lola lifted the phone's receiver and called the front desk.

No, the woman who answered assured her. She hadn't seen a young woman leave Lola's room. And she added, with an air of disapproval that wafted from the phone, that she hadn't realized Lola had a guest. Guests were extra. Did Lola know that?

"I'll pay," Lola snapped.

She stood in the middle of the room and turned slowly, a few inches at a time, taking in everything. But nothing was amiss. Shrink-wrapped Styrofoam cups stood beside the empty plastic ice bucket. The remote sat undisturbed atop the television. The card seeking guest comments was still squared off next to the lamp on the nightstand. Lola's duffel sat mute and unhelpful on its stand near the door, next to the matching stand that had held Mai's bag. Now that bag, like its owner, was gone.

# FORTY-TWO

She pulled out her new phone and texted Munro.

*Mai missing.*

Then it hit her: Melena.

She'd left her alone with Bryce and Galon, either one of whom might have had something to do with Sariah's killing. That silly warning not to say anything about Mai. What woman didn't share secrets with her husband? And what husband didn't pass along secrets to his best friend? She'd been so wrapped up in her own confusion that she hadn't adequately considered the consequences to Melena. How long had it been since she'd left Melena? An hour? Two?

But first, Mai. Lola's hand hovered over the phone, forefinger resting on 9. She could press it, follow it up with the 1 and another 1. But even before she'd met Charlie, she'd known all about law enforcement's skeptical attitude, too frequently justified, when grown people went missing, especially if nothing pointed to a crime.

She moved her finger away from the numbers, back to the letters, and texted Jan. Better safe than sorry, she thought. *Might not be home soon after all.*

In the time it took her to type, a flurry of messages from Munro arrived.

*Who?*

*What's going on?*

*Where r u?*

And then, with a journalist's instinct to fear the worst: *Call cops.*

Another slew of texts, these from Jan.

*WTF?*

*Margaret expects you.*

*No way, Wicks.*

*Can't believe you'd do this.*

*Don't even bother coming back.*

Lola thumbed Jan's number, bracing for the explanation. But an explanation would take time she didn't have. She clicked off, ran to the car, tossed the phone onto the dash, and turned the key in the ignition.

She peeled out of the parking lot, leaving rubber on the pavement, the phone sliding off the dash and ricocheting off the door onto the floor. Went full East Coast driver on the interstate, all the old skills back, full employment for horn and middle finger. Gave quick thanks for her cheap suburban digs as opposed to the fancy and farther-away downtown hotel. It took her all of ten minutes to get to Camellia, and that only because she glimpsed a cop car's light bar ahead of her as she took the exit. She passed the cop, and the poor sucker who'd gotten caught, at a sedate twenty-five, foot quivering on the accelerator, stomping it as soon as the cop car was out of sight.

The car swung wide around the damnable curves of Camellia's streets. The radio blared storm warnings. *Be okay*, she pleaded. Melena, so slight and whispery and dangerously disoriented by mourning. Her hulking, brooding husband. And Galon, not as physically intimidating as Bryce, but with a skier's lithe fitness. Melena wouldn't stand a chance against either of them.

Finally, the house. No sign of the black Suburban. Maybe the men were gone. Lola hesitated at the door. What if they weren't?

"Lola?"

Melena came around a corner of the house, peeling off a pair of muddy work gloves. Probably covering plants or whatever you were supposed to do to protect them as bad weather approached. Even though she was sure Melena had told her that Bryce was the gardener. Which didn't matter now.

"I—Melena, where's Bryce?"

"He and Galon are on their way back to my sister's house. Lola, are you all right?"

Relief nearly knocked Lola off her feet. She braced herself against the front door. "Melena, I think you'd better come with me. Right away."

Melena tilted her head. "How mysterious! Where are we going? And, why? I need to clean up, of course. I've just been out turning the compost pile."

"No time. Just come with me." Lola cast a glance down the street, expecting to see the black Suburban headed her way, heedless to the niceties of a speed limit. How much time had she wasted due to the speed trap? How much was she wasting now? She took Melena's elbow and steered her toward the car. "Please."

Melena stopped in the middle of the walk.

"You're scaring me."

A car turned onto the street. Lola's heart thudded. Not the Suburban. A quivering sigh escaped her. Melena's eyes widened, still puzzled but with the dawning recognition of something seriously amiss. Lola watched the wheels turn. *Hurry, hurry.*

Melena held up a forefinger. "One second." She stepped into the house and returned, shrugging into a warm coat, brushing past Lola to toss a purse into the back seat. Lola eyeballed the coat enviously. Her windbreaker was fast becoming inadequate.

Melena pulled on a pair of slim leather gloves with something approaching a snap, and finally Lola saw the uber-efficient carpooling, activity-organizing, meal-managing PTA mom she'd expected to interview before that eons-ago phone call from Munro announcing Sariah's murder.

"Whatever's going on, you're in no shape to drive. You'd better give me the keys."

Lola surrendered them. "If that's what it takes to get you out of here, fine."

# FORTY-THREE

"Where are we going? And why?"

"Where? I don't know. For now, let's just get as far away from your house as possible. As to why—" Lola wondered about the wisdom of letting Melena drive. How would she react to Lola's suspicions about Bryce and Galon? She started with the now more pressing matter of Mai.

"Mai's missing. I got back to the room and she was gone."

"Missing? Oh, Lola. She probably went for a walk. She has to be all turned around because of the time change."

Lola didn't want to take the time to go into the missing bag, the desk clerk's mystification. "Melena, did you say anything to Bryce?"

A "no" so long and drawn out as to be patently unbelievable. Followed by another, predicable, "why?"

"You'd better pull over."

They'd ended up in an industrial district, featureless warehouses lining wide streets designed for semi trucks, deserted at this hour. The wind screamed past, funneled by the warehouse walls, lashing at the rental car. The interstate ran nearby, the road elevated, bright ribbons of headlights illuminating its path, traffic moving fast and purposeful, late workers finally on their way home, others headed for the supermarket to stock up on mass quantities of milk and bread and eggs before the snow started. So many cars. So many people. So many places for a girl to disappear.

The radio squawked the obligatory caution. "Eight inches or more … dangerous wind chill … essential travel only after ten … "

Melena touched a gloved finger to the button. The wind's shriek took over where the announcer had left off, issuing its own elemental warning, far more effective.

Lola needed to get this conversation over as quickly as possible, and then get herself and Melena somewhere safe. And she needed to find Mai. What if the girl were outdoors somewhere, spectacularly unequipped to handle cold let alone a full-on blizzard. Still, she soft-pedaled her news to the extent possible.

"You know how I told you that Mai might know something that could help Trang? Frank. Maybe something that could free him? Melena, I think it's about Bryce."

Lola had expected denial. Anger. Fear. Anything but the hope that raised Melena's voice to a near-normal level.

"Does Bryce know something that could help him?"

Lola hadn't thought about it that way. But no, fear had coated Mai's words whenever she mentioned Bryce. "Maybe. Melena, I know I told you not to say anything to Bryce. But I have ask you again—are you sure you didn't say something? To him or to Galon? I won't be mad. I promise." Fingers crossed behind her back. Time enough later for Melena to feel betrayed. Right now, she needed Melena to trust her. Snowflakes struck the windshield, dissolved, struck again. This time, they stuck.

Melena sucked in that rabbity underlip and looked away. "I might have said something. That his sister was alive." She swung on Lola, eyes bulging and bright. "Oh, Lola, it was such wonderful news! Especially in the midst of such horror. Bryce has suffered so much these past few days. I couldn't help but share it with him. Right then and there, as soon as I told him, we made a prayer of thanks."

Go slow, Lola warned herself. Dole out the information in tiny doses. Don't let her know—yet—that you suspect her husband. Or Galon.

A semi rumbled past, so loud as to give Lola an excuse to wait a moment longer before she spoke again. Headlights flooded the car's interior as the driver braked and swung wide around them, casting a look of annoyance from his lofty perch.

"Melena, did you tell Bryce where I was staying?"

"No. But I told him about coffee tomorrow. Maybe he figured it out. That's the only motel nearby. Lola!" Melena's eyes brightened. She bounced in her seat like a little girl. "I think I can find Mai!"

She threw the car into gear and surprised Lola by heading deeper still into the industrial park, the interstate receding behind them. The wipers swish-thumped, the view ahead clearing and disappearing, black, then white, then black again. The car picked up speed, fishtailing a little in the snow.

"Melena?"

"I'll bet he couldn't wait to meet her. He probably wondered, just like me, if she'd recognize him after all these years. He'd want to show her all of his favorite sights, just like she showed us Hanoi, all those years ago. There's a place he likes to go...." She flashed Lola a radiant smile. "Relax. I think I know exactly where Mai is."

---

313

The buildings thinned out, then disappeared entirely. The road ran straight and lonely through a flat expanse of desert. A building reared before them, pale domes against a black sky. The castle she'd seen from the sky as the plane coasted toward the airport. What had Tynslee called it? Melena supplied the answer.

"Bryce loves the lake, even crazy old SaltAir."

He did? Tynslee's parents had described the place as dangerous, populated during concerts by druggies. Well, nobody was populating it now. It looked closed for the winter, windows black, a chain-link fence surrounding it.

Melena swung the car around SaltAir and pointed it across a parking lot, pulling up at the far side. Beyond the lot, a gunmetal-gray expanse heaved and sighed. The lake. *Hush now, hush now,* the wipers whispered. Snow glittered in the headlights. Melena killed the engine.

"They're probably down here somewhere. Let's find them." She leaned forward and yanked the lever that popped the trunk.

Lola peered into the blackness. "I don't see his car. I don't see any cars at all. And it's cold. And dark. Melena, are you sure about this? Why would anyone come here in this kind of weather?"

But Melena was already out, rummaging around in the trunk. Lola opened her door. A gust grabbed at it. She got out, leaning into the wind, slitting her eyes against the snow. She stood on a vast salt flat, the snow fast filling the cracks in the earth beneath her feet, the lake disappearing into darkness. The highway was far behind them now, its reassuring stripes of light revealed only when the wind parted the curtains of snow.

"Lola?"

She turned and saw Melena, a tire iron swinging from the end of her arm.

314

The wind pried a hank of Melena's hair free and blew it across her face. Lola couldn't see her expression. Didn't need to. Animal instinct took over. She whirled to run. Took a long step.

The tire caught her across the back of the legs. She went down, rolling, curling around herself, arms cradling her head, Charlie's voice in her ears: *Always protect your head.* They could fix everything else. But not head injuries.

Charlie hadn't said anything about knees. That's where the iron struck next. Lola, even as she screamed, marveled at the precise sensation of shattering bone.

She rolled away, wondering where the next blow would fall. It didn't. She couldn't trust her voice yet, but she opened her eyes.

Melena stood above her, twirling the tire iron like a baton. Even through her pain, Lola was impressed. That thing was heavy.

"CrossFit." Melena nodded. "Sariah and I went together."

Lola remembered her condescending assumption about pink dumbbells and lavender leotards. Switched out that image for one involving kettleballs and buckets of sweat. Damn the Mormon modesty, Lola thought. If Melena had been sleeveless the first time they'd met, she might have seen the musculature concealed beneath the prim drape of her blouse. Might have been more wary. She rejected the thought even as it came. Approximately a million years would have passed before she'd ever have imagined that the soft-spoken, diffident woman with the wounded eyes was capable of this. And if she was capable of *this*—

"You killed Sariah." Lola wrenched her voice out of its low groan. Her knee, her knee. She felt the blood ballooning within the confines of flesh, testing the seams of her jeans. She'd sprained her ankle once in an eerily similar situation. At the time, she'd thought that had hurt. Now she'd give anything for a simple sprain.

Melena rested the tire iron on her shoulder, rifle-like, oblivious to the wind seemingly intent upon wrecking her careful hairstyle. "What was your first clue?"

Great, thought Lola. A killer, and batshit crazy, too. Logic wasn't going to work. Maybe if she could keep her talking long enough. And ... what? Get the tire iron away from her? Wrestle her to the ground? Lola tried an ill-advised experiment. She flexed her calf muscle. At the motion, the bits and pieces of bone floating around in her knee ground together. "Aiiieeeeeeeee."

Melena halted. "Sorry about that."

"Doubtful," Lola managed.

But that "sorry." Flippant though it was, it was a nod to normalcy. If you hurt someone, you apologized. She wondered if Melena had apologized to Sariah before ...

"Why?" she asked through clenched teeth.

Melena tossed the tire iron from hand to hand. Probably something else she'd learned in CrossFit. Lola had spent nearly the last decade of her life among people whose daily lives involved holding down two-hundred-fifty-pound calves, stretching barbed wire tight against fence posts, bucking sixty-pound bales of hay. They thought gyms were stupid. So had Lola—until now.

"Would you mind putting that down? I'm not going anywhere."

"Nice try."

Lola rolled onto her back in a series of infinitesimal moves, each one ramping up the pain to dizzying levels. She lay panting for a few moments, then inched onto her elbows, as close to a sitting position as she could get, and gasped the word again: "Why?"

"Sariah? Why should I tell you?"

Lola knew that some people believed bad news should be broken gently, if at all. Doctors couched reality for terminal conditions: "Not compatible with life." Rejections from literary agents routinely began with a paragraph of praise, followed by an ominous "But."

Lola always liked to start with the worst-case scenario. That way, she reasoned, you were never disappointed, and sometimes even surprised with better news. She lobbed the worst at Melena.

"Because you're going to kill me."

Melena cocked her head this way and that, as though she were trying to decide among shades of beige for new drapes. Flakes glinted in her hair.

"Yes," she said finally. "I am."

# FORTY-FOUR

"Actually," she added, "you're going to kill yourself. Just like Mai."

Lola had thought she was already in maximum pain. She'd been wrong. She'd forgotten about the laceration of emotional injury.

"Mai's dead?"

Melena extended her left arm and shook it, exposing a thin band of flesh between sleeve and glove, circled by a dainty gold watch. She held her wrist close to her face. "If she isn't yet, she will be soon."

"She just found her brother. How could you do this?"

"I didn't do anything. She killed herself. Just like I said. Just like you're going to."

"Like hell I am. What am I going to do? Shoot myself? Cut my throat? Hit myself in the head with that tire iron? Anyhow, nobody will believe it." The wind drove a mix of grit and snow into her face, down her throat. She turned her head and spat.

"Yes, they will." Melena took a small plastic bottle from her pocket and shook it. Pills rattled within. "You're a junkie."

Lola sat up straighter. Her knee screamed anew. "How did—?"

Melena put the pills back in her pocket and twirled the tire iron again. Lola wished she'd put it down. "You showed up asking all those questions. So I told Bryce I had things to do to buy, food and flowers and such, to get ready for the funeral, and I followed you. You went to my sister's house—I don't even want to think about how you figured out where she lived—and you talked to Tynslee. You went to Pioneer Park. I saw you buy pills from that... that... " Lola watched a series of words come into Melena's head; watched her reject them all as unacceptably foul. "That homosexual."

The park. The way her attacker had swept her feet from beneath her with a stick to the back of the knees. Just like the tire iron.

"You went to the park another day."

"Because you did. You kept hanging around."

And Melena kept showing up. The invitation to Starbucks after the funeral. Keeping an eye on her, even—maybe especially—after the night in the park.

"Jesus." Realization cut through the pain. "You were going to kill me that night."

"No. I just wanted to scare you. Get you to leave town."

"I bit you."

Melena turned sideways and let the wind lift her hair, revealing the mangled ear so adeptly hidden.

Lola allowed herself a moment's satisfaction. At least she'd drawn blood. "I thought you were a man. That parka."

Melena preened. "Galon's. I took it from his house."

So that explained the bay rum. Implicating Galon with the parka, just as she had Trang with the hockey stick. Bitch.

Lola made another leap.

"It was you. Not Malachi. You're the one who called Munro about the pills. And the police in Vietnam." Munro had said only that he knew the voice on the phone wasn't his son's. Lola hadn't thought to ask him whether the voice was male or female.

Another moue of pride. "Guilty as charged. Do you have any idea how difficult it is to get word from here to the police in Vietnam?"

"But…" Lola brushed snow away from her face. "How did you know I was going there? I didn't tell anybody."

Melena's smile was frightful. "Oh, yes you did."

Of course she had. Munro. Who'd either said something to Malachi, or maybe Malachi had looked at his father's phone and figured it out and told Tynslee, and maybe Melena had overheard them talking, or had drawn the girl into her solicitous confidence—there were so many ways she could have found out. And under the circumstances, none of them mattered now. The only thing that mattered was to keep Melena talking, until… until what? Lola hadn't had the great good sense to dial 911 (*shut up, Charlie*). She'd told Munro only that Mai was missing. Even if he figured out who Mai was, and then came looking for her, he'd have no way of guessing that she'd ended up outside this fun-house palace on the edge of the lake. Talking was just a way of postponing the inevitable. On the other hand, given the alternative—

"What did you do to Mai? Why did you kill Sariah? And the cop? Did you try to kill him, too? Why?"

"Too many questions. It's getting cold." Melena made a show of withdrawing deeper into the warmth of the woolen coat. Lola, still in her fall jacket, lengthened her immediate wish list: Melena dead, or at least incapacitated. Melena's coat; even though the woman was so small it probably wouldn't fit, it would make a lovely blanket. And those gloves; she'd take them, too.

Melena lifted a leather-sheathed finger. Lola's longing for the gloves rose to first on her list.

"Pay attention. You're not very good at that, are you?"

Until that moment, Lola would have disagreed with her. Ten— no, nearly twenty—years of experience as a journalist, doing nothing but paying attention every minute of every hour she was on the job. But Melena had a point. She'd let heartache distract her to the point where she'd missed something crucial, some flash of lunacy behind the twitchy, vulnerable mien. Rabbits were prey, and nothing about this moment suggested that Melena Shumway was anything but pure predator, eyes glittering, lower lip caught in her sharp little teeth, tasting blood, feral.

"Handcart," said Lola.

Melena released her lip. Licked away the scarlet droplet. "What?"

Those people who'd crossed the desert on foot, Lola thought. Melena's forebears. They must have faced weather like this. And its opposite, the hundred-degree days with no water in sight, the mothers' milk drying in their breasts, the babies going limp in their arms. Strong stock, Lola had thought when she'd first read about them. Possessed of the kind of faith she'd never understood. Now she thought, maybe just possessed.

Melena apparently tired of waiting for an answer. "I didn't do anything to Mai. She ate a bunch of pills. Just like you're going to. Grief about her brother being in jail and all."

Lola thought of the girl, so recently reunited with the brother she thought she'd never see again. Of Trang, of the hope he must have derived from seeing her. Now his sister was dead in a strange land, only hours removed from their recent joy.

"Where is she?"

"At our house. In her brother's room."

"What's she doing there?"

"I stopped by the motel."

"But how did you know which room—never mind." Melena had already proven herself adept at getting information she wasn't supposed to have. In another life, under different circumstances, she'd have made a great reporter.

"When I go home," Melena said, "I'm going to find her in his room. When I call the police, I'm going to say that she told me she wanted to take a nap there, to sleep off her jet lag. And to be close to his things, to the brother she remembered, not the murderer he's turned out to be. She's overcome with shame about that. So she takes the only way out." Melena pulled a sad face, grotesque in its clownishness.

"And what about me? I've got no reason to kill myself."

"Oh, but you must have one. That's what this note will show."

"What note?"

Melena went to the car and retrieved her purse from the back seat. It was the kind with several compartments and pockets designed to hold a phone, glasses, keys. She searched through them. "Here," she said. She held out Lola's business card. "Remember this?"

It was the one Lola had started to leave at Melena's back door the morning Sariah's body was discovered. *I'm so sorry*, she'd written. And then left off when she realized that Melena's back door was unlocked.

She'd dropped the card. Melena must have found it, saved it.

"Whatever you were sorry for, that's why you killed yourself." Melena scraped a patch of earth free of snow, placed the card on the ground tantalizingly out of reach, and anchored it with a rock. She returned the purse to the car and came back and stood over Lola. The tire iron began its lazy swing.

"Wait!" Lola was afraid Melena would change her mind about the pills and simply bash her in the head. "No one will believe this. Why would I kill myself out here? And what happened to my knee? What about my car? You've got to drive it back, right? Whoever finds me will know that I didn't just walk all the way out here."

The tire iron stopped. "You're right."

Lola took an easier breath.

"But it doesn't matter. I'll leave the car someplace near Pioneer Park with the keys in it. Somebody'll grab it. The police will think that somebody came along out here, found the car, and helped themselves. As to the knee, maybe you fell down. Bashed it on a rock. Who knows? No one's going to care."

"That'll never work." But Lola knew it was hopeless. Melena, who must have planned Sariah's murder with infinite attention to detail, had crossed the line from logic to madness. She wouldn't be able to talk her out of anything.

Melena wrenched the top off the pill bottle. "Open your mouth."

Lola pressed her lips together. The iron tapped her head. Her mouth fell open.

"That's a good girl. Head back. Come on, don't be stupid. You think your knee hurts? This'll hurt worse."

*Protect your head.* Charlie again. *Protect your head.* From external blows, he meant. He'd never given her any advice about swallowing pills. A few dropped into her mouth.

Lola shifted the pills to one side of her mouth and tried to fake a gulp. One of pills slid down her throat anyway.

"Don't swallow them. Chew them. They work quicker that way."

How would *you* know? Something Lola was smart enough not to ask. She moved her jaws around.

"Open up."

Lola shifted the pills under her tongue and opened her mouth. "Stick your tongue out." She stuck.

Lena pinched it between two gloved fingers and yanked it upwards, face screwed up in distaste. "Hah. I thought so."

The tire iron clapped smartly against Lola's head. Her ears rang.

"Let's try this again. Here's a few more. Let's see some real chewing this time. Yes. Like that. All right, now. Down the hatch. All of them this time. Done? Good. Here's some more."

Tap.

Chew.

Swallow.

Tap.

Lola waited for the familiar lassitude, the thing she'd always loved about the pills. It would come so much faster with the chewing.

"I'm so sorry," she murmured.

"That's right. Just like what you wrote."

"I'm so sorry, Margaret."

"Who?" Melena stood over her. She took Lola's bare hand in her gloved one and folded Lola's around the empty bottle. "Fingerprints," she said. She took the bottle back, held it high, and let it go. It fell in slow motion.

The snow would rinse away the prints, would dissolve the business card. But Melena appeared well beyond caring.

"Just tell me why. Why kill Sariah?"

"Because she was going to tell."

"About Trang being gay? But"—Lola struggled to piece together a longer sentence—"he and Tynslee were getting married. No one was going to find out."

"No. Not him."

Above her, Melena's outline blurred, edges melding with falling snow, her voice seemingly issuing from some separate place.

"Sariah said everyone had suffered enough. That she'd lived a lie her whole life and she wasn't going to force it on the kids, too. That everyone needed to come clean and let the church leaders do what they wanted. That it was the only way any of us would find happiness. But what about my happiness? She never gave that a moment's thought."

The words flowed over Lola, who was still stuck on Melena's previous utterance.

"Not Trang? Who are we talking about?"

Had she spoken? She thought she'd heard her voice. Couldn't be sure.

"Frank? Who cares about Frank? It wasn't enough that God gave me one homosexual in my life. He sent me a homosexual son, too. Although maybe that's not Frank's fault. Maybe he was infected in my diseased household. And you—you had to bring that girl here. To tell everyone about how blind I am. I thought it was women I had to worry about. I knew he was fooling around, even back then. And no way was I going to bring a teenage girl into our house, make it even easier for him. I didn't know. I didn't know."

Lola rallied for a very great effort. "Melena, what are you talking about?"

"Bryce. I'm talking about my homosexual husband, Bryce."

# FORTY-FIVE

THE CAR DISAPPEARED IN a churn of white. Lola knew it was impossible, but she imagined she heard the mocking rattle of her phone, sliding around on the car floor.

The decibels in her knee subsided from a scream to a murmur. All those times she'd taken the pills to sleep, she'd forgotten about their original purpose as painkillers. Nice.

Then: *No.*

She didn't dare succumb. Somebody would eventually look for her, but no one would think to look in this place. By the time they found her, she might be dead. Would be. The only question now, would she freeze before the pills did her in?

Unfair. All those times she'd wanted to die. Now that she didn't want to, here came Death, grinning like a fool.

"Go away."

He ignored her. Took a seat close by. Settled in. Got comfortable.

She stuck her fingers down her throat and retched. Nothing came up. She tried again. Farther. Some coffee-stained liquid. A few white crumbles. Not enough. The knee roared back to life. She lay back. Heard Charlie again, after he'd come home from dealing with yet another fatal overdose.

*He was on his back, smothered by his own vomit. All his friends had to do was turn him on his side. He'd be alive.*

Lola rolled onto her side, face pillowed in the snow, and waited for the knee to shut up.

"You, too," she said to Death's cackle.

If nothing else, she had to leave a message. She fumbled in the jacket pocket where she always kept a notebook and pen. Hah. Melena hadn't thought of everything. She scratched at the paper, working at an *M*. Nothing. The pen had frozen in the cold.

Maybe the police would see the *M* shape dug into the paper. She should finish the word, at least. *Melena*. Or, better still, *Margaret*. So that if nothing else, her daughter would know her mother's last thought was of her. Or would she just see it as the beginning of a suicide note, proof of her mother's purposeful removal?

Another chortle from Death, that bastard. It wasn't enough that he sought her for himself—and that, for too long, she'd encouraged him. Now he wanted the world to know that she'd chosen him.

She had to let Margaret know she'd changed her mind. She patted hopelessly at her pockets, hoping to feel a cold-defying pencil. Nothing.

*Wait.* Something.

The little burner phone she'd gotten in Vietnam.

*Pleasepleaseplase.* She held it against her chest before daring a look. Its screen lit up. Power! A single bar, but power, nonetheless. Along with a red light warning that the battery was low.

327

Lola punched the numbers with fingers gone fat and frozen, and heard the sweetest words ever spoken on the planet.

"911. What is your emergency?"

———————

First things first.

She pulled Melena's address out of her ass.

"There's a dead girl there. Her name is Mai. Melena Shumway killed her. She killed Sariah Ballard, too."

"What is your name and the location you're calling from?"

"Lola Wicks. L-o-...never mind. I'm at the lake..."

The phone went dead.

Death slid beside her, put an arm around her, pulled her close.

I'm sorry, Margaret.

I'm sorry, Jan.

I'm sorry, everybody.

But Charlie, oh, Charlie. She'd get to see him again.

That's good. Right? It's good, isn't it? Where are you? She reached for him, hands scrabbling through the snow. But he pushed her away, so hard she could almost feel it, leaving her alone in the censorious blackness.

# FORTY-SIX

IT WAS DARK, AND then it was light. So much light, prying at Lola's eyelids, forcing its way between them.

Lola squeezed them tight. Because when you were dead, you walked toward the light, right? No light, no Death. Fooled you, sucker.

But what if she was already in the light? What if he'd grabbed her and hauled her off to heaven, all sunshine and puffy clouds and glowing halos?

Heaven? Her? Not a chance.

The other place then. Flames. They gave off light, too. Except that she didn't believe in that place, any more than she believed in heaven. But then, she'd been wrong about a lot of things. So many things. Maybe she was wrong about being dead.

"Does she seem awake to you?"

Jan.

Oh, yeah. She was definitely wrong.

"Huh." A shadow over her eyes, as though from a hand held close. A man's voice. Brush of palm against her lips. Charlie? Her heart leapt.

"She was out before. But now she's faking. Her breathing's all jerky."

Poor old heart. Another blow. Not Charlie after all. That guy. The mean one. Jan's friend. Munro. Her breath left her in a long sigh.

"Hey, Wicks." Jan again. "We're on to you. Come on back from wherever you've gone."

Breath filled her lungs. So they worked, along with the heart. What the hell.

Lola Wicks rejoined the world.

---

"Welcome back."

Lola could have sworn Jan's braid was shorter, as if she'd chewed a couple of inches right off. Her freckles were dark constellations on a chalky surface. And whatever she was doing in pursuit of a smile wasn't working. Her mouth went all lopsided. Her nose was red; her eyes, damp. "Damn allergies."

Lola tried to say something. Her throat hurt.

"Don't talk. They pumped your stomach. Not a sight easily forgotten." Munro looked entirely too pleased to deliver the news, albeit in a shaking voice.

Jan took her cue. "There was charcoal all around your mouth. You looked like a Halloween decoration."

"Hospital?" Lola mouthed.

"Duh. Your knee is about in a million pieces. She really clocked you. You're going to need a ton of surgery. The *Express*'s insurance company is probably going to put out a contract on you." Jan sounded more cheerful by the moment.

"The knee is the least of your worries. The cops found you just in time." Despite his jaunty words, the skin around Munro's mouth and eyes was drawn tight.

"How?" Lola managed the word, which turned into "ow."

"Thank the kids. All the dispatcher got out of you was 'the lake.' It's a big lake," said Jan.

"Seventeen hundred square miles," added Munro, the local expert. "They could have looked for days."

"Kids?"

"Trang's girlfriend—I mean, not his girlfriend. His friend. Whatever she is."

"Tynslee," Lola croaked.

"Right. Tynslee remembered you asking about that castle thing."

"SaltAir," Munro supplied.

"And how the moms used to take all of the kids there when they were little."

"And the dads." Munro's mood darkened apace with Jan's increasing cheer. "I guess Galon and Bryce have been together ever since high school. Just like Trang and Malachi. Except they didn't dare come out. So they married best friends. Lived next door. At some point the women must have figured it out, and given the way things are here, they decided it was better to just grin and bear it."

Jan took up the narrative. "Until Trang kept talking about going to Vietnam for his mission. Melena couldn't chance it, even though she knew he probably wouldn't be sent there, and even if he were, he'd be with his mission partner twenty-four/seven. She was too afraid he'd find his sister, and that his sister would tell how they left her behind. That from there, people would look at Bryce thinking he'd cheated on Melena with a woman in Vietnam. And if they looked at him hard enough, it wouldn't be long until they figured out who he was really cheating with."

A new voice in the room. "Tynslee's mom would have been fine with it. Maybe not fine, but she was tired of all the sneaking around. She said to let the church leaders do whatever they wanted. But for my mom, it was the last straw. She'd put up with it all those years. To see it go public, though—she couldn't handle that. And so she went after Sariah and me."

Trang stepped into view.

"Trang!" Lola started to sit up. "Oh, owwwwwwww."

"They let me out yesterday. You were still under."

"I'm glad. But your sister. I'm so—so—" Her throat closed on *sorry*.

Jan moved to Lola's side. "Shhh. Now that you're awake, someone's here to see you."

"Margaret? Margaret?" Lola made another abortive attempt at sitting up.

Jan nudged her back down. "Here. Let the bed do the work for you." She fooled around with some sort of control. The bed went lower, then raised, higher than before, each movement sending the pain in her knee stratospheric.

Lola batted at her. "Get out of the way. I want to see my daughter."

Jan dropped the controls and moved to the wall, along with Munro and Trang.

Lola heard the squeak of wheels, soft-soled footsteps. Two nurses wheeled a bed into the room and began to maneuver it beside hers.

"Oh, no." The words escaped Lola's ravaged throat in a whisper. Had something happened to Margaret? "Oh, please, no."

Only Jan understood. "It's not what you think—" she began.

But the person in the other bed lifted her head, and with that small motion tore one last word from Lola's throat.

"Mai?"

───────

"Hello."

If possible, Mai's voice sounded worse than Lola's.

"No talking. Either of you," one of the nurses said. He stood six feet and more in his white clogs and wore super-size green scrubs.

"Your phone call," Munro said. "It saved her. She was near-comatose but not dead when the cops got there."

Lola cut her eyes toward the nurse. He shook his massive head. She made a scribbling gesture with her hand, willing him to bring her a pen and paper. Jan, as usual, was ahead of her. "You want to know about Melena. In jail. On attempted murder charges in Mai's case. She hasn't 'fessed up to killing Sariah—yet—but they'll probably charge her anyway after they interview you. Another reason for you to save your voice."

Lola let her head fall back on the pillow. She closed her eyes.

The nurse's voice reached her from somewhere high above. "Rest. That's a good idea. Both of these women need it. I'll bring Miss Mai back to her room. The rest of you, clear out."

# FORTY-SEVEN

THE DISTRICT ATTORNEY HAD indeed slapped Melena with a murder charge, about two minutes after he finished scanning the transcript of the police interview with Lola. They'd found the knife used to kill Sariah—and another used on the cop, whose condition was improving by the day—in Melena's compost heap, just as Lola, remembering Melena's muddy garden gloves, had suggested.

"It took more than two minutes," Galon corrected Bryce.

"By the end of the day, though."

The two men fidgeted at the end of Lola's hospital bed, bearers of the worst sort of good news. Especially for Bryce, now married to a murderer. An *accused* murderer. Still. Something loosened inside Lola, anxiety gusting away, dissipating into the general hospital miasma of rubbing alcohol, uneaten food, and faint tang of urine.

Trang was free. Melena would answer for Sariah's death. It had been worth it. She looked at her leg, a Frankenstein limb of bruised, mustard-colored flesh, shading purple along a line of raised and puckered stitches that formed a mountain range in miniature running from the top of her shin up onto her thigh. Gruesome as its outer appearance was, X-rays had revealed a far more frightful interior: metal rods forming a scaffolding that purportedly held everything together. Lola hadn't had the nerve to ask the surgeon if she'd run again. It was worth it, she told herself again, hoping that this time she'd believe it.

*It was,* Charlie breathed into her ear. *Of course, if you'd listened to me and called the cops sooner…*

Lola waved him back and focused on Galon and Bryce. "What's the exact charge?" Plain old *murder* was a layman's term, one eliciting poorly disguised eye rolls among the criminal law cognoscenti.

"Aggravated murder," Bryce said. "It's more serious than just murder. She could get the death penalty." He bent and braced both hands against the bed.

"You need to sit down." Galon pulled two plastic chairs from their station along the wall. "They won't execute a woman. He told you. Don't go there."

Lola nodded agreement. Sometimes paternalism had its benefits. But she could tell Bryce had gone there the minute he'd heard the charge, that he remained imprisoned in that dark place echoing with *if only.*

If only—what? If insomnia had nudged him awake earlier, perhaps in time to interrupt Melena's deadly journey across the lawn, hockey stick in hand? If he'd somehow divined his wife's increasing frustration with the fakery of their marriage, her horror at what exposure would mean? If, years earlier, before her resentment festered into madness, he'd found the courage to do the unthinkable, to live his life openly as a gay man?

He and Galon settled into the inadequate chairs pulled so close together that their thighs touched. Like kids, Lola thought, still pretending there was nothing between them but taking every opportunity for even the slightest intimacy. They'd come of age before gay pride and PFLAG and marriage equality, with the cautionary tales of Matthew Shepard and other savage learn-your-lesson attacks, all of it layered with an unforgiving faith that mandated they marry, produce children, and become active in the church that despised them.

As a white woman married to an Indian man, Lola had had her share of uneasy moments. Now, considering the condemnation that faced Galon and Bryce every moment of every day, she was embarrassed by even those small discomfitures. Yet given everything they were dealing with, they'd taken the time to visit her, showing up right at ten o'clock for the morning shift of visiting hours.

Jan and Munro would stop by in the evening, they told her. The young people, all of them—Mai and Trang, Tynslee and Malachi and Kwesi—were under orders to stay away.

"Mai and Trang need time together," Bryce said. "They're letting him stay in the hospital with her. And the rest just need to get back to their normal lives. Whatever 'normal' is going to be now."

They looked at each other and then away, apprehension darkening their faces. Kwesi and Tynslee had lost their mother. No doubt some people would still view Trang with suspicion despite his release. And, by the time Melena either pleaded guilty or went to trial, news of Galon's and Bryce's long involvement would become public.

Another wave of compassion briefly distracted Lola from the jackhammering pain in her knee. The nurse padded into the room. "Bad today?"

"Like being punched from the inside. By somebody—a whole host of somebodies—wearing brass knuckles."

The nurse pointed to the stupid pain scale on the wall, the one with a smiley face at one end and a Edvard Munch-style screaming visage at the other.

"Where are we today? One to ten."

"Try twelve."

"You know I can give you something for that."

Yes*yesyesyesoh*please*yes.*

"No, thank you."

Who said that? Surely not her. Because she wasn't that strong. She wanted the pills, God, yes, she did. But the shakes and chills that had tormented her in Vietnam had only just started to subside when she'd returned to Salt Lake. She didn't want to go through all of that again. She must have said something, maybe just a shake of the head, that caused the nurse to shrug and walk away.

*Good.*

"Knock it off, Charlie."

"Uh, it's Galon." The men glanced at one another. "Maybe we should go."

"No. Please. Stay." *Don't leave me alone with this.* The gang inside her knee switched from brass knuckles to switchblades. Lola gripped the edges of her mattress. The sounds of a busy urban hospital—the purposeful squeak of rubber-soled shoes, the unending ringing of the phone at the nurses' station, the beeping and whooshing of the machines that signified life, the self-important murmurings of doctors translated with no-bullshit briskness by the nurses who swept into the rooms in their wake—mounted an aural assault. Sweat traced Lola's hairline and dampened the sheet beneath her.

She gathered herself with an enormous effort, focusing on the faint scent of bay rum.

"I thought it was you. In the park."

Galon started. "What?"

"Someone attacked me. Held a knife to my throat. The person smelled like you. But she told me it was her."

The men stared at her with bewilderment.

"You were in the park that night, though. I saw you by the restrooms. Kissing." Lola forced her mind back to the moment. That flash of familiarity. The glimpse of the sculpted blond hair, the cleft chin, just as she'd seen in the photo of Galon in Melena's house—not enough to connect it with the man barely seen in the darkness, but a nudge nonetheless.

And then, to get the cop off her back, she'd sent him to roust them from their tryst.

"That's why," she gasped.

"Why what?"

"Never mind." Too ashamed to tell them what she'd done, how her craven attempt to divert the cop had nearly gotten the cop killed, Melena doing everything within her power to keep her husband and his lover from the exposure of being busted.

Her knee throbbed as though in punishment. Lola tried to regain her composure. She looked at the floor, studied the pastel landscapes in their silvery fake-wood frames on the wall, every color in the room chosen to soothe. None of it a match for the hard gleam of the stainless steel machines, the yellowish translucence of the plastic tubing, the chairs of industrial orange plastic. Galon and Bryce waited.

She went for distraction. "It seems crazy. Having to sneak around in the park like that."

"We had our hunting trip," Bryce said. "We take one every year." He put a shy hand over Galon's.

"How very *Brokeback*," Lola murmured.

"A movie we couldn't see, not even to rent. They wouldn't stock it in the stores here," Galon said.

*Haven't you ever heard of the internet?* Lola wanted to ask. Although she figured they didn't dare. She knew she was prying, yet she couldn't help herself. "But to keep it going all these years? That takes more than a hunting trip or two."

Living next door, seeing each other every day but never being able to touch except for rare moments in the park, sex—delicious, scorching, holler-out-loud and break-the-bed sex—only on the once- or twice-annual getaways? Lola wondered how long she and Charlie would have lasted under such conditions. Well. She'd already lasted five months, hadn't she? And a lifetime of celibacy yawned ahead of her. Alice Kicking Woman's words came back to her: *Find yourself a man. Doesn't need to be a husband.*

Her deepening blush went unnoticed. Bryce's fingers twined with Galon's. Galon leaned his shoulder against Bryce. The emotion on their faces so naked that Lola looked away.

"Every day," Bryce said. "Every single day, I told him I loved him."

"He did."

A shadow in the doorway. The men jerked apart. A different nurse, a small starchy woman, one who looked as though she would have preferred the old-style uniform of stiff white dress and peaked cap rather than the sloppiness of scrubs. She tightened the blood pressure cuff around Lola's arm to the point of pain and jabbed the thermometer into her ear with a little too much enthusiasm.

She raked Bryce and Galon with a knowing gaze. "Ten minutes," she snapped. "Or you could go now. You're tiring her out."

Bryce trundled to his feet. Lola shook her head at him. "Wait." She had to know. The nurse left the room. "How did you tell him?"

Bryce shrugged. "It sounds silly."

Silly? Had she told Charlie every day that she loved him? "Tell me."

"Every day, I left a stone on his doorstep."

Galon's hand made a small, caressing movement. "Each morning, when I went out to get the paper, it would be there. A new stone. And I'd know. That he'd taken the trouble to get up early, find a stone, walk across the lawn, leave it there."

Realization dawned. Lola turned to Bryce. "That's what you were doing. That morning when you found Sariah."

"Yes. I dropped the stone, though. On the walkway."

"But I found it anyway. In the midst of that awful day, that reminder. You can't imagine what that meant," Galon said.

Lola could. "All those cairns."

"Yes. I saved every stone."

"What about Sariah and Melena? Did they know what those were?"

"Melena knew for longer, I think. Even though she didn't get it right at first." A sad smile flitted across Bryce's face. "Mai told me she saw me one day in Vietnam. That she thought I was looking for a woman. That Melena might have seen me, too."

Galon reached for his hand again. "Sariah, too. She never said anything directly. But one day, we were all out on the lawn, the four of us. And Melena said something about the cairns. 'How many more of those are you going to build? The place is starting to look like Stonehenge.' Something like that. And Sariah—she had this way; she'd smile, but underneath that smile, there was steel—she said, 'He can build as many as he wants. They're beautiful.' And she looked at me when she said it, and then she looked at Bryce. So, yes, I think she knew for quite a while."

# FORTY-EIGHT

Jan reverted to form once it had been established that Lola would live. There'd been too many months of too many broken promises, so Lola was going to have to prove herself again—and again, and again—before Jan found her way back to trust. Fair enough.

No fun, though. And especially no fun on the trip back to Montana. Jan had driven Lola's truck to Salt Lake, a trip that, as she reminded Lola at least every twenty minutes, had only taken a little over eight hours. But on the return journey, every bathroom break—and given their mutual coffee consumption, there were many—required a complicated descent from the truck, and then the hop on crutches across the parking lot along with a fair amount of cursing from both parties.

For the first couple hundred miles, those untoward phrases were the only words exchanged. Jan might have lost her trust in Lola, but Lola's shoulder ached beneath the weight of a chip of its own. After all, if Jan hadn't badgered her into taking the assignment from *Families of Faith*, her knee would still be intact. For starters. The silence lasted into Idaho, where the mountains, as though abashed by the grandeur to the south, lowered themselves into decorous foothills. At their base, the land flattened out into fields, now brown, that in summer would be green with acres of potatoes and legumes that bore testament to big agriculture.

Lola ground her teeth in boredom. She tried to sleep but the urgent distress in her knee forbade it.

"Are you sure?" the doctor had asked when she'd refused painkillers upon being discharged.

"Positive."

Skepticism and understanding alternated across his face. "You'll have a rough go of it."

"Really?"

He'd fumbled for words of reassurance before he caught her sarcasm. Lola was nobody's favorite patient. The hospital couldn't discharge her fast enough. The tall nurse stopped Jan as she pushed Lola's wheelchair toward the waiting pickup. He handed Lola a squeeze ball.

"We usually give these to people with arm injuries to build their strength back up."

"And yet." Lola pointed to her knee.

His voice sharpened. "Just trying to help. I thought it might take your mind off the pain."

As Lola hoisted herself out of the chair, she could have sworn she heard him mutter, "Or you could stuff it up your ass."

As the miles passed, Lola squeezed and squeezed, longing for a distraction from both the pain and the endless brown fields. At this rate, she thought, she'd have muscles like Popeye by the time they got to Magpie.

Jan cleared her throat. "I guess we should talk."

Only Lola knew, and knew because she herself wasn't the talk-it-through type, what those words cost Jan. She stopped squeezing and tried to assume an attentive yet dignified position, difficult when one's lap was a mess of candy wrappers and bags of the junk food she'd insisted upon buying the last time they'd stopped for gas.

"I probably shouldn't have gotten so mad at that text you sent. But I thought you were bailing on us. Again."

Lola's earlier silence had aimed to punish. Now, she offered an explanation.

"Bail? I didn't freaking bail. It was you. All of you. You kicked me out. Banished me! I could barely keep it together at home and you made me leave."

"Oh, please." Jan looked remarkably unconcerned at the accusation. She wasn't even chewing her braid. She did, in fact, reach for the open bag of Cheetos in Lola's lap and help herself to a handful.

"Mmm. Love these things. Especially the way they turn your fingers orange." She licked them. "Just like old times, huh? The two of us heading off to a story, eating crap."

Old times. Lola barely remembered them. The last time they'd chased a story together, Charlie had been alive. He'd hated her penchant for road food. She remembered the way she'd slide her orange-stained fingers into her pockets as she sauntered into the house after one of those trips, how she'd hurry into the bathroom to wash away the evidence. But he'd always find out. An errant wrapper on the floor of the truck, the smudge of orange on the gearshift. Lola's face felt funny. She realized she was smiling. Her chest hurt, as it did whenever she thought of Charlie. But a new emotion had crept in, soft and fond.

She puzzled over it. Was this how things were going to go? Would warmth ever replace the pain? Did she want it to?

She mused so long and hard that she forgot about her tirade until Jan spoke again. If she'd thought Jan's lighthearted Cheetos remark meant she was going to get off easy, she'd been mistaken.

"We banished you? That's a good one. You banished yourself. You crawled down into some deep, stinking sewer of grief and pulled the manhole cover over you. Kept all of us out. Even though we were hurting, too. The whole rez. Do you know what it meant to them, Charlie being the first Indian sheriff in a white county? All the aunties who helped raise him up. Even me. Don't forget, I knew him way before you did. He always dealt with me straight, never tried to bullshit me the way a lot of sources did. And Margaret! You left that child without a father or a mother, either. By the time you went off to Utah, it didn't make a damn bit of difference what the reason was. Your being gone was no different than your being around."

"I didn't go off to Utah. I was sent," Lola sulked.

"Because we knew it would get you off your ass. And?"

"And what?"

"Admit we were right."

Lola grabbed a handful of Cheetos and stuffed them in her mouth. "Can't," she mumbled around them. "Mouth full."

"Say it," Jan insisted.

"Mmph, mmmph."

"Good enough," Jan said.

And each turned her head away from the other to hide their respective smiles.

———

It was late afternoon when they crossed the Montana line, dusk when they left the interstate, and full dark by the time they got to

Magpie. The sign in Nell's Cafe had long been turned to *Closed*. A clerk stood lonely in the interior glow of the convenience store.

Past the harsh glare of streetlights, the waxing moon took over, silvering the snowy ridgelines, casting the coulees in deep shadow. Lola looked west, toward the black wall of the Front. Her breath caught. She cracked her window. Caught the scent of sage.

The truck rounded a curve and approached the turnoff to the ranch. Lola forgot she was angry. Her heart did a marimba solo in her chest. Margaret.

Jan slowed not a bit.

"What the—?"

"She's at Lena's."

After that, it was back to the sullen silence. But lighter, somehow. A smile kept forcing its way to Lola's lips as the moonlight highlighted the MacPhersons' herd of registered Angus, the horses that the Eckmans couldn't bear to sell even though there were far too many for the occasional ranch chore that still relied on them. She wished they'd stopped at the house to pick up Bub.

The reservation town was, if possible, more moribund than Magpie. The school, the site of so many community events, seemingly something every night, stood black. Jan turned into the parking lot and pulled around to the front rather than continuing on to the large lot behind it that everybody used. "Margaret forgot her bookbag," she said by way of explanation. "Her teacher said she'd leave it outside the front door."

Lola slumped. Was she never going to get to see her daughter?

Jan stopped the truck. "Crap," she said. She pulled out her phone. "I just got a text from Jorkki. Probably some story he wants me to chase tomorrow. I have to deal with this. You get it. It'll be good practice for you, getting out of the truck by yourself."

Like hell, Lola thought.

Margaret's purple book bag leaned against the brick wall, maybe a dozen feet away. It might as well have been a mile. Lola opened the door, stuck the crutches out, and leaned them against the side of the truck. Then she turned her back to the door and slowly lowered one foot to the snow-sheeted pavement and grabbed the crutches, positioning them under arms already rubbed raw, berating herself for ignoring Charlie's occasional advice to add upper-body strength training to her running regimen. Her arms quivered. The knee upped the pain ante.

"Ow-ow," swing. "Ow-ow," hop.

She advanced upon the bookbag.

Swing. Hop. Almost there.

A final swing. She transferred a crutch to her other hand and held tight to both as she leaned down to grab the bag.

The door swung open. Light flooded the sidewalk. A small girl and a small dog shot from the crowd within and knocked Lola Wicks right on her ass.

---

The aunties installed Lola at a long table, slapping down a stack of fry bread before her, along with a bowl filled to the brim with bison stew.

Alice Kicking Woman sat on one side, Margaret on the other, as close as she could be without crawling into her mother's lap, emitting peals of laughter every time she rubbed her mother's shorn head. Under the table, Bub lay across Lola's good foot, raising his head occasionally to catch a bit of bison slipped to him by Margaret. Lola leaned over to bury her nose in her daughter's hair, a habit since Margaret's infancy.

"Mom. Stop smelling me. People will see." A complaint since Margaret had learned to talk, one lacking just enough outrage to undercut its veracity.

"No one's paying attention." Lola pointed out the obvious. The school cafeteria was packed, most of the tables filled, with a line still snaking before the steam trays. The trays held the usual suspects at any reservation feast—the stew, fry bread, and macaroni and cheese, alongside stacks of bologna-and-cheese sandwiches, and cups of sweet sodas and instant lemonade. Most of the people still in line were young, the elders having been served first as per protocol.

"You didn't really think the aunties would pass up the chance for a celebration, did you?" Jan sat across the table. She snagged a piece of fry bread from Lola's stack. Powdered sugar whitened her lips.

"I don't deserve it." Lola spoke low, beneath the room's hubbub. But Alice overheard.

"You went away broken. You came home healed."

"Healing." A small correction, one that did not risk an insult to an elder.

Alice nodded understanding. "That's enough."

Enough for a celebration, especially given the reservation's penchant to mark the smallest occasion with a full-on feed. But there was more to it than that. Waging a lopsided battle against unemployment and poverty, alcoholism and drug abuse, an underfunded Indian Health Service and a housing shortage that verged on criminal, the reservation took pride in marking every victory, no matter how small.

A soldier returned alive from Afghanistan or Iraq. A successful completion of rehab. Graduation—every last one, from elementary school on up through the big door prizes of law school, medical school, or a PhD. Lola had heard more times than she could count about the daylong hurrah that accompanied Charlie's election as sheriff.

"Wonder what he would think of this?" The words escaped unbidden. No need to specify whom.

Margaret took her hand. "I wish he were here."

*Me, too,* Lola would have said, but for the tears clogging her throat.

Alice's sharp elbow punctured her self-pity. "He'd be glad to see you with family."

Family.

Lola looked around the room, at the aunties and elders who'd insisted—rightly—that only the act of leaving would underscore the value of what she had at home. At Jan, more like a sister than a friend. Even Jorkki, a few seats away, his wispy hair shining white among all the dark heads surrounding him, had looked after her in his fashion, assigning her one impossible-to-screw-up feature after another while he delayed his retirement and labored overtime to put out the paper and cover the stories she'd normally have written.

As an only child whose parents were long dead, Lola had limited her concept of family to Charlie and Margaret. Now she realized the short-sightedness of that view. Family meant the people who surrounded you, who put up with your bullshit—up to a point—and called you on it when you crossed the line. It meant blood relations when they fit the bill, and others when the shared DNA let you down.

She thought of Trang and Mai, determined to find one another after so many years apart. Because they were family. Of Tynslee and Kwesi and Trang and Malachi, forming their own little band against the strictures they faced. Of Malachi and Munro, who despite her instinctive dislike of him had unhesitatingly stepped up in support of his son. Of Bryce and Galon, their secret bond of longer duration than most of the church-approved marriages that were held up as the only true way. Of poor Sariah, who loved her family so much that she was willing to defy convention on their behalf.

And Melena, the dark side of family, willing to do battle for an image even if it meant destroying those she loved. For far too long, Lola herself had wallowed in a different sort of darkness—not one that lashed out in violence but withdrew into grief, obstinately pulling away from the strong arms surrounding her.

"I'm so sorry."

"Sorry about what?"

A familiar voice. But in an impossible place. "Munro?"

She turned, only to be confronted with the retreating back of a lanky figure, hair flying as he hurried away. It had to be a mistake.

It wasn't. He rounded the table and wedged himself in beside Jan.

"What the hell—I mean, what brings you here?" Lola hadn't expected a test of her newfound humility quite this soon.

He shoveled up some bison stew and closed his eyes in appreciation. "God, that beats those airline peanuts," he said. "I almost wished I'd driven. What with the time I had to wait in the security line in Salt Lake, and then getting the rental car in Great Falls and driving up here, it took just about as long."

"You did the right thing," Jan assured him. "Believe me, the drive's no fun. Although in my case, it might have had something to do with the company."

"Why are you here?" Lola had made her single stab at good manners. If people wanted her healed, they'd have to deal with the old Lola.

"Had some time on my hands. I quit the magazine."

"Wow." So Munro had a backbone after all. Which deserved her grudging "Congratulations."

"And…"

Lola got a bad feeling. "And what?"

Munro and Jan shared a conspiratorial smile. Jan spoke first. "You know how Jorkki's retiring?"

"And how I'm out of work?" Munro added.

Lola's fry bread fell into her stew. "No. Oh, no. No, no, no."

"Maybe. Maybe, maybe, maybe. It's not a done deal. I'm just here for an interview. By the way, Anne Peterson says thanks. She's really going to town on the story. Nice of you to hand over your notes. I didn't figure you for the type." That gunslinger's grin.

Alice's elbow again, so sharp that Lola jumped. Which had the unwelcome effect of getting Munro's and Jan's attention just as Lena said, not bothering to keep her voice down at all, "He looks good. You don't snap him up, maybe I will."

"She can't," Jan said. "He'll be her boss. Forbidden fruit. He's all yours."

*Forbidden fruit.* Something twanged within Lola. A feeling too long forgotten and now rushing back with far too much intensity She started to cross her legs. Her knee asserted itself. She made a stab at dignity.

"I'm not snapping up anything except some dessert. Come on, Margaret. I think I saw Lena's chocolate cake."

She crutched away, Margaret trailing reluctantly, twisting to study the stranger in their midst. Lola directed her attention to the cake. "That piece. And that one. Can you take them back to the table, please? I'm going to get some air."

She slipped through a side door, trading the overheated gym and its good-humored racket for the crystalline silence of a Rocky Mountain night. The moon wobbled atop the Front, a pale balloon about to break free and soar up and up, seeking a place among the great glittering panoply of stars.

Yellow light, man-made and pedestrian, splashed across her.

"Thought I'd find you here." The door closed behind Munro.

He stood beside her, so close she could feel the warmth of his body, the cumulus cloud of his breath mingling with her own. The masculine scent of Scotch and cigarettes. That damnable thrum within.

He lifted his chin toward the Front. "Do you ever get used to it?"

She shook her head. "Never."

Just like I'll never get used to Charlie being gone. A vow, a promise, a solemn pact ...

*Oh, cut the crap, Lola. You're already forgetting me. Not forgetting, but looking ahead. As you should. You're back on your feet. You'll be fine. I don't know about him, though. Poor guy.*

A final time, she whirled. A final time, nothing.

Nothing but the soft, absolving laughter of Charlie's goodbye.

**THE END**

## ACKNOWLEDGMENTS

Thanks the team at Midnight Ink—acquisitions editor Terri Bischoff, an able shepherd for Lola along her journey; production editor Sandy Sullivan, for smoothing the stumbles from the manuscript; publicist Jake-Ryan Kent; cover designer Ellen Lawson; interior designer Bob Gaul; and copywriter Alisha Bjorklund. And thanks to my agent, Barbara Braun. Two wonderful critique groups, the Badass Women Writers and the Creel crew, gave invaluable suggestions on the novel, and Stephen Paul Dark in particular helped with some Salt Lake City details. If mistakes remain, they are mine. Nguyen Ngoc Lan proved such a wonderful guide to Vietnam that I can't wait to return. And speaking of wishing I could return, Willapa Bay AiR provided a month of near-solitude between ocean and bay where I drafted this book. Finally, profound gratitude to Scott for shouldering household duties when I went back to work full-time in the middle of writing it. Every writer should have such support.

© Slikati Photography/Missoula, MT

## ABOUT THE AUTHOR

Veteran journalist Gwen Florio has covered stories ranging from the shootings at Columbine High School and the trial of Oklahoma City bomber Timothy McVeigh to the glitz of the Miss America pageant and the more practical Miss Navajo contest, whose participants slaughter a sheep. She's reported from Afghanistan, Iraq, and Somalia, as well as Lost Springs, Wyoming (population three). Her journalism has been nominated three times for the Pulitzer Prize and her short fiction for the Pushcart Prize. Learn more at http://gwenflorio.net/.